His blue gaze met hers, direct and powerful. "How long has it been?"

"Has it been for what?"

"Since you've been out on a date?"

Sam took such a deep sip of water she nearly drowned. "I could ask you the same thing."

"My answer's easy. A week."

"Oh." She put the glass down. "I thought you said you didn't have that much free time."

"I was exaggerating. I'm a writer." That grin again. "Given to hyperbole and all that."

Was he…flirting with her? Was that why everything within her seemed touched with fever? Why her stomach couldn't stop flip-flopping? Why she alternately wanted to run—and to stay?

It was simply because he was right. She hadn't been out on a date in forever. She wasn't used to this kind of head-on attention from a man. Especially a man as good at the head-on thing as he was.

"So which would you rather?" Flynn asked. "A date? Or an interview?"

The interview, her mind urged. *Say interview.* The business. The bakery needed the increase in revenue. Her personal life could wait, just as it always had. The business came first.

"A date."

Dear Reader,

Christmas. Is there a more magical time of year? To me, it's the season of miracles. Of possibilities. In the Midwest, where I live, the first snowfall of the year is as eagerly awaited as Santa's arrival. Though I'm more than done with the cold weather by the middle of January, the entire month of December seems like something almost otherworldly after those first flakes start to drift to the ground.

A major part of the holiday for me is the food. I love to cook (which is why my blog at www.shirleyjump.blogspot.com is all about food!), and throughout the holiday season I'm cooking pretty much nonstop. Cookies, breads, stews—you name it, I'm making it. I get the kids involved, and not only serve the food to my family, but share a lot of it with my friends, too (and, hey, that keeps me from gaining all that weight!).

So it seemed appropriate to write a book that featured holiday food, and I wrapped that story in the magical theme of Christmas and the possibility of love. I hope you enjoy Sam and Flynn's story, and if you have a moment between the gift-wrapping and mugs of hot cocoa, drop me an e-mail at shirley@shirleyjump.com and share your favorite moment from the story!

Wishing you all the best this holiday season,

Shirley

SHIRLEY JUMP

Marry-Me Christmas

TORONTO • NEW YORK • LONDON
AMSTERDAM • PARIS • SYDNEY • HAMBURG
STOCKHOLM • ATHENS • TOKYO • MILAN • MADRID
PRAGUE • WARSAW • BUDAPEST • AUCKLAND

Recycling programs
for this product may
not exist in your area.

ISBN-13: 978-0-373-17557-4
ISBN-10:   0-373-17557-4

MARRY-ME CHRISTMAS

First North American Publication 2008.

Copyright © 2008 by Shirley Kawa-Jump, LLC.

New York Times bestselling author **Shirley Jump** didn't have the willpower to diet or the talent to master under-eye concealer, so she bowed out of a career in television and opted instead for a career where she could be paid to eat at her desk—writing. At first, seeking revenge on her children for their grocery-store tantrums, she sold embarrassing essays about them to anthologies. However it wasn't enough to feed her growing addiction to writing funny. So she turned to the world of romance novels, where messes are (usually) cleaned up before The End. In the worlds Shirley gets to create and control, the children listen to their parents, the husbands always remember holidays and the housework is magically done by elves. Though she's thrilled to see her books in stores around the world, Shirley mostly writes because it gives her an excuse to avoid cleaning the toilets, and it helps feed her shoe habit. To learn more, visit her Web site at www.shirleyjump.com.

Praise for Shirley Jump...

"Jump's office romance gives the collection a kick, with fiery writing."
—*PublishersWeekly.com,* on *New York Times* bestselling anthology *Sugar and Spice*

"Shirley Jump always succeeds in getting the plot, the characters, the settings and the emotions right."
—*CataRomance.com*

"Shirley Jump begins THE WEDDING PLANNERS with *Sweetheart Lost and Found.* It's smart, funny, and quite moving at times, and the characters have a lot of depth."
—*Romantic Times BOOKreviews*

A *Bride* FOR ALL *Seasons*

Would your perfect wedding be in the **spring**,
when flowers are starting to blossom and
it's the perfect season for new beginnings?

Or perhaps a balmy garden wedding,
set off by a riot of color that makes the
summer bride glow with the joys of a happy future?

Do you dream of being a **fall** bride, walking down the aisle
amid the dazzling reds and burnished golds of falling leaves?

Or of a **winter** wedding dusted with glistening white
snowflakes, celebrated by the ringing of frosty church bells?

With Harlequin Romance® you can have them all!
And, best of all, you can experience the
rush of falling in love with a gorgeous groom....

In April we celebrated spring with:
The Bride's Baby
by **Liz Fielding**

In June we kicked off summer with:
Saying Yes to the Millionaire
by **Fiona Harper**

In September we enjoyed a fall wedding in:
The Millionaire's Proposal
by **Trish Wylie**

And don't miss Christmas wedding bells this month:
Marry-Me Christmas
by **Shirley Jump**

Visit http://abrideforallseasons.blogspot.com
to find out more.

CHAPTER ONE

FLYNN MACGREGOR hated Riverbend, Indiana, from the second his Lexus stalled at the single stop light in the quaint town center, right beneath the gaily decorated Christmas swags of pine needles and red bows. The entire snow-dusted town seemed like something out of a movie.

There were people walking to and fro with wrapped gifts, stores bedecked with holiday decorations, and even snowflakes, falling at a slow and steady pace, as if some set decorator was standing in the clouds with a giant shaker.

Okay, so *hated* might be a strong word. Detested, perhaps. Loathed. Either way, he didn't want to be here, especially when he'd been forced into the decision.

His editor at *Food Lovers* magazine had assigned him this story in Riverbend, knowing Flynn, of everyone on staff, could get the job done. Write an incisive, unique piece on the little bakery—a bakery rumored to have cookies that inspired people to fall in love, his editor had said. So here he was, spending the Christmas holiday holed up in the middle of nowhere penning one more of the stories that had made him famous.

Flynn scowled. He couldn't complain. Those stories had been his bread and butter forever, a very lucrative butter at that. And after that little fiasco in June, he needed to get his edge back, reestablish his position at the top of the writer pack. To do that, he'd do what he always did—suck it up, feign great joy at the festive spirit surrounding him and get to work.

Then he could get back to Boston, back to Mimi, and back to civilization. This town, with its Norman Rockwell looks, had to be as far from civilization as Mars was from Earth. Not that he had anything against quaint, but he lived in a world of iPods, e-mail and high-speed Internet connections. Riverbend looked like the kind of place that thought Bluetooth was a dental disease.

So, here he was, at the Joyful Creations Bakery.

Oh, joy.

He pushed his car to the side of the road, then grabbed his notebook and headed across the street. The crowd in front of the Joyful Creations Bakery blocked most of the plateglass window, but Flynn could see that storefront, too, had not been spared by the town's festive elves. A trio of lighted wreaths hung in the window, one of them even forming the *O* in the business's name..

"Nauseatingly cute," Flynn muttered under his breath.

He circumvented the line that stretched out the door, around the bakery and all the way to the corner of Larch Street. Ignoring the snow falling from the sky, couples stood together—most of the men looking none too keen on the idea of being dragged off to a bakery purported to be a food love source, while groups of women chatted excitedly about the "romance cookies."

It took sheer willpower for Flynn not to roll his eyes. The airline magazine that had first broken the story had clearly created an epidemic. By the time this piece hit *Food Lovers'* Valentine's Day issue, the shop would be overrun with the lovelorn. He hoped the owner was prepared for the onslaught. Flynn knew, from personal experience, how a too-fast rocket to success could be as destructive as a too-quick drop to the bottom.

Regardless, he was here to do a job, not offer a business consultation.

He brushed by a woman holding a toddler and entered Joyful Creations. A blast of warm air and holiday music greeted him like he'd jumped into a Christmas bath. The scent of fresh-baked bread, coupled with vanilla, cinnamon and a hint of raspberry, assaulted his senses. The waiting patrons were surely impressed, but Flynn had seen all this and smelled all this before.

"Hey, no cutting," the woman said.

"I'm not buying anything," he replied, and kept going. Get in, get the story, get out. Get back to Boston. Hopefully before Mimi even noticed he was gone. *If* Mimi even noticed he was gone.

"Why would you battle this crowd if you weren't going to buy anything?" the woman asked, shuffling the kid to the other hip.

"For…" Flynn turned toward the counter where two women were busy filling orders as quickly as they were being shouted over the din. One, gray-haired and petite, the other, tall and blond, curvy, with the kind of hips that said she didn't spend her days obsessing over having two pieces of celery or one.

Wow. The airline magazine hadn't run a photo of Samantha Barnett with their story, just one of the cookies. But clearly, she was the owner that the writer had described as "energetic, friendly, youthful."

"Her," Flynn said.

"Sam? Good luck with that." The woman laughed, then turned back to her kid, playing with his nose. Pretending the thing was a button or something. Flynn had no experience with other people's children and had no intention of starting now, so he moved away.

It took the navigational skills of a fleet admiral to wade

through the crowd inside the shop, but a few minutes later, Flynn had managed to reach the glass counter. He stood to the far right, away from the line of paying customers, most of them looking like they'd come straight from placing a personal ad. "Are you Samantha Barnett?"

The blonde looked up. Little tendrils of her hair were beginning to escape her ponytail, as if the first few strands were thinking of making a break for the border. She wore little makeup, just a dash of red lip gloss and a dusting of mascara. He suspected the slight hint of crimson in her cheeks was natural, a flush from the frantic pace of the warm bakery. A long white apron with the words *Joyful Creations* scrolled across the middle in a curled red script hugged her frame, covering dark denim jeans and a soft green V-neck sweater. "I'm sorry, sir, you'll have to get into the line."

"I'm not here to buy anything."

That made her pause. Stop putting reindeer-shaped cookies into a white box. "Do you have a delivery or some mail for me?"

He shook his head. Vowed to buy a new dress coat, if he looked like a mailman in this one. "I just want to talk to you."

"Now is not a good time." She let out a little laugh. "I'm kind of busy."

"Yeah, well, I'm on a deadline." He fished a business card out of his pocket and slid it across the glass case. "Flynn MacGregor with *Food Lovers* magazine. Maybe you've heard of it?"

Her face lit up, as so many others before hers had. Everyone had heard of *Food Lovers*. It was *the* magazine about the food industry, carried in every grocery store and bookstore, read by thirty million people nationwide. A print mention in its pages was the equivalent of starring in a movie.

Even if *Food Lovers* magazine's focus had shifted, ever since Tony Reynolds had taken over as editor a year ago. His insistence on finding the story behind the story, the dish on every chef, restaurant and food business, had given the magazine more of a tabloid feel, but also tripled readership in a matter of months.

At first, Flynn hadn't minded doing what Tony wanted. But as each story became more and more invasive of people's personal lives, Flynn's job had begun to grate on him. More than once he had thought about quitting. But Flynn MacGregor hadn't gotten to where he was by turning tail just because he butted heads with an editor or ran into a roadblock ot two.

"Wow," Samantha said, clearly not bothered by *Food Lovers'* reputation. "You want to talk to me? What about?"

"Your bakery. Why you got into this business. What makes Joyful Creations special…" As he ran through his usual pre-interview spiel, Flynn bit back his impatience. Reminded himself this was his four hundredth interview, but probably her first or second. Flynn could recite the questions without even needing to write them down ahead of time. Heck, he could practically write her answers for her. She got into baking because she loved people, loved food. The best part about being in business in a small town was the customers. Yada-yada-yada.

As for the cookies that made people fall in love, Flynn put no stock in things like that. He'd seen soups that supposedly made women go into labor, cakes that were rumored to jump-start diets, appetizers bandied about as the next best aphrodisiac. None of which had proven to be true, but still, the magazine had run a charming piece in its pages, appealing to its vast readership.

While he was here, he'd track down a few of the couples who owed their happiness to the sugar-and-flour concoctions, then put some kind of cutesy spin on the story. The art department would fancy up the headline with dancing gingerbread men or something, and they'd all walk away thinking Joyful

Creations was the best thing to come along since Cupid and his trademark bow.

"That's pretty much how it works, Miss Barnett," Flynn finished, wrapping up his sugarcoated version of the article process.

The bakery owner nodded. "Sounds great. Relatively painless."

"Sam? I hate to interrupt," another woman cut in, just as Flynn was getting ready to ask his first question, "but I really need to pick up my order. I have a preschool waiting. And you know preschoolers. They want their sugar."

Samantha Barnett snapped to attention, back to her customer. "Oh, sure, Rachel. Sorry about that. Two dozen, right?"

The other woman, a petite brunette, grinned. "And one extra, for the teacher."

"Of course." Samantha smiled, finished putting the reindeer into the box, then tied it with a thin red ribbon and handed the white container across the counter. "Here you go."

"Will you put it on my tab?"

Samantha waved off the words. "Consider it a Christmas gift to the Bumblebees."

Not a smart way to run a business, giving away profits like that, but Flynn kept that to himself. He wasn't her financial consultant. "The interview, Miss Barnett?"

Behind them, the line groaned. Samantha brushed her bangs off her forehead. "Can I meet with you later today? Maybe after the shop closes? I'm swamped right now."

She had help, didn't she? On top of that, he had somewhere else he wanted to go before beginning that long drive back to Boston, not endless amounts of time to wait around for pre-schoolers to get their sugar rush. "And I'm on deadline."

The next person had slipped into the space vacated by Miss Bumblebee, a tall senior citizen in a flap-eared flannel cap and a Carhartt jacket. He ambled up to the counter, leaned one arm on the glass case and made himself at home, like he was planning on spending an hour or two there. "Hiya, Samantha. Heard about the article in that airline magazine. Congratulations! You really put our town on the map, not that you weren't a destination from the start, what with those cookies and all." He leaned forward, cupping a beefy hand around his mouth. "Though I'm not so sure I want all these tourists to stay. They're causing quite the traffic jam."

Samantha chuckled. "Thanks, Earl. And sorry I can't do anything about the traffic. Except fill the orders as fast as I can." She slid a glance Flynn's way.

"You give me my interview, Miss Barnett, and I'll be out of your hair."

"Give me a few hours, Mr. MacGregor, and I'll give you whatever you want."

He knew there was no innuendo in her words, but the male part of him heard one all the same. He cleared his throat and took a step back. "I have to get back on the road. Today. So why don't you just cooperate with me and we can both be happy?"

"I have customers to wait on, and it looks like now you're going to have a long wait either way." She gestured toward the windows with her chin as her hands worked beneath the counter, shoveling muffins into a bag. "You might as well make yourself comfortable."

Flynn turned and looked through the glass. And saw yet another reason to hate Riverbend.

A blizzard.

By noon, Sam was already so exhausted, she was sure she'd collapse face-first into the double-layer cinnamon streusel. But she pasted a smile on her face, kept handing out cookies and pastries, all while dispensing directions to her staff. She'd called in her seasonal part-timers, and everyone else she could think of, right down to Mary, who did the weekend cleaning, to help keep up with the sudden influx of tourists. It seemed every person in a three-state area had read the article and turned out to see if Joyful Creations would live up to its reputation of bringing love to people who tried Grandma Joy's Secret Recipe Cherry Chocolate Chunk Cookies.

Sam had long heard the rumors about her grandmother's cookies—after all, they were the very treats Grandma Joy had served to Grandpa Neil when they had first met—but had never quite believed all the people who credited the tiny desserts for their happy unions. Then a reporter from *Travelers* magazine had tried them on a trip through town and immediately fallen in love with one of the local women. The two of them had run off to Jamaica and gotten married the very next weekend. Afterward, the reporter had raved about the cookies and his happy ending in the airline publication, launching Sam's shop to national fame, and turning a rumor into a fact.

Ever since, things hadn't slowed down. Sam had worked a lot of hours before—but this was ridiculous. Nearly every spare moment was spent at the bakery, working, restocking and filling orders. But it was all for a larger goal, so she kept pushing, knowing the bigger reward was on the horizon.

"I can't decide." The platinum-blond woman, dressed head to toe in couture, put a leather-gloved finger to her lips. "How many calories did you say were in the peanut butter kiss cookies?"

The smile was beginning to hurt Sam's face. "About one hundred and ten per cookie."

"And those special cherry chocolate chunk ones?"

"About a hundred and fifty."

"Do those cookies really work? Those love ones?"

"That's what people say, ma'am."

"Well, it would really have to be worth the calories. That's a lot to work off in the gym, you know, if I don't meet Mr. Right. And if I meet Mr. Wrong—" the woman threw up her hands "—well that's even more time on the treadmill."

Sam bit her lip, then pushed the smile up further.

"Do you happen to know the fat grams? I'm on a very strict diet. My doctor doesn't want me to have more than twenty-two grams of fat per day."

From what Sam could see, the woman didn't have twenty-two grams of fat in her entire body, but she kept that to herself. "I don't know the grams of fat offhand, ma'am, but I assure you, none of these cookies have that many per serving."

The gloved finger to the lips again. She tipped her head to the right, then the left, her pageboy swinging with the indecision. Behind her, the entire line shifted and groaned in annoyance. "I still don't know."

"Why don't you buy one of each?" Sam said. "Have one today and one tomorrow."

"That's a wonderful idea." The woman beamed, as if Sam were Einstein. She handed her money across the glass case to Ginny while Sam wrapped the cookies in wax paper and slid them into a bright white Joyful Creations box, then tied a thin red ribbon around the box. "But…"

"But what?"

"How can I decide which one to have today?"

Sam just smiled, told the woman to have a merry Christmas, and moved on to the next customer. Four hundred of Grandma Joy's secret recipe cherry chocolate chunk cookies later, the line had finally thinned. Sam bent over, taking a moment to straighten the trays, whisk away a few crumbs and bring order back to the display.

Then, through the glass she glimpsed a pair of designer men's shoes, their glossy finish marred by road salt, dots of dried snow. Her gaze traveled upward. Pressed trousers, a dark gray cashmere dress coat. White shirt. Crimson tie.

He was back. Flynn MacGregor.

Blue eyes, so deep, so dark, they were the color of the sky when a thunderstorm came rolling through. Black, wavy hair that had been tamed with a close cut. And a face set in rigid stone. "I have waited. For hours. Watched dozens of customers come through here, thinking you have the answer to love, marriage and apparently the beginnings of the earth." He let out a breath of displeasure. "I had no idea you could get such bonuses with your coffee cake."

His droll manner told her it wasn't a joke, nor a compliment. "I don't purport to offer anything other than baked goods, Mr. MacGregor."

"That's not what the people in that line thought. That very *long* line, I might add. One that took nearly three hours to clear out. And now—" he flicked out a wrist and glanced at his watch "—I'm never going to get to where I needed to go today if I don't get this interview done. Now."

"I don't think you're going to be able to make it farther than a few miles. I doubt the roads are clear. The weather is still pretty bad."

"My editor is from the mailman school of thought. Neither blizzard nor earthquake shall stop a deadline."

She eyed him. "And I take it you agree with his philosophy?"

"I didn't get to where I am in my career by letting a little snow stop me." He leaned forward. "So, do you have time *now*, Miss Barnett?"

Clearly, Sam's best bet was to fit in with his plans. Business had slowed enough for her to give the reporter some time anyway. "Sure. And it'd be great to sit down for a minute."

Sam turned toward her great-aunt. "Aunt Ginny, could you handle the counter for a little while?"

The older woman gave her a grin. "Absolutely."

Sam pivoted back to Flynn. The man was handsome enough, even if he was about as warm and fuzzy as a hedgehog. But, he had come all the way from Boston, and Lord knew she could use the publicity. The airline magazine story had been a great boon, but Sam was a smart enough business person to know that kind of PR wouldn't last long. "Can I get you some coffee? A Danish? Muffin? Cookies?"

"I'd like a sampling of the house specialties. And some coffee would be nice."

He had good looks, but he had all the friendliness of a brick wall. His words came out clear, direct, to the point. No wasted syllables, no wide smiles.

Nevertheless, he offered the one gift Sam had been dreaming about for years. A positive profile of the bakery in the widely popular *Food Lovers* magazine would be just the kickoff she needed to launch the new locations she'd been hoping to open this year. Heck, the exposure she'd hoped and prayed for ever since she'd taken over the bakery. Coupled with the boost in business the airline magazine's story had given her, Joyful Creations was on its way to nationwide prominence.

And she was on her way out of Riverbend.

Finally.

Not to mention, she'd also have the financial security she needed to fund her grandmother's long-term care needs. It was all right here.

In Flynn MacGregor. If that didn't prove Santa existed, Sam wasn't sure what did.

She hummed snippets of Christmas carols as she filled a holly-decorated plate with a variety of the bakery's best treats.

Gingerbread cookies, pecan bars, cranberry orange muffins, white mocha fudge, peppermint chocolate bark, frosted sugar Santa cookies—she piled them all on until the plate threatened to spill.

"Don't forget some of these," Ginny said, handing Sam a couple cherry chocolate chunk cookies.

"Aunt Ginny, I don't think he needs—"

"He came here for the story about the special cookies, didn't he?" Her great-aunt gave her a wide smile. "And if the stories are true, you never know what might happen if he takes a bite."

"You don't seriously believe—"

"I do, and you should, too." Ginny wagged a finger. "Why, your grandmother and grandfather never would have fallen in love if not for this recipe. I wouldn't have married your Uncle Larry if it hadn't been for these cookies. Why, look at all the proof around you in this town. You just don't believe in them because you've never tried them."

"That's because I'm too busy baking to eat." Sam sighed, accepted the two cookies and added them to the plate. What was the harm, really? There was nothing to that legend. Regardless of what Aunt Ginny thought.

Balancing the plate, Sam crossed the room and placed the treats and a steaming mug of coffee before the reporter. "Here you are, Mr.—"

And she lost the next word. Completely forgot his name.

He had taken off his coat and was sitting at one of the small round café tables in the corner, by the plate-glass windows that faced the town square. He had that air about him of wealth, all in the telltale signs of expensive fabric, perfectly fitting clothing, the way he carried himself. His sleeves were rolled up, exposing defined, muscled hands and forearms, fingers long enough to play piano, touch a woman and—

Whoa. She was staring.

"Mr. MacGregor," she finished. Fast. "Enjoy." Sam took a couple steps back. "Uh, enjoy."

He turned to her and a grin flashed across his face so quickly, she could have almost sworn she'd imagined it. But no, it had been there. A thank-you, perhaps. Or maybe amusement at her discomfit?

Either way, his smile changed his entire face. Softened his features. Made Sam's pulse race in a way it hadn't in a long time.

"You already said that," he said.

Okay, it had been amusement. Now she was embarrassed.

"Did I? Sorry. You, ah, make me nervous." No way would she admit public humiliation.

"I do? Why?"

"I haven't had a real reporter in the shop before. Well, except for Joey from the *Riverbend Times*, but that doesn't count. He's nineteen and still in college, and he's usually just here to get a cup of decaf because regular coffee makes him so hyper he can hardly write." She was babbling. What was wrong with her? Samantha Barnett never babbled. Never got unnerved.

Way to make a first impression, Sam.

"I should get back in the kitchen," Sam said, thumbing in that direction.

"I need to interview you. Remember? And I'd prefer not to shout my questions."

Now she'd annoyed him. "All right. Let me grab a cup of coffee. Unlike Joey, I *do* need the caffeine."

He let out a laugh. Okay, so it had been about a half a syllable long, but still, Sam took that as a good sign. A beginning. If he liked her and liked the food, maybe this Flynn guy would write a kick-butt review, and all her Christmas wishes would be granted.

But as she walked away, he started drumming his fingers on the table, tapping out his impatience one digit at a time.

Ginny tapped her on the shoulder when she reached the coffeepot. "Sam, I forget to mention something earlier."

"If it's about getting me to share Grandma's special recipe cookies with a man again—"

"No, no, it's about that magazine he's with. He said *Food Lovers*, didn't he?"

Sam poured some coffee into a mug. "Yes. It's huge. Everybody reads it, well, except for me. I never get time to read anything."

Ginny made a face. "Well, I read it, or at least I used to. Years ago, *Food Lovers* used to just be about food, you know, recipes and things like that, but lately, it's become more…"

"More what?" Sam prompted.

Her aunt paused a moment longer, then let out a breath. "Like those newspapers you see in the checkout stand. A lot of the stories are about the personal lives of the people who own the restaurants and the bakeries, not the food they serve. It's kind of…intrusive."

"What's wrong with writing stories about the people who own the businesses?"

Ginny shrugged. "Just be careful," she said, laying a hand on Sam's. "I know how you guard your privacy, and your grandmother's. I might not agree with your decision, but you're my niece, so I support you no matter what."

Sam drew Aunt Ginny into a hug. "Thank you."

"Anything for you, Sam," she said, then drew back. She glanced over the counter at Flynn MacGregor. "There's one other thing you need to be careful of, too."

"What's that?"

Ginny grinned. "He's awfully cute. That could be the kind of trouble you've been needing, dear niece, for a long time."

Sam grabbed her coffee mug. "Adding a relationship into my life, as busy as it is?" She shook her head. "That would be like adding way too much yeast to a batter. In the end, you get nothing but a mess."

CHAPTER TWO

SAM RETURNED with her coffee, Aunt Ginny's words of wisdom still ringing in her head, and slipped into the opposite seat from Flynn MacGregor. He had a pad of paper open beside him, turned to a blank page, with a ready pen. He'd sampled the coffee, but none of the baked goods. Not so much as a crumb of Santa's beard on the frosted sugar cookies. Nary a bite from Grandma's special cookies—the ones he'd presumably come all this way to write about.

Sam's spirits fell, but she didn't let it show. Maybe he wanted to talk to her first. Or maybe he was, as Aunt Ginny had cautioned, here solely for the story behind the bakery.

Her story.

"Are you ready *now?*" he asked.

"Completely."

"Good. Tell me the history of the bakery."

Sam folded her hands on the table. "Joyful Creations was opened in 1948 by my grandmother Joy and grandfather Neil Barnett. My grandmother was an amazing cook. She made the most incredible cookies for our family every holiday. I remember one time I went over to her house, and she had 'invent a cookie' day. She just opened her cabinets, and she and I—"

"The bakery, Miss Barnett. Can we stick to that topic?"

"Oh, yes. Of course." Sam wanted to kick herself. Babbling again. "My grandfather thought my grandmother was so good, she should share those talents with Riverbend. So they opened the bakery."

He jotted down the information as she talked, his pen skimming across the page in an indecipherable scrawl.

Sam leaned forward. "Are you going to be able to read that later?"

He looked up. "This? It's my own kind of shorthand. No vowels, abbreviations only I know for certain words."

She chuckled. "It's like my recipes. Some of them have been handed down for generations. My grandmother never really kept precise records and some of them just say 'pecs' or 'CC.' They're like a puzzle."

He arched a brow. "Pecs? CC?"

"Pecans. And CC was shorthand for chocolate chips." Sam smiled. "It took me weeks to figure out some of them, after I took over the bakery. I should have paid more attention when I was little."

His brows knitted in confusion. "I read it was a third-generation business. What happened to the second generation?"

"My parents died in a car accident when I was in middle school. I went to live with my grandparents. Grandpa Neil died ten years ago." Sam splayed her palms on the table and bit her lip. Flynn MacGregor didn't need to know more than that.

"And your grandmother? Is she still alive?"

Sam hated lying. It wasn't in her nature to do so. But now she was in a position where telling the truth opened a bucket of worms that could get out of hand. "She is, but no longer working in the bakery."

He wrote that down. "I'd like to interview her, too."

"You can't."

Flynn looked up. "Why?"

"She's…ill." That was all he needed to know. Joy's privacy was her own. This reporter could keep the story focused on the present.

Nevertheless, he made a note, a little note of mmm-hmm under his breath. Sam shifted in her chair. "Don't you want to try a cranberry orange muffin?"

"In a minute."

"But—"

"I'm writing an article, Miss Barnett, not a review."

She shifted some more. Maybe her unease stemmed from his presence. The airline magazine had done the interview part over the phone. The reporter had come in and bought some cookies, then found his happy ending, unbeknownst to Sam, at a different time. Talking to someone she couldn't see, and answering a few quick questions, had been easy. This face-to-face thing was much more difficult.

More distracting. Because this reporter had a deep blue, piercing gaze.

The bell over the door jingled and a whoosh of cold air burst into the room. "Sam!"

"Mrs. Meyers, how can I help you?"

"I need more cookies. My dog ate the box I brought home. I didn't even get a chance to feed the batch I bought to my Carl and that man is in the grumpiest of moods." Eileen Meyers swung her gaze heavenward. "He's hanging the Christmas lights."

"In this weather?"

"You know my husband. The man is as stubborn as a tick on a hunting dog, Sam. There are days I wonder why I'm even buying those cookies."

"Because they're your husband's favorites," Sam reminded her. Eileen had been in the day before, plunked down her money, her love for her husband still clear, even in a marriage that had celebrated its silver anniversary, and was edging its way toward gold.

Eileen harrumphed, but a smile played at the edge of her lips. "Will you get me another dozen?"

"Ginny can help you, Mrs. Meyers."

Eileen laid a hand on Sam's arm, her brown eyes filled with entreaty. "I love your Aunt Ginny, Sam, I do, but you know my Carl better than I do some days. He says you're the only one who can pick out the cookies he likes best."

Across from her, Flynn MacGregor's pen tapped once against his notepad. A reminder of where her attention should be.

"Please, Sam?" Eileen's hand held tight to Sam's arm. "It'll mean the world to Carl."

"This will just take a minute," she told Flynn. "Is that all right?"

"Of course." A smile as fake as the spray-paint snow on the windows whipped across his face. "I've already waited for that massive line of customers to go down. Dealt with my car breaking down, and a blizzard blowing through town, which has undoubtedly delayed my leaving, too. What's one more box of cookies?"

Sam filled Eileen's order as quickly as she could, trying to head off Eileen's attempts at conversation. And failing miserably. Eileen was one of those people who couldn't buy a newspaper without engaging in a rundown of her life story. By the time she had paid for her cookies, she'd told Sam—again—all about how she and Mr. Meyers had met, what he'd done to sweep her off her feet and how he'd lost his romantic touch long ago.

"Are you done playing advice columnist?" Flynn asked when Eileen finally left.

"I'm sorry. Things have been especially crazy here since word got out about those cookies." Sam gestured toward the plate, where the trio of Grandma's special recipe still sat, untouched.

"The ones that are purported to make people fall in love?"

She shrugged. "That's what people say."

"I take it you don't believe the rumors?"

She laughed. "I don't know. Maybe it's true. If two people find a happy ending because they eat my grandmother's cookies, then I think it's wonderful. For them, and for business."

Flynn arched a brow. "Happy endings? Over cookies?"

"Not much of a romantic, are you?"

"No. I'm a practical man. I do my job, and I don't dabble in all this—" he waved his hand "—fanciful stuff."

"Me, too." Sam laughed, the chuckle escaping her with a nervous clatter. "Well, not the man part."

"Of course." He nodded.

What was with this guy? He was as serious as a wreath without any decorations. Sam laced her fingers together and tried to get comfortable in the chair, but more, under his scrutiny. The sooner this interview was over, the better. "What else did you need to know?"

"How long have you been working here?"

"All my life. Basically, ever since I could walk. But I took over full-time when I was nineteen."

Surprise dropped his jaw. "Nineteen? Isn't that awfully young? What kind of business person could you be at that age?"

"You do what have to, Mr. MacGregor." She sipped at her coffee, avoiding his piercing gaze. He had a way of looking at a woman like he could see right through her. Like Superman's X-ray vision, only he wasn't looking at the color of her underwear, but at the secrets of her soul.

She pushed the plate closer to him. "I think you'd really like the sugar frosted cookies. They're a Joyful Creations specialty."

Again, he bypassed the plate in front of him, in favor of his notes. "Did you go to culinary school?"

She shook her head. "I couldn't. I was working here. Full-time."

"Having no life, you mean."

She bristled. "I enjoy my job."

"I'm sure you do." He flipped a page on his notepad, bringing him to a clean sheet of paper.

"What's that supposed to mean?"

"I'm not here to tell you how to run your business."

"And yet, you're judging me and you hardly know me."

Flynn folded his hands over his pad. "Miss Barnett, I've been covering this industry for a long time. Talked to hundreds of bakers and chefs. This is the kind of business that consumes you." He let out a laugh, another short, nearly bitter sound that barely became a full chuckle. "Pun intended."

"My business doesn't consume me." But as the words left her mouth, she knew Joyful Creations had, indeed, done that very thing, particularly in the last few weeks. The business had taken away her weekends. Vacations. Eaten up friendships, nights out, dates. Left her with this empty feeling, as if she'd missed a half of herself.

The half that had watched her friends grow up. Get married. Start families. While she had toiled in the bakery, telling herself there'd be time down the road. As one year passed, then two, then five, and Sam hit twenty-five, and tried not to tell herself she'd missed too much already. She had plenty of time—down the road.

There was a reason she worked so hard. A very important reason. And once she'd reached her goals, she'd take time off.

She would.

"I watched you earlier. And I've watched you as you've talked about this business. I can see the stars in your eyes," he went on. "The *Travelers'* magazine article has probably put the lofty idea in your head that you can become the next McDonald's or Mrs. Fields Cookies."

"It hasn't," Sam leapt to say, then checked her defensive tone. "Well, maybe a little. Did you see those lines? It's been that way nonstop for two weeks. I'm sure you've seen many businesses that became mega-successes after something like that. Don't you think it's possible for me to hit the big time?"

"I have seen it happen," he conceded. "And let me be the first to warn you to be careful what you wish for."

She leaned back in her chair and stared at him, incredulous. Ever since she'd met him, he'd been nothing but grouchy, and now here he was, trying to tell her how to run her own company. "Who put coal in your stocking this morning?"

"I'm just being honest. I believe in calling the shots I see."

"So do I, Mr. MacGregor," Sam said, rising. If she didn't leave this table in the next five seconds, she'd be saying things to this man that she didn't want to see in print. "And while we're on the subject of our respective industries, I think yours has made you as jaded and as bitter as a bushel of lemons." She gestured toward his still-full plate, and frustration surged inside her. With the busy day, with him, and especially with his refusal to try the very baked goods he was writing about yet already judging. "Maybe you should have started with the cookies first. A little sugar goes a long way toward making people happy. And you, sir, could use a lot of that."

CHAPTER THREE

"WELL, I WAS WRONG."

Flynn bit back the urge to curse. "What do you mean, wrong?"

"I replaced the air filter. And it turned out, that wasn't it. That means, I was wrong." Earl Klein shrugged. "It happens." He put out his hands, as if that explained why Flynn's car was sitting inside Earl's Tire and Repair on a lift six feet off the ground, a jumble of parts scattered below.

"Did you fix it?" Flynn asked. Of all the people to end up with, Earl would have been Flynn's last choice. He had asked around once he left the bakery, and it turned out the hunting cap guy he'd seen earlier owned the closest garage to Flynn's broken-down car. Although, given how circular a conversation with Earl was turning out to be, Flynn was beginning to regret his choice.

Earl stared at Flynn like he had all the intelligence of a duck. "Does your car *look* fixed?"

"Well, no, but I was hoping—"

"Your fuel filter needs to be replaced. I usually have one for your model on hand, but used my last one yesterday. Damnedest thing, too. Paulie Lennox comes in here, his car was running fine, then all of a sudden—"

"I don't care about Paulie Lennox. I don't even know him."

"Oh, you'd know him if you see him. He's six foot seven. Tallest man in Riverbend. Sings in the church choir. Voice of an angel. Ain't that weird for a guy that big? Must have organ pipes in his chest."

Flynn gritted his teeth. "How long?"

"How long are his vocal cords? Damned if I know. I'm no doctor."

"No, I meant how long until my car is fixed?"

"Oh, that." Earl turned around and looked at the Lexus as if it might tell him. "Day. Maybe two. Gotta wait for the part. You know, 'cept for Paulie, we don't get many of those fancy-dancy cars in here. If you'da come in here with a Ford, or Chevy pickup, I'd have you fixed up a couple minutes. But this, well, this requires what we call special treatment."

Flynn hoped like hell this guy would give the Lexus special treatment, considering what the car cost. "Did you order the part? Or can you go get it?"

"I ordered it. Can't go get it."

Flynn wanted to bang his head into a brick wall. He'd probably get further in the conversation if he did. This was like playing Ping-Pong by himself. "Why can't you go get the part?"

Earl leaned in closer to Flynn. "Have you looked outside, son? It's *snowing*. Blizzard's on its way into town, hell, it's already here. Only an idiot would drive in this. And I'm no idiot."

Flynn would beg to differ. "It's four days before Christmas."

"That don't change the icy roads. Old Man Winter, he doesn't have the same calendar as you and me."

Flynn dug deep for more patience. "Is there another garage in town?"

Earl's face frowned in offense. "Now, I'm going to pretend you didn't even ask that, because you're from out of town. My garage is the best one for miles, and the only one."

Of course. Flynn groaned. "I have some place I need to go. As soon as possible."

That was if he even decided to make that stop in southern Indiana. On the drive out here from Boston, it had seemed like a good idea, but the closer Flynn got to the Midwest, the more he began to second-guess his impromptu decision. That was why he had yet to make any promises he couldn't keep. Better not to say a word. That way, no one was disappointed. Again.

"Well, that ain't happenin', is it?" Earl grinned. "You best get down to Betsy's Bed and Breakfast. She'll put you up and feed you, too." He patted his stomach. "That woman can cook. And she's real pretty, too. But she's spoken for. So don't go thinking you can ask her out. Me and Betsy, we have an understanding." Earl wiggled a shaggy gray brow. "Thanks to those cookies of Sam's, which helped us out a lot. Brought me and Betsy together, they did."

Flynn put up his hands, hoping to ward off the mental picture that brought up. "I don't want to know about it. Just point me in the general direction."

Thirty seconds later, Flynn was back outside, battling an increasingly more powerful wind. The snow had multiplied and six more inches of the thick wet stuff now coated the sidewalks. The earlier tourist crowds had apparently gotten the hint and left for their hotels or real cities. Traffic, what there was left in Riverbend, had slowed to a crawl. Within minutes, the damp snow had seeped through Flynn's shoes and he was slogging through slush, ruining five-hundred-dollar dress shoes. Damn it. What he wouldn't do for a sled dog team right now.

"Do you need a ride?"

He turned to see Samantha Barnett at the wheel of an older model Jeep Cherokee. Or what he thought was Samantha Barnett. She was bundled in a blue parka-type jacket that obscured most of her delicate features, the hood covering all of her blond hair. But the smile—that 100-watt smile he'd seen earlier in the bakery—that he could see.

Only a fool would say no to that. And to the dry, warm vehicle.

"Sure." He opened the door and climbed inside. Holiday music pumped from the stereo, filling the interior of the Jeep like stuffing in a turkey. Again, Flynn got that Norman Rockwell feeling. "Is this town for real?" he asked as Sam put the Jeep in gear and they passed yet another decorated window display—this one complete with a moving Santa's workshop.

"What do you mean?"

"It's a bit too jolly, don't you think? I mean, it's almost nauseating."

"Nauseating? It's Christmas. People are feeling…festive."

"Festive? In this?" He gestured out the window. "My feet are soaked, nearly frostbitten, I'm sure. My car is being worked on by the village idiot, I'm on a deadline that I can't miss and I'm being held hostage in a town that thinks Christmas is the be-all and end-all."

"Well, isn't it?"

"There are three hundred and sixty-four other days in the year, you know."

Sam stared at him. Never before had she met anyone with as little Christmas spirit as Flynn MacGregor. "Don't you celebrate Christmas? Put up a tree? Drink a little eggnog?"

Flynn didn't answer. Instead he glanced out the window. "Do you know a place called Betsy's Bed and Breakfast?"

"Of course I do. It's a small town. Everyone knows everyone else, and everything. You burn your toast in the morning and Mrs. Beedleman over on Oak Street is on your doorstep, lending you her toaster before lunch." Sam smiled. "I'm on my way to make a couple of deliveries, so I have time. Besides, driving you to Betsy's is the least I can do to say I'm sorry for being so short with you earlier." She took a left, using caution as she made the turn and navigated through the downtown intersection. "I guess I'm just a little protective when it comes to the bakery."

"Most business owners are." He kept watching out the window. "Is that a *live* reindeer I see in the park? This town is Christmas gone overboard."

She turned to him. "You're kind of grumpy, aren't you? This whole anti-Christmas thing, the way you jumped on me about my business... Grumpy."

He sat back. "No. Just...honest."

She shrugged. "I call it grumpy."

"Honest. Direct. To the point."

She flashed another glance his way. "You know who else was grumpy? Ebenezer Scrooge. Remember him? He got a pretty bad preview of his future."

Flynn rolled his eyes. "That was fiction. I'm talking real life."

"Uh-huh. Let me know when the ghost of Christmas Future comes knocking on your door."

"When he does, I'll know it's time to put away the scotch."

Samantha laughed. Her laughter had a light, musical sound to it. Like the holiday carols coming from the stereo. Flynn tried hard not to like the sound, but...

He did.

"Listen, you had a rough day," Sam said, "so you're excused for any and all grumpiness. And don't worry, you're in good hands with Earl."

Flynn let out a short gust of disbelief. "I'd be in better hands with a troop of baboons."

"Oh, Earl's not so bad. He's really easygoing. You just gotta get used to him. And, indulge him by listening to his stories once in a while. Nothing makes him happier than that. You might even get a discount on your service if you suffer through his account of the blizzard of '78 and how he baked

a turkey, even though the power was out for four days." She
shot him a grin.

"I don't have time for other people's stories."

"You're a reporter, isn't your whole mission to get the story?"

"Just the ones they pay me for." That pay had been lucrative, ever since he turned in his first article. Flynn had risen
to the top of his field, becoming well-known in the magazine
industry for being the go-to guy for getting the job done—on
time, and right on the word count.

Then he'd hit a road bump, a big one, with the celebrity chef
back in June. His editor had lost faith in Flynn, but worse—

Flynn had temporarily lost faith in himself.

He refused to get sucked into that emotional vortex again.
He'd gotten to the top by staying out of the story, and he'd do
that again here. Get in and out, as fast as possible.

And then make one stop, one very important stop, before
heading back to Boston.

But he couldn't do either if he didn't shake off that silly
whisper of conscience, write the story his editor wanted and
get it in on time, no matter what it took.

The interior of the Jeep had reached a comfortable temperature and Sam pulled off one glove, then the other. Her
hands, he noticed, were slim and delicate, the nails short and
no-nonsense, not polished. She tugged on the zipper of the
parka, but it stuck. "Oh, this coat," she muttered, still tugging
with one hand while she drove with the other.

"Let me." He reached over, intending only to help her,
but his hand brushed against hers, and instant heat exploded
in that touch. Flynn's hand jerked upward. He hadn't reacted
with such instantaneous attraction to a woman—a woman
he'd just met—in a long time. Granted, Samantha Barnett
was beautiful, but there was something about her.
Something indefinable. A brightness to her smile, to her per-

sonality, that seemed to draw him in, make him forget his reporter's objectivity.

Not smart. If there was one thing Flynn prided himself on being, it was smart.

Controlled. He didn't let things get out of hand, get crazy. By keeping tight reins on his life, on himself, he was able to manage everything. The one time he had lost control, he'd nearly lost his career.

He cleared his throat. He clasped the tiny silver zipper and pulled. After a slight catch, the fastener gave way, parting the front of the coat with a low-pitched hum as it slid down.

Beneath the coat, she wore a soft green sweater that dipped in a slight *V* at the neck and skimmed over her curves. From the second he'd met Samantha Barnett, Flynn had noticed the way the green of the sweater enhanced the green in her eyes, offset the golden tones in her hair. But now, without the cover of the apron, he noticed twice as much.

And noticed even more about her.

The scent of her perfume…cinnamon, vanilla, honey—or was it simply the leftover scents of the bakery?—wafted up to tease at his senses. Would her skin taste the same? Taste as good as the baked delights in the cases of the shop?

Flynn drew back. Shook himself.

Get back on track, back in work mode.

Getting distracted by a woman was not part of the plan. It *never* was. He did not get emotionally involved. Did not let himself care, about the people in the story, about people in general. That was how he stayed in control of his life.

No way was he deviating from the road he had laid for himself. Even Mimi, with her need for no real tie, no commitment, fit into what he needed. A woman like Samantha Barnett, who had small-town, commitment values written all over her, would not. "Your, ah, zipper is all fixed."

"Thanks." She flashed that smile his way again.

That was when Flynn MacGregor realized he had a problem. He'd been distracted from the minute he'd walked into that bakery.

Betsy's Bed and Breakfast was located less than six blocks from Earl's repair shop, but with Flynn MacGregor so close, the ride seemed to take ten hours instead of ten minutes. Sam was aware of his every breath, his every movement. She kept her eyes on the road, not just because visibility had become nearly zero, but because it seemed as if the only thing she saw in her peripheral vision was Flynn.

She hadn't been out on a date in—

Well, a long time. Too much work, too little personal life. That must be why her every thought seemed to revolve around him. Why she'd become hyperaware of the woodsy notes of his cologne. Why her gaze kept straying to his hands, his broad shoulders, the cleft in his jaw.

This ride was a prime opportunity to impress him. To tell him more about the bakery. Not flirt. Not that him jumping in to help with her zipper was flirting…except she had held her breath when he'd gotten so close. Noted the fit of his jacket. The flecks of gold in his eyes. The way the last rays of sun glinted in his hair.

Business, Sam. Business.

"Have you interviewed many bakery owners?" she asked. Then wanted to kick herself. She hadn't exactly hit the witty jackpot with that one.

"A few. Mostly, I cover high-end restaurants. Or, I did." He gave her a wry grin, one that made her wonder about the use of the past tense. "All those chefs courting heart attacks, trying to maintain their five-star ratings."

Sam stopped the Jeep, the four-wheel drive working hard

to grip the icy roads, and let a mother and her three children cross the street. Sam recognized Linda Powell, and waved to her through the front window. The littlest Powell waved back, a small red mittened hand bringing a smile to Sam's face. "Is the restaurant business really that competitive?"

He snorted. "Are you kidding? In some cities, these places campaign all year to garner those ratings. They agonize over their menus, stress over the tiniest ingredients, sometimes shipping in a certain fish from one pocket of the world because the chef insists absolutely nothing else will do. Every detail is obsessed over, nitpicked at like it's life and death. They'll accept nothing less than the unqualified best. A bad review can close a place, a good review can skyrocket it to the top."

"But…that's ridiculous." She halted at a stop sign, waiting to make the right onto Maple Street. The Jeep's wipers clicked back and forth, wiping snow off the frosty glass. "A review is simply one person's opinion."

"Ah, but people like me are paid to be the experts." Flynn put a hand on his chest, affecting a dramatic posture. "They live or die by our words."

They had reached Betsy's Bed and Breakfast, where a small hand-painted sign out front announced the converted Victorian's vacancies. Sam stopped in front of the quaint home and parked alongside the front walk. Betsy, a complete Christmas fanatic, had decked the entire porch in holiday flare, with a moving Santa, twinkling lights and even a lighted sleigh and reindeer on the roof.

"And what about me?" Sam asked, turning to Flynn before he exited the Jeep. "What do you think will be my fate? Do you think I'll skyrocket to the top?"

Flynn studied her for a long time, his gaze unreadable in the darkening day, a storm in his blue eyes rivaling the one in the sky. "That, Miss Barnett, is still to be determined."

CHAPTER FOUR

BETSY WILLIAMS, the owner of the bed and breakfast, greeted Flynn with bells on. Literally.

The buxom, wide woman hurried across the foyer and put out her arms, the bells on her house slippers jingling and jangling as she moved, like a one-person reindeer symphony. "Welcome! It's so nice to have another guest! At Betsy's Bed and Breakfast, there's always room for one more!"

Flynn would have turned and run, except Samantha Barnett was standing behind him, blocking the sole exit. "I'm only here until my car is fixed."

And hopefully not a single second longer.

"As long as you want, my heart and home are open to you." She beamed, bright red lips spreading across her face and revealing even, white teeth. Her hand shot out, and she pumped his in greeting, extracting his name and reason for coming to Riverbend in quick succession. "Oh, that's just so exciting!" Betsy said. "Now, tell me what you want for breakfast. Waffles, French toast or eggs?"

Flynn forced a smile to his face. "Surprise me."

Betsy squealed. "I'll delight you, is what I'll do. And I'll have plenty of baked goods to choose from, too, won't I, Sam?"

"You're my first delivery of the day, Betsy. Not to mention, my best customer."

Betsy hustled around and took Flynn's arm, practically hauling him toward the front parlor. "I was her *only* customer, don't you know, back when she first took over. So many people didn't think a girl, still practically a teenager, could run a shop like that. And she did have her mishaps, didn't you, Sam? A few burned things and well, that one teeny-weeny explosion, but you moved past those little setbacks." Betsy beamed. "You're a regular baker now, even if you had no formal training."

Flynn glanced over at Samantha. Her smile seemed held on by strings.

"And those romance cookies, why they worked for me and my Earl. Oh, he's such a cutie, isn't he?" Betsy barreled on, saving Flynn from having to offer an opinion. "Those cookies have fixed up many a person who has come through my door. I serve them every morning on the buffet table." Betsy wagged a finger at him. "If you're looking for love, Mr. MacGregor, you be sure to try those cookies."

"I'm fine, thank you."

She assessed him like a Christmas ham. "I don't see a ring. That means you need the cookies." Betsy nodded. "And our Sam, here, she's available."

"Betsy, Mr. MacGregor needs a room," Sam interjected.

"Oh, my goodness, I almost forgot! And here I am, the hostess and everything." Betsy tsk-tsked herself. "And you need to get back to work, missy, right?"

"I do," Sam replied. "Business is booming lately."

"Well, why wouldn't it? Where else are people going to go to get their cookies? You're the only bakery for miles and miles!" Betsy grinned, as if she'd just paid Samantha a huge compliment. Flynn supposed, in her own way, Betsy thought she had, but he could see the sting in Samantha's eyes. The implication that her success was due solely to a lack of competition, not hard work and expertise. Maybe Betsy still saw Sam as that young kid who burned the muffins.

For a second, his chest constricted with sympathy, then he yanked the emotion back. The first rule in reporting was not to get involved with the story, stay above the fray.

He'd used that as a yardstick to measure every personal decision he'd ever made. After years of sticking to that mantra like tape to a present, Flynn wasn't about to start caring now. To start putting his heart into the mix. He did not cross those boundaries.

Ever.

He didn't care if Riverbend had issues with Sam Barnett or vice versa. Didn't care if her business was going gangbusters or going bust. He'd made a very good living without ever putting his heart into a story, because Flynn MacGregor had learned a long time ago that doing so meant putting his emotions through a meat grinder. He'd rather write about kitchen implements than experience them.

"I'd like to get settled, Miss Williams," Flynn said. "And find out how to log onto your network."

"Network?" She frowned, then propped a fist on her ample hip. "I'll have you know Betsy's Bed and Breakfast is not a chain."

"*Internet* network," Flynn said. "I wanted to check my e-mail."

"Oh, that." She crossed to a side table, to straighten the green-feathered hat on a stuffed cat in an elf costume, then walked back to Flynn. "I don't have one of those either."

"Well, then your dial-up connection. That'll do."

"Dial-up to what? Anytime we need to talk to somebody, we either walk on down to their house or call 'em on the phone." Betsy wagged a finger at him. "By the way, local calls are free at Betsy's Bed and Breakfast, but there is an extra charge for any long distance. The parlor phone is the one set aside for guest usage."

Flynn pivoted back toward Samantha. "There *is* an Internet connection in this town, isn't there?"

"Well, yes, but…" Samantha gave him a smile. "It's not very reliable, so most people here don't bother with it."

He truly had landed in the middle of nowhere. Flynn bit back his impatience, but it surged forward all the same. "What *exactly* does that mean?"

"Meaning when there's a storm, like there is now, the Internet is the first to go."

"What about cable? Satellite?"

"Not here, not yet. Companies look for demand before they start investing the dollars in technology and, well, Riverbend has never been big on embracing that kind of thing." Samantha shrugged.

"How the hell do you do business out here?"

"Most people still do things the old-fashioned way, I suppose. Face-to-face, with a smile and handshake."

A headache began to pound in Flynn's temples. He rubbed at his forehead. He couldn't miss his deadline. Absolutely could not. It wasn't just that *Food Lovers* was holding the Valentine's Day issue especially for this article, and being late would risk raising Tony's ire. Flynn had already earned a slot on the ire list.

There was more than his career to consider. In the last few months since that interview that had blown up in his face, Flynn had found himself searching for—

A connection. To a past he thought he'd shut off, closed like a closet door full of memories no one wanted to look at. He'd done everything he could to take care of that past, to assuage his guilt. But suddenly throwing money at it wasn't enough.

He needed to go in person, even if he wasn't so sure his

shoes on that doorstep would be very welcome. Either way, one glance out the window at the storm that had become a frenzy of white, told him the chances of leaving today—even if his car was fixed—were nil.

Until the storm eased, he'd work. Write up this thing about magic elves baking love cookies, or whatever the secret was, turn it over to his editor, and then he could get back to the meat that fed his paycheck and his constant hunger to find the scoop—scathing restaurant reviews exposing the true underbelly of the food industry.

"How am I supposed to work without an Internet connection?" he said.

"We have electricity," Betsy said, her voice high and helpful. "You can plug in a computer. That's good enough, isn't it?" Upstairs, someone called Betsy's name, mentioning an emergency. She sighed. "Oh, Lord, not again." She toodled a wave, then headed up the stairs, while her slippers sang their jarring song.

Flynn turned back to Samantha. "If Scrooge's ghosts do come visit me, they better bring a connection to civilization. And if they can't, just put me out of my misery. Because this place is Jingle Hell."

"He's awful, Aunt Ginny." Sam shuddered. "He hates this town, hates me, I think, and even hates Christmas."

"But he's easy on the eyes. That kind of evens things out, doesn't it?" Ginny Weatherby, who had worked at Joyful Creations for nearly twelve years, smiled at her niece. The two of them were in the back of the bakery, cleaning up and putting it to rights after the busy day. The front half of Joyful Creations was dark, silent, the sign in the window turned to Closed, leaving them in relative peace and quiet. "Your grandmother would have agreed."

"Grandma liked everyone who came through this door." Sam groaned. "I think he purposely sets out to frustrate me. How am I supposed to give him a good interview? I'm afraid I'll say something I'll regret."

"Oh, you're smart enough not to do that, Sam. I'm sure you'll do fine."

"I don't want him to find out about Grandma," Sam said.

Ginny's gaze softened. "Would it be so bad for people to know?"

Sam toyed with the handle on the sprayer. "I just want people to remember her the way she was, Aunt Ginny."

"They will, Sam." She put a hand on her niece's shoulder. "You need to trust that people of this town are your friends, that they love and care about you, and your grandmother."

"I'll think about it," Sam said. Though she had thought about the same question a hundred times over the past five years, and come back to the same answer. She didn't want people's pity. And most of all, she didn't want them to be hurt when they found out the Joy Barnett they knew and loved was no longer there. "For now, I'm more worried about that Flynn guy. He gets on my last nerve, I swear."

Ginny loaded the dishwasher and pushed a few buttons. "Give him cookies. That'll sweeten him up."

"I did. He wouldn't eat them." Sam sprayed disinfectant on the countertops and wiped them down, using the opportunity to work out some of her frustrations.

Aunt Ginny made a face. "Well, then I don't trust him. Any man who won't eat a plate of cookies, there's something wrong. Unless he's diabetic, then he has an excuse. Did you check for a medical ID bracelet?"

"No. Maybe I should have looked for a jerk bracelet."

"Have some patience, dear." She patted her niece's hand. "This guy could give the shop lots of great publicity."

"I'm trying to be patient."

"And you never know, he could be the one."

Sam rolled her eyes. "Stop trying to fix me up with every man who walks through that door."

Aunt Ginny took off her apron and hung it on a hook by the door, then crossed to her niece. The gentle twinkle of love shone in her light green eyes. "Your mother wouldn't want to see you living your life alone, dear, and neither would your grandmother."

"I'm not alone. I have you."

Sam would forever be grateful to her Aunt Ginny, who had moved to Riverbend from Florida a few months after Sam took over the bakery. Not much of a baker, she hadn't exactly stepped into her sister Joy's shoes, instead becoming the friend and helper Sam needed most. Though making cookies had never been her favorite thing to do, she'd been an enthusiastic supporter of the business, and especially of Sam.

Ginny pursed her lips. "Not the same thing and you know it."

"It's good enough for now. You know why I have to pour everything into the business." Sam went back to wiping, concentrating on creating concentric circles of shine, instead of the thoughts weighing on her. The ones that crept up when she least expected them—reminding her that she had stayed in this shop instead of going to college, getting married, having a family. The part that every so often wondered what if…she didn't have these responsibilities, these expectations?

But she did, so she kept on wiping, and cleaning.

Ginny's hand on her shoulder was a soft reminder that they had visited this topic dozens of times. "You don't have to pour everything into here, dear. Leave some room for you."

"I will," Sam promised, though she didn't mean it. Ginny didn't understand—and never really had—the all-consuming pressure Sam felt to increase business, and revenues.

Grandma Joy deserved the best care—and the only way to pay for that was by bringing in more money. Not think about possibilities that couldn't happen.

"And as far as this reporter goes," Ginny said, grabbing her coat as she waited for Sam to finish putting away the cleaning products, "I think it's time you tried the cranberry orange bread. The frosted loaf, not the plain one. I haven't met a person yet that didn't rave about it."

Sam let out a breath, relieved Ginny hadn't suggested sweetening him up with a date, or something else Sam definitely didn't have time or room in her life for. "Okay. I'll bring some over to Betsy's in the morning. Try to sweeten him up."

"And wear your hair up. Put in your hoop earrings, and for God's sake," Aunt Ginny added, wagging a finger, "wear some lipstick."

"Ginny, this isn't a beauty contest, it's an interview."

Ginny grinned. "I didn't get to this age without learning a thing or two about men. And if there's one thing I know, it's to use your assets, Sam," she said, shutting off the lights and closing the shop but not the subject, "every last one."

Flynn woke up in a bad mood.

He flipped open his cell phone, prayed for at least one signal bar, and got none. Moved around the frilly room, over to the lace-curtained window, still nothing. Pushing aside a trio of chubby Santas on the sill, Flynn opened the window, stuck the phone outside as far as his arm would reach and still had zero signal. Where was he? Mars? Soon as he got back to Boston, he was switching wireless carriers. Apparently this one's promise of service "anywhere" didn't include small Indiana towns in the middle of nowhere.

Flynn gave up on his cell phone, got dressed and went downstairs. The scent of freshly brewed coffee drew him like a dog to a bone, pulling him along, straight to the dining room. Several guests sat at one long table, chatting among themselves. Swags of pine ran down the center, punctuated by fat pinecones, puffy stuffed snowmen with goofy grins, unlit red pillar candles. A platoon of Santa plates had been joined by an army of snowman coffee mugs and a cavalry of snowflake-handled silverware. The Christmas invasion had flooded the table, leaving no survivors of ordinary life.

He'd walked into the North Pole. Any minute, he expected dancing elves to serve the muffins.

"Good morning, good morning!" Betsy came jingle-jangling out of the kitchen, her arms wide again. Did the woman have some kind of congenital disease that kept her limbs from hanging at her sides?

"Coffee?" he asked. Pleaded, really.

"On the sideboard. Fresh and hot! Do you want me to get you a cup?"

"I'll help myself. Thanks." He walked over to the poinsettia-ringed carafe, filled a Mrs. Claus mug, then sipped deeply. It took a few minutes for the caffeine to hit his brain.

"I don't know what your travel plans are, but the plows are just now getting to work, and the Indianapolis airport is closed for a couple more hours. They're predicting more snow. I'm so excited. It'll be a white Christmas, for sure!" Betsy applauded the joyful news.

"Thank you for the update." A little snow wouldn't stop him from getting the story out of Samantha Barnett. It might delay his trip down to southern Indiana, but the job—

Nothing delayed the job.

"No problem. It's just one of the many services I provide for my customers. No tip necessary." She beamed. "Oh, and Mr. MacGregor, we'll be singing Christmas carols in the parlor after breakfast, if you'd like to join us."

He'd rather do *anything* but that. "Uh, no. I—"

The front door opened. Flynn turned. Samantha Barnett, her arms loaded with boxes, entered the house. Excellent timing. Flynn hurried forward, taking the top few from her.

"Thanks. I thought I might lose those." She flashed him a smile that slammed into Flynn with more force than the caffeine's punch.

He told himself it didn't matter, that it hadn't affected him at all. Instead, he put on the friendly face that had won over many an interview subject. "It's not often that I get to come to the rescue of baked goods. Or that they come to mine."

"My goodness, Mr. MacGregor. Did you just make a joke? Because I didn't think you had it in you." Samantha paused in laying the boxes on a small table in the dining room. "Sorry. Sometimes my mouth gets ahead of my brain."

Betsy handed Samantha a set of serving platters, but didn't linger to chat, because one of the guests called her over to ask her a question about local events.

"It's this town," Flynn said after Betsy was gone, keeping his voice low, lest she overhear and come back to argue. "It's like bad lighting on an actress. It brings out the worst in me."

Samantha bristled. "Riverbend? It's not perfect, but I can't imagine why anyone would hate it. You really should give this place a chance before you condemn it. You never know, it might grow on you."

"So do skin rashes."

"You *are* Scrooge," she whispered. "Don't let Betsy hear you say that. People around here are proud of their town."

"I know. She's been trying to recruit me for the caroling crew all morning."

Samantha gave him a nonchalant shrug. "It might do you some good. Infuse you with some Christmas cheer."

Flynn let that subject drop. Infusing wasn't on his menu.

He didn't settle in, didn't get to know the locals. Of course, once he came in and ripped apart the local steakhouse in the pages of *Food Lovers*, he wasn't exactly invited back for tea anyway. "You know, there's a big world out there that offers a lot of great things like *civilization*, Internet connections, cellular towers, reliable public transportation. All without paying the price of Christmas carols in the parlor."

Samantha placed the last of the baked goods on the platters and let out a long sigh. "All my life I've dreamed of seeing that world, but…"

"This bakery is as binding as a straightjacket." He'd written that story a hundred times. Shop owners complaining about how small-business life drained them, yet they stayed in the field.

But he understood them. He might not be braising roasts or reducing sauces, but he knew the spirit that drove entrepreneurs. That hunger to climb your own way to the top. To be the only one who fueled success. It didn't matter what it took—long hours, financial worries, constant demands—to make it from the bottom to the top of the food chain.

Because he had done it himself, and his climb had paid off handsomely. Flynn had become known as the top writer for the food industry and his ambition had created a career that allowed him to call his own shots. Because he was the one that got the story, no matter what it took. No matter how many hours, how many weekends, how many holidays.

He remained unencumbered, without so much as a mortgage, a wife, kids. And though he may have lost his footing this summer—that was a temporary setback. He'd be back on top, after this piece.

"It's not just that the bakery keeps me tied down," Samantha said. "I have other reasons for staying here."

Her tone, almost melancholy, drew him. He could hear the

scoop underlying the words, note them like a bloodhound on the trail of a robber. "Like what?"

She quickly pulled herself together. "You're interviewing me about Joyful Creations, Mr. MacGregor, not my personal life." A smile crossed her face, but it was one that had a clear No Trespassing sign. "Let's stick to that, okay?"

"Certainly. Business only, that's the way I like things, too."

Except…she'd intrigued him with the way she'd shut that door so firmly. Most people Flynn interviewed spilled their guts as easily as a two-year-old with an overfilled cup of milk. Samantha Barnett clearly wouldn't be letting a single drop spill.

And he wouldn't let a drop of sympathy spill, either. He refused to fall for whatever had brought that wisp of emotion to her eyes. To let her move past his reporter curiosity.

Except…a part of him did wonder about the story behind the story. He had to be crazy. Clearly made delusional by all this Christmas spirit surrounding him. That was it.

Except, Flynn wasn't a Christmas spirit kind of guy.

"How's the weather out there?" Flynn asked, even though he already knew the answer. His comment was simply meant to retreat to neutral ground. He'd circle around to the article in a while, once he got his head back in the game.

"The storm has eased a bit, but they're expecting another front to move in, later this morning."

"If Earl's got the part for my car, that gives me just enough time to get out of town, if you have time for us to finish our interview before I have to go."

Samantha laughed. "Go and do what? The road travel will be awful again in a couple of hours, not that it's all that great right now to begin with. You might as well stay. In fact, I don't think you'll have a choice."

"There's always a choice, Miss Barnett."

"Well, unless you convince the National Guard to convoy you out, Mr. MacGregor, I think your only choice is to stay put." She closed the last of the boxes and stacked them into a pile. "I have to get back to the shop, but if you want to finish your interview, I'll be free at lunch for twenty minutes or so."

He'd be here all day, from the sounds of it. Have hours and hours of time to kill. He could, most likely, get what he needed from Samantha Barnett in twenty minutes. But the idea of rushing the questions, scribbling down the answers over a corned beef on rye—

Simply didn't appeal like it normally did. He must be in need of a vacation. Why else would he not be in a rush to meet his deadline? To move on to the next headline?

"No," he said.

"No?" One eyebrow perked up.

"I want more than that."

"More?" Now the other eyebrow arched.

"Dinner." The noise from the other bed-and-breakfast guests had risen, so Flynn took a step closer, and caught the scent of vanilla in her hair. Had he just said that word? Offered a dinner date?

Yes, he had, and now, he found himself lowering his voice, not for intimacy he told himself, but for privacy. Yet, everything about their closeness, the words, spelled otherwise. "A long, lingering dinner. No rushing out to fill boxes with cranberry muffins or to bring frosted reindeer to screaming three-year-olds."

"Just you and me…"

"And my pen and notepad. This is an interview, not a date, Miss Barnett," Flynn added, clarifying as much for himself as for her.

"Of course." Her gaze lingered on his, direct and clear. "But either way, would you do me one favor?"

"What?"

"Stop calling me Miss Barnett. I feel like a schoolteacher, or worse, the lone spinster in town, when you do that. My name is Samantha, but my friends call me Sam. Let's start with that."

He nodded. "Sam it is." Her name slipped off his tongue as easily as a whisper.

"And one more thing." She picked up a cookie from one of the platters and held it out to him. "I'm not leaving here until I know you've tasted my wares."

His grin quirked up on one side. "That could be taken in many ways, Sam."

She brought the cookie to his lips. "The only way I'm meaning is the white chocolate chip kind, Mr. MacGregor."

"Call me Flynn, and I'll do whatever you ask." Was he *flirting*? He never did that. Ever. Maybe Betsy had spiked the coffee.

"Flynn," she said, so softly, he was sure he'd never heard his name spoken like that before, "please take a bite."

"These aren't those special romance cookies, are they?"

"No," Sam said. "Although my Great-Aunt Ginny thinks I should give one to every eligible male that crosses my path."

Her face colored, and he knew she regretted sharing that tidbit. So. Samantha Barnett's life was a bit lonelier than she wanted to admit.

"You've never tried them?" he asked. Then wondered why he cared.

"No. But I assure you, Flynn, that my white chocolate macadamia nut cookies are just as delicious." A smile crossed her lips. "And even better, there's absolutely no danger of falling in love if you eat one."

Before he could tell himself that it was far smarter to resist, to ignore whatever silly, impractical feelings Sam had awakened in him, Flynn found his lips parting and his mouth accepting the sweet morsel.

The minute the cookie hit his palate, Flynn knew this interview would be unlike any other.

And that would be a problem indeed.

CHAPTER FIVE

SAM CHANGED into a dress. Out of a dress. Into jeans. Out of jeans. Into a skirt. Out of the skirt and back into the jeans. Finally, she settled on a deep green sweater with pearl beading around the collar and black slacks, with pointy-toed dress boots. Nothing too sexy, or that screamed trying to impress the guy.

Even if she was.

Though she couldn't say why. Flynn MacGregor had been incredibly disagreeable, and not at all her kind of man. Even if he did have nice hands. Deep blue eyes. Broad shoulders. And a way of entering a room that commanded attention.

All that changing and fussing over her appearance made her ten minutes late. She entered Hall's Steaks and Ribs, brushing the snow from her hair and shoulders, half expecting Flynn to make a note in his notebook about the Joyful Creations' owner's lack of punctuality. Instead, he simply gave her a nod, not so much as a smile, and rose to pull out her chair. "Is it still snowing?"

Okay, so she was a little disappointed that he hadn't said she looked pretty. Hadn't acknowledged her one iota as a woman.

She was here for an interview, not a date. To grow her business. "It's a light snow now. The weatherman said we'll only get another inch or two tonight."

"Good. Hopefully Earl has my car fixed and I can get back on the road in the morning." Flynn took the opposite seat, then handed one of the menus to Sam.

She put it to the side. "Thank you. But I already know what I want."

"Eat here often?"

"When there's only one restaurant in town, this is pretty much *the* date hot spot." Sam felt her face heat. Why had she mentioned dates?

"Are you here often? On dates?" He glanced around the dark cranberry-and-gold room, decorated in a passably good imitation of Italianate style, considering the building was a modern A-frame. The restaurant was crowded, the hum of conversation providing a steady buzz beneath the instrumental Christmas carols playing on the sound system.

"Me?" Sam laughed. "Yeah, in all my spare time. Like those five minutes I had back in 2005."

He let out a chuff. "Probably the same five I had."

A waitress came by their table—a willowy blonde on the Riverbend High School pep squad whose name temporarily eluded Sam's memory—and dropped off two glasses of water, but didn't pause long enough to take their orders.

"You must travel a lot for your job," Sam said.

Flynn took a sip and nodded. "About half the year I'm on the road. The other half I'm behind a computer."

"So I'm not the only workaholic in the room?"

"My job demands long hours."

Sam arched a brow. "Oh, I get it. You're a special case. Whereas I'm…" She trailed off, leaving him to fill in the blank.

"Ambitious, too." He tipped his glass toward her, in a touché gesture.

"Exactly. Then you can understand why I want to expand the shop."

"I do. I just think you should understand what you're getting yourself into when you start pursuing fame, fortune, the American dream."

"I do." The way he'd said the words, though, made Sam feel as if what she wanted was wrong. That she was being self-serving. Had she expressed her dream wrong? No, she hadn't. He'd simply misinterpreted her.

Besides, Flynn MacGregor didn't know the whole story, nor did he need to. She *had* to get out of Riverbend. Away, not just from this town, but from things she couldn't change, things she'd given up on a long time ago. The life she'd wished she could have had, and had put on hold for so long, it had slipped through her fingers. Maybe then—

Maybe then she'd find peace.

Flynn picked up his menu and studied the two pages of offerings. "And where do you fit into that equation?"

"What's that supposed to mean?"

"Exactly what I said." His voice was slightly muffled by the vinyl-bound menu.

"You mean, free time for me?"

Flynn put the menu down. "From what I've heard around town, you're not exactly…the social butterfly. You work. And you work. And you *work*. You're like a squirrel providing for a never-ending winter."

"You write for this industry. Of everyone, you should know how demanding a bakery can be."

"That's what the classified ads are for. To hire people to bake."

"People around here," Sam began, then lowered her voice, realizing how many of those very people were situated right beside her, "expect the baked goods to be made by a family member. Third generation, and all that."

He scoffed. "Oh come on. In this age of automation, you

don't actually think that everyone believes you're truly popping on every last gumdrop button?"

She stared at him, as if he was insane. "But I do."

"Who is going to know if you do it, or a monkey from the zoo does?" Flynn asked.

"Well…I will, for one."

"And the harm in that is…?" He put out his hands. "You might actually have some free time to see a movie? Go out on a date? Have a life?"

She shifted in her chair. His words sprung like tiny darts, hitting at the very issues Sam did her best to avoid. "I have a life."

Flynn arched a brow. "You want me to write the story for you? Young, ambitious restaurateur, or in your case—" he waved a hand in her direction "—baker, goes into the business thinking she'll be *different*." He put special emphasis on the last word, tainting it with disgust.

"My circumstances were different."

But Flynn went on, as if he hadn't even heard her. "She thinks she'll find a way to balance having an outside life with work. That she'll be the one to learn from her peers, to balance the business with reality. That she, and only she, can find the secret to rocketing to the top while still holding on to some semblance of normality." He leaned forward, crossing his arms on the table. "Am I close?"

"No." The lie whistled through her lips.

"Listen, I admire your dedication, I really do. But let me save you the peek at the ending. You won't end up any different than anyone else. You'll look back five, ten, twenty years from now, and think 'where the hell did my life go?'"

"Who made you judge and jury over me?" Sam's grip curled around her water glass, the temptation to throw the beverage in his face growing by the second. "I'm doing what I have to do."

"Do you?"

"What?"

"Have to?"

His piercing gaze seemed to ask the very questions she never did. The ones that plagued her late at night when she was alone in the house her grandmother used to own, pacing the floors, wondering…

What if.

Before she had to come up with an answer, the waitress returned, introduced herself as Holli with an i and took out a notepad. "What can I get you?"

"Lasagna with extra sauce on the side," Sam said, grateful for the change in subject.

"I'll have the same." Flynn handed his menu to Holli, who gave each of them a perky smile before heading to the kitchen. "Enough of me giving you the ugly truth about your future. I'm not here to play psychic."

"And I'm not asking for your advice."

"True." A grin quirked up one side of his mouth. "I get the feeling you're not the kind of person who would take my advice, even if I gave it."

His smile was contagious, and she found herself answering with one of her own. He had charm, she had to give him that. Grudgingly. "I might. Depending on what you had to say."

"Admit it. You're stubborn."

"I am not." She paused. "Too stubborn."

He laughed then, surprising her, and by the look on his face, probably even himself. "Now there's a line I should quote." He dug out his pen and paper.

Disappointment curdled in Sam's stomach. "Are you always after the story?"

He glanced up. "That's my job."

"Yeah, but…just like you were saying to me, don't you ever take a moment for you?"

His blue gaze met hers, direct and powerful. "You mean treat this as a date, instead of an interview?"

"Well—" Sam shifted again "—not *that* exactly."

The grin returned, wider this time. "How long *has* it been?"

"Has it been for what?"

"Since you've been out on a date?"

Sam took such a deep sip of water, she nearly drowned. "I could ask you the same thing."

"My answer's easy. A week."

"Oh." She put the glass down. "I thought you said you didn't have that much free time."

"I was exaggerating. I'm a writer." That grin again. "Given to hyperbole and all that."

Was he…flirting with her? Holy cow. Was that why everything within her seemed touched with fever? Why her gut couldn't stop flip-flopping? Why she alternately wanted to run—and to stay?

It was simply because he was right. She hadn't been out on a date in forever. She wasn't used to this kind of head-on attention from a man. Especially a man as good at the head-on thing as he was.

"So which would you rather?" Flynn asked. "A date? Or an interview?"

The interview, her mind urged. Say interview. The business. The bakery needed the increase in revenue. Her personal life could wait, just as it always had. The business came first.

"A date."

Had she really just said that? Out loud? To the man who held the future of Joyful Creations in his pen? Sam's face heated, and her feet scrambled back, ready to make a fast exit.

But instead of making a note on his ubiquitous notepad, Flynn leaned back in his chair and smiled. "You surprise me,

Samantha Barnett. Just when I think you're all work and no fun, you opt for a little fun."

"Maybe I'm not the cardboard character you think."

"Maybe you're not." His voice had dropped into a range that tickled at her gut, sent her thoughts down a whole other path that drifted away from fun and into man-and-woman-alone territory. He pushed the notepad to the side, then leaned forward, his gaze connecting with hers. When he did that, it seemed as if the entire room, heck, the entire world, dropped away. "Well, if this *was* a date, and we were back in Boston, instead of the pits of Christmastown here, do you want to know what we'd be doing?"

"Yes," Sam replied, curiosity pricking at her like a pin. "Why not?"

He thought a second, considering her. "Well, since you haven't been out on a date in a while, our first date should be something extraordinary."

"Extraordinary?" she echoed.

"A limo, for starters. Door-to-door service."

"A limo?" She arched a brow. "On a reporter's salary?"

"I've done very well in my field. And they tend to reward that handsomely."

Quite handsomely if the expensive suit, cashmere coat and Italian leather shoes were any indication. "What next, after the limo?"

"Dinner, maybe at Top of the Hub, a restaurant at the top of the Prudential building in Boston. Lobster, perhaps? With champagne, of course."

"Of course," she said, grinning, caught in the web of the fantasy, already imagining herself whisked away in the long black car, up the elevator to the restaurant, sipping the golden bubbly drink. "And after dinner?"

"Dancing. At this little jazz club I know where the lights

are dimmed, music is low and sexy and there's only enough room for me to hold you close. Very, very close."

Sam swallowed. Her heart raced, the sound thundering in her head. "That sounds like quite the place."

"A world away from this one."

A world away. The world she had dreamed of once, back when she'd thought she was going to college, going places—

Going somewhere other than Riverbend and the bakery.

For just a second, Sam allowed her mind to wander, to picture a different future. One without the bakery to worry about, without the future of several potential additional locations to fret over. Without other people to worry about, to care for.

What if she were free of all that and could pursue a love life, a marriage, a family? A man who looked at her with desire like Flynn did—

And she had time to react, to date him? To live her life like other women did?

Guilt smacked her hard. She didn't have time to dally with those thoughts. Too many people were depending on her. Later, Sam reminded herself with an inward sigh.

Later, it would be her turn.

Sam looked away, breaking eye contact with Flynn MacGregor. With the temptation he offered, as easily as a coin in his palm. She toyed with her silverware, willing her heart to slow, her breath to return to normal, and most of all, her head to come down from the clouds. "Well, that would be nice. If I lived somewhere else besides here."

"If you did. Which you don't." Flynn cleared his throat, as if he, too, wanted to get back to business, to put some distance between them. "So, tell me. Why the lasagna?"

Of all the questions he could have asked, that one had to be the last one Sam would have expected. "I like lasagna, and the way they make it here is even better than my grandmother did—does," she corrected herself. Darn. She had to be more careful. Sam brushed her hair off her face and opted for another topic, trying to stay on safe, middle ground. "Don't you meet many women who like lasagna?"

That made him laugh. Flynn MacGregor's laugh was deep and rich, like good chocolate. "No. Definitely not. Most of the women I know spend their entire day obsessing about how to whittle their waists down to the next single digit."

Sam patted her hips. "Well, as you can see, that's definitely not me. My waist has never been considered whittled. Though maybe if I did cut back on the—"

"Don't." Flynn's steady gaze met hers. "Enjoy the lasagna. Your waist is perfect just the way it is."

Heat pooled in Sam's gut. Other men had looked at her with desire of course. She'd had boyfriends who had made her feel wanted, even pretty, but never before had a single sentence set off a blast of fireworks in her veins. And here was this big-city playboy, seeing her as a sexy woman.

"You don't have to butter me up," she said. "I already agreed to the interview."

He leaned forward in his seat, his blue eyes assessing her intently. "I'm not buttering you up for anything at all. You look beautiful tonight, Sam."

A trill of joy ran through Sam, skating down her spine. "Well then, thank you." She felt a blush fill her face, and she cursed under her breath. Time to get the focus off herself. Every time he looked at her like that, she got distracted from what was important. "I've told you plenty about me. It's your turn."

He paused. "I'm from Boston. I write for a magazine. I live alone, have no pets."

She laughed. "You're not a man who shares a lot about himself, are you?"

"Just the facts, ma'am." He smiled.

But behind that smile, an invisible wall had been erected. Curiosity rose in Sam. What made Flynn MacGregor tick? What made him smile? Until tonight, he'd rarely done so. When his mouth did curve into a grin, the gesture transformed his face, his eyes, and seemed to make him into an entirely different person. The kind of person she would—under other circumstances—want to get to know.

Not today. Despite their agreement to put the interview on hold, she reminded herself to watch her words. Aunt Ginny's warning about *Food Lovers'* tendency to want the story behind the story came back to Sam. She'd have to be on guard tonight. Flynn MacGregor could be doing all this simply to get her to open up.

And not because he wanted her.

She should be happy. For one, she had no time for a relationship. She had a business to run, a business that was on the cusp of taking off and becoming something so much bigger than this little town, that corner location. She had people depending on her to take Joyful Creations to the next level—and getting sidetracked by dating was just not part of the recipe.

But what if it could be?

The lasagna arrived, and Flynn immediately took a bite of the steaming Italian food. "It pays to follow the locals when ordering food. This is delicious."

"I know. It may say steaks and ribs on the sign out front, but the owner is a full-blooded Italian, so that's his specialty, which also explains the décor. I think he just has the other things on the menu, because that's what tourists expect when they come to Indiana. Not that we get many in Riverbend, at least until the last few weeks."

"Because of the airline magazine's mention of the shop."

Sam buttered two pieces of bread, and handed one slice to Flynn, who thanked her. "That article, and the boost in business, was a blessing and a half, but one that has kept us hopping from sunup to sundown. In fact, after I leave here, I'm going back to the shop to get a start on tomorrow's baking."

"Tonight? But you already put in a long day, didn't you?"

"That's the life of a baker. No free time."

"And yet, you want more."

"I'm not a sugar addict, Flynn. I'm a success addict." She shot him a smile.

Flynn pulled his notepad over and jotted down those words. If anything reminded her this wasn't a date, that did. A flicker of disappointment ran through her, but Sam brushed it off.

For a minute, he'd given her the gift of a normal life. Let her feel again like a normal woman, a beautiful woman. That would be enough. For a while.

A really long while.

"Why?" he asked.

"Why does anyone want success?" Sam bent her head and took a bite of food, chewed and swallowed. "To prove you did well with your business."

"That's all? No other reason?"

No other reason she wanted in print. "That's all." She signaled to Holli to box up her dinner and pushed her plate to the side, her appetite gone. But that wasn't what had her wanting to get out of the restaurant so bad. It was the way Flynn kept studying her, as if he could see behind every answer she'd given him, as if he knew she was holding something back. "Is that all you need? Because I really have to get back to the shop."

"Sure. Thank you for your time, Miss—" He paused. "Sam."

She reached into her purse to pull out some money for dinner but Flynn stopped her with a touch of his hand on hers. A surge of electricity ran up her arm.

"My treat," he said.

"I thought you said this wasn't a date."

"It's not. I have an expense account."

Once again, disappointment whistled through her as brisk and fast as winter's winds. "Oh. Well, in that case, thank you." Sam rose and grabbed her coat off the back of her chair. "If you have any other questions, call me at the shop. That's pretty much where I live." She turned to go.

"Wait."

Sam pivoted back, part of her still hoping—some insane part—that all this really had been a date, and not an interview. "Yes?"

"You mentioned something about having dial-up Internet access at Joyful Creations. Do you think I could come by tonight, if you're going to be there anyway, and access my e-mail?" A grin flashed on Flynn's face. "I'm having acute withdrawal symptoms. Fever, aches, pains, the whole nine yards."

She'd been wrong.

He wanted her—but for her Internet connection only. That was for the best. Even if it didn't feel that way.

"Certainly," Sam said. "Like I said, that shop is my life."

CHAPTER SIX

FLYNN STARED at the picture for a long time. The edges had yellowed, the image cracked over the years, but the memories were as fresh as yesterday. Two boys smiling, their hair tousled by the wind whisking up the Atlantic and onto Savin Hill Beach, their grins as wide as the Frisbees they held in their hands. One day, out of thousands, but that one day—

Had been a good one.

Flynn put the picture back in his wallet, flipped open his cell phone and scrolled through his contact list until he got to the name Liam.

Flynn shut the phone without dialing. He didn't have a signal anyway. Not that he would have called if he had. He hadn't dialed that number in over a year.

Liam hadn't answered his calls in two.

He'd driven all this way, with a crazy idea that maybe Liam would see him if Flynn called. If he said he was a few towns away, and asked if Liam wanted to see him? Or maybe if he just showed up on Liam's doorstep and surprised him, saying "hey, it's Christmas, why don't we just put all this behind us?"

Flynn shook his head. Maybe too much time had passed to heal old wounds.

Flynn rose and put his wallet into his back pocket. He swallowed back the memories, the whiff of nostalgia—had it been nostalgia or something else?—that had hit him for a brief second, then grabbed his laptop and headed out of the bed and breakfast and over to Sam's shop.

From outside the window, he could see her inside, softly lit by a single overhead light, the golden glow spreading over her features. If he hadn't known better, he'd have thought she was an image from a Christmas card—the painted kind famous for their lighting and muted colors.

Flynn shook off the thought. What was with him today? He was going soft, that was for sure. First, the picture, followed by the quick detour down Memory Lane, then the temptation to call Liam, and finally the comparison of this woman to an artist's impression, for Pete's sake. He was not the emotional type. Clearly, he needed to get out of this odd little town and back to the city. He entered the shop, his presence announced by a set of jingle bells above the entrance.

Jingle bells. He scoffed. Of course.

"I'm in the kitchen," Sam called to him.

He headed through the darkened shop, pulled as much by her voice as by the scent of baked goods. The quiet notes of vanilla, mixed with the more pungent song of nutmeg, all muted by the melody of fruits and nuts. The scents triggered a memory but it was gone before he could grasp it. "Smells good in here."

She looked up and brushed a tendril of blond hair off her forehead with the back of her hand. "Thanks. I'm usually too busy to notice anything other than how low the flour supply is getting."

He slipped onto a stainless steel stool in the corner and laid his laptop on the small desk beside him. "Don't you take breaks to taste the cookies? Dip into the muffins?"

"Me? No. I rarely have time."

"Didn't we already have this discussion about all work and no play…?" He let the old axiom trail off, tossing her a grin.

She gestured toward his computer. "Hey, speak for yourself, Mr. Nose to the Grindstone."

Right. Get back to work. Flynn had no intentions of missing this deadline, because doing so meant putting his road trip on hold, and even though he wasn't so sure of the reception he'd receive, he knew it was time to see Liam. That meant he needed to check in with the office and get a head start on writing his article. Procrastinating wasn't going to restore his reputation at the magazine, nor was it going to get him any closer to seeing Liam. "Speaking of which…Can I use your Internet connection?"

"If you get lucky." Sam colored. "I, ah, didn't mean that the way it came out. I meant—"

"If the lines are working."

"Yes." She nearly breathed her relief.

"I wouldn't have thought anything else."

But hadn't he, for just a second? Samantha Barnett was an attractive woman. Curvaceous, friendly and she was surrounded by the perfume of cookies. Any man with a pulse would be enticed by her, as he had been—very much so—at dinner a little while ago. Mimi had never seemed so far away.

Not that he and Mimi had what anyone would really call a relationship. They were more…convenience daters. When either of them needed someone to attend a function or to see a movie with, they picked up the phone. Days could go by before they talked to each other, the strings as loose as untied shoelaces. Mimi liked it that way, and so did Flynn.

Samantha Barnett, who wore her small-town roots like a coat, was definitely not a convenience dater. He'd do best to keep his heart out of that particular cookie jar.

Flynn cleared his throat, turned to his bag and unpacked his laptop, plugging the machine into the outlet on the wall and the telephone line into his modem. Sam gave him a phone number to dial and connect to her provider. He typed in all the information, then waited for the magic to happen.

Nothing. No familiar musical tones of dialing. No screeching of the modem. No hiss of a telephone line. Just an error message.

He tried again. A third time. Powered down the computer, powered it back up and tried connecting a fourth time.

"No luck?" Sam asked.

"Are you sure we're not on Mars?"

Sam laughed. "Pretty sure. Though there are days…" She tossed him a smile, while her hands kept busy dropping balls of chocolate chip cookie dough onto a baking sheet. "That remoteness, that disconnect from city life, is all part of the charm of Riverbend, though. And what draws those droves of tourists."

Flynn shot her a look of disdain. "All five of them? Not counting your temporary flood, of course."

"Actually, it's pretty busy here in the summer. And you saw the lines outside the shop today. People from big cities really like the rural location, and the fact that we have lots of lakes nearby for boating and camping."

"The cityfolk roughing it, huh?"

"Yep. Except we have running water here." Again, another grin. He noticed that when she smiled, her green eyes sparkled with gold flecks. They were the color of the forest just after a storm, when the sun was beginning to peek through the clouds.

Or maybe that was just the reflection from the overhead lights. Yeah, that was it.

Flynn gave up on his computer and shut the laptop's cover. He rose and crossed to Sam. Was it the light? Or was it her eyes? "Why do you live here?"

She paused in making cookies, as if surprised by the question. The scent of vanilla wafted up from the dough. "I grew up here."

He took another step closer. Only because he still couldn't decide what caused the gold flecks in her eyes. Mother Nature or sixty watts. He'd been intrigued all night, first in the restaurant and now, wondering, pondering…thinking almost nonstop about her. A bad sign in too many ways to count, but he told himself if he could just solve this mystery of her eyes, the thoughts would stop. "Okay, then why did you stay? You didn't have to keep the business open. You could have closed it and moved on."

She opened her mouth, then shut it again, as if she had never considered this question before. "Joyful Creations has been in my family for three generations. My family was depending on me to keep it open."

Another step. Flynn inhaled, and he swore he could almost taste the air around Sam. It tasted like…

Sugar cookies.

"What did you say?" Sam said.

Had he said that out loud? Damn. What the hell was wrong with him? He did *not* get emotionally involved with his interview subjects.

He did *not* lose his focus.

He did *not* forget the story. He went after it, whatever the cost.

Flynn backed up three steps, returned to his laptop and flipped up the top. It took a few seconds for the hibernating screen to come back to life. Several long, agonizing seconds of silence that Flynn didn't bother to fill. "If it's all the same to you, I'd like to work here for a little while. That way, if I have any questions while I'm writing, I can just ask them." Meaning, he intended to probe deeper into the clues she'd dropped at dinner, but he didn't say that. "And, I can try to connect to the Internet again."

"Sure." Her voice had a slight, confused lilt at the end. She put the sheet of cookies into the oven, then started filling another one.

Keeping his back to her, Flynn sought the familiarity of his word processing program. He tugged his notepad out of his bag and began typing. The words did what they always did—provided a cold, objective distance. It was as if the bright white of the screen and the stark blackness of the letters erased all emotion, scrubbed away any sense of Flynn's personality. He became an outside observer, reporting facts.

And nothing else.

He wrote for ten minutes, his fingers moving so fast, the words swam before his eyes. Usually, when he wrote a story, pulling the paragraphs out of his brain was like using camels to drag a mule through the mud. He'd never been a fast writer, more a deliberate one.

But this time, it seemed as if his brain couldn't keep up with his hands. He wrote until his fingers began to hurt from the furious movement across the keyboard. When he sat back and looked at the page count, he was stunned to see he had five solid pages in the file already.

Flynn scrolled up to the opening paragraph, expecting his usual "Established in blah-blah year, this business" opening, followed by the punch of personal information, the tabloid zing he was known for. Nearly all his stories had that straightforward, get-to-the-facts approach that led to the one nugget everyone else had missed. It was what his editor liked about him. He delivered the information, with a minimal peppering of adjectives.

"Can I read it?" Sam asked.

He hadn't even realized she had moved up behind him. But now he was aware, very aware. He jerked back to the real world, to the scent of fresh-baked cookies, and to Samantha Barnett, standing right behind him.

"Uh, sure. Keep in mind it's a first draft," he said. "And it's just the facts, none of the fluff kind of thing the airline magazine…" His voice trailed off as his eyes connected with the first few paragraphs on the screen.

"Visions of sugar plums dance in the air. The sweet perfume of chocolate hangs like a cloud. And standing amidst the magic of this Christmas joy, like the star atop a tree, is the owner of Joyful Creations, Samantha Barnett.

"She knows every customer by name, and has a smile for everyone who walks through the door of her shop, no matter how many muffins she's baked or how many cookies she's boxed that day. She's as sweet as the treats in her cases…."

Flynn slammed the top of the laptop shut. What the *hell* was that?

"Wow." A slow smile spread across Sam's face. "And here I thought you were going to write one of those scathing exposés, the kind I've heard the magazine is famous for. I mean, you barely tasted any of the food here and…"

"And what?" he asked, scowling. He did *not* write that kind of drivel. He was known as a bulldog, the writer that went for the jugular, got the story at all costs. Not this sweet-penning novelist wanna-be.

"And well…it didn't seem like you liked me."

He didn't know how to answer that. *Did* he like her? And what did it matter if he did or didn't? He'd be leaving this town the second his car was fixed and the roads were clear. After that, Samantha Barnett would simply be one more file among the dozens in his cabinet. "I don't like this town. It's a little too remote for me." That didn't answer the question of whether he liked her, he realized.

Either way, his editor was expecting a Flynn MacGregor story. The kind free of emotion, but steeped in details no other publication had been able to find. Flynn dug and discovered, doing whatever it took to get the real story. That chase was what had thrilled him from his first days as a cub reporter at a news-paper, and it was what had made him a legend at the magazine.

Getting the story was a game—a game he played damn well.

Sam crossed her arms over her chest and stared at him. "Ever since you arrived here, I've been trying to figure you out. Aunt Ginny would tell me that if I had any common sense at all, I'd keep my mouth shut, but I've never been very good at that."

He had turned toward her, and when they'd both been reading the story on his computer, the distance between them had closed. Now Flynn found himself watching that mouth. A sassy mouth, indeed. "And I suppose you're about to tell me exactly what you think of me? Point out all my faults?"

"You do have a few." She inhaled, and the *V* of her sweater peeked open just enough to peak his desire.

She had more than a sassy mouth, that was for sure. He reached out and tipped her chin upward. "What if I do the same for you?"

She swallowed, but held his gaze. Desire burned in his veins, pounding an insistent call in his brain. Everything within him wanted to kiss her, take her in his arms, end this torturous curiosity about what she'd feel like. Taste like.

And yet, at the same time, the reporter side of him tried to shush that desire, told him to take advantage of the moment, to use it to exploit the vulnerable moment.

"I'm not the one going around with a chip the size of Ohio on my shoulder," she said.

"Maybe I have a good reason for that chip."

"At Christmas? No one has a good reason to be grumpy at Christmas."

He released her jaw. "Some people do."

The clock above them ticked, one second, two. Three. Then Sam's voice, as quiet as snow falling. "Why?"

The clock got in another four ticks before Flynn answered. "Let's just say I never stayed in one place long enough for Santa to find me."

"Why?"

A one-word question. One that, in normal conversation, might have prompted a heartfelt discussion. Some big sharing moment over a couple cups of coffee and a slice of streusel. But Flynn wasn't a coffee-and-streusel kind of guy. He hadn't done show-and-tell in first grade, and he wasn't going to do it now.

The oven timer buzzed, announcing another batch of cookies was done. And so was this conversation. Somehow it had gotten turned around, and Flynn was off his game, off his center of gravity. He needed to retreat and regroup.

"The story is about you, not me," Flynn said. "When you get a job as a reporter, then you get to ask the questions."

Without bothering to pack it in the bag, he picked up his laptop, yanked the cord out of the outlet and headed out of the warm and cozy shop. And into a biting cold, the kind he knew as well as his own name.

This was the world where Flynn found comfort, not the one he'd just left.

Today her grandmother thought she was the maid.

Sam told herself not to be disappointed. Every time she drove over to Heritage Nursing Home, she steeled herself for that light of confusion in Joy Barnett's eyes, that "Do I know you?" greeting instead of the hugs and love Sam craved like oxygen.

And every time disappointment hit her like a snowplow.

"Have you cleaned the bathroom?" Joy asked. "I'm afraid I made a mess of the sink when I washed my face. I'm sorry."

Sam worked up a smile. "Yes, I cleaned it."

It took all Sam had not to release the sigh in her throat. How she wanted things to change, to turn back the clock. There used to be days when her grandmother had recognized her, before the Alzheimer's had robbed her grandmother of the very joy that she had been named for. The smiles of recognition, the friendships, the family members, and most of all the memories. It was as if she'd become a disconnected boat, floating alone in a vast ocean with no recognizable land, no horizon.

So Sam had, with reluctance, finally put Grandma Joy into Heritage Nursing Home. The care there was good, but Sam had visited another, much more expensive facility several miles away from Riverbend. The bakery simply didn't make enough money, at least with a single location, to pay for Grandma Joy's care at the other facility, one that boasted a special Alzheimer's treatment center with a nostalgic setting, an aromatherapy program and several hands-on patient involvement programs designed to help stimulate memory and brain activity. It might not bring her grandmother back to who she used to be, but Sam hoped the other facility would give her grandmother a better quality of life than Heritage Nursing Home, which was nice, but offered none of those specialized care options.

After all Grandma Joy had done for Sam, from taking her in as a child to raising her with the kind of love that could only be called a gift, Sam would do anything to make the rest of Joy's years happy, stress-free and as wonderful as possible. There might not be any way to bring back the grandmother she remembered, but if this other center could help ease the fearful world of unfamiliarity that Joy endured, then Sam would sacrifice anything to bring that to the woman she considered almost a mother.

Including living her own life. For a while longer.

Grandma Joy looked at Sam expectantly, as if she thought

Sam might whip out a broom and start sweeping the floor. Sam held out a box. "Here, I brought you something."

Joy took the white container and beamed. "Oh, aren't you sweet." She flipped open the lid and peeked inside. "How did you know these were my favorite?"

Sam's smile faltered. Her throat burned. "Your grand-daughter told me."

Grandma Joy looked up, a coconut macaroon in her hand. "My granddaughter? I have a granddaughter?"

Sam nodded. Tears blurred her vision. "Her name is Samantha."

Joy repeated the name softly, then thought for a moment. "Samantha, of course. But Sam's just a baby. She can't hardly talk, so she can't tell you about my favorite cookies, silly. She is the cutest thing, though. Everyone who meets her just loves her. She comes to the bakery with me every day." She leaned forward. "Did I tell you I own a bakery?"

"Yes, you did."

"My husband and I started it when we first got married. So much work, but oh, we've had a lot of fun. Sam loves being there, she really does. She's my little helper. Someday, Sam and I are going to run it together." Joy sat back in the rose-patterned armchair. As her thoughts drifted, her gaze drifted out the window, to the snow-covered grounds. The white flakes glistened like crystals, hung in long strings of diamonds from the trees. She sighed. "That will be a wonderful day."

"Yes," Sam said, closing her eyes, because it was too painful to look at the same view as her grandmother, "it will."

Sam Barnett was leaving something out of her personal recipe. Flynn had rewritten the article into one more closely resem-bling the kind he normally wrote—where that poetic thing had come from last night, he had no idea—and realized not all the whys had been answered. There was still something, he wasn't sure what, that he needed to know. But the bulldog in him knew he'd yet to find that missing piece.

He had to dig deeper. Keep pawing at her, until he got her to expose those personal bits that would give his article the meat it needed. The kind of tidbits *Food Lovers'* readers ate like candy.

It was, after all, what he was known for. What would put him right back on top. Then why had he hesitated? Normally, he did his interviews, in and out in a day, two at most. He never lingered. Never let a subject rattle him like she had last night.

Damn it, get a hold of yourself. Get the story, and get out of town.

Flynn rose, stretching the kinks out of his back he'd picked up from sitting in the uncomfortable wooden chair at the tiny desk in his room. He crossed to the window and parted the lacy curtains. Outside, snow had started to fall.

Again.

Where the hell was he? Nome, Alaska? For Pete's sake, all it did was snow here.

He pulled on his coat, and hurried downstairs. Betsy, who was sitting behind the piano in the front parlor, tried to talk him into joining the out-of-tune sing-along with the other guests, but Flynn waved a goodbye and headed out of the bed and breakfast, turning up his collar against the blast of cold and ice. By the time he made it to Earl's garage, his shoes and socks were soaked through, and his toes had become ten Popsicles.

"Well, howdy-ho," Earl said when Flynn entered the concrete-and-brick structure. He had on his plaid earflap hat and a thick Carhartt jacket. "What are you doing here?"

"Picking up my car."

"Now why would you want to do that?"

"So I can go back to Boston." First making a side trip, but he didn't share that information with Earl.

"Tomorrow is Christmas Eve," Earl said. "You got family in Boston?"

Flynn bit back his impatience at the change in subject. By now, he'd learned the only way to get a straight answer out of the auto mechanic was to take the Crazy Eights route. "All I have back there is an apartment and a doorman."

"A doorman?" Earl thought about that for a second. "Can't say I've ever heard of anyone having their doorman over for Christmas mornin'. He must be really good at opening your door."

Flynn sighed. This was going nowhere. "My car?"

"Oh, that. The part's on order."

"It hasn't arrived yet?"

"Oh, it arrived." Earl scratched under one earflap.

"And?"

"And I sent it back."

Flynn sighed again, this time longer and louder. "Why would you do that?"

"Because I'm getting old. Forgot my glasses on Tuesday."

Flynn resisted the urge to scream in frustration. "And what would that have to do with my car?"

"Made me order the wrong part. I got my two's all mixed up with my seven's. But don't you worry," Earl said, patting his breast pocket, "I brought my glasses today. So you'll be all set to leave by Friday at the latest."

"Can't you fix it now?"

"Nope. Gotta go work the tree lot at the Methodist church." Earl patted his hat down farther on the top of his head, then strode out of the shop, waving at Flynn to follow. "The ladies' bingo group is coming by at three to get their trees, and they're counting on my muscles to help them out. I can't be late."

Earl strode off, leaving Flynn stuck. He should have been

mad. Should have pitched a fit, threatened to sue or have his car towed to another garage. He could have done any of the above.

But he didn't. For some reason, he wasn't as stressed about the missing part as he should have been. He chalked it up to still needing more information from Sam.

As his path carried him toward the bakery again, something pretty damned close to anticipation rose in his chest. If there was one thing Flynn needed from Santa this year, it was a renewed dose of his reporter's objectivity.

CHAPTER SEVEN

A PAY PHONE.

Who'd have thought those things still existed?

Flynn's hand rested on the receiver. Stumbling upon the phone on his way to the bakery had taken him by surprise. In his opposite hand, he jingled several coins, and debated. Finally, he picked up the phone, dropped in several quarters and began to dial. He made it through nine of the ten digits that would connect him to Liam's dorm room before he hung up.

It had to be this town that had him feeling so sentimental. Especially considering he was surrounded by so much Christmas spirit, it was like being in the company of a woman wearing too much perfume. Even the pay phone was wrapped in garland, a little red bow hanging from the handle. That must be what had him thinking of mending fences so broken down, it would take a fleet of cement trucks to build them up again.

Would Liam see him when he arrived in town this week? Assuming, that was, that his car ever got fixed. Or would Liam slam the door in his face? Maybe it was better not to know.

The change dropped to the bottom of the phone. Flynn dug it out of the slot and redeposited the coins, then added some more change to reach his editor at *Food Lovers* magazine.

But while he waited for the four dollars in quarters to

connect him, he realized the money would have been better spent on a lifetime supply of candy canes. At least then he could have used them to sweeten Tony Reynolds up—

Because at this point he could use every tool in Santa's arsenal to assuage the inevitable storm that was about to come.

"Where the hell is that bakery piece?" Tony Reynolds barked into the phone. "We held the damned issue to get this piece in there because you promised to get it to me, remember? Or did you lose your brain back in June, too?"

Flynn winced. Even now, he couldn't tell Tony why he had walked out in the middle of the interview of the year, ticking off a celebrity chef. It was intended to be the cover story for the magazine, one they had advertised for the last three months, a coup that Tony had worked his butt off to finesse, promising the celebrity chef everything from a lifetime subscription to the magazine to a limo ride to the interview.

Flynn hadn't just dropped the ball at that interview—he'd hurled it through the window. He'd been working day and night to get back to the top ever since.

He hadn't expected to walk into that room, meet "Mondo," the chef to the stars, and see one of the first foster fathers he'd ever had. A man he and Liam had lived with for a total of six months before the man had decided the two boys were too much for the man and his wife, who were busy making a go of their restaurant, and he'd asked the department of children's services to find them another home.

The recognition had hit Flynn so hard, he'd never even made it into the room. Never said a word to the man. He'd made up some excuse to Tony about a bout of food poisoning, but the damage had been done. Mondo had stalked out of the building, furious about being stood up, and refused to reschedule.

Flynn had worked too damned hard building his reputation

to let that one mistake ruin everything, which explained why he was the one out on assignment at Christmas while all the other writers were at home, toasting marshmallows or whatever people did with their families the day before Christmas Eve.

"I'll have the story," Flynn said. "You know I will."

"Yeah, I do. We're all allowed one mistake, huh?" Tony chuckled, calmer now that he'd blown off some steam. "You're the only guy who'll work on Christmas, too. Hell, you *never* take a day off. What is it, Flynn? You got some extra ambition gene the rest of us missed?"

"Maybe so." That drive to succeed had fueled him for so many years, had been a constantly burning fire, unquenchable by hundreds of cover stories, thousands of scoops. Then he'd faltered, and he'd been working himself to the bone to recover ever since. There'd be no messing up again. "I'll have the story, Tony," he repeated. "You can count on me."

"That's what makes you my personal Santa, Flynn." Tony laughed, then disconnected.

Flynn hung up the receiver. For a moment there, he'd let himself get sidetracked by Samantha Barnett. Hell, last night he'd even talked about *dating* her, got caught up in a whole champagne-and-lobster fantasy. No more.

He needed to eviscerate the emotion from this job. Get back to business. Then he could get out of this town, and get back to his priorities.

Sam hadn't spent this much time outside the bakery in…well, forever. She could thank Aunt Ginny's matchmaking, though she didn't want to be matched with anyone at all, but she was grateful for the break from work. The minute Flynn MacGregor had entered Joyful Creations and said he needed to talk to her, Ginny had practically shoved Sam out the door and told the two of them to go ice skating.

"Do you know how to do this?" she asked Flynn.

He paused in lacing up the black skates. "Not really. Do you?"

"You can't grow up in rural Indiana without learning to ice skate. There's practically a pond in every backyard." She rose, balancing on her rented skates, then waited for Flynn to finish. Several dozen children and their parents were already skating on a small pond down the street from the park that was set up every winter as a makeshift rink.

He stood, teetering on the thin blades, reaching for the arms of the bench. "This isn't as easy as it looks."

She laughed. "Is anything ever as easy as it looks?"

"I suppose not." He rose again, then let go, taking his time until he was balanced. "Okay, I'm ready to go."

"If you've ever Rollerbladed before—" She cut off her words when she saw his dubious look. "Okay, so you're not the Rollerblading type."

"Limos, champagne and lobster, remember?"

Oh, yeah. She remembered. Very well. In fact, she hadn't been thinking of much but that since their date—no, it hadn't been a date, had it?—last night.

They made their way through the compacted snow on the bank and down to the ice. Sam stepped onto the rink first, then put out her hand. Flynn hesitated for a second, then took her hand and joined her, with a lot of wobbling. Even through two pairs of gloves—his and hers—a surge of electricity ran up Sam's arm when Flynn touched her. This was *so* not in the plan for the day.

"Okay, so where do we start?" he asked. "Hopefully, it's not a position that lands me on my butt."

She laughed. "I can't promise that."

"Then I can't promise to be nice in my article."

She couldn't tell if he was joking or not. She hoped he was. But just in case, she held on to him, even as part of her told her to let go, because every touch awakened a stirring of feelings she hadn't expected. "First, pretend you're on a scooter. Take a step, glide, take a step, glide. Put your arms in front of you to balance."

He let go of her and did as she said, while Sam skated backward, a few feet before him. He wobbled back and forth, scowling at first, frustrated with the whole process. "I give up."

She laughed. "So soon?"

He swayed like a palm tree in a hurricane. "You said you wouldn't let me—"

She caught him just before he fell, the two of them colliding together in that close—very, very close—position of the dancing he had mentioned last night. Hyperawareness pulsed through her, and she tried to pull back, but Flynn's balance still depended on her, and she found her body fitting into the crook of his, as naturally as a missing puzzle piece.

"Fall," he finished, his voice low and husky.

"I didn't," she answered, nearly in a whisper.

He bent down to look at her, his mouth inches from hers, and Sam held her breath, desire coursing through her, the heat overriding the cold air. "Thank you."

"You're…you're welcome."

A crowd of teenagers whipped past them, laughing and chattering, their loud voices jerking Sam back to reality. She inserted some distance between them, locking her arms to keep herself from closing that space again.

"Let's try this again," Flynn said. He started moving forward, one scoot at a time, while Sam slid backward, her gaze first on their feet, and the milky white surface holding them up, then, as Flynn began to master the movement, she allowed her gaze to travel up, connecting with him.

He was intoxicating. Tempting. Her skate skipped across a dent in the ice, and she tripped. Flynn's grip tightened on hers. "Careful," he said.

"I'm trying," Sam said. Trying her best.

"Do you do this often?"

They swished around the rink, going in a wide circle, circumventing the other skaters with an easy shift of hips. "Not often enough. I love to skate. Love the outdoors."

"You? An outdoorsy girl?"

She laughed. "I didn't say I was Outdoorsy Girl, but I do like to do things outside. Garden, skate, swim."

"Swim?" Heat rose in his gaze, the kind that told her he was picturing her in a swimsuit, imagining her body in the water. Another wave of desire coursed through Sam.

"You must have gone swimming a lot, growing up near an ocean."

A shadow dropped over his face. "I used to. But then I…moved."

"Oh." Flynn didn't seem to want to continue that line of questions, so Sam moved on. "What made you get into writing about restaurants?" She grinned. "Do you just like food?"

"I do," he acknowledged. Flynn began to glide forward, his steps becoming a little surer, even as his conversation stayed at a near standstill. "As to the restaurant business, I have some personal acquaintance with it."

Something cold and distant had entered Flynn's gaze, like a wall sliding between them. Not that he'd ever been that open to begin with, but Sam had begun to feel like they were sort of making headway, and now—

He had gone back to being as impersonal as that first day. Was it because the issue wasn't with her…

But with him?

"What happened in your life?" she asked, emotionally and

physically invading his space by sliding her body a little closer, not letting him back down this time, or back away. She sensed a chink in his armor, a slight open window, something that told her there was more to Flynn MacGregor than a man who didn't want to sing "Jingle Bells."

"Nothing."

"I don't believe you. And I don't believe all that hooey about seeing one too many restaurateurs give up their lives to their restaurants. This all seems so personal to you, Flynn. Why?"

Sam was sure, given the choice, he would have moved away, but he was stuck on the ice, stuck holding on to her. He paused a long time, so long she wasn't sure he was going to answer. "I know someone who chose their business over their family."

"Over…you?"

Flynn swung his body to the side, breaking eye contact. He had clear natural athletic ability, which had allowed him to pick up the ice skating quickly, and he let go of one of her hands. "I'm not in Riverbend to talk about me."

"Does every second of our time together have to be about the article?"

"No." But he didn't elaborate. Another group of teenagers whooshed past them, their raucous noise a stark contrast to the tight tension between Flynn and Sam.

She sighed. He was as closemouthed as a snapping turtle. Why? Perhaps she had treaded too close to very personal waters. Could she really blame him for pushing her off? If he had started asking about her grandmother, she would have likely done the same. "I guess it's not too fun to be on the other end of the interview, huh?"

A slight grin quirked up one side of his mouth. "It's not a position I like being in, no."

"Join the club. I know it's good for business and all, but…" She toed at the ice, stopping one skate so that she swung around to skate beside him instead of in front of him, figuring then he'd let go of her hand, but he didn't. "But it's uncomfortable all the same."

"Why?"

"I'm afraid I'll say something I'll regret. And you—" She cut the words off.

"And I'll what?"

Sam cursed the slip of tongue. Now she had to answer. "You'll write one of those tabloid type stories."

"The ones the magazine, and I, am known for."

She watched the ice pass beneath her, solid and hard, cold. "Yes."

"You don't trust me?"

She glanced at him. "Should I?"

The same group of teenagers hurried past them, one brushing past Flynn, causing him to wobble. "Let's take a break for a little while."

"Sure." They made their way off the ice and over to the park bench where they had stored their shoes. The bench sat beneath two trees, long bared by winter's cold. Before them, the skaters continued in repeating circles.

As soon as they sat down on the small bench, the tiny seat making for tight quarters, the tension between them ratcheted up another couple of notches. Sam wished for someone else to come along and defuse the situation. For the teens to rush by, for Aunt Ginny to pop out of the woods, for Earl to amble by, heck, anyone.

"Listen, ah, I didn't mean to pry," she said, diverting back to the earlier topic. It would be best not to make an enemy of this man. "Your personal life is your own."

"And I didn't mean to bite your head off. I'm just not used to women who take such an interest in me personally."

"I'm not, I mean…" She felt her face heat again. Damn.

Why did he have to look at her so directly, with those blue X-ray eyes? "What are they interested in?"

"Let me put it this way. They're not looking for deep, meaningful relationships when they date me."

"And neither are you?"

He chuckled. "No. That's not me, at all."

"Oh." Disappointment settled in her stomach. She couldn't have said why. For one, he was here as a reporter, not as a potential boyfriend. For another, Flynn MacGregor was leaving town in a day, maybe two, and he wasn't the kind who believed in permanence, settling down.

Besides, when did she have time to do either? She couldn't have a relationship, even if she wanted to. Guilt pricked at her conscience, for even thinking she could. She had priorities. Priorities that did not include a man.

Yet, he was tempting, very much so, especially when he was this close. She could see why women would be attracted to him. He had a curious mix of mystery and charm, of aloofness, yet a hint of vulnerability, as if there was something there, something wounded, that he was trying to cover.

"I'm just not the settling down kind," Flynn said. "And most of the women I date understand that." He draped one arm over the back of the bench, then leaned a little closer to Sam. "But I bet you aren't like that at all, are you? The kind that would understand a guy like me."

"We may be more alike than you think," she said quietly.

"You think so?"

She could only nod in response. The noise of the skaters on the pond seemed to disappear, the world becoming just the two of them.

"Maybe you're right." His voice was deep, the timbre seeming to reach crevices in Sam's heart that hadn't been touched in a long time. And all he'd said was three words.

Geez. She really needed to get out more.

Flynn closed the gap between them. For the first time, Sam noticed how the light blue of his dress shirt seemed to make the blue of his eyes richer, deeper. Her pulse began to race, thudding through her veins. "There's only one way to find out."

Sam swallowed hard, her heart beating so loud, she was sure Flynn could hear the pounding. "Find out what?"

"If you would be interested in me."

He caught a tendril of her hair between his gloved fingers, letting it slip through the leather. "We've been dancing around the subject all week."

"Have we?" she asked, the slight catch of laughter in her voice, a clear giveaway of her nerves. "Or is this…"

"What?" he prompted.

"Nothing," she said, not wanting to voice her greatest fear, not wanting to break the sweet, yet dangerous tension.

The silence between them stretched one second. Two. Three. Heat filled the few inches separating them, building like a fever. Sam gazed up at Flynn, her breath caught somewhere in her throat, as if her lungs had forgotten their job. He released her hair, then pulled off his glove and cupped her jaw, using the same hand that had slid down her zipper. A hundred times over the last couple of days she had stolen glimpses of his hands, fascinated by the definition of his fingers, the implied power in his grip, and now, now, he was touching her, just as she'd pictured, and she leaned into the touch, into his thumb tracing along her bottom lip, the desire building and building.

Flynn leaned forward. Slow. Tentative. Taking his time. Because he was unsure? Waiting for her response? His gaze never left hers. Then his fingers slipped down to her neck, dancing along the sensitive skin of her throat—

And he kissed her.

CHAPTER EIGHT

FLYNN HADN'T INTENDED to kiss Samantha Barnett—he could honestly say in all the years he had covered the restaurant business that he had never kissed anyone that he had interviewed. But something had come over him, and the temptation to taste those lips—to see if his theory about neither of them being interested in the other would hold up—had overwhelmed him.

He knew it wasn't her grandmother's cookies; he hadn't even eaten any of those. And either way, truth be told, he'd wanted to kiss Sam pretty much from minute one. Okay, maybe minute two. And now that he finally had—

The experience had lived up to his every expectation. And then some. Kissing Samantha Barnett was like coming home, only Flynn had never really experienced a home, just dreamed of one. She was soft, and welcoming, warm and giving, and yet, she inspired a passion in him, a craving, for more.

But that would be unwise. He was a bulldog, the one who got the article at all costs, not the puppy cowed by a sweet treat.

So Flynn pulled back. "That, ah, won't be part of the article."

"Good." Sam let out a little laugh. "I definitely don't need Bakery Owner Kisses Reporter in Exchange for Good PR as part of the headline." She traced a line along the edge of the painted green bench. "Then what was that? Research?"

He chuckled. When was the last time he'd laughed, really laughed? Hell, if he couldn't remember, then it had definitely been too long. Sam was intoxicating, in more ways than one, and that was dangerous ground to tread. "No, not part of the research. Though, if there is a line of work that lets me kiss you as part of my job—"

"Sorry, no. I'm not part of anyone's resume."

"Pity. And here I was all ready to fill out a job application, too."

What was he saying? He needed to grab hold of his objectivity, and not let go.

A smile slid across her lips, and something that approached joy ballooned in Flynn's chest. The feeling was foreign, new. "You're turning into a joke a minute, Flynn MacGregor. Before you know it, you'll be appearing on a late night comedy special."

"Oh, yeah, that's me. Flynn the comic." He chuckled. Again. Twice in the space of one minute. That had to be an all-time personal record.

He watched her join him in laughter, and the temptation to kiss her again rose inside him, fast and furious. Flynn jerked his attention away and began to unlace his skates. "I should probably get back to work."

"All work and no play?"

He looked up at her. "I could say the same for you."

"Oh, I play. Sometimes."

"When?" He moved closer to her, ignoring the warning bells in his head reminding him he should be working, not flirting. "Is there a nonbusiness side to Samantha Barnett?"

It was a pure research question. The kind he could use to delve deeper, expose a vulnerable vein. He'd done it a hundred times—

Except this time he found his attention not on how he would write up her answer, or what his next question would be, but on whether her answer would be something that would interest him, too. Something they could do together.

She brushed her bangs out of her face, revealing more of her heart-shaped countenance. "Well, Christmas, for sure. I love this time of year."

"I think it's a prerequisite for living in this town."

"You might learn to love the holiday, too," she said. "In fact, if you're looking for something to cultivate your feelings for Christmas, you could go to the Riverbend Winterfest."

"Winterfest?"

Sam nodded, her eyes shining with excitement, a fever Flynn could almost imagine catching. "The town recently started holding this really big Christmas celebration. C. J. Hamilton does it up big, bringing in all kinds of decorations and moving props. He dresses up as Santa, and his wife is Mrs. Claus. Even Earl gets into the spirit. This year, I hear he's dressing up as an elf and handing out candy canes to all the kids who come to Santa's workshop. That alone should be worth the price of admission, which is free anyway. It's a really fun time."

What it sounded like was another date. Another temptation. Another opportunity to be alone with Samantha Barnett.

And a bad idea.

"It's, ah, not really my cup of tea. Besides, I should probably be working on my article." He slipped off his skates and put his shoes back on, as a visual and physical reminder of getting out of here.

"The Winterfest starts at night. You have plenty of time to do your article and anything else you might want to accomplish today." She took off her own skates, then met his gaze. He found himself watching her mouth move, fantasizing about kissing her again. And again. "You should reconsider. You'll be missing something really cool. Trust me, Winterfest is fun for more than just kids. I love going."

"I'm not much of a Christmas person."

"Oh. Well, it was just an idea."

"I didn't mean to offend you."

"You didn't." She tied her skates together, then slid her feet into her boots.

"It's just…" He paused. "Where I grew up, Christmas wasn't a big deal."

Sam smiled. "When I was a kid, Christmas was the biggest day of the year. My family was total Christmas-holics, and after my parents died, my grandmother did Christmas up even bigger, as if to make up for losing my mother and father." Her smile died on her lips, and her gaze drifted to the skaters rounding the rink. "I miss those days."

"What happened?"

"My grandmother isn't there like she used to be."

Flynn opened his mouth, as if he intended to ask her what she meant by that, then closed it again. Sam regretted saying anything at all. She had done her best to keep her grand-mother's condition private, from everyone in town. Not just to protect Grandma Joy, but to prevent the inevitable ques-tions. The visitors who would stop by to see Joy, and be hurt that she didn't know them. The pity parties, the people who wanted to help lift the burden from Sam's shoulders.

No one understood this burden couldn't be lifted. Her grandmother didn't remember her. Didn't know her. No amount of sympathy would ever change that.

So Sam kept the details to herself, told people Joy was happily living a life at a retirement home, and buried herself in her work. Carrying on her family's legacy, living up to gen-erations of expectations—not from her grandmother, but from this town. There'd been a Barnett behind the stove at Joyful Creations since it had opened, and that's what customers expected when they walked in the door.

Even if a part of Sam wanted to walk out that door one day and keep on walking. To pretend that she didn't have those responsibilities waiting for her every morning. To imagine a different life, one that was more—

Complete.

"This Winterfest thing is probably the social event of the year, huh?" Flynn said, drawing Sam out of her thoughts.

"It is. People look forward to it. Myself included." She laughed. "I spend days baking like crazy before it, to supply the festival's stand, while a few people work the downtown shop. We get a lot of out-of-towners for Winterfest, so it's a busy day for all the stores around here." Sam rose and put a fist on her hip. "It's a big deal, for those who dare to go. So, do you?"

One corner of Flynn's mouth curved up. "Are you challenging me?" He took a few steps closer, the distance between them shrinking from feet to inches in an instant. He flipped at the laces on her skates, dangling from her fingers, hanging near her hips. Sam inhaled and her breath caught in her throat, held, waiting, for—

What? For Flynn to make a move? For him to kiss her again?

Oh, how she wished he would, even as another part of her wished he wouldn't.

He distracted her, awakened her to the possibilities she had laid aside for so long. He had this way of forcing her to open her eyes, to confront issues she'd much rather leave at the door.

"I am," she said, the two words nearly a breath.

"I should…" Flynn began, his body so close she could feel the heat emanating from his skin, and the answering heat rising inside her. Then the grin widened, and before Sam could second-guess her challenge, it was too late. "Suddenly I can't think of anything else I should do, but go with you."

CHAPTER NINE

FLYNN SHOULD HAVE put the pieces together sooner. He used to be really good at that. Figuring out what parts of the story people held back. And why.

But this time, his objectivity had been compromised. By his attraction to Sam? By the town? By that one assignment going so horribly awry? Whatever it was, Flynn had lost his tight hold on his life, and that had caused him to stop paying attention to the details.

Until now.

Until he'd returned to the bed and breakfast after ice skating, and Betsy Williams had started chatting up a storm, first pointing out a photo on the wall of Sam and her grandmother, then telling tales about the two of them working together, then finally segueing into rumors about the cookies.

"You wouldn't believe how fast people are eating those cookies up," Betsy was saying as Flynn helped her carry the dishes out to the dining room table and set up for dinner.

Betsy had pronounced Flynn a "sweet boy" for volunteering, having no idea of his ulterior motive. How many times had he employed a similar tactic? Using a nice gesture as a way to get more information out of someone? Never before had it bothered him. He was doing his job, just as he should.

But today, every dish he carried, every fork he laid on the table, while Betsy chattered on, seemed to nag at him, like stones on his back.

"I feel like I'm running *The Dating Game* right in my little B and B," Betsy went on. "Maybe I should open a wedding chapel next door." She laughed. "Oh, wouldn't Sam's grandmother get such a kick out of this, if she could see what was happening with that bakery."

"Where is Sam's grandmother, by the way?"

Betsy shut the door of the dining room hutch and turned back to Flynn, a silver bread platter in her hands. "She didn't tell you?"

Flynn shrugged, feigning nonchalance. "We didn't talk much about her."

"Oh, well, that's because Sam hardly ever talks about Joy. No one in this town does, either, though they like to speculate, being a small town and all."

"Why?"

"Well…" Betsy looked around, as if she expected Sam to appear in the dining room at any second. "I don't know the whole story, but I heard from Estelle, who heard from Carolyn, who heard from Louise, that Joy isn't really living at a retirement home and playing golf every day."

A tide rose in Flynn's chest. This was the missing piece, the nugget he searched for in every story, the one that made headlines, the one that earned his reputation on every article. He could feel it, with an instinct bred from years on the job. "Really? Where is she?"

"No one's really sure because we never see Joy anymore, and if you ask Sam or Ginny, they just put on a brave face and keep on sticking to that retirement home story. But you know…" Again, Betsy looked around, then returned her attention to Flynn. "Before she 'retired,' Joy was getting real forgetful. Doing things like wandering around town in her night-gown, showing up to work at the bakery in the middle of the night, telling Earl, a man she's known all her life, that she didn't know him. We just thought she was overworked, you know? That bakery, it's a handful, I'm sure. I know, because I have this bed and breakfast. It's a lot for one woman."

The pieces of the story assembled in Flynn's head, and he could nearly write the article already, see the bold letters of the headline leaping from the pages. His editor would be crowing with joy when this came across the transom. "You think Joy went to a home for people with Alzheimer's?"

"Maybe. I mean, where else could she be? And that leaves poor Sam with hardly no family, except for her Aunt Ginny." Betsy pressed a hand to her heart. She sighed, then looked back at the photo on the wall, taken outside of Joyful Creations. "Well, she does have that shop. That place has been her real family, for a long time. And you know, I think that's the saddest part of all."

A couple burst through the bed and breakfast's doors just then, giggling and feeding each other bites of the special cherry chocolate chunk cookies. The reporter in Flynn knew his job was to pursue that couple—they personified the kind of happily-ever-after that would be perfect for his article—but another part of him was still tuned to Betsy's words, even as she said something about getting pies in the oven and hurried off to the kitchen.

Flynn pulled his notepad out of his back pocket, and took two steps toward the couple. Then he paused, stopping by the black-and-white photograph of Sam and her grandmother, one photo among the several dozen crowding Betsy's wall. Even back then, Sam was smiling, beaming, really, with pride, standing beneath the curved banner of the store's name. And the woman beside her, an older version of Sam, reflected the same joy and pride.

Flynn's notepad weighed heavy in his palm. He knew where the rest of his story lay. The problem?

Deciding whether it would be worth the price he'd pay to go after it.

"We fell in love, just like that." The couple beamed and leaned into each other, looking so happy, they could have been an ad for a jewelry store.

Flynn had spent his afternoon tracking down couples who attributed their romances to the legendary cherry chocolate chunk cookies from Joyful Creations. The process had been easy. After talking to the duo at the bed and breakfast, he'd simply asked Betsy for recommendations. One chat led to another and to another. In a small town, just about everyone had a neighbor, a sister, a friend who believed the treats were the reason for their marital bliss.

Every single one of them thanked the legendary Joy Barnett for their bliss. They extolled the virtues of Sam, for carrying on Joy's legacy, during Joy's retirement.

Retirement.

There was no retirement, of that Flynn was sure. Every reporter's instinct he had told him so. Sam was trying to keep the truth the secret.

The question was why.

Finding that out would make for an interesting story. A very interesting story, indeed.

"Did you know the cookies were supposed to make people fall in love?" he asked.

"Well, it wasn't a *known* fact," the woman said, "not until the magazine story came out. But now everyone in Riverbend knows. And, all over the country, too."

"So this was just kind of a coincidence?"

"Not at all. We went out on a date, we had cookies and we fell in love."

Flynn kept himself from saying anything about the possibility that a sugar high might have led to a hasty infatuation. He just jotted down the quote, thanked the couple for their time and left their small Cape house. The snow had frozen enough to keep from soaking his pants and shoes as he walked through the streets of Riverbend and back to the bakery to meet Sam. He had everything he needed for his article—

Except the story of Sam's grandmother.

He could, of course, write the article without it. Just turn around, go back to the bed and breakfast, plug in what he had and leave it at that. But it wouldn't be the article his editor was expecting, nor would it be the kind of article he was known for.

Flynn MacGregor didn't quit until he got to the real story. He made a lot of enemies that way, but he also made a lot of reader fans, and a hell of a lot of money.

The magazine was called *Food Lovers* because its readers loved to know the real story behind the food. They didn't just want recipes and tips on choosing a knife; they wanted to know what kind of childhood their favorite chef had, or whether that restaurant failed because the hostess divorced the owner.

And that meant Flynn would find out what happened to Sam's grandmother. He'd want to know—because his readers would eat it up. Pun intended.

Since Sam had agreed to meet Flynn downtown, he stopped by the pay phone again. His cell still wasn't having any luck finding a signal, and calling from Betsy's meant using the public phone in the front parlor—with the carolers hanging on his every word.

So he deposited his change into the public phone, and dialed Mimi's number. On the other end, three rings, then a distracted, "Hello?"

"Mimi? It's Flynn."

The sounds of music, laughing and bubbly conversation carried over the line, nearly drowning out Mimi's response. "Flynn MacGregor, I can't believe you didn't show up at my Christmas party. Didn't even RSVP. That's so totally rude."

"I told you, I had to go out of town on assignment."

Mimi let out a gust. "Again? You know I can never keep track of your schedule."

"I don't expect you to." But a part of him was disappointed that once again, Mimi hadn't paid attention. Hadn't even cared.

Sam wouldn't do that to someone. Sam would have noticed. Sam would have baked him a box of cookies to take along for the ride, for Pete's sake.

Where did that come from? He didn't need a woman like Sam. He liked his life unencumbered. He could come and go as he pleased. No one waiting for him, no one expecting him to make a home, settle down.

"Listen, Flynn, I can't talk right now. I have, like, fifty people here." Then Mimi was gone, the congestion of people silenced with a click.

"Everything okay back in Boston?"

Flynn turned. Sam stood behind him, bundled as always in her thick, marshmallowlike jacket. Mimi, who followed every fashion tip espoused by the editors of *Vogue*, would never have worn anything even close. She preferred sleek, impractical coats in a rainbow of colors that accented her attire like diamonds on a necklace. "It's the same as always," he said.

"Ready to go to the Winterfest?"

Flynn would have rather taken a dip in Boston Harbor than

spend his evening at the town's homage to all things Christmas. But what else did he have to do? Spending a little more time with Samantha Barnett could only help him fill in those few more details he wanted. Maybe get her to open up, tell him about her grandmother without him having to probe.

Hell, who was he kidding?

The details Flynn was interested in had less to do with his article and more to do with the way she filled out her sweater, the way her smile curved across her face, and the way her laughter seemed to draw him in and make him wonder if maybe he'd been missing out on something for the last thirty years of his life.

Even as he told himself not to get emotionally involved, to hold himself back.

Not to make the same mistake twice.

They headed down the sidewalk, past several shops that were so decorated for Christmas, they could have been advertisements for the holiday. A toy store, a deli, a church. On every light pole hung a red banner advertising the Riverbend Winterfest, while white lights sparkled in the branches of tiny saplings that lined the street. People hurried by them, chattering about Christmas, while children stopped to peer into the windows of the shops, their hands cupped over their eyes to see deeper inside.

Flynn took Sam's hand. It seemed a natural thing to do, something dozens of other couples were doing. She glanced over at him, a slight look of surprise on her face, but didn't pull away. His larger palm engulfed hers, yet a tingle of warm electricity sizzled up his arm at her touch.

"This way." She tugged him down a side street.

When he turned, he saw the park where he'd seen the live reindeer earlier. Only now it had been transformed into a mega-winter wonderland with the atmosphere of a carnival, taken to the nth degree. The grassy area was filled with people, and looked like something straight out of a movie. Hundreds of lighted Christmas displays, featuring every image associated with the holiday that a human being could imagine and hook up to ten gazillion watts, ringed the central gazebo, while little stands from local vendors sold everything from Riverbend T-shirts to hot pretzels.

Sam stopped walking and let out a sigh. "Isn't it perfect? It's like every child's dream of the perfect Christmas day."

And it was. At one end, by a small shed, Santa Claus held court, with Mrs. Claus by his side. To the right, the live reindeer was in his pen, chomping a carrot. On the roof of the shed, someone had installed a lighted sleigh and eight painted fake reindeer. He bit back a laugh. "You weren't lying, were you?"

"I told you he was dressing up as an elf."

Earl Klein, in an oversized elf costume, looking more like the Jolly Green Giant than one of Santa's helpers, stood to the front of the small shed, handing out candy canes and greeting all the children. Throughout the park, a sound system played a jaunty, tinny selection of Christmas carols, carrying through the air with the scent of hot chocolate and peppermint. Hundreds of people milled around the Winterfest, chatting happily, visiting the petting zoo, greeting old friends, hugging family members.

"People really get into this thing, don't they?"

"I told you, it's a big deal."

"It's…unbelievable."

Sam laughed. "No, it's fun, that's what it is."

Everything Sam had promised him was here. The Riverbend Winterfest was, indeed, the perfect Christmas celebration, all in one place.

"Let's hit the games first. There's a prize every time." Sam pointed toward a set of dart games, with stuffed animal prizes dangling from the roof. "How's your aim?"

He chuckled. "Terrible."

"Good thing there's a prize every time then."

Before he could protest, or think twice, Flynn found himself plunking down a couple bucks to throw a trio of darts at some small balloons. A few minutes later, he was rewarded with a tiny stuffed Santa, which he handed to Sam. "Your prize, m'lady."

"Oh, it's all yours. A souvenir from your time in Riverbend."

He ticktocked the miniature jolly guy back and forth. "He'd be my one and only Christmas decoration."

Sam closed her hand over his, and over the toy. "Well, you gotta start somewhere, don't you?"

Did he? Flynn stuffed the toy in his pocket, more disconcerted than he could remember being before. And all over a Santa no bigger than the palm of his hand. This was crazy.

He walked through the displays, tasting the pretzels, riding on a few of the rides, with Sam by his side, telling himself he should be asking her questions, probing deeper for his article, but he kept getting distracted…by the one thing he'd never thought he'd find in this town.

A good time.

They paused by the Joyful Creations booth, manned by Sam's Aunt Ginny. "Well, hello there. Are you two having a good time?"

"We are," Sam answered, sparing Flynn.

"Would you like to try some cookies?" her aunt asked, holding up a platter. "The shop's specialty, perhaps?"

Sam shot her a glare.

"No, I'm good. Thank you." After interviewing that couple earlier, Flynn wasn't taking any chances on having those cherry chocolate chunk cookies. Not that he believed the rumors, but—

Just in case.

Turning his life upside down by falling in love would be completely insane. So he'd stick to the story, and avoid the desserts. Yep. That was the plan. Except...

He wasn't doing so well in that department thus far. He couldn't help but admire Sam's curves, the way her hair danced around her shoulders as he followed her away from the booth and over to the carousel, where they stood and watched some children ride wooden ponies in a circle.

"There's something I've been meaning to ask you," Sam said.

"Shoot."

"Boston's really far from Indiana. Did you really drive all the way out here, just to interview me?"

"Well...not exactly."

"What do you mean?" They started walking again, weaving in and out among the crowds, the scents of hot chocolate, peppermint and popcorn wrapping around them like a blanket.

"I drove so I had the freedom to make another stop." Assuming, that was, that he was welcome.

"To visit family?"

Flynn shrugged. "Something like that."

"Do you have much family back home in Boston?"

The fun moments they'd been having dissolved as quickly as snow under direct sunlight. "No." He paused. "Yes."

Why hadn't he stopped at no? Where had that compulsion to qualify his answer come from? Now he was opening a door he had kept shut for years. A door he had never opened to anyone else.

"Yes and no?" She smiled. "Now, that's an interesting family."

"My brother used to live there...but we don't talk." That was an understatement and a half. Flynn could have said more, but he didn't. Why and how he and Liam had drifted apart required starting at the beginning, and Flynn refused to go back there. For anyone.

"Oh. I'm sorry."

"Yeah."

Whoa, there was an answer, Flynn. He could see the question marks in Sam's eyes, the inevitable "why" lingering in her gaze, but she didn't voice the question, and he didn't volunteer the answer.

He paused beside a hayride station, watching the children in line, thinking Sam would let the conversation go. Hoping she would. But when he racked his brain for another topic, he came up with…nothing.

"Older or younger?" she asked.

"What do you mean?"

"Is your brother older or younger? I'm an only child, so I've never had a sibling." She sighed. "I always wondered what it would be like, though I had cousins around a lot when I was a kid. They were sort of like brothers and sisters."

"He's younger. In his last year of college."

"Wow. A lot younger, huh?"

"Just four years. He got a late start on going to Purdue." What was this, show-and-tell? He'd never told anyone this much about Liam—ever. Yet, Sam's openness, her friendly, easy questions, made talking about his brother seem like the most natural thing in the world. Like he had a normal background. A normal family. A normal personal story to tell. Like so many of the ones surrounding them.

When the truth was completely the opposite.

"He's at Purdue? But, that's not far from here."

"I know."

"You could stop and see him for the holidays. The drive isn't too bad, maybe an hour and a half…" Her voice trailed off as she read his face, which must have said he wasn't going to go down that conversational road, because he'd already visited it and turned around. "You probably know that, too."

"I do."

Let the topic drop, he thought. Don't press it. He didn't want to talk about Liam, because doing that would lead to a conversation about his past. And that wasn't a door he wanted to open.

But Sam apparently didn't possess mind-reading skills.

"If your brother is still in school, then he's probably not married, is he?" Then she paused, and a blush filled her face. "I never thought to ask if you were. I just assumed, because you kissed me…"

"I'm not married." They stopped at a snack stand and ordered two coffees to go. "Not now. Not then, and not ever. I'm not a marrying kind of guy."

She cocked an elbow on the counter and tossed him a grin. "What's the matter? Are you scared of the big, bad altar?"

"No. It's just…" This time, he did have the sense to cut himself off before he started opening any more painful doors. He handed her a foam cup, then took his and started walking again.

"Just what?"

He took a long gulp of the coffee. The hot caffeine nearly seared his throat. "Some of us are meant for settling down, and some aren't."

"The nomadic freelancer?"

"Something like that."

Sam tipped her head and studied him, apparently not put off by his short answers. "Funny, it's hard to see you as a nomad."

He snorted. "You think I'm some two-point-five kids, German-shepherd-in-the-suburbs guy?"

"I think…you'd fit into a town like this better than you think." Her green eyes pierced through the shell that Flynn thought had been like steel-plated armor, but apparently, around her, had a few unprotected areas. "And that you're secretly more of a golden retriever guy."

"You have the golden retriever part right." He got to his feet. "But I'd never fit into a place like this. And I know that from personal experience."

He knew the truth. And knew he couldn't keep on walking around this Winterfest and pretend he was part of that world. That he could be some normal family guy, like all the others he saw. Sipping cocoa, laughing, singing. Acting like this was just another merry Christmas, one more out of dozens.

Whereas Flynn had never learned to have one in the first place. He tossed his half-full coffee into a nearby trash can.

"I have to go. I have work to do," Flynn said. "Sorry."

She pivoted toward him. The tease was still in her eyes, because she didn't understand, didn't see what this would cost him. How he couldn't experience this, and then walk away from it at the end.

It would have been better not to go at all.

"Not so fast, mister," she said. "There's more to this than just you not wanting to play pin-the-nose-on-Rudolph, isn't there?"

Flynn glanced over his shoulder at the Christmas paradise. The music and the scents streamed outward, calling to him like a siren. "I'm just not in the mood for holly jolly right now. I have work to do."

Then he left, before he could be tempted into something he knew he'd regret, by a woman who was surrounded by a cloud of cinnamon and vanilla. A woman who made all of that seem so possible—when Flynn knew the truth.

CHAPTER TEN

SAM HAD TO BE CRAZY.

Here she was, walking the streets of Riverbend long after the Winterfest had ended. Her breath escaped her in bursts of white clouds, and though she had her hood up and her coat zipped all the way to the neck, the cold still managed to seep through the thick fabric. If she was smart, she'd go home and go to sleep. After all, she had to be up bright and early tomorrow morning to start baking, and begin the whole vicious work cycle all over again.

Just as she had every day of her life for the past umpteen years.

But after leaving the Winterfest, still confused about Flynn's early exit, she'd headed back to the house where she'd grown up. Once there, a restlessness had invaded her, and she'd been unable to sleep. She'd paced for half an hour, then finally given up, slipped back into her coat and boots and headed out into the cold.

The bracing winter air stung her cheeks like icy mosquitoes, while the dryness sucked the moisture from her lips, but she kept walking, increasing her stride. Silence blanketed Riverbend, with all the residents snug in their proverbial beds. Sam loved this time of day, when she could be alone, with her thoughts, her town, herself. Her steps faltered when she noticed a familiar figure outlined under the warm glow of a porch light.

Flynn.

Apparently she wasn't the only one who couldn't sleep.

Sam hesitated, then strode up the walkway of Betsy's Bed and Breakfast. "I thought a good night's sleep was guaranteed."

He scoffed. "Guess I better ask Betsy for a refund."

"Well," Sam began, suddenly uncomfortable under his piercing blue gaze, "I suppose I should get back to my walk."

"At this hour? Isn't that a little dangerous?"

She laughed. "In Riverbend? Our crime rate is so low, it's not even a number."

He shook his head. "I didn't think places like that existed."

"Walk with me, and you can see for yourself."

What had made her offer that? She'd gone out with the express intention of being alone. And here she'd gone and invited Flynn MacGregor along. The more time she spent with this man, the more she revealed about herself. Too much time, and she'd be exposing secrets she didn't want in print.

He was in town for one reason—for a story, and nothing more. Tonight, after she'd gone home, she'd unearthed some back issues of *Food Lovers* that had sat in her den, unread for months and months. Sam had skimmed them and found exactly what Aunt Ginny had said—most of the articles were more focused on the personal lives of their subjects than their products or business.

Sam's heart had sunk. Even as she knew better, she'd hoped for something different. Many of the articles had had Flynn MacGregor's byline. The worst ones, in fact. The ones that were the harshest, the ones that had the most blaring head-lines about businesses rocked by divorces, by deaths of a partner or a hidden bankruptcy.

And now, she knew, she'd end up the same way.

He wasn't really interested in her. How could she think anything different? He was using the kisses, using his charm, for one reason only.

To get the story.

He was a reporter.

Not a friend.

Just because he'd kissed her, and she'd kissed him back, didn't change anything.

Except…it did. She found herself liking him, even despite knowing all this. She sensed something about him, a vulnerability. It pulled at Sam, and told her there was a story beneath him, too. The problem was whether she was willing to take the risk of getting close to him to find out what that story was.

"A walk sounds good," Flynn said, ending Sam's internal debate. "It'll let me see the town with new eyes."

Maybe this wouldn't be such a bad idea after all. Perhaps if she showed him a softer, quieter side of town, he'd feature Riverbend in his article—and not her.

Uh-huh. And maybe she was just some naive country bumpkin, after all.

Flynn rose, buttoned his coat tighter against the cold, then hurried down the stairs. "Promise not to drag me to any hometown festivals? Or force me to ooh and ahh over the decorations?"

Sam crossed her heart. "Scout's honor."

A slight smile played on his lips. "Were you ever a Girl Scout?"

"Four years. I had to drop out because I needed to help in the bakery after school." They began to walk, falling into stride together. The town was silent, save for the occasional car or barking dog. Beneath their feet, snow crunched like cornflakes in a cereal bowl. "How about you? Were you ever in Boy Scouts?"

"No. I never…had time."

The pause in the middle of the sentence made her wonder. What was he leaving out? But he didn't seem inclined to share, and she couldn't badger him when she didn't want him to do the same to her, so she let it go.

Just as he had at the Winterfest, Flynn's hand dropped down and sought hers again, and he held onto her as they walked. It seemed so normal, so wonderful, and yet, she tried not to enjoy the feeling, tried to remind herself that he wasn't staying and she didn't have time for a relationship.

And most of all, that Flynn had ulterior motives for getting close to her.

Above them, heavy snow creaked in the branches of the trees, threatening to break under the extra weight. An SUV passed them, its tires crunching on the icy roads, red lights winking when the car turned right.

"I love the houses when they're decorated for the holidays." Sam sighed. "It looks so…magical."

Flynn glanced up at the cascade of lights around them. Had he ever taken the time to notice Christmas lights before? The way they twinkled in the ebony darkness? The play of white and red against shrubs and siding, the dancing rainbow of bulbs running along gutters, edging the houses with an almost mystical brilliance? "They're…nice. I guess."

Okay, they were *very* nice, but he kept that to himself. He refused to fall in love with this town, because places like this—seasons like this—didn't last.

"When I was little, my father hated hanging the lights, or at least that's what he always said. I think it's because he took them down so fast at the end of the year, they were a jumbled mess every December. My mother would be out there, helping him, reminding him that he shouldn't curse in front of his daughter." Sam laughed softly. "But once they were up, he'd hoist me onto his shoulders and take me outside, even if I was already in my pajamas, to see them. And that's when I got to make a wish."

"A wish?"

"Yep. The first time the lights are turned on, my father said, was the most magical time, and he told me it was like birthday candles. Make a wish for Christmas and it would come true. I was a kid, so I was always wishing for a toy." Sam's smile faltered. "If I'd known…I would have wished for something else."

"Known what?"

"Known I wouldn't have had that many Christmases with him." She let out a breath, which became a cloud, framing her face in a soft mist. "I wish they were still alive."

"I'm sorry." And he was, because he knew her feelings.

She shrugged, as if she was over the loss, but Flynn saw a glistening in her eyes. "It's okay. My grandparents were there, and they were wonderful. The best substitute I could have asked for. What about your family? Did they hang lights every year? And curse their way through the process?"

"No."

They paused at a stop sign, even though there was no traffic. Sam turned to look at him, clearly surprised by his single-word answer. Flynn stepped off the curb and continued the walk.

"Did you live in an apartment? Is that why you didn't hang lights?"

What was with this woman? She was like a terrier with a new bone. She refused to give up on a topic. "No, that wasn't it. I just didn't celebrate Christmas much as a kid."

Sam halted on the sidewalk. "Really? Why?"

Flynn scowled. "I thought we were taking a walk. Not writing my biography."

The winter wind slithered between them, building an icy wall faster than a colony of ants could invade a picnic. Sam's hand slipped out of his and she stepped to the left, not a noticeable difference, but enough to send a signal.

He'd stopped getting personal, and she'd stopped connecting. He should be glad. He didn't want any kind of personal connection, anything that took him from the controlled path he'd always carefully maintained.

Then why did the bitter taste of disappointment pool in his gut?

"So, you said earlier you had some more questions to ask me," Sam said. "Did you remember what else you needed to know?"

Now that the time was here, and Sam was looking at him, waiting for him to ask the questions he knew he should—the kind he'd asked a hundred times before—

Flynn hesitated.

"Let's not talk business tonight. Let's just enjoy the walk."

She laughed, the sound as refreshing as lemonade on a hot summer day. "The intrepid reporter, getting sentimental? Dare I think the Winterfest actually got to you?"

No. *She'd* gotten to him. Every time he should be thinking about his job, he thought about kissing her. Every time he thought he was focused, he got distracted. And right now, when he was supposed to be taking the actions that would put his career back on top, everything within him started to rebel. For a man like Flynn, who lived life on a leash, that could only mean trouble.

"We have time anyway. It turns out my car won't be ready for another day or two." He thumbed in the general direction of Earl's shop. "So it looks like I'm stuck here."

She let out another little laugh. "You make it sound like you've been sentenced to a chain gang."

"Nah. Just Alcatraz."

She pressed a hand to her chest. "Flynn MacGregor, did you just make another joke?"

He grinned. "Not on purpose."

Flynn didn't know how they had done it, but their path had taken them to the park where the Winterfest had been held. On purpose? By accident?

He paused at the entrance. The lighted displays—gingerbread men, snowmen, Christmas trees, teddy bears—had all been left on, layering the grounds with silent, twinkling enchantment. The people were gone, Santa and Mrs. Claus back at home, the stands and games shut up for the night. Only the reindeer remained, chomping on some hay in his pen. The blanket of night gave everything a spirit of magic, as if anything could happen, as if, on this night, wishes could come true.

What would he have given to have gone to something like this as a kid? To have been able to bring Liam to Santa's Workshop, to let him sit on Santa's lap, and tell Santa what he wanted—

And even more, have Santa actually deliver what he and Liam really desired?

The one thing neither of them had ever had. The only gift ripped away, time after time.

A home. A family. A place he could depend on, knowing it would be there this December 25th and the next, and that there would be someone there who would hang the lights and string garland on the tree.

Flynn shook his head. Damn. He hadn't intended to think about those days. Ever.

He felt a soft hand on his back. "Flynn? Are you all right?"

Sam. Her voice so gentle it called to him like a salve.

Maybe it was the timing. The darkness, punctuated by the sparkling holiday lights. Or maybe it was something more. Flynn didn't pause long enough to question why, he just turned toward Samantha Barnett and gave in to the desire that wrapped between them as tight as a bow on a present, and kissed her again.

When Flynn's lips met hers, Sam nearly stumbled backward in surprise. Then a wave of desire rocked her, and she leaned into him, her mouth parting against his. Their tongues danced, their bodies pressed together, heat building in crashing waves, even through the thick fabric of her winter coat.

His fingers tangled in her hair and her hood fell down, but she didn't feel the bite of winter, only the whoosh of desire as Flynn gently tugged her even closer.

Had she ever felt this treasured? Like she was the only woman in the world? The most special gift he had ever held? When he released her, disappointment slid all the way to her toes.

"We keep doing that," he said. "And we probably shouldn't."

"Yeah." Though right now, Sam couldn't think of a single reason why. "Not that I'm complaining," she added.

"I'm not complaining, either," he said. "And even though I know I shouldn't, because it shoots my reporter's objectivity all to hell, I couldn't resist." He caught a tendril of her hair and let it slip slowly through his grasp. "You are a very desirable woman."

"Oh, yeah, I'm a totally hot beauty right now." Sam ran a hand down her puffy jacket and let out a laugh. "I mean, I'm a walking marshmallow in this coat and even without it, I'm no skinny-minny, not to mention I—"

He put a finger to her lips. "You're beautiful, just the way you are. Skinny doesn't automatically mean gorgeous. Nor was it your jacket that attracted me to you."

A shiver of pleasure ran down her spine. She hadn't been fishing for a compliment, but the words sent her heart singing.

"Good, because if you were turned on by this thing, I'd be worried about you." She let out a laugh, but still it shook at the end. Flynn MacGregor had unnerved her, without a doubt.

"Do you find it that hard to believe that I'd be attracted to you?"

Sam broke away from Flynn and crossed to one of the displays, silent and immobile, but still lit, giving the town an all-night Christmas picture. She ran a hand down the lighted gingerbread mother, then up and over the circular heads of the little gingerbread children, all of them plump and happy in their wooden splendor.

"No…" But her voice trailed off, into the cold. Because she did. Flynn, the charming city man, who had surely dated women miles away from Sam, finding her attractive, seemed so unbelievable, yet very, very heady.

Silence held them in its uncomfortable grip for a long time, then Flynn came up behind her. "Who broke your heart, Samantha?"

"Is this on the record?" she asked, without turning around.

"Do you think that little of me, that I'd actually put your personal life into the story?"

She pivoted. "Would you, if you thought it would add more depth? Get you on the cover?"

He hesitated for only a fraction of a second, but it was enough to give her the answer she needed. Had any of this been real? Had he wanted her for her? Or for the story?

She needed to remember the truth. Behind every move Flynn MacGregor made, was an ulterior motive.

Sam's heart shattered in that instant. And even as Flynn said "no," Sam was already heading out of the park and back home.

Alone in the cold.

CHAPTER ELEVEN

THE MAN WAS LIKE A VIRUS.

Okay, maybe not a virus, but Flynn MacGregor had a tendency to be everywhere. Just when Sam thought she'd have a moment to breathe without him, he showed up, and disconcerted her all over again.

Heck, she'd been disconcerted ever since that kiss last night, not to mention the one before that, and all the times she'd thought about kissing him in between. She'd gone home, gone to bed, then tossed and turned for an hour, alternately berating herself for getting swept up in the moment and reliving the way his lips had moved against hers. The way he had awakened something inside of her that she'd thought didn't even exist.

The way he'd made her feel not just pretty, but beautiful. And then undone it all with the way he'd hesitated in his answer to her question.

He'd been at Joyful Creations first thing in the morning, which had surprised her, considering the way they'd ended things last night—or rather the way she had ended the evening. She half expected him to get out his notepad and start asking questions, but instead he'd come into the kitchen and simply kept her company for the last few minutes.

Which had set her off-kilter, made her lose her concentration more than once.

What *did* he want?

"Uh, Sam, I'm not here to tell you how to do your job, but aren't you supposed to crack the eggs *before* you add them to the batter?" Flynn asked.

Sam looked down at the bowl, where three eggs sat, mocking her distractedness with their white oval shells. "Oh. Yeah." Her face flushed.

She fished the eggs out and cracked the shells against the edge, then turned on the professional-sized mixer, several times larger than one used in a regular kitchen. Instead of watching Flynn, she watched the dough turn and consume the yellow yolks.

"Why are you working today?" he asked. "It's Christmas Eve. How busy could you possibly be the day before Christmas?"

She turned off the mixer and reached for the sugar, measuring it into a large cup and pouring the crystals into the wide metal bowl. "You'd be surprised how many people have parties and need last-minute desserts. Or want Danishes for Christmas morning breakfast. It'll be busy in here. Though I do close early." She turned on the mixer and began incorporating the ingredients. "Technically, today's supposed to be my day off, but—" She shrugged, as if what he thought didn't matter. Sam turned away, feigning the study of a recipe in a book, before she started measuring her dry ingredients into a second bowl. She already knew the recipe by heart, but used the book as a way to avoid Flynn.

She'd do well to remember their roles. She was the story. He was the reporter. Getting any more personal with him than she already had would be a mistake.

If she did, she might end up spilling her personal beans,

and he'd use her grandmother's story to throw in some human interest angle for his story about the bakery, making it national news, which would spread Grandma Joy's personal info all over Riverbend. She'd seen it happen too many times to other people—they became news charity cases. Sam refused to become another headline on Flynn's wall.

Flynn MacGregor would be gone in a day, two at most. She could keep her secrets safe that long. Protect her grandmother's privacy. She didn't want people knowing what had happened, realizing that Joy had lost the very memories that had once made her such a treasured part of this town.

That wouldn't do Joy or the people who loved her any good. All it would end up doing was creating a stirring of sympathy and a rush to "do something," when really, nothing could be done.

Flynn leaned against the doorjamb, his arms crossed over his chest. "Bet you haven't taken a Christmas Eve off, in…"

Sam began dropping teaspoonfuls of cookie dough onto cookie sheets. "About as long as you haven't."

"Touché." He moved closer to her. "Then why not take the day off?"

She paused in making cookies and studied him. "Are you suggesting we play hooky?"

"Exactly."

"But that would be…crazy. I never do that."

"Me neither."

She stared at him, stunned by the thought. All these years, heck, most of her life, she'd been working here full-time—more than full-time—and she couldn't even imagine the thought of leaving here for no good reason other than because she felt like it, and here she was thinking of doing exactly that for the second time in two days. "What would we do all day?"

Flynn cleared his throat. "Well, seeing as I have two

choices—hanging out at Betsy's and listening to her struggle through Christmas carols or go to Earl's garage and hear his long-winded stories—both options painful in their own aural way," he said, wincing, "I thought I'd see if you…"

"What?" she asked when he didn't finish.

"Nothing. It's a crazy idea."

She tapped her lips, suddenly feeling game. It took her a second, but she put together the elements before her—guy, day of the year—and came up with what he'd been about to say. "Let me guess. You haven't bought a single Christmas present yet and wondered if I'd go shopping with you."

He shrugged. "Yeah."

Spending the day alone with Flynn would be a bad idea. She had enough work to do to keep her busy for a week, and he—

Well, he had this way of disrupting her equilibrium every time he entered a room. Sam prided herself on never letting those kinds of things happen. She was a levelheaded, practical businesswoman who made smart, well-thought-out decisions. Who put the right decision ahead of her personal temptations.

And Flynn could be dangerous if she let him get too close, a threat to everything she had worked so hard to build.

Yet, as she looked at his face, she saw a flicker—so brief it could have been a trick of the light—of vulnerability and her heart went out to him. Then the look was gone, and he was back to his stalwart, standoffish self.

Was it just because they had shared a kiss? Or was it because she thought, just for a moment, that she had seen a kindred spirit in him? The man who'd left the Winterfest, unable to stay around the Christmas celebration, the man who she'd noticed appreciating the lights last night even if he wouldn't admit enjoying the twinkles, the same man who could barely talk about his own family?

Could it be that there was far more to Flynn MacGregor than met the eye? And maybe she had misjudged him?

She thought of the few hints of his life that he had given her, the way he seemed to avoid Christmas like most people avoided friends with the flu, and wondered whether he, like her, had reasons behind it all.

"You need a day off, more than anybody I know," he said, interrupting her thoughts. "And I need to shop. Since you're not very good at taking time off, and I really stink at shopping, the only solution is to work together. I don't know about you, but I could use a break." He took a step closer. "What do you say, Sam?"

"I have cookies to—"

"There will always be cookies to bake." Flynn took another step closer. "Come on, take the day off. For no reason, other than you just want to."

"And help you shop."

Flynn moved a little closer still, his hand inches from hers, triggering the memory of his kiss. "Something like that."

She knew she should say no. Knew she should stay right here, running the shop, baking cookies, filling orders. Except she didn't want to.

The craving for normalcy rose inside Sam, fast and fierce, tempered by guilt that she should stay. But the yearning for a life outside this bakery, doing ordinary things like shopping and dating, overpowered her, and she found herself tugging the apron off and tossing it onto the counter.

"Well, to be honest," Sam said, as everything inside her rebelled against the idea of working one more minute, "I haven't finished all my shopping yet, either."

"Let me guess. Too busy working to get to the store?"

"Something like that," she said, repeating his words. She didn't tell him that Christmas had lost its sparkle a long time ago. When her grandmother started forgetting holidays, when every day at the Heritage Nursing Home ran in Joy's head one after another, like an endless stream of Tuesdays. Without a husband, or a family, Sam just didn't have the desire to shop and celebrate like she used to. She still put up the tree, and made the attempt, but it wasn't the same.

"Yeah, me, too," Flynn said.

But as the two of them cleaned up the kitchen, then left the little shop, while Aunt Ginny offered—with a knowing wink—to stay behind with the temporary workers and cover the day's customers, Sam began to worry that she'd just made a huge mistake.

What had he been thinking?

Flynn could name on one hand the number of people he needed to shop for. Mimi. Liam. Who probably wouldn't even open the gift anyway. Maybe his editor. Most years, Flynn just dropped off a fruit basket for the office, if he even thought of that.

Hey, he was a guy. Gift-giving wasn't exactly his forte.

He knew why he'd proposed the shopping trip. It hadn't been about escaping Betsy's piano playing. Or Earl's stories. He'd been looking for something to fill the day, the hours until his car was fixed, and spending that time with Sam had seemed like a good idea when he'd been standing in the back of her little shop, wrapped in the scent of cookies. The deep green of her eyes.

He could tell himself it was because he still wanted to get to the heart of his story, to find out about her grandmother. To finish those final pieces of his article.

But that wasn't it at all.

He wanted to be with her, craved her presence, in a way he'd never craved anything before. She represented all the things he hadn't thought existed. Small towns, with families where parents raised their children, made a life based on love and commitment.

The kind of life he'd dreamed of, and never imagined he could have. For just a little while longer, before he had to go back to real life, he'd hold on to that dream.

Now, they wandered the aisles of a cramped antiques shop, looking at trinkets he had no use for and furniture he'd never bring to his apartment, not that he was home enough to even use the furniture he already had. He picked up a white dish that looked like it had beads imbedded in the edge, then set it down again. Fingered the fringe on the edge of a lamp so gaudy, he couldn't even imagine what sight-challenged artist had designed it in the first place—or why.

"Finding anything?" Sam asked. Her arms were laden with purchases. A wide painted bowl, a leather-bound book, a hand-cut glass vase and an intricate wrought-iron wine rack. Everything she'd picked out looked tasteful and perfect, the kinds of things he could imagine in his own home, if he ever bought a house.

"Nope."

A smile curved across her face. "You're totally out of your league, aren't you?"

"Well…" He looked around the shop. "Yeah."

"And I bet this isn't exactly your kind of place, is it?"

"Not quite. I was thinking something more…fancy. Maybe a jewelry shop?" A bracelet or some earrings, he knew would make Mimi happy. Other than that, he had no idea which way her tastes ran.

It occurred to him that he had probably spent more time inside Sam's bakery than he had inside Mimi's apartment. He'd have an easier time buying Sam a home decoration than his own girlfriend, if that was even the label he could put on Mimi.

Sam thought about that for a second. "I know where we

can go. Let me just purchase these. Then we can head down to Indianapolis. There's civilization there. Meaning a mall." She gave him a grin.

"Civilization." Flynn drew in a deep breath, as if he could suck up the city from here. "That's the one thing I'd pay about anything to have."

He should have been excited, but for some reason, the expected lilt of anticipation didn't rise in his chest. Even the knowledge that his car would be ready tomorrow—meaning he could leave—didn't excite him like it should.

He attributed it to a lack of sleep, or too many renditions of "Jingle Bells" ringing in his ears from Betsy's overactive piano fingers. Because he certainly hadn't started to like this town. There was *no way* Riverbend was beginning to grow on him.

He'd feel better when he got to the city. Away from this overdone home of all things Christmas. Back to the cold, impersonal world he knew.

Flynn took several of the items from Sam's arms, earning a surprised thank-you, and a few minutes later, she had paid and they were inside her Jeep, on their way out of town. The snow had started up again, falling in thick, heavy flakes. "Does it ever stop snowing around here?"

"Welcome to the Midwest. Although this month, we are getting a record amount of snow, so you're getting a treat." She shot him a smile. "You're from the East Coast. Don't you get a lot of snow, too?"

"I live in the city. I guess I don't notice as much."

"This storm is supposed to stop tomorrow. And we should be fine. I have four-wheel drive on the Jeep. If not—" Sam looked over at him "—are you up for an adventure?"

Flynn glanced down at his dress shoes and cashmere coat. "I'm not exactly prepared for much beyond a dinner party."

"Well, then, Flynn MacGregor," she said with that laugh

in her voice that rang as easily as church bells, "you better hope nothing goes wrong on our expedition."

Sam should have kept her mouth shut.

Twenty miles outside of town, the Jeep suddenly got hard to steer. Sam attributed the stubborn wheel to the icy roads, until she saw steam coming from the hood. She pulled over, wrestling with the steering wheel to get the Jeep to come to a stop at the side of the road.

"Overheated?" Flynn asked.

"Maybe. I have no idea what's wrong. Are you handy with cars?"

"Are you kidding me? If I was, I would have fixed my own and been gone long before now."

Steam curled in twin vicious clouds from under the hood, spreading outward in a mysterious burst that spelled certain doom for the engine. Sam sighed. "Well. That doesn't look good."

"Let me take a look under the hood."

"I thought you said you weren't good with cars."

"I'm not, but considering we have zero options here, I figure I can't make it any worse." He gestured toward the windshield. "Pop the hood. Maybe I'll get some mechanical vibes from the engine."

Sam pulled the latch for the Jeep's hood, then waited inside while Flynn got out and went around to the front of the car. When the worst of the steam had cleared, Flynn leaned in to look at the engine. One minute passed. Two. She heard him tinker with something.

Finally, Sam climbed out of the Jeep and joined him at the front of the SUV. "Did you find anything?"

"Radiator fluid is fine. But your oil is low." He held up a dipstick.

Furious gusts of wind blew into Sam and Flynn, and snow drifts skittered across the highway in white sheets. Sam shivered and raised her voice over the howling storm. "I don't think that's the problem. Do you?"

"No." Flynn slid the long skinny stick back into place, then leaned farther inside. Another chilly thirty seconds passed. "I'm no expert, but I'd say *that's* your problem." He pointed into the dark depths of the engine.

"I don't see anything."

"Right there."

Sam moved over, until her shoulder brushed against his, and despite the cold and the bulky layers of her coat, a jolt of electricity ran through her. For a second, she forgot about the engine. Awareness of the man beside her slammed into Sam like a tidal wave.

"Do you see the problem?"

Oh, yes. She did. All six foot two of him.

"It's right there," Flynn said.

Get a grip, Sam.

They were stuck in the middle of nowhere, with a blizzard bearing down on them. This was not the time to go off on a hot man tangent, not when she had a major hot car problem.

"Uh, is it that what you're talking about?" Sam pointed at a frayed belt buried deep in the engine.

"Yep. Like I said, I'm no mechanic, but even I know a broken belt is a problem. Whichever belt this is, it's an important one."

The snow continued to fall, building up so fast, the engine was already covered with a fluffy white blanket. Flynn ran a hand over his hair, mussing the straight lines, and sending a spray of flakes to the ground. "We need to get out of the storm."

They hurried back inside the Jeep. Sam shuddered and rubbed her hands up and down her arms. "It's getting cold out there."

"And we can't stay in the car. It's not running and it won't hold whatever heat it has for very long." Flynn flipped out his cell phone, held it up toward the angry gray sky, then let out a curse. "Is there anywhere around here that has a cell tower?"

Sam gave him a smile. "We were driving *toward* civilization, if that helps."

"Well, we're going to need something approaching civilization or we'll become Popsicles pretty soon."

Sam looked out the window. The blizzard had picked up steam, and no cars were on the road. She should have checked the weather forecast before deciding on this impromptu shopping trip. Clearly, it had been a bad idea. And now, they were stranded, with nowhere to go.

Then, a little way down the road, she spied a familiar orange sign, tacked to a light pole. Serendipity, or a miracle, Sam didn't question which it was.

"My father used to hunt in this area when I was a little girl," Sam said. "I never went with him, but I know he and his friends used to stay overnight sometimes. That means there must be a hunters' cabin out here somewhere."

Flynn cupped a hand over his eyes and peered out into the white. "That's the problem. It's somewhere."

"It's better than staying here and freezing to death."

"True."

"Riverbend is twenty miles behind us. The next town is thirty miles south. Either we find the cabin or hope someone else was stupid enough not to check the weather before getting on the road."

"What are the chances of that?" Flynn asked. He took one more look down the road, in both directions. Empty, as far as the eye could see, visibility closing to almost nothing. "Well, you told me to be up for an adventure. I guess this is it."

CHAPTER TWELVE

IT TOOK THEM CLOSE to an hour to find the rustic cabin, nestled deep in the woods off the highway. By that time, Flynn's shoes were ruined, and the snow had soaked through his gabardine pants, all the way to his knees. His coat, which had seemed warm enough for the season when he bought it, turned out to be little protection against the biting winter wind.

But then again, when he'd bought the cashmere coat, it hadn't been with the intention of traipsing through the woods, searching for a hunters' cabin.

Sam was better prepared for the weather, in her thick parka and boots. Still, her face was red and she looked ready to collapse by the time they spied the small wood structure.

"Finally," Sam said, the word escaping with a cloud of breath. She hurried forward, pumping her arms to help her navigate the deep snow. "I can feel the heat already."

He grabbed her sleeve. "Wait. We should gather some dry wood so we can start a fire."

Sam drew up short. "Of course. I can't believe I didn't think of that. Maybe there will be some over there—"

"No. You go inside and I'll get the wood." He gestured toward the cabin.

She gave him a dubious look. "You are hardly dressed to go gallivanting through the forest looking for firewood."

"I'm not letting you go gallivanting through the forest, either," Flynn said as they continued through the woods, stopping when they reached the stoop of the cabin—if the few slats of wood under a one-foot overhang could even be called a stoop.

"Oh, I get it. This is you playing the gentleman. I'm supposed to wait inside, because I'm the girl, is that it?"

"Well…yeah."

"I can take care of myself."

"I have no doubt that you can. And that I can take care of you, too." This woman could sure be stubborn when she wanted to be. It was probably what made her such a good business owner, what had gotten her through those difficult years when she was young, but damn it, he wasn't going to let her go running off in the woods alone.

Sam laughed. "You, take care of me? I probably have more survival skills in my left foot than you have in your—"

He put a finger to her lips, and when he did, he became acutely aware that they were alone in the woods. That it had been twelve hours since he'd kissed her. And how very much he wanted to kiss her again. "You don't know me as well as you think you do. So why don't you go inside, and let me do this?"

She considered him for a long moment, then shrugged concession. "Do you want my boots?"

He grinned. "I think your feet are just a bit smaller than mine."

"All the more reason why I—"

"I'm not arguing this." He'd take care of her whether she liked it or not, not out of some macho need to be the guy, but because she was the kind of woman who deserved to have a man take care of her—and the first woman to tell him she didn't. Flynn reached forward and pulled open the cabin door.

The outside light spilled into the cabin, illuminating part of the interior. "Let's go inside, and I'll light a candle or something for you, then I can go looking for firewood."

Sam started to laugh.

"What's so funny?"

"Apparently, you don't have to go far, Superman." She pointed inside the small, musty building. Against the wall, a pile of wood had been stacked in a pyramid. "But at least I know you would have taken care of me, if I needed you to."

He would have, even if he'd had to go back into the woods barefoot, but he didn't say that. She might be great at the helm of her bakery, but out here, he knew what to do.

"Well, that's a start. I'll get a fire going, then load us up, in case we're stuck here for a while." Flynn stomped the snow off his shoes, then crossed to the fireplace. He rubbed his hands together to bring some feeling back into his fingers, then laid the kindling in the cold cavern. Flynn found a box of matches on the mantel, and a few moments later had a tiny flame licking at the edges of the small sticks.

He kept his back to Sam, feeding the flame, one piece of wood at a time. It was far easier to do that than to consider the fire brewing behind him.

One he hadn't counted on when he'd first arrived in Riverbend. One he hadn't counted on at all.

It wasn't the flames that had Sam amazed so much as how fast Flynn MacGregor coaxed them from the wood. Of all the people she would have listed as least likely to be able to build a fire, he would have topped the list. And yet, here he was, stoking the fire and building it gradually, like he'd been a Boy Scout all his life.

Flynn MacGregor. The same man who'd walked into Riverbend wearing expensive leather shoes and a cashmere coat. The one who'd hated small-town life, and seemed like he'd never been more than five minutes outside of a city. And here he was, bringing in wood from the forest, laying it by the fire to dry, then expertly tending to the fireplace, warming the tiny cabin so fast, Sam could hardly remember being cold.

Well, it was Christmas. The season of miracles, after all.

The cabin was small, about a fifteen foot square, and not exactly five-star accommodations. Rough pine walls had been nailed together enough to block the weather, but not so well that they kept out all drafts. There was no insulation, no drywall. Nothing fancy that would make anyone mistake this hunting cabin for anything more than a temporary stopping place. A kitchen table and two chairs sat on one end of the single-room cabin, and a threadbare cushion covered a log-framed couch on the other. Against the far wall, a set of bunk beds with plastic mattresses, apparently made for sleeping bags instead of fine linens, waited for weary hunters. In the kitchen, a shelf of canned goods sat beside two pots and a couple of spoons. Sam suspected she wouldn't find much more than a few forks and knives in the single drawer beside a rudimentary dry sink.

As Flynn worked on the fire, she grabbed a few jarred candles from the shelf, then lit them and set them around the room. She also found a hurricane lamp and after a lot of fiddling, got it to light.

Okay, so the whole atmosphere was oddly romantic, but Sam ignored the flickering flames, the soft glow. They were here to get out of the storm. A temporary place to get warm. Soon, the storm would stop and they could make a plan.

When Flynn was done, he swung the sofa around to face the fire. A cozy sitting place, just for the two of them. "It's not the Ritz, but it should do until the storm blows over."

"It's great. Thank you."

"You're welcome."

They were quiet, the only sound in the room coming from the crackling of the logs and the occasional soft thud of a snow chunk falling from the roof. For the first time, Sam became aware that they were alone. Totally alone.

And as much as she hoped otherwise, it could be hours. Many, many hours, until the storm ended and she could get a tow truck to pick up the Jeep. That meant they'd be stuck here, for an indefinite period of time.

"You should come over here and get warm." Flynn took off his damp coat and draped it over the arm of the sofa. "And take off whatever is wet, so you don't get sick."

"I'm fine." Way over here. Bundled up. Not so tempted to kiss him then.

Flynn crossed to her and placed a palm against her cheek. The touch warmed her, not just because of body heat, but because every time Flynn MacGregor touched her, he seemed to set off some kind of instant thermal jump inside her. "You're freezing. Come on, sit by the fire. And don't argue with me."

Sam's protests were cut off by Flynn taking her hand and leading her over to the sofa. She stood there, her palms outstretched to greet the heat emanating in waves, still a human marshmallow, until Flynn slipped between her and the fire and began to unzip her coat. "What are you doing?"

"Your coat is soaked. I know it's waterproof, but that doesn't mean it's completely impervious to snow." He slipped his hands under the fabric and over her shoulders, sliding the heavy fabric off. His gaze caught hers, and heat rose in her chest. Desire quivered in her gut, then coiled tight against her nerves. Her breath caught, held. Flynn's thumbs ran over her collarbone, sending a tingle down her spine.

His gaze captured hers. A second passed. Another.

"What are we doing here?" The words whispered out of her.

"Getting out of the storm."

"Is that what we're really doing?"

Flynn released her and stepped away, bending to retrieve her coat from the floor. "Yes. That's all."

Sam moved closer to the fire, running her arms up and down her sleeves, warding off a chill she didn't feel. Behind her, Flynn pulled one of the kitchen chairs closer to the flames, and draped her jacket over the back, leaving it to dry in the heat. She expected him to join her at the fire, but he paused for a long second behind her, then she heard his footsteps recede.

A moment later, he was in the kitchen, going through the canned goods, pulling one after another off the shelves until finding whatever he was looking for.

Sam remained where she was, trying to calm the turbulent waters in her gut. What was it with this man? Was it just that he was a stranger? A sexy city guy who offered something new and different? Or had she simply been cooped up with that mixer too long?

Every time she was near him, she forgot the hundreds of reasons she shouldn't get involved with him. Most of all, she forgot reason number one. When Flynn drew near, when his gaze captured hers, she lost track of her goals—with the business, this article, her future, her family—and that was reason enough not to get distracted by him.

Flynn brushed past her, a pot in one hand, and a long-handled contraption in the other. He set up the handled thing near the fire, then attached the pot, swinging it out and over the flames. They licked eagerly at the bottom of the pan, heating whatever was in there as easily as they had Sam.

She watched him cook, stunned, speechless. He seemed to know exactly what he was doing, because a few minutes later, he swung the pot back, took it off the handle and brought it back to the kitchen.

Well. She hadn't expected that. Flynn *cooking?*

"Spaghetti surprise," Flynn said, returning and holding a plate out to Sam.

She bit back a laugh at the sight of canned spaghetti topped with crushed saltines. "You are very inventive, Mr. MacGregor. I had no idea you could do all this, or come up with a recipe for dinner, based on what was in there."

"Hey, I had to be inventive when I was—" He cut off the sentence. "There wasn't much to work with in the kitchen."

What had he been about to say? What personal tidbits was he leaving out? Every time she got close, he seemed to shut the door on himself. Because he didn't want her to get to know him? Or because there were things about himself that he didn't want to share?

She had no right to criticize him, Sam realized. She'd yet to tell him the truth about her grandmother. Heck, she'd yet to tell the town the truth about her grandmother, the same customers who patronized Joyful Creations every day, and asked about Joy just as often.

Sam thanked him, for the food, but deep down inside, she was even more grateful for the diversion.

They took seats on opposite ends of the sofa and began to eat. The odd dish turned out to be far more appetizing than it had looked. "Where did you learn this particular recipe?"

Flynn picked at his dish, but didn't take another bite. He let out a long breath, then put his plate down on his knee. He hesitated, as if warring with himself about the answer, before finally speaking. "Foster care."

"Foster care? You were in foster care?" Again, another major surprise. Not something she would have associated with him.

At all.

"Let's just say not all the places I lived were the best, so I learned how to take care of myself. And sometimes, I was taking care of my brother, too."

"Sometimes?"

"Not every foster family wanted the two-for-one deal."

The words slammed into Sam. She may have lost her parents when she was young—far too young, she'd always thought—but she had grown up in a happy, two-parent home, first with her parents and then later with Grandma Joy and Grandpa Neil. She'd always had grandparents around, a town she'd known all her life, lots of people who loved her. Stability.

She'd never had to live with strangers. Never had to concoct spaghetti surprise.

Sam laid a hand on his arm. "I'm so sorry, Flynn."

He shrugged. "I turned out okay. And I learned some cooking skills."

At what price? Sam looked at Flynn with new eyes. Knowing his past, or at least the little he had shared so far, explained so much. The way he'd reacted to Riverbend. The way he held himself back from people, didn't engage, didn't connect. All along, she'd faulted him, thinking he was disagreeable, only after the story, when he'd simply been someone who probably hadn't had a chance to find a home. To find people to connect with. Sympathy rode through her in a wave, and she made a vow.

A vow to give Flynn MacGregor the best darn Christmas ever. Assuming, that was, that he let her. And they ever got out of this cabin and the storm.

"What happened to your parents?" she asked.

He made a face, as if he didn't want to talk about the subject, then let out a long breath. "I've never talked to anyone, besides Liam, about my childhood."

"Oh." She didn't know if that meant he didn't want her to

ask, or if he meant the opposite. She simply waited, allowing Flynn to call whatever shots he wanted.

"It's not an easy topic for me." He picked at his food, but didn't eat, as if the twist of noodles on his plate held some answers she couldn't see. Before them, a log split, the fissure hissing and spitting sparks. "My mother was…not the most responsible person on the planet. She never knew who my father was. Mine or Liam's."

Again, Sam reached out a hand to Flynn, laying her palm gently on his wrist. She was here, and she would listen. That, she suspected, was what he needed most right this second.

"She was an addict. Nothing too heavy when I was born, but by the time Liam came along, she was doing cocaine. Nothing could get her to stop, not even getting pregnant. They tested him for drugs in his system at birth, and that was it. We were yanked out of the house, and even though she made a stab at getting clean a few times, it never stuck. So we bounced around the foster care system all our lives. She overdosed before we were in high school."

Sam gasped. "Oh, Flynn, that's awful. I can't even imagine."

"Don't. Because whatever picture you come up with, it's probably not half as bad as the reality. I'm not saying all foster care is terrible, because there are a lot of good foster families out there, but Liam and I never seemed to hit the family lottery. We were…" He shrugged. "Difficult."

"You were traumatized."

"Yeah, well, in those days, that wasn't what they called it."

Her heart broke for him, and even though she knew it was impossible, Sam wished she could go back in time, and make up for all those years. Take away all the rejections, the shuffling from place to place. Somehow give Flynn and his brother the home they'd never had. "And Liam? Did he do okay?"

A smile filled Flynn's face. Clearly, he loved his brother. "He's at Purdue University, going for a master's in engineering. He's smart as hell. And thank God, he's turned out just fine."

"Because you were there for him."

"Not enough," Flynn said quietly. "Not enough."

She heard the guilt in his voice. That was an emotion she understood, too well. "Are you still planning on seeing him before you go back to Boston?"

Flynn rose and grabbed a log, tossing it onto the fire. He watched the flames curl around the wood, accepting it and devouring the bark, then eating into the wood. "No."

"Why not?"

"We lost touch when he went away to college. It was always hard for Liam, and he was younger, so he didn't always understand. I tried my best..." Flynn rose, dusted his hands together. "I just tried my best."

"I'm sure you've done plenty, Flynn."

He shook his head. "I watched out for Liam when I could, but we weren't always together. That hurt him, more than me. It's made him...distant. It's like an old joke. You think I'm detached?" He looked up at her, his face no joke, but filled with the pain of separation, of losing the sole family member he had. "You should meet my brother."

"Oh, Flynn," Sam said, reaching for him where he stood, but he didn't want the comfort, not yet. It was as if he needed to say the words, get them out in one painful pass.

"Everything we went through was so much harder on him because he was younger. I can't take those years back. I can't undo the damage." Flynn ran a hand through his hair and sighed, the sound pouring from him like concrete. "All I can do is make it up to him the best way I know how. Keep taking care of him, but this time with dollars."

Guilt lined Flynn's face, and his shoulders sagged beneath

a burden only he could feel. For a moment, she wanted to reach out, to tell him she shared that burden. That she felt that pain every time she brought her grandmother cookies, a new sweater or simply made sure the nurses and staff had her favorite blanket on her bed. Instead, Sam kept her secrets walled inside. "You pay for everything for him?"

Flynn shrugged. "Yeah. But he…won't talk to me."

"Maybe…" She paused. "Maybe he wants you, not the money."

"Maybe. Maybe not." Flynn returned to the sofa and picked up his plate again. "Fire's doing well, don't you think?"

"It is." The heat was so good, it was making her drowsy. Sam tucked her legs beneath her, and leaned closer to Flynn. She let the subject of his brother drop. She certainly didn't have a right to tell others how to handle their relationships with loved ones when she wasn't taking anyone's advice, either. "Who taught you to build a fire?"

"There was one house," Flynn said, stirring his food, "we stayed at for almost a year. The father there, he was into camping. Loved the outdoors. He took my brother and me a few times, and made sure we knew how to survive." Flynn scoffed, then his voice softened, going so quiet Sam had to strain to hear him. "Turned out, that was the one skill I'd need the most."

"What do you mean?"

Flynn rose, forcing her touch to drop away, and crossed to the kitchen, depositing his plate on the counter. "Considering how well you bake, I'm sure you're a hell of a cook, Sam. You probably would have done a better job than me."

The subject of his childhood was closed. He couldn't have made that any clearer if he'd hung up a sign. Sam could hardly blame him. She'd been hanging No Trespassing signs around her own heart for years.

But for the first time, she began to wonder if maybe the time had come to take a few of the signs down. And take a chance again.

CHAPTER THIRTEEN

WHAT HAD HE been thinking?

For five minutes there, Flynn had lost control. Had opened the door to a past he'd vowed never to visit. Not again. Instead of continuing the conversation, he melted some snow over the fire and used it to wash the dishes and put them back.

But that only killed a few minutes.

Long, potentially endless hours stretched before him. Alone with Samantha Barnett. A woman he told himself, over and over again, that he wouldn't get involved with. Wouldn't open himself up to, emotionally.

Except for those kisses. Yeah, there had been that. And the fact that he wanted to repeat those. Again and again. Wanted still to take her in his arms, even as he knew he shouldn't.

What he should really be doing, instead of spilling his guts over some lousy canned spaghetti, was getting the story his editor was paying him to find. Start probing *Sam* for answers instead of spitting out his own every five seconds like some crazy self-pity candy machine.

"Do you need some help?"

Sam's voice, soft as silk, over his shoulder. "No, I've got it."

"Listen, I didn't mean to intrude earlier. If you don't want to talk about your childhood, I understand."

"Like I said, it's not my favorite subject."

"Then how about we spend the rest of our time here doing something else?"

The invitation in her voice brought the roar of desire, one he'd barely been holding back, to life again. Flynn laid the last dish on the shelf and turned to her. "I don't think—"

And saw that Sam was holding a deck of cards. "I found these in one of the drawers. Are you up for some gin rummy?"

She'd meant card games. Not kissing. Not anything else.

He should have been grateful, but, damn it, he wasn't.

What did he want? Flynn crossed the room, following behind Sam's curvy figure, and knew, without a doubt what he wanted.

Everything.

He wanted to get the story, get out of Indiana, go back to Boston, keep his job, and—

Have this moment with Sam. To forget that he was Flynn MacGregor, a man who'd never known this kind of sweet simplicity, the kind that she believed in as devoutly as children believed in Santa Claus. To surrender to the same beliefs, and just…

Have a merry Christmas.

In the last few days, that Christmas spirit had started to rub off on him, as silly as the thought was. The possibility that Flynn, of all people, could have what Riverbend offered began to feel…real. It sounded so easy. But for Flynn, nothing had ever been that easy.

Still, he ended up at the kitchen table with Sam, who dealt the cards. He vaguely remembered how to play gin rummy, and fanned his cards in front of him.

"Flynn? Your turn. Lay down or discard."

"Oh, yeah. Sorry." He discarded an ace he'd really wanted to keep, which Sam promptly picked up and used to make her own triplet of aces, crowing with delight over the find. Three minutes later, Sam had trounced him at cards.

She leaned forward to collect his cards, getting ready to deal again. "Your mind's not in the game, MacGregor," she teased. "You keep playing like that and—"

Flynn leaned forward, cupped a hand around her neck, and kissed her again. The fire crackled softly, sending quiet waves of heat over them, but there was already plenty of heat brewing in the kitchen. Flynn's fingers tangled in Sam's blond mane, dancing up and down the tender skin of her neck, while his mouth captured the sweet taste of hers.

Her tongue darted into his mouth, dancing a slow, sensual tango, which only served to inflame the desire in his gut. Flynn groaned, sliding out of his chair to get closer. His hand drifted down, over her shoulder, along her arm, sliding around to cup her breast through the thick fabric of her sweater.

Sam arched against him, responding with a fervor that matched his own. She whispered his name into his mouth, and Flynn nearly came undone.

Had he ever known anyone this sexy? A woman who could make him fall apart with a kiss, the mere mention of his name?

Sam curved into him, her arms going around his back, holding him tight, as if she couldn't bring him close enough. His kiss deepened, wanting more of her, so much more than he could have.

Finally, reluctantly, he pulled back. "If we, ah—" he caught his breath "—don't stop, we'll probably end up finding ways to pass the time that we hadn't intended."

Sam's green gaze was steady on his, deep, still filled with desire. Against his chest, her heart hammered a matching beat. "And that would be bad."

"Very." Though he was having trouble thinking of very many reasons right now.

"Because…"

"We don't know each other very well."

"There is that."

He traced a finger down her cheek, along her jawline, fighting the growing desire to kiss her again, to taste that sweet skin. "And we should probably be thinking about ways of getting out of here."

Sam sighed. "Yeah, we probably should."

And he should be focusing on his job. On what was important. Kissing a woman he had no intention of staying with didn't even make the list.

So, he tried. He picked up the deck of cards, dealt them out again and tried to concentrate on the game.

And failed miserably.

A rock band drummed in Sam's head. Pounding, pounding, calling her name…

"Sam! You in there?"

She jerked awake, just in time to see Earl stumble into the cabin, along with a flurry of snow and a barking dog. Beside her, Flynn popped to his feet. The two of them had fallen asleep after playing cards, the heat of the fire and the exhaustion of the day finally catching up with them. "Earl?"

"You're alive! Well, thank the Lord in heaven. I thought sure I'd be finding myself two Popsicles in the woods." Earl brushed a load of snow off the top of his hat. The golden retriever started running around the cabin, sniffing every corner, his tail wagging, as if he'd just latched on to his own personal treasure trove.

"What are you doing here?" Flynn asked. He had already disentangled himself from Sam, and gotten off the sofa.

Had Earl seen them like that, lying in each other's arms? And how had they fallen asleep like that? Sam remembered sitting on the sofa, talking lazily with Flynn about when the storm might end...

And then nothing.

Earl stared at them like they were idiots. "Looking for you."

"How did you know we were here?" Sam said.

"Ol' Earl's not as dumb as he looks. Plus, your man here told Betsy he was going shopping. And you, Sam, told your Aunt Ginny you'd be back this afternoon. She called Betsy, looking for you, all worried that you weren't back yet. Me and Betsy, we were gettin' cozy—" Earl paused, cast a glance at the sofa, then cleared his throat "—we were talking, just talking, and we put two and two together, and got thirty-one."

Earl had seen them. Great. He'd tell Betsy, and the next thing Sam knew, the whole town would be planning her wedding.

Flynn shook his head. "Two and two adds up to four, Earl."

Earl removed his cap and gave Flynn a grin. "Not when you and Sam are on highway thirty-one, it don't."

"Whatever math you're using," Sam said, crossing to give Earl a hug, "I'm glad you found us. We were worried we'd be stuck here forever."

Earl's face reddened, from collar to hairline. "Aww, it was nothing, Sam. Really." He stepped out of the embrace, twirling his cap in his hands.

The golden retriever, done with his search of the cabin, came bounding over to them, pausing by Sam for an ear-scratch, before heading to Flynn and jumping on him. Flynn looked surprised for a second, then patted the dog. In response, the golden retriever licked Flynn's face then jumped down again. Flynn swiped at his jaw. "What's the dog for?"

"That's Paulie Lennox's worthless mutt. Supposed to be good for tracking, but Gracie there, she didn't find nothin' but two black squirrels. If I'd had my shotgun, we'd all be having squirrel for dinner—"

Flynn blanched.

Earl chuckled and clapped him on the shoulder. "Just kidding there, city boy. I draw the line at animals that climb trees."

"We have that in common."

"See? Told you that you'd fit into this town." Earl plopped his hat back on his head. "Are you two about ready to leave? Or you thinking of moving in here? I gotta admit, it's mighty cozy here. Maybe this summer me and my Betsy…" He colored again. "Well. Time to go."

A flicker of sadness ran through Sam. She should be glad to be getting out of the cabin. Back home. Her Aunt Ginny was undoubtedly worried sick, and things at the bakery were probably insane without her there.

But as they doused the fire, tidied the cabin, and headed out the door, Sam couldn't help but feel a little regret that the small oasis she'd found with Flynn MacGregor had come to an end. They were going back to the real world.

And soon, he'd be going back to his.

"Good news," Earl said, while he drove them back to town, in a pickup truck that had been built long before Flynn had been born. "Your part came in while you were out traipsing through the woods."

"My part?"

"My goodness, boy, I think the snow has damaged your frontal lobe." Earl looked over at him. "For your car. I put it in and your car is running like a dream again. I told you ol' Earl would take care of you. Now you can hightail it out of town. And just in time for Christmas tomorrow."

Christmas.

He'd be heading back to Boston. To his apartment. Alone.

He should have been happy, but he was inexplicably disappointed. Irritated, even. Like he wished the part hadn't arrived. That his car would remain on Earl's lift for a couple more days. What was up with that?

Mimi would have already flown to Paris, or Monte Carlo, or wherever it was that she had chosen to spend her holiday this year. Mimi didn't do holidays—except New Year's Eve, which was an occasion to host a social event, and get noticed by people in the business. Flynn tended to avoid Mimi's parties, the crush of strangers, because they were always more of a networking tool than a celebration.

And Liam? Liam was probably with his friends, or a girl-friend. Flynn hadn't talked to his brother in so long, he wasn't quite sure. The chances of Liam still being on campus tomorrow were about zero.

Most years, Flynn didn't mind that his Christmases were anything but conventional. He couldn't remember the last time he'd had anything even remotely resembling a tradi-tional December 25th.

In fact, most years, Flynn *preferred* to be alone on holidays. It gave him time to catch up, to clear out his desk, go through the backlog of e-mails, and most of all—

Pretend he didn't care that there was no one's house to drive to for a turkey dinner and a slew of presents to open. That it didn't matter that Liam hadn't returned his calls. Or that he hadn't called Liam, either. Because for a while there, the brothers had lost touch and stopped relying on each other because it was easier than connecting and being torn apart again and again.

It was this town. And most of all, Samantha Barnett. The two of them had gotten him dreaming of something he'd never really had—a real Christmas.

He fished his cell phone out of his pocket and flipped it open. He scrolled through the list of contacts until he got to Liam's name. The four letters stared back at him, simple and plain.

"Oh, look," Sam said from her position in the backseat. "You finally have a signal. If there's anyone you want to call." Her gaze met his in the rearview mirror. "Tomorrow's Christmas, Flynn."

He had a signal. He could make a call, if he needed to, as Sam had said. The phone weighed heavy against his palm. He ran his thumb over the send button, but didn't press the green circle.

"Gas station coming up in a few miles," Earl said. "I need to stop and fill the ol' bucket up."

"Great," Sam said. "I could really use a cup of coffee. Flynn? How about you?"

"Huh?"

"Coffee?"

"Yeah. That sounds like a good idea."

But when they finally did pull over, Earl got out to pump gas, and instead of staying behind to make a call, Flynn offered to head inside to get the coffee, leaving his phone on the dashboard.

CHAPTER FOURTEEN

SAM WAS FORCED to go straight home. Earl refused to drop her off at the bakery. He told her in no uncertain terms that it was Christmas Eve and no fool in her right mind worked the night before Christmas. "And you, my dear Sam, are no fool," Earl said. "You have yourself a merry Christmas. I'll get your Jeep on December twenty-sixth, and fix it up, good as new."

"Thanks, Earl." Sam left the truck, and traipsed up her stairs, Flynn behind her. She unlocked the door, then paused. "Do you want to come in for a while?"

Earl tooted his horn, then pulled away, tossing Sam a grin and a wave as he did. "Looks like my ride has left me," Flynn said.

"Everyone in this town is a matchmaker," Sam muttered.

"What?"

"Nothing."

Flynn cast a glance at the dark sky. "I should probably get back to Betsy's. Finish my article, get packed…" His voice trailed off. He toed at the porch. "Earl's got my car ready, so I can get on the road."

"It's Christmas Eve, Flynn. Surely you aren't thinking of driving home tonight."

Flynn flicked out his wrist and checked his watch. "It's a fourteen-, or fifteen-hour drive back to Boston. The longer I stay here, the longer it is 'til I get my article turned in. I could take a chance on getting it e-mailed from here, but the Internet connection is too spotty. So I should—"

"Should what? Hurry home for a Christmas that's no Christmas at all?" She leaned against the open door and faced him. No way was she going to let him go without making a good attempt to get this man to enjoy the holiday. Not after what he'd told her back in the cabin. He, of everyone she knew, deserved more than that. "What's waiting for you back in Boston? An empty apartment? A half a bottle of wine in a refrigerator filled with take-out boxes?"

"I doubt my fridge is filled with anything. I don't eat at home often enough to even leave the leftovers in there."

"Exactly my point."

He thumbed in the direction behind him. "My car is—"

"Still going to be ready the day after Christmas. You should stay here. And have a Christmas, a real one, for once. Look at this town. It's Christmas personified. Where else are you going to find a bed-and-breakfast owner wearing jingle bells, for Pete's sake?"

He quirked a grin at her. "Are you trying to convince me to stay?"

"I'm offering you the deal of the year. A holiday you won't forget." She'd do whatever it took tomorrow—bake a ham, light the candles, sing the carols—if it would give Flynn the Christmas she suspected he had yet to have.

He shook his head, the slight smile still playing at his lips, as if he could tell he was being beaten at his own game. "And what will *you* be doing this Christmas?"

"Spending the morning with my Aunt Ginny and then..." Sam's voice trailed off. She may want to give Flynn MacGregor a Christmas, but in the end, he was still a reporter, and she was still a woman who wanted to keep a few personal details private

"And then what?"

"I visit other family members."

He studied her. "You don't trust me."

"Should I?"

"Why shouldn't you?"

"Let's be real here, Flynn. You want me for the story, not for me. And you'll be gone after the holiday. I can't afford to have my heart broken."

"So instead you don't risk it at all."

She met his gaze, seeing in him the same distance that he had maintained from the minute he'd pulled into town. Every once in a while, Flynn had let down his guard—like he had back in the cabin—but most of the time, he had a wall up as unscalable as Alcatraz. "I say what we have here, Mr. MacGregor, is a clear case of the pot calling the kettle black."

He chuckled. "Touché, Miss Barnett." Then he took a step closer, winnowing the gap between them into inches. "Perhaps we should just say goodbye now, rather than delay the inevitable."

"Maybe we should."

"That would be the wisest course."

She didn't move. Didn't breathe. "It would."

"And yet…" He paused. "I'm not leaving."

"You're not?"

"I want what you're offering." A shadow flickered in his eyes, like he'd briefly wandered into a bright room that exposed every vulnerable corner of his soul. "I want a Christmas. Just this once."

Resisting those four words was impossible. Even if it meant opening her heart, being vulnerable and maybe being left alone—and sorry—at the end of all of this.

She'd do it for the boy who hadn't had a Christmas. She'd

do it because she saw something in his eyes that bordered on the same longing she had felt ever since Grandma Joy had left.

"I can give you that," Sam whispered. "I can."

Flynn MacGregor had stepped into the one fantasy he'd never allowed himself to have.

A seven-foot Christmas tree stood in the living room, hung with unlit multicolored lights. A string of gold beads draped concentric festive necklaces down the deep green pine branches. Not a single ornament matched. Every one of them, Flynn was sure, from the tiny nutcracker to the delicate gilded bird, was the kind that had a history. A story behind it. An angel held court over the tree, a permanent patient smile on her porcelain face, arms spread wide, as if welcoming Flynn to the room.

Beneath the tree, dozens of wrapped presents waited for tomorrow. For loved ones, for friends. There wasn't one, Flynn knew, for him, but for just a second, he could pretend that this tree was his own. That he would wake up tomorrow in this house and the sun would hit those branches, gilding them with a Christmas morning kiss. That Sam would flick on the tree lights, he would make a wish—

And it would come true.

Damn. He was getting sentimental.

And most of all, forgetting why he had come to this town in the first place.

"I can make some coffee," Sam was saying, "or if you're hungry…"

"Do you have…" He paused. This was insane. He was a reasonable man. A man who never, ever, got emotional. Out of sorts. But something about that tree, that damned tree, had him feeling—

Nostalgic.

Craving things he'd never desired before.

"What?" Sam asked.

Flynn swallowed. Pushed the words past his throat. "Hot chocolate?"

She laughed. "Of course."

He followed her into the kitchen and found this room just as festive as the other. Instead of annoying him, as the town and Betsy's house had when he'd first arrived, Sam's home seemed to wrap him with comfort. Her kitchen, warmly decorated in rich earth tones of russet brown and sage green, held a collection of rustic Santas, marching across the top of the maple cabinets. A quartet of holly-decorated place mats waited for guests at the small oval table, which was ringed with chairs tied with crimson velvet bows. It was beautiful. Picturesque, even.

Oh, boy. He was really getting soft now. Next, he'd be breaking out into song.

Outside the window, a light snow began to fall, the porch light making the white flakes sparkle against the night like tiny stars. Flynn shook his head and let out a soft gust.

"What?" Sam asked, handing him a mug of hot chocolate.

Flynn looked down. Whipped cream curled in an *S* on top of the hot liquid. In a snowman-painted mug. "Of course."

"Of course, what?"

He turned toward her. "It's like you ordered up a Christmas, and it arrived straight out of the catalog, and into your house."

"This? This is nothing. I didn't have enough time this year, because the publicity from that article has kept me so busy at the bakery, to even put up all the decorations. I haven't even turned on the lights once yet. You should see my house when I really—"

He cut off her words with his own mouth, scooping her against him with his free arm. Just as fast, he released her.

What had come over him? Every time he turned around, he was kissing her. "Sorry."

"Sorry for kissing me? Was it that bad?"

"No. Not for that." He turned away, heading for the back door. He watched the snow fall and sipped at the hot cocoa. Perfectly chocolately, just the right temperature.

Suddenly, guilt rocketed through him. Here he was, standing in the perfect kitchen, enjoying the perfect cup of hot cocoa, with a woman who could be anyone's wife, when he was far from the kind of man who would make a good husband.

For a moment there, he'd actually pictured himself staying. Enjoying the holiday. Being here, in this crazy town for longer than just one more night.

Who was he kidding? Flynn MacGregor was a nomad. A man who didn't stick, any more than the flakes falling to the ground. In a month or two, or even three, they would melt and be gone, as if they had never existed.

He would be wise to do the same. Instead of thinking he could have what he'd never even dared to dream of.

Especially when this was his last chance to get what he had really come for. What he needed, if he hoped to make that final payment on Liam's tuition, and do what he'd promised Liam he'd do since that day on the beach.

Take care of his brother for as long as he needed him.

Flynn took another sip of hot chocolate, but the drink had lost its sweetness. He shifted position, and something poked him in the chest.

His notepad.

His job. He was supposed to be asking questions. Somehow, he'd lost his compass, forgotten his focus, and Flynn knew exactly when that had happened.

When he'd lost the tight hold on his emotions, let down his

guard and kissed Samantha Barnett. He cleared his throat, tugged the notepad and pen from the breast pocket of his jacket and flipped to a clean sheet. Back in work mode, and out of making-mistake mode. Hadn't he learned his lesson back in June? He couldn't afford another mistake like that.

He turned around, back to Sam. "You owe me a few answers, Miss Barnett, remember?"

He worked a smile to his face as he said the words, but he knew Sam caught the no-nonsense tone, the formal name usage. Shadows washed over her features.

Flynn had done what he wanted. He'd erased those kisses, undone them as easily as if he'd painted over the past with a wide brush. Leaving this room, filled with so many rich colors, as pale as an old sheet.

He was so tempted to put the notepad back, to leave the subject alone. Just walk out that door and write a nice, sweet article about a happy baker in the middle of Indiana making cookies that had made dozens of couples fall in love.

And watch his career go right down the toilet.

"Yesterday," he began, clicking his pen on, "I wrote up a draft of my article, and when I finished the piece, I realized there were a few holes."

"Holes?" Sam crossed to the refrigerator, pulled out a selection of cold cuts and condiments, then headed for the breadbox. "Like what?"

"I wanted to ask about your grandmother."

Sam bristled. "I told you. She doesn't work at the bakery anymore."

"Because she lives in a rest home now?"

Her features froze, and a chill whipped through the room. "How do you know about that?"

"This is a small town, like you said. Everyone knows everything." A flicker of regret ran through him. Maybe he shouldn't have said anything. Clearly, this was a subject Sam wanted him to leave untouched.

But he couldn't. Every instinct inside him told him this was where his story lay. If he didn't pursue this line of questioning, he'd surely run his career into the ground.

"I don't want to talk about my grandmother," Sam said. She opened the package of ham, unwrapped a couple slices of cheese, all the while avoiding looking at him.

"She founded the bakery," Flynn said. "She's where everything began. I think people would want to know—"

Sam wheeled around. "I don't give a damn what people want to know! Let them remember her the way she was, not as this—"

She cut off the words, as if realizing she'd let too much slip already.

"As this invalid who doesn't remember the very dream she helped create?" Flynn finished.

And hated himself.

Tears pooled in Sam's eyes. "Don't. Don't print that."

"It's the truth, Sam. It's—"

"I don't care what it is. I don't care if this is the story that gets you the big headline." She snorted, disgust mixing with the beginnings of tears. "That's all I am to you, isn't it? That's all this was about? A headline?"

"No. That's not it. There's more to this story than that."

"Right." She shook her head. "Tell me you weren't planning on writing some dream falling into a tragedy? Or are you going to pretend that you had something else planned from the beginning? Some happy little piece? I read your articles in the magazine, Flynn, but I kept thinking—" her voice broke and damn, now he really hated himself, really, really did "—you'd be different, that you wouldn't do that to *me*."

The man in Flynn—the one who had kissed Sam, had held

her in front of the fire in that cabin—wanted to retreat, to end the conversation before he hit at the raw nerves he knew ran beneath a difficult subject. Hell, he could write the book on raw nerves. And he could see, in Sam's eyes, in the set of her shoulders, that this wasn't something she wanted to talk about. But the reporter in Flynn had to keep going. "I'm not trying to hurt you, Sam. I'm just trying to get to the truth."

Sam wheeled back to face him. "Why? So you can get your headline by dragging my family's personal pain onto the cover? Blasting that news all over town, so people can pity her, pity me? No, I don't think so." Sam slapped the bread onto the counter, twisting off the tie in fast, furious spins, then yanked open the drawer for a butter knife.

Damn. He should have trusted his gut. Should have let this go. But he'd already asked the question, he couldn't retrace those steps. "Trust me, Sam. I'll handle the story nicely. I'll—"

"Trust you? I hardly know you." Sam began to assemble a sandwich, layering ham and cheese, spreading mayonnaise on a slice of bread.

The words slapped him. Although, it seemed like he knew Sam better than he knew anyone in his immediate circle. How could that be? He'd been in this town for a matter of days, and yet, he had shared more with her—and felt as if she had opened up to him—than he had shared in his life.

"Nor do you know my family, or what I've been through," she went on, "so I would appreciate it if you would stick to the cookies, the bakery, and nothing else."

Defensiveness raised the notes in her voice, and maybe if he didn't have someone else depending on him, he would have re-treated, would have let the subject drop. But that wasn't the case. And he couldn't afford to let emotion, or sympathy, sway him.

"I need more than just the story of the cookies," Flynn said, deciding he had to push this. He had no time left, and no options. He knew what he had for an article already—and he knew what his readers and his editor expected. And it wasn't what Flynn had written. "My editor sent me here to get the whole story, and I'm either getting that, or no story."

"What is that supposed to mean?"

"That I'll go find another bakery to profile in the Valentine's Day issue. You're not the only one baking cookies."

The icy words shattered any remaining warmth between them and Flynn wanted to take them back, but he couldn't. He'd played his trump card, and now it lay heavy in the air between them. Her gaze would have cut him, if it had been a knife.

They had done what he'd expected. Severed the emotional tie.

"You'd seriously do that? Just to get the story?"

"Listen," he said, taking two steps closer, "I'm not here to write some kind of mean-hearted exposé. I know you love your grandmother, I know you want to protect her privacy. But readers want to know what happened to her, too. Heck, the *town* wants to know. Don't you think people worry, care? Want to help?"

"Why? The people who love her already know. That's all that matters."

He moved closer, seeing so much of himself in the way she had closed off the world, insulating herself and her grandmother from everyone else. As if she thought doing so would make it all go away. He knew those walls, knew them so well, he could have told Sam what kind of bricks she'd used to build them. "Did you ever think that maybe people worry and wonder because they care about you, too? That they'll want to help if they know?"

"Help how?" Sam shot back, her voice breaking. She stepped away from him, pacing the kitchen, gesturing with her hands, as if trying to ward off the emotion puddling in her eyes. "What are they going to do? Send in their best memories to my grandmother, care of the Alzheimer's ward? It's not going to work. She's forgotten me. Forgotten her recipes. Forgotten everything that mattered." Sam turned away, placing a palm against the cabinets, as if seeking strength in the solid wood. "Seeing her is like ripping my own heart out. You tell me why I'd want to share that pain with the rest of America." Her voice broke, the rest of the sentence tearing from her throat. "With *anyone*."

Tears threatened to spill from Sam's emerald eyes. Flynn told himself he didn't care. He told himself that he needed to write down what she'd just said, because they were damned good quotes. Exactly the kind his story needed.

Instead, he dropped the pen to the counter, crossed to Sam and took her in his arms. When he did, it tipped the scales on her emotions, and two tears ran down her cheeks. She remained stiff, unyielding, but he held her tight. "Don't," she whispered. "Don't."

"Okay." And he held her anyway. She cried, and he kept on holding her, her head against his shoulder.

"She doesn't know me," Sam said, her voice muffled, thick. "She doesn't know who I am."

"And you're carrying this all by yourself."

"I have my aunt Ginny."

"Sam," Flynn said, his voice warm against her hair, "that's not sharing the burden, not really. And you know it. You carry this bakery, this house, your grandmother, all on your shoulders. Why?"

She turned away, spinning out of his arms, crossing back to the sandwiches, but she didn't pick up the knife or top the ham with a slice of bread. She just gripped the countertop like a life preserver. "Because I have to. Because if I rely on anyone else…"

Her voice trailed off, fading into the heavy silence of the kitchen.

And then Flynn knew, knew as well as he knew the back of his own hand, what the answer was. Because Sam was him, in so many ways. His heart broke for her, and he wished he could do something, anything to ease her pain. But Flynn MacGregor couldn't fix Sam's situation any more than he could fix his own. "Because if you rely on anyone else, they might let you down."

"I…" She stopped, caught her breath. "Yes."

He let out a half laugh. "We're two of a kind, aren't we? Neither one of us wants to put our trust in other people, just in case things don't last. Only, you have more faith than me."

"Me?"

"You still live in the fairy tale," Flynn said, waving at her kitchen, at the Christmas paradise that surrounded them. "And I…I gave up on that a long time ago."

"You don't have to, Flynn. It still exists."

"Maybe for you," he said, a smile that felt bitter crossing his face. "You can reach out, to the town, you can lean on other people, and you can try to connect with your grandmother, and try to build that bridge."

"How am I supposed to do that?" She swiped at her face, brushing away the remaining tears. "Last time I went there, she thought I was the maid."

Flynn might not be able to fix everything for Sam, but he could help with this. A little. Maybe. "This fall I did a story on a chef whose wife had Alzheimer's," he said. "It was heart-breaking for him, because the restaurant, everything, had always been all about her. His whole life was about her. When I interviewed him, he didn't want to talk about the restaurant at all. He only wanted to tell me about this photo album he was making. It had all the moments of their life. From the day they met through the day their kids were born, through every day they spent in the restaurant. He'd go over to her room, every single afternoon and flip through that book. It didn't bring her back all the way, but there were days, he said, when she would look at him, and know him."

Sam glanced up at him. "Really?"

Flynn nodded. Even now, months after writing the story, it still moved his heart, and tightened his chest. He remembered that man, the tender way he'd loved his wife, as if it were yesterday. *That* had been the kind of article Flynn wanted to write, but it wasn't what he'd ended up writing.

Instead, he'd done the kind of piece he'd always done. A story on how a dream had died, along with the woman's memories, and the man's inattention, because he wasn't at the restaurant as often as he should be. Because he was with his wife.

How would it have felt to write the other story? The kind he'd written a few days ago in the back of Sam's shop?

Sam's gaze, still watery, met his. "And what kind of story will you write about me? One as sweet as what you just told me?"

He swallowed hard. What could he tell her? The truth would hurt, and lying would only delay the inevitable. So he just didn't answer at all.

"Thanks for the hot chocolate," Flynn said, placing the mug on the counter before it got too comfortable in his grasp. "But I have to go."

Then he grabbed his coat and headed out the door. Because the one thing he couldn't do was break Samantha Barnett's heart on Christmas Eve.

CHAPTER FIFTEEN

"MERRY CHRISTMAS," Sam whispered, pressing a kiss to her grandmother's cheek.

Joy stirred, then swung her gaze over to Sam's. "Is it Christmas?"

Sam nodded, then pulled up the chair beside her grandmother's bed and took a seat. On the opposite side of the room, Grandma Joy's roommate snored loudly, under a red-and-green plaid blanket. Sam reached for her grandmother's hand, then pulled back, not wanting to scare her by becoming too familiar too quickly. "Yes, it's Christmas."

"Oh, that's my favorite day of the year." Joy sat up in the bed, pushing her short white hair out of her eyes.

"I know." Sam smiled. God, how she missed those days, when her grandmother would decorate the house and pour every ounce of energy into making the holiday merry. The house would ring with the sound of singing, the halls would be filled with the scents of baking. Both generations of Barnett woman had loved Christmas, and passed that holiday spirit on to Sam. "They're having a piano player come today, to play for everyone here. For the holiday party."

Her grandmother smiled. "That will be nice."

"Do you want me to help you get ready?"

"Of course. I'll want to look my prettiest for the party."

Sam tried to keep her spirits up, to not let the lack of recognition dampen her Christmas, but every year she came to Heritage Nursing Home and every year, it seemed to be the same story. There had been holidays, in the beginning, before the Alzheimer's had gotten so bad that her grandmother had to be hospitalized, when Joy would remember, but then, it seemed as if the entire world became strange, and though Sam kept praying for a miracle, for a window to open, if only briefly—

It didn't.

But was it possible, Sam wondered, as Flynn had told her, to help push that window open? For a long time, Sam had tried, by bringing in her grandmother's favorite things from home, and hanging pictures of loved ones around the room, but then she'd given up, frustrated and depressed. Maybe it was time she tried again. In a bigger way than ever before.

"I brought you a gift," Sam said.

"For me?" Grandma Joy smiled. "Thank you."

Sam held her breath and put the wrapped package into her grandmother's hands. What if Flynn had been wrong? What if this was the worst idea ever?

Joy removed the bow, smiling over the fancy gold-and-white fabric decoration, then undid the bright, holiday packaging. She ran a hand over the leather album. "A book?"

"Of sorts. It's a story." Sam swallowed. "About you. And…" She took in a breath. "Me."

"Us?" Confusion knitted Grandma Joy's brows. She looked down again at the thick brown cover, then opened the book and began to turn the pages.

Page after page, Joy and Sam's lives flashed by in a series of images. A young Joy working at the bakery with her husband in the first few days after it opened. More pictures of her, as a new mother, with baby Emma in her arms, then handing out baked goods at a church fund-raiser, then, at Emma's wedding. Joy paused when she reached the picture of herself holding a newborn Sam, her face beaming with pride. Her fingers drifted lightly over the image of her grandbaby. "So beautiful," she whispered.

Sam could only nod. This was too painful. Flynn had been wrong. How could she possibly sit here and watch her grandmother not remember the most important days of her life?

Joy turned another page, to images of Sam in kindergarten, then the second-grade class play, then to older pictures of Sam, after her parents had died and she had gone to live just with her grandparents. Middle school science fair, high school awards nights, and so many pictures of Sam working with Joy at the bakery, others at church on Easter, in front of Christmas trees. Joy paused, over and over again, mute, simply tracing over the pictures, her fingers dancing down faces.

Sam shifted in her chair. She was tempted to leave. She couldn't watch this for one more second. She half rose, opening her mouth to say goodbye, when her grandmother reached out a hand.

"This one, do you remember it?"

Sam dropped back down. "Do I remember...?" She leaned forward and looked into the album. It was one of the last pictures of her and her grandmother, before her grandmother had been admitted to Heritage Nursing Home. They stood together, arm in arm, in front of the bakery, beaming. Still a team then, thinking they'd run things together. A good day, one of the few Joy had had left. "Yes."

"My sister Ginny took the picture."

Sam's breath caught in her throat. "Yes, she did." Six months before everything had changed, when Aunt Ginny had come up for a visit, not realizing that things would get so bad so fast later and Sam would be forced into taking over the bakery, but Sam didn't mention that part. There were certain things she was glad her grandmother had forgotten.

Her grandmother smiled. "It's a beautiful picture."

Sam exhaled, deflating like a balloon. "Yeah. It is." And now she did rise, tears clogging her throat, burning her eyes. She couldn't spend another Christmas being mistaken for a stranger. Her heart hurt too much.

This was why she couldn't stay in Riverbend. This was why she couldn't give her heart to anyone else. Because she didn't have it in her to see it fall apart, crumble so easily. Not again.

"It's so beautiful," Grandma Joy repeated, "just like my granddaughter." She reached out a hand—long, graceful fingers exactly like Sam's—and grasped Sam's wrist before Sam could walk away. She stared at Sam, for a long, long time, then she smiled, her eyes lighting in a way Sam hadn't seen them brighten in so, so long. "Just like you, Samantha."

"Did you…did you just say my name?" Sam asked.

"Of course. You're my granddaughter, aren't you?"

Sam nodded, mute, tears spilling over, blurring her vision. She sank down again, this time onto the soft mattress, and reached out, drawing her grandmother into one more hug.

And when Grandma Joy's arms went around her, fierce and tight, Samantha Barnett started believing in Christmas miracles again.

Betsy was singing.

If Flynn didn't know better, he'd have sworn a cow was dying in the front parlor of the bed and breakfast. He headed downstairs on Christmas morning, going straight for the coffeepot. In the parlor, the few remaining guests were gathered around the piano, joining Betsy in a rousing and agonizingly off-key rendition of "O Little Town of Bethlehem."

From the dining room, Flynn watched the group. He stood

on the periphery, never more aware he was on the outside. How long had he lived like this? Outside of normal people's lives?

Living another kind of normal. One that he now realized was far from normal.

The front door to Betsy's opened and Sam walked in, her arms laden with boxes from the bakery. Flynn put down his coffee and hurried over to help her. "I thought you were under Doctor Earl's orders not to work on Christmas Eve."

"I baked these ahead of time. And besides, it's not Christmas Eve anymore, it's Christmas Day. So merry Christmas." She gave him a smile.

A smile? After the way things had ended between them yesterday? Flynn didn't question the facial gesture, but wondered. Why the change?

"But you *are* working, even on Christmas?" he said.

"I'm delivering, not working." She thought about it for a second. "Okay, yes. But only for a little while. And, I had an ulterior motive."

He unpacked a box of Danishes, laying them in a concentric circle on a silver-plated platter. It reminded him of the first time he'd done this, right after arriving in town. That seemed like a hundred years ago, as if he'd met Sam a lifetime ago. Before yesterday, he'd thought…

Thought maybe there was a chance they could have something. What that something could be, he wasn't sure, because he lived on the East Coast and she lived in the Midwest, and their worlds were as opposite as the North and South Poles.

And then he'd gone and driven a wedge between them yesterday. Had made it clear where his priorities lay—with his job.

If there'd been another choice, Flynn would have grabbed it in a second. Another choice…

He looked at Sam, her face bright and happy, her hair seeming like gold above the red sweater she wore, and wished for a miracle. It was Christmas, after all. Maybe a miracle would come along.

Uh-huh. And maybe Santa would just sweep on through the front door, too. Best to abandon that train of thought before it derailed his plans to leave.

"Ulterior motive?" he asked.

"You left last night before I could give you your Christmas gift."

That drew Flynn up short. "You bought me a *Christmas gift*?"

"Well, I had to sort of improvise, and your gift is, ah—" she looked at her watch "—not quite here yet, because what I bought you is still in my Jeep, which is on the side of the road."

"You bought me a gift yesterday?" He couldn't have been more surprised if Santa himself had marched in and handed him a present.

"Of course. It's Christmas. Everyone should have a gift on Christmas. I was going to give it before you—"

Even though he knew he shouldn't, even though he'd just vowed a half second ago to stay away from her, Flynn surged forward, cupped her face with both his hands and kissed her. "Thank you."

She laughed. "You don't even know what I got you. You could hate it."

"It doesn't matter. It's the thought that counts." She had thought of him. Thought about whether he would have a merry Christmas. Who had worried about his Christmas? Ever? Flynn couldn't remember anyone ever doing that. Most holiday seasons, he and Liam had been between homes, shuffled off by the system to some emergency place, a temporary landing, before they'd be off to the next family. But no one had latched on to the boys who rebelled, who didn't connect, fit in with their little blond-haired boys and girls.

The fact that Sam, a woman he had met a few days ago, would go to so much trouble, for him, blasted against him.

He might not be a little kid anymore, and no longer cared if there was a gift under the tree, or heck, a tree in his living room, but to know that someone had taken the time to plan a gift like that…

It touched him more than he had thought possible.

A fierce longing tugged at him, and the urge to leave dissipated. Instead, he found himself wanting to stay. Here, in this town. This crazy, Christmas-frantic town.

"Are you speaking in trite phrases now, Flynn MacGregor?"

"I, ah, think this town is rubbing off on me."

Sam laughed again. "You must be catching pneumonia or something."

"I've caught something," Flynn said, tracing Sam's lips with his fingertips. Wanting to kiss her again. Wanting to do much more than that, but painfully aware that they were in Betsy's dining room.

"Come on in, Flynn, Sam!" Betsy called. "And join us!"

Sam's eyes danced with a dare. "Are you feeling truly festive?"

He cringed. "Singing with Betsy might be pushing it."

Sam grabbed one of his hands and pulled him toward the parlor. "It'll be good for you, Flynn."

And as he stood by the piano a moment later with an assortment of strangers, his arm wrapped around Sam's waist, joining in on "Jingle Bells," a swell of holiday spirit started in Flynn's chest and began to grow, as if the music itself was pounding Christmas right into him. Somehow, he seemed to know the words, or at least snippets of them, to every song. Perhaps he'd absorbed them over the years, some kind of holiday osmosis, and he added his baritone to the rest of the singers. Sam leaned her head against his shoulder, and for those moments, everything seemed completely perfect in Flynn's world.

A truth whispered in his ear, one he wasn't prepared to hear. He loved this woman.

Loved her. It didn't matter that it had happened in four days, four weeks or four years. The feeling ran so deep, and so strong, Flynn could no longer ignore it.

For the first time in his life, he wanted depth, he wanted a real relationship, no more convenience dating, the kind of flighty relationship he'd had with Mimi. She was surely off in some foreign country, probably flirting with someone else, which didn't bother Flynn one bit.

He had everything he wanted right here with him.

Never before had he fallen in love, but he recognized the emotion as clearly as his own name. His arm tightened around Sam's waist, and he vowed that as soon as the song ended, he would pull Sam aside and tell her.

Another set of chimes joined in with the piano. It took a moment for anyone to realize the sound was coming from the doorbell, and not Betsy's feet. "Oh, someone's here," Betsy said. "I hope whoever it is, sings tenor!"

"I'll get it," Flynn said, releasing Sam to cross the front parlor, head into the hall and down to the door. He expected one of the guest's relatives. Or maybe Earl, here to chide Sam about making a delivery on Christmas Day.

But when Flynn pulled open the door, he found a gift no one could have fit under a tree. And one he wasn't so sure was glad to be here.

His brother.

"What are you doing here?"

"I was invited," Liam said. He picked up a suitcase that had been sitting by his feet. A suitcase? Why? Was he intending to stay a while?

Confusion waged a war in Flynn's gut. Who had called Liam? Why? And what had made Liam drive all the way up here?

The tension between them ran as thick as syrup. Flynn knew the choice was his. He could step aside, let Liam pass and leave the moment as it was, or he could do something about it.

Liam hoisted the suitcase higher in his grip and moved forward, making the decision for him. Before his younger brother could pass, Flynn reached out and drew Liam into a tight embrace. "Hi, Liam."

Liam stiffened, then patted Flynn's back in a gesture meant more for a stranger than a relative. "Hi, Flynn."

Damn, how he had missed his brother. It didn't matter if two years or two minutes had passed, whether they were in their twenties or still in elementary school. A fierce love rose in Flynn's chest, and he held tight for a long moment, his mind whipping back to the beach, to the two of them together against the wind, swearing to always be together. Always.

Flynn clapped his brother hard on the back, then released him. He swept his gaze over Liam, who was thinner than Flynn remembered, but still had the same tall, dark good looks. His hair was curlier, his eyes tended more toward green than blue, but otherwise, the two shared a lot of the same characteristics. "It's good to see you."

Really good.

"Yeah. Same to you." Liam came inside and shut the door behind him, then dropped the suitcase to the floor. Behind them, the caroling continued, segueing into "We Wish You a Merry Christmas." Liam shuffled from foot to foot, ran a hand through his hair. "Singing, huh?"

"Yeah."

Some more silence extended between them. If one of them

didn't say something, Flynn knew they never would. There'd been too many phone calls, too many visits, that had been filled with awkward small talk and anguished pauses, and nothing of substance. He cleared his throat. "Listen, Liam, about the last time we saw each other—"

"You don't have to say anything."

"Yeah, I do." Flynn ran a hand over his face, then met his brother's gaze. "All I've been trying to do is take care of you. But you make it damned hard sometimes."

Liam shook his head, and a flush of frustration rose in his cheeks. "Flynn, I'm all grown up now. I can take care of myself."

"I know, but…" Flynn let out a breath.

"There's no buts. You keep on trying to throw money at me. I don't want that, Flynn. I want—" Liam cut off his sentence and let out a low curse.

"You want what?" Flynn prompted when Liam didn't continue. Behind them, the group had moved onto "O Little Town of Bethlehem."

Liam stared at his shoes for a long while, then finally looked up and met Flynn's gaze. "I want you, big brother. Not your damned money."

There. It was out. The truth. Liam needed the one thing Flynn had always held back, kept tucked away. His heart. His emotions.

And what good had it done him? Left him alone, estranged from his brother, living one holiday after another without anyone.

Flynn ran a hand along the woodwork, fingers tracing the thick oak. "I was wrong, Liam. I pushed you away…."

"Because I was a reminder of all we went through," Liam said, finishing the sentence.

"Yeah." Here he'd thought he'd been controlling his life. Controlling his emotions. When all he'd done was shove them in a closet and ignore them.

Liam's gaze met his older sibling's. In that moment, a

shared history unfurled between them, a mental *This is Your Life*, that played in an instant, then came around full circle to the two of them, together then, together now. "Yeah, me, too."

There was no need for words, no need for anything other than that assent. They knew, because they'd been there. Because they shared the same DNA. And heck, because they were guys. Blubbering for hours simply wasn't the way they handled things.

Flynn reached out, and drew his brother to him again, in an even tighter embrace this time, one that lasted longer, and made up for the last two years. "Merry Christmas, Liam."

Flynn couldn't hear his brother's response, because he was holding him too tight. But it didn't matter. He didn't need to hear the words to know his little brother felt the same.

Because this time, Liam hugged him back.

"Oh, we have another guest!" Betsy exclaimed from behind them. "At Betsy's Bed and Breakfast—"

"There's always room for one more," Flynn finished for her.

Betsy grinned. "Absolutely!"

Flynn picked up his brother's suitcase. "Come on in, make yourself at home."

Liam gave Flynn a dubious glance, as he watched Betsy hurry forward, her house slippers jingle-jangling, her mouth going nonstop about the town, the Christmas activities planned for the day, the dinner menu, the local call policy. "Is it always like this here?"

"Yep. And that's the beauty of the place. Hang around for the Christmas carols," Flynn said. "They're the best part."

Liam glanced over at him, eyes wide. Flynn just laughed, and it felt damned good to do so.

CHAPTER SIXTEEN

SAM SLIPPED OUT Betsy's back door. She'd seen Flynn greet his brother and knew she had done what she wanted to do. She had given Flynn the merry Christmas she had intended.

The wind stung her face as soon as she stepped outside, and at first, she couldn't understand why the cold hurt so bad, until she realized her cheeks were covered with tears, and winter's wrath had turned them to ice. She swiped at her face with her glove, then walked the few blocks to the bakery, opting for the peace of the shop, instead of heading to Aunt Ginny's house.

She let herself inside Joyful Creations, turning on a single light. Then she headed to the case, filled a plate with all the treats she never had time to eat, put on a pot of coffee, and when it was ready, she took her snack out to one of the café tables, as if she were a customer.

She sat down, and for the first time in a long time, enjoyed the fruits of her labor. Outside the window, a soft snow began to fall, a dusting, really, just enough to sparkle for the holiday.

The door opened and Earl poked his head in. "What on earth are you doing, Sam? It's Christmas."

She smiled. "I could say the same to you."

"I'm on my way over to Betsy's. I've got her Christmas gift out here."

"Out there?" Sam rose out of her chair and peeked through the window. "You bought her a truck?"

"Hell no. I bought her what's in the back of my truck." Earl beamed with pride at his thoughtfulness. "A new washer machine."

"Oh. How romantic."

"My Betsy is practical. She's gonna love it. You'll see." He adjusted his hat, then gave Sam another disapproving glance. "You aren't planning on spending your holiday in here, now are you?"

"No. I'm going to my Aunt Ginny's."

"Good. You need to do more for yourself. You don't want to make this place your life, Sam. We need you around this town more than we need a bakery." He tipped his head toward her to emphasize the point. "If you see Joy today at that fancy retirement place, please give her my best. I sure do miss seeing her 'round here."

Sam drew in a breath. Flynn was right. It was time to tell the people of this town about Grandma Joy. Everyone in Riverbend cared about her—hadn't they made that obvious a hundred times over? And they'd cared about her grandmother, and would continue to care—regardless of what had happened, and whether Grandma remembered them or not. "No, Earl. My grandmother doesn't live in a retirement village. She never did." Sam paused. "Grandma Joy lives at Heritage Nursing Home, in the Alzheimer's unit."

Earl looked at her in shock for a long moment, then he nodded somberly, as if he'd expected to hear that. "I saw her mind going, long time ago. I wondered how long it would be. I'm sorry, Sam. But you made the right decision." He ambled into the store, and gave her a hug.

Sam's heart filled, the love of the people of Riverbend bursting in her chest. "Thanks, Earl." She brushed away a few tears, but this time, they weren't tears of sorrow, just tears of gratitude for the comfort of others.

"Don't think nothing of it. Maybe me and Betsy, we'll head on over there, see her today."

"She probably won't remember you."

Earl waved a hand in dismissal. "That's okay. Half the time I don't remember my own name." He grinned. "And if your grandma doesn't know me, it won't bother me none. Why, it'll be like making a new friend every time I go up there."

After a final warning not to work all day, Earl wished her a merry Christmas then headed out the door. Sam watched him go, feeling lighter than she had in a long time. Flynn had been right. Sharing the burden suddenly made it a lot easier to bear.

Now if she could only find a way to have it all—a life and carry on her grandmother's legacy, she'd be all set. Sam sighed, then took Earl's advice, and turned out the lights.

Flynn paused on Sam's doorstep, shifting the scratchy gift in his hands to his opposite arm. He rang the bell and waited. What if she wasn't home? What if she'd gone to her aunt's house? What if—

But then the door opened and Sam stood on the other side, a roll of wrapping paper in one hand. "Flynn."

"You're still here. I thought you might have gone to your aunt's already."

She held up the wrapping paper. "Working too much, not enough time to wrap gifts. So, I'm running late. What are you doing here?"

"I came here to say Merry Christmas."

"Merry Christmas, Flynn." A smile crossed her lips. "I think we already had this conversation this morning."

"It worked pretty well the first time, didn't it?" He grinned. "This is for you. It's, ah, not much, because there's not exactly many shopping options on Christmas Day, and yesterday's shopping trip was ended prematurely."

She laid the wrapping paper against the door, then took the wreath from his hands, the smile on her face widening. "A Christmas wreath?"

"I noticed you didn't have one on your front door. There was this guy selling them on the corner of Main this morning, and when I saw them, I—"

"*You* noticed I didn't have a wreath?"

"Is that so unusual?"

She hung the wreath on her front door, straightened the red velvet bow, then turned back to him, shutting the door behind her. "For one, you're a guy. For another, of everyone in town—"

"I had the least Christmas spirit."

"Well, yeah." She arched a brow. "Had?"

Flynn crossed to Sam, taking her hands in his. "I changed my mind about the holiday."

"What changed your mind?"

"Well, it sure wasn't Betsy's singing. Or her jingle bell slippers." He grinned. "It was you."

"Me? How could I do that?"

He reached up and cupped her jaw, tracing her bottom lip with his thumb. "Thank you for bringing my brother here. When you did that, you showed me what was important. That I had my priorities as backward as a man could get them."

Confusion warred in her green eyes.

"I wrote my article early this morning, and sent it in to my editor. Turns out one of the guests at Betsy's had a national broadband connection on his laptop, and we got it to work by sitting in the backyard, freezing our butts off." He chuckled. "Doesn't matter. The article is done, and gone. No going back. But I still wanted you to read it.

Either way, no matter what happens, I'm not changing a word."

Her face fell, and she stepped away. "Just be kind, Flynn. That's all I ask."

He fished the papers he'd printed that morning on his portable printer out of his pocket and handed them to Sam. "Read it, and then judge, Sam."

She took the sheaf of pages, then turned away from him, crossing into the living room. She sank onto one of the sofas, flicked on a lamp and began to read.

Flynn already knew the words on the page. It hadn't been all that hard to recall them from the first draft. His heart had committed those earlier pages to memory, and when he'd sat down to write, the article had poured from him, as easily as water from a faucet. *Visions of sugar plums dance...*

Long minutes passed, without Sam saying a word. She read, turning the pages slowly, while Flynn's breath held, his lungs tight. Finally, she looked up, her green eyes watery.

Damn. Had he written the piece wrong? Had he, despite his best intentions, still ruined everything?

"Flynn. It's—" she drew in a breath, searching for words "—wonderful."

He exhaled. "It's not what my editor wants. Or what my readers expect. It's not, in fact, at all what I was paid to write. I'll probably be fired." He grinned. "So if you're looking for a little help making cookies...I might need a job on the twenty-sixth."

"But...why? Why would you do this?"

He crossed to the sofa and sat down beside her. "I realized that my career didn't matter if it cost me peace of mind. Happiness." He drew in a breath. "Happiness with you, Sam, because...I love you."

Her eyes widened. "You love me?"

Flynn felt a goofy grin take over his face, the kind that made his jaw go slack with happiness. "Yes. I do. And I know it sounds crazy because I've only known you for a matter of days, but one of those days was spent stuck in a cabin in the woods, so that's like triple time, because we were alone so much, and—"

She surged forward, the papers on her lap falling to the floor, and kissed him. "Oh, Flynn. I love you, too."

Joy exploded in his chest. She loved him, too. Holy cow. This was what other men felt when a woman said those words? This was what made them settle down, have kids, buy a house in the suburbs? No wonder.

And what the heck had he been doing all this time, denying himself this? Thinking he was happier alone?

"All my life," he said, "I've controlled my emotions, held them back, because I thought it was easier not to feel, not to open my heart to other people—"

"Because protecting your heart kept it from getting it hurt," Sam finished. "But in the end, all it did was leave you alone. And unhappy."

He nodded. He placed a hand against her cheek, seeing so much of himself in her eyes. "You did the same thing."

"And got the same result." She worked a smile to her face, but it fell flat. "I don't want to be alone anymore, Flynn."

Flynn opened his arms, and drew Sam against his chest. "You won't be, Sam. And neither will I."

They held each other for a long time, while the snow fell softly outside, and the fire crackled in the fireplace. In all his life, Flynn could have never imagined a Christmas gift as wonderful as this.

Sam drew back, her gaze going over Flynn's shoulder. "I forgot to turn on the lights for the Christmas tree." She rose, pulling Flynn up with her, and they crossed to the seven-foot spruce.

Flynn ran a hand down the tree, his touch skipping over the history of Sam's life contained in the dozens and dozens of ornaments. Someday, he'd know the story behind every one of these. Because he would be with her for next Christmas and the one after that, and they would hang these ornaments together. He could hear her telling him that her grandmother had baked those salt dough gingerbread men, and her Aunt Ginny had made those macramé birds. That she'd bought the cable car on a trip to San Francisco, found the pinecone on a long hike in the woods. The joy in his heart tripled, for the future he could finally see, one with Sam by his side.

"Here," Sam said, handing him a switch. "You can do it. And don't forget to make a wish."

Flynn smiled. "I don't need to. My wish already came true." He pressed the button for the lights into Sam's palm. "You make the wish."

She closed her eyes, whispered a few words, then pressed the button. The lights came on, illuminating the tree with a burst of tiny white lights. A second later, they began to blink in a synchronized dance. "My favorite moment," she said. "The first time. It's like that's when Christmas really starts."

"What did you wish for?"

"If I tell you," she said, grinning, "it might not come true."

"If you wished for me to marry you," Flynn replied, swinging Sam back into his arms, "then that's one wish that's going to come true, because there's no way I'm letting you get away, Samantha Barnett."

Surprise arched her brows again. "You move fast, Flynn MacGregor."

"There's another thing you should know about me. When I see something I want, I go after it."

She smiled, then a moment passed, and the smile fell from her face. "I can't marry you, Flynn. It wouldn't be fair to you."

"What do you mean, it wouldn't be fair? We can find a way to make anything work, Sam."

"Do you want to know what I wished for?" She leaned her head against his chest. Flynn inhaled, catching the scent of sugar cookies. For the rest of his life, he'd associate that scent with Sam. "I wished for a way to have everything I wanted."

"I'm not enough?" He chuckled.

She looked up at him, sorrow filling her gaze. "I can't afford to pay for the treatment my grandmother needs, not without expanding Joyful Creations beyond the bounds of Riverbend. To expand, I have to work more hours. And if I'm working more hours, I won't be much of a wife, or a mother, if we ever have children."

Children. He hadn't thought of having kids—had never pictured himself with his own children at all—but now that Sam had said the word, he realized he did want a family.

A big family. A dog. A house. The whole enchilada.

But Sam was right. She couldn't have a life, and run multiple locations, not in such a demanding field. Hadn't he seen that when he'd went to live at Mondo's house? The chef and his wife had never been home, and eventually, called children's services to give back the foster children they'd taken in. Their best intentions had been undone by a work schedule that didn't allow for a family. He'd heard the same story over and over again. So many families tried to make it work, but in an industry that required early mornings and late nights, it was almost impossible. Some could work it out, but so many were forced to choose between business and home.

And as for Sam, if she had more than one location, along with the demands that came with those early years of still building her business?

He didn't see how she could have it all, either. Not unless...

"What if there was another way to expand Joyful Creations beyond Riverbend?" he said.

"Another way? What are you talking about?"

"It would require having Internet service," Flynn said with a grin. "Reliable postal service."

"Now *that* we have."

"Good." The idea exploded in his head, all those years of covering the food industry, and learning from chefs and experts coalescing at once. "What if you started a Web site? To sell, not just the regular cookies and desserts, but also the 'love cookies'? They already have a national reputation, and once my article runs—"

"I thought you said your editor would hate it."

"If he does, I'll just sell it somewhere else. It's a good article, Sam. A damned good article. I'll sell it, and in the process, make Joyful Creations even more famous."

"Ship the cookies. And stay here." Sam thought about that, pacing as she talked aloud. "It could work. I wouldn't have to move away from my grandmother or my aunt, and if I needed to increase production, I could always rent more space from the shop next door. They have a back room they don't use. My overhead would be low, the hours I'd have to put in…" She spun back toward him. "It could work."

"And you could have it all, Sam. Stay here, have a family." He grinned. "Have me, if you want."

"Of course I do." She crossed back to him, slipping into his arms as if she had always been there, fitting as easily as a link in a chain. "You're part of the package, Flynn MacGregor."

He leaned down and kissed her, capturing the taste of vanilla, the scent of cinnamon, the sweetness of Sam. Everything he'd ever wanted, in one beautiful, wonderful Christmas gift. "You know what people are going to say, don't you?"

"Hmm…what?"

"That we fell in love because of those cookies."

"But we never even ate any."

"No one knows if we did or not. And if it's rumored that we did…"

Sam grinned. "It'll be good for business."

"As long as it's good for us, I'm okay with that." Then Flynn kissed the woman he loved again, while the lights from the tree cast their golden light on her face. For the first time in his life, Flynn MacGregor believed in Santa Claus, because the jolly man had finally listened and given him the perfect gift.

The *only* gift he'd ever really wanted for Christmas—

A home.

* * * * *

Silhouette Desire kicks off 2009 with
MAN OF THE MONTH, *a yearlong program*
featuring incredible heroes by stellar authors.

When navy SEAL Hunter Cabot returns home for some
much-needed R & R, he discovers he's a married man.
There's just one problem: he's never met his "bride."

Enjoy this sneak peek at Maureen Child's
AN OFFICER AND A MILLIONAIRE.
Available January 2009 from Silhouette Desire.

One

Hunter Cabot, Navy SEAL, had a healing bullet wound in his side, thirty days' leave and, apparently, a wife he'd never met.

On the drive into his hometown of Springville, California, he stopped for gas at Charlie Evans's service station. That's where the trouble started.

"Hunter! Man, it's good to see you! Margie didn't tell us you were coming home."

"Margie?" Hunter leaned back against the front fender of his black pickup truck and winced as his side gave a small twinge of pain. Silently then, he watched as the man he'd known since high school filled his tank.

Charlie grinned, shook his head and pumped gas. "Guess your wife was lookin' for a little 'alone' time with you, huh?"

"My—" Hunter couldn't even say the word. *Wife?* He didn't have a wife. "Look, Charlie…"

"Don't blame her, of course," his friend said with a wink as he finished up and put the gas cap back on. "You being gone all the time with the SEALs must be hard on the ol' love life."

He'd never had any complaints, Hunter thought, frowning at the man still talking a mile a minute. "What're you—"

"Bet Margie's anxious to see you. She told us all about that

R and R trip you two took to Bali." Charlie's dark brown eyebrows lifted and wiggled.

"Charlie…"

"Hey, it's okay, you don't have to say a thing, man."

What the hell could he say? Hunter shook his head, paid for his gas and as he left, told himself Charlie was just losing it. Maybe the guy had been smelling gas fumes too long.

But as it turned out, it wasn't just Charlie. Stopped at a red light on Main Street, Hunter glanced out his window to smile at Mrs. Harker, his second-grade teacher who was now at least a hundred years old. In the middle of the crosswalk, the old lady stopped and shouted, "Hunter Cabot, you've got yourself a wonderful wife. I hope you appreciate her."

Scowling now, he only nodded at the old woman—the only teacher who'd ever scared the crap out of him. What the hell was going on here? Was everyone but him nuts?

His temper beginning to boil, he put up with a few more comments about his "wife" on the drive through town before finally pulling into the wide, circular drive leading to the Cabot mansion. Hunter didn't have a clue what was going on, but he planned to get to the bottom of it. Fast.

He grabbed his duffel bag, stalked into the house and paid no attention to the housekeeper, who ran at him, fluttering both hands. "Mr. Hunter!"

"Sorry, Sophie," he called out over his shoulder as he took the stairs two at a time. "Need a shower, then we'll talk."

He marched down the long, carpeted hallway to the rooms that were always kept ready for him. In his suite, Hunter tossed the duffel down and stopped dead. The shower in his bathroom was running. His *wife?*

Anger and curiosity boiled in his gut, creating a churning mass that had him moving forward without even thinking, about it. He opened the bathroom door to a wall of steam and the sound of a woman singing—off-key. Margie, no doubt.

Well, if she was his wife...Hunter walked across the room, yanked the shower door open and stared in at a curvy, naked, temptingly wet woman.

She whirled to face him, slapping her arms across her naked body while she gave a short, terrified scream.

Hunter smiled. "Hi, honey. I'm home."

* * * * *

Be sure to look for
AN OFFICER AND A MILLIONAIRE
by USA TODAY bestselling author Maureen Child.
Available January 2009 from Silhouette Desire.

CELEBRATE
60 YEARS
OF PURE READING PLEASURE
WITH **HARLEQUIN**®!

We'll be spotlighting a different series
every month throughout 2009
to celebrate our 60th anniversary.
Look for Silhouette Desire® in January!

MAN of the
MONTH

Collect all 12 books in the Silhouette Desire®
Man of the Month continuity, starting in
January 2009 with *An Officer and a Millionaire*
by *USA TODAY* bestselling author
Maureen Child.

*Look for one new Man of the Month title
every month in 2009!*

Silhouette®

SPECIAL EDITION™

The Bravos meet the Jones Gang
as two of Christine Rimmer's famous
Special Edition families come together
in one very special book.

THE STRANGER
AND TESSA JONES

by

CHRISTINE RIMMER

Snowed in with an amnesiac stranger during a
freak blizzard, Tessa Jones soon finds out her
guest is none other than heartbreaker Ash Bravo.
And that's when things really heat up....

*Available January 2009
wherever you buy books.*

Silhouette®

Romantic SUSPENSE

**Sparked by Danger,
Fueled by Passion.**

Justine Davis

Baby's Watch

THE COLTONS
~FAMILY FIRST~

Former bad boy Ryder Colton has never felt a connection to much, so he's shocked when he feels one to the baby he helps deliver, and her mother. Ana Morales doesn't quite trust this stranger, but when her daughter is taken by a smuggling ring, she teams up with him in the hope of rescuing her baby. With nowhere to turn she has no choice but to trust Ryder with her life...and her heart.

Available January 2009 wherever books are sold.

Look for the final installment of
the Coltons: Family First miniseries,
A Hero of Her Own by Carla Cassidy in February 2009.

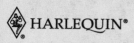
HARLEQUIN®

American ★ Romance®

TINA LEONARD
The Texas
Ranger's Twins

Men Made in America

The promise of a million dollars has lured
Texas Ranger Dane Morgan back to his family
ranch. But he can't be forced into marriage to
single mother of twin girls, Suzy Wintertone,
who is tempting as she is sweet—can he?

**Available January 2009
wherever books are sold.**

LOVE, HOME & HAPPINESS

www.eHarlequin.com

HAR75245

REQUEST YOUR FREE BOOKS!
2 FREE NOVELS PLUS 2
FREE GIFTS!

HARLEQUIN ROMANCE®

From the Heart, For the Heart

YES! Please send me 2 FREE Harlequin Romance® novels and my 2 FREE gifts (gifts are worth about $10). After receiving them, if I don't wish to receive any more books, I can return the shipping statement marked "cancel". If I don't cancel, I will receive 4 brand-new novels every month and be billed just $3.32 per book in the U.S. or $3.80 per book in Canada, plus 25¢ shipping and handling per book and applicable taxes, if any*. That's a savings of over 15% off the cover price! I understand that accepting the 2 free books and gifts places me under no obligation to buy anything. I can always return a shipment and cancel at any time. Even if I never buy another book, the two free books and gifts are mine to keep forever.

114 HDN ERQW   314 HDN ERQ9

Name	(PLEASE PRINT)	
Address		Apt. #
City	State/Prov.	Zip/Postal Code

Signature (if under 18, a parent or guardian must sign)

Mail to the **Harlequin Reader Service:**
IN U.S.A.: P.O. Box 1867, Buffalo, NY 14240-1867
IN CANADA: P.O. Box 609, Fort Erie, Ontario L2A 5X3

Not valid to current subscribers of Harlequin Romance books.

Want to try two free books from another line?
Call 1-800-873-8635 or visit www.morefreebooks.com.

* Terms and prices subject to change without notice. N.Y. residents add applicable sales tax. Canadian residents will be charged applicable provincial taxes and GST. Offer not valid in Quebec. This offer is limited to one order per household. All orders subject to approval. Credit or debit balances in a customer's account(s) may be offset by any other outstanding balance owed by or to the customer. Please allow 4 to 6 weeks for delivery. Offer available while quantities last.

Your Privacy: Harlequin Books is committed to protecting your privacy. Our Privacy Policy is available online at www.eHarlequin.com or upon request from the Reader Service. From time to time we make our lists of customers available to reputable third parties who may have a product or service of interest to you. If you would prefer we not share your name and address, please check here. ☐

HR08R

You're invited to join our Tell Harlequin Reader Panel!

By joining our new reader panel you will:

- Receive Harlequin® books—they are FREE and yours to keep with no obligation to purchase anything!
- Participate in fun online surveys
- Exchange opinions and ideas with women just like you
- Have a say in our new book ideas and help us publish the best in women's fiction

In addition, you will have a chance to win great prizes and receive special gifts! See Web site for details. Some conditions apply. Space is limited.

To join, visit us at
www.TellHarlequin.com.

HARLEQUIN *Romance*

Coming Next Month

**Harlequin Romance® rings in the New Year in style this month.
Ball gowns, tiaras and six dashing heroes will ensure
your New Year starts with a bang!**

#4069 LUKE: THE COWBOY HEIR Patricia Thayer
The Texas Brotherhood

In *The Texas Brotherhood* series, Luke returns to Mustang Valley, where blond beauty Tess is waiting for him—waiting to fight for the place she and her little daughter call home. The businessman in Luke would evict them without a care—but the man in him has different ideas.

#4070 NANNY TO THE BILLIONAIRE'S SON Barbara McMahon
In Her Shoes...

It's New Year's Eve. Sam has her hands on the hottest ticket in town, and finds herself dancing with billionaire Mac! But when the clock chimes twelve, reality strikes! Her stolen night has cost Sam her job, but Mac comes to the rescue.

#4071 THE SNOW-KISSED BRIDE Linda Goodnight
Heart to Heart

A secluded cabin in the Rocky Mountains is the perfect place for Melody to hide from the world. But now ex-army ranger John needs her help to find a missing child—she knows the unforgiving mountains better than anyone. Soon something about this mysterious beauty captures the rugged ranger's heart....

#4072 CINDERELLA AND THE SHEIKH Natasha Oakley
The Brides of Amrah Kingdom

In the first of the *Brides of Amrah Kingdom* duet, Pollyanna has come to Amrah to relive her great-grandmother's adventure. Journeying through the desert with the magnificent Sheikh Rashid feels like a dream! As the fairy-tale trip draws to an end, Pollyanna's adventure with Rashid has only just begun....

#4073 PROMOTED: SECRETARY TO BRIDE! Jennie Adams
9 to 5

With a new dress and a borrowed pair of shoes on her feet, mousy Molly is transformed for a posh work party. But will it be enough to catch the eye of her brooding boss, Jarrod?

#4074 THE RANCHER'S RUNAWAY PRINCESS Donna Alward
Western Weddings

Brooding ranch-owner Brody keeps his heart out of reach. But vivacious stable-manager Lucy has brought joy to his hardened soul. Lucy has found the man who makes her feel as though she belongs—only she hasn't told him she's a princess!

HRCNM1208BPA

"My sister and brother are my responsibility now. Take me to them—please," Rachel said in a slow, deliberate voice.

For a long moment Michael stared at her, his gaze hard, unyielding. Pieces of their past flashed into Rachel's thoughts, coming together like a patchwork quilt. There had been other times when their gazes had clashed in silent battle, and times when they had connected in mutual care. Blinking, she looked away.

"Actually, don't bother. I can find them," she said. She headed for the gangplank, more resolved than ever to remain in control, not to let Michael get to her.

"They're in the main salon," he said.

Rachel kept walking. All she wanted to do was leave. She'd known when she returned to Magnolia Blossom that she would probably see Michael again, but not this soon. She hadn't been prepared for the emotional impact. Now she wondered if she would ever have been prepared.

Books by Margaret Daley

Love Inspired

MARGARET DALEY

feels she has been blessed. She has been married for thirty-one years to her husband, Mike, whom she met in college. He is a terrific support and her best friend. They have one son, Shaun, who is married to his high school sweetheart.

She has been writing for many years and loves to tell a story. When she was a little girl, she would play with her dolls and make up stories about their lives. Now she writes these stories down. She especially enjoys weaving stories about families and how faith in God can sustain a person when things get tough. When she isn't writing, she is fortunate to be a teacher for students with special needs. She has taught for over twenty years and loves working with her students. She has also been a Special Olympics coach and participated in many sports with her students.

THE COURAGE
TO DREAM

MARGARET DALEY

Published by Steeple Hill Books™

STEEPLE HILL BOOKS

ISBN 0-373-87212-7

THE COURAGE TO DREAM

Visit us at www.steeplehill.com

Printed in U.S.A.

Trust in the Lord with all thine heart and lean not
unto thine own understanding. In all thy ways
acknowledge Him, and He shall direct thy paths.
—*Proverbs* 3:5-6

To my son, Shaun, and his new wife, Katie.
May you two have a long and wonderful marriage.

Chapter One

"I wondered when you would finally show up, Rachel." Michael Hunter stopped several feet from her on the river landing.

There was none of the remembered warmth in his voice, and Rachel Peters shuddered in the heat of the day. "I came as soon as I found out." Everything around her seemed to come to a standstill, the breeze, the flow of the river, the chirping of the birds, her heartbeat.

"We couldn't wait for you. We buried Flora yesterday."

"I was working halfway around the world as a guest chef on a cruise." The tightness in her throat prevented her from explaining further. She'd only found out the day before about Aunt Flora's death. Her aunt had been like a mother to her. It had taken more than a week for the message from the family lawyer to finally catch up with Rachel. She hadn't even had time to think about her aunt's death, much less grieve properly. Swallowing hard, Rachel asked, "How are Amy and Shaun?"

"Do you care?"

The hostility in his question sparked her anger, but she was determined not to let him see his effect on her. "Where are my sister and brother?" she asked in an even voice, suppressing her rage.

Michael gestured toward the riverboat. "They're with Garrett. Why?"

"Why? Because I've come to take them home."

"Whose home? Aunt Flora's or yours, wherever that may be?"

"I don't have to defend myself or my lifestyle to you."

The harsh glint in his eyes intensified. "They've been through a lot this past week. I think it'll be better if they stay with me for a while."

"You!" Her anger began to infuse her voice, her expression.

"Yes, me. I know Amy and Shaun. Can you honestly say the same?"

"They're *my* family."

"And that automatically gives you the right to decide what's best for them?"

"Yes."

"Where were you when Shaun broke his arm or Amy went on her first date?"

Rachel clamped her teeth together so tightly that

pain radiated down her neck. "They're my responsibility now. Take me to them—please," she said in a slow, deliberate voice.

For a long moment he stared at her, his gaze hard, unyielding. Pieces of their past came together in her mind like a patchwork quilt. There had been other times when their gazes had clashed in silent battle and times when they had connected in friendship and mutual affection. The blare of a boat's horn startled Rachel, the pieces of the quilt unraveling. Blinking, she looked away from Michael.

"Don't bother. I'm sure I can find them." She headed for the gangplank, more resolved than ever to remain in control and not let Michael get to her.

"They're in the main salon."

Rachel kept walking, feeling the scorch of his regard on her back. All she wanted was to get her sister and brother and leave. She'd known when she returned to Magnolia Blossom, Mississippi, that she would probably see Michael again, but she hadn't been prepared for the emotional impact of their meeting.

Remembering the location of the main salon, Rachel went straight to it. She paused in the doorway to scan the room that had once been beautiful and grand. Amy, Shaun and Michael's son, Garrett, sat at a table, their voices low, their heads bent together. When Amy glanced up and stopped talking, Rachel entered the salon, realizing the next few minutes might be even more difficult than the last ones.

It had been almost a year since she'd seen Amy and Shaun. She'd talked to them on the phone, but it wasn't the same. They've grown up a lot in that time. I don't know them very well, she thought, fighting a surge of panic. Once or twice a year isn't enough time to know what they're feeling, thinking, to be a family.

"Hello, Shaun. Amy." Rachel attempted a smile that quivered at the corners of her mouth, the tension in the air as thick as the humidity that draped her. When neither one said anything, she turned to Michael's son, hoping he would break the taut silence. "I'm Rachel Peters, Amy and Shaun's sister."

"I'm Garrett. Nice to meet you." The young boy stood and extended his hand.

The similarities between father and son disarmed her. It was as though she was staring at a younger version of Michael, more relaxed, more carefree—like he had once been around her. Then she remembered his marriage to Mary Lou and the betrayal she'd felt when she'd heard about it. She realized she had no right to feel that way, but sometimes emotions weren't easy to control. The memory gnawed at her composure until she determinedly pushed it away.

"What are you doing here?" Amy's question cut into the silence like a sharpened butcher's knife into a piece of thick meat.

Rachel looked at her sixteen-year-old sister. Amy's expression was defiant, and for a moment Rachel didn't know how to answer her. "Aunt Flora asked me to take care of you two if anything ever happened to her. I promised her I would.''

At the time she hadn't thought she would ever really have to take care of her brother and sister. She had only been concerned with making her aunt feel better.

Amy shot to her feet. ''We're doing just fine the way things are now. Michael doesn't mind us staying with him. Go back to wherever you came from. Shaun and I don't wanna leave.''

Rachel glanced from her sister to her eight-year-old brother then back to her sister, not sure what to do. ''I'm not going back just yet. I've come to take you to Aunt Flora's.''

Amy pushed back her chair, its scraping sound reverberating in the silence. Standing behind Shaun, she placed her hands on his shoulders. ''We don't need your help. I'm sure you have better things to do than baby-sit us.''

Michael walked into the salon, sharpening Rachel's awareness of the hostility in the room. Her nape tingled, and the humid air felt even heavier and more oppressive. ''Let's go home and we'll discuss everything there. I'm not going to make any decisions without talking it over with you two first.''

Amy began to say something, but Michael interrupted. ''I think that's a good idea. Your sister has come a long way, and y'all have a lot to talk about.''

Amy clamped her lips together in a pout.

Shaun looked at Garrett, who nodded. Shaun rose,

touching Amy's arm. "C'mon, I need to check on my fish anyway."

Amy didn't move. Her pout deepened as she folded her arms across her chest.

"This was your aunt's wish," Michael said in a gentle tone. "Y'all are welcome to visit anytime. My home is always open."

When Amy's bottom lip started to tremble, she bit it. Drawing in a long breath, she said, "Oh, all right— for the time being." She rushed past Rachel and Michael.

As the two boys followed Amy from the salon, Rachel started to thank Michael, but the sight of his hard stare caused the words to die in her throat. His gaze cut through her as though she were beneath his consideration.

"I didn't do it for you, Rachel. Amy and Shaun don't need to feel any more torn apart than they already are. But my offer still stands. They're welcome to stay with me and Garrett anytime."

"We'll do fine once everything settles down." She stopped short of telling him that they didn't need his help. Since returning to Magnolia Blossom, she wasn't sure of anything.

One brow arched as he studied her. A slow, chilling smile appeared on his face. "I hope so—for Amy and Shaun's sake."

Michael had once been her best friend, but she didn't know this man before her now. The realization saddened her. Puzzled by her feelings, she hurried toward the door. "I'd better go. I don't want to keep them waiting."

"No, I wouldn't do that."

The condemning tone of his voice stopped her at the door. He had always been able to provoke her. She couldn't afford to let him incite her. Over the years she had learned to control her emotions. Gripping the doorjamb, she calmly murmured goodbye, then left the salon to find her sister and brother.

Amy and Shaun stood on the landing below. Her sister still had her arms crossed over her chest with a frown lining her brow while her brother was skipping rocks across the water with Garrett. Observing them, Rachel was overwhelmed. She was not only trying to come to terms with the death of her aunt, whom she loved dearly, but with the fact that she was the only person her younger sister and brother could depend on. Since leaving Magnolia Blossom she'd had her life planned. Now she had no earthly idea what the future held. The thought scared her to death.

When Michael came out onto the deck behind her, she felt his regard and shivered in the warm air. With no more than a glance at him, she hurried down the stairs.

Michael watched Rachel stop on the landing to gather her sister and brother. Anger held him rigid, his hands gripping the railing. Until he had seen Rachel, he hadn't realized how angry he was. He'd thought he'd gotten over her years before, but the

memory of her last day in Magnolia Blossom assailed
him. She'd walked away from him and the town and
had never once looked back. He had to find a way to
get past his anger because he loved Amy and Shaun
and wanted to be there for them in their time of need.

*Lord, help me to overcome this sudden feeling of
anger at Rachel. She's a part of my past, where I
want to keep her. I need to be strong for Amy and
Shaun, but I'm afraid I can't do it without Your guidance.*

"Rachel, Flora knew you would do what was best
for Shaun and Amy," the family lawyer said as he
closed the file and leaned back in his chair.

Rachel rose, feeling sorrow, pain, confusion. "But
that's the problem, Robert. I don't *know* what's best."

"Give it some time. Don't rush things."

Rachel smoothed a strand of black hair that had
strayed from her compact French braid. After gath-
ering her clutch purse, she shook Robert Davenport's
hand. "I don't think Shaun or Amy will let me do
anything but take it slowly. I'm finding my sister and
brother are as strong-willed as Aunt Flora was."

"Then I guess you'll be staying a while."

"Yes." The one word sounded like a death sentence.

"I'll be out to the house in a couple of days. There
are some more papers you'll need to sign. We'll need
to work out guardianship. From conversations with

Flora, living with your parents isn't an option for Amy and Shaun.''

Her control faltered, emotions constricting her throat. The enormous responsibility she had agreed to take on hit her with overwhelming force. ''No, my parents don't live in a place conducive to raising children. I tried reaching them, but I haven't gotten a response from their base camp in the Amazon.''

When Rachel stepped outside Robert's office, a hot blast of summer air fogged her sunglasses. She moved them down the bridge of her nose and took a moment to scan the small, sleepy Southern town, nestled along the banks of the Mississippi River near Natchez.

An old man across the street waved to Rachel, and she returned the greeting. A couple passed her on the sidewalk and offered her their condolences. Everyone knew everyone. For two short years as a teenager she had been a part of this town, made to feel welcome because of her aunt. Rachel's chest tightened, and she drew in several deep breaths.

Magnolia Blossom—stifling, confining. She hadn't wanted to be a part of this town. She had left ten years ago because she'd refused to put down roots.

A bright yellow sign caught Rachel's attention. Helen's Southern Delight. Suddenly Rachel needed to be with a person who cared. Helen had been there for her in the past.

When Rachel entered the café with its booths along one wall and a jukebox on the other side, Helen came from behind the counter to hug her. "Well, sugar, it's 'bout time you stepped into my place."

Sitting at the counter, Rachel felt as though she were eighteen again and seeking Helen's advice about going to Paris to study cooking. She scanned the café where her dreams had been cultivated and realized in all these years Helen hadn't changed the fifties decor.

Helen stood back from the counter, eyeing Rachel in her no-nonsense manner, placing her hands on her plump hips. "I'll certainly say you don't eat all that delicious food I hear you've learned to cook. You're skin and bones, sugar."

"I can always count on you to speak your mind. I'm glad some things haven't changed in this world."

Helen smiled, the corners of her eyes crinkling. "Hey, maybe you can show me one of your fancy recipes while you're here. I hear that you do divine things with chicken."

"I doubt there's anything I could show you about cooking, Helen. The basis of all my recipes came from working with you at this café."

Helen stared at Rachel with one of her probing looks. "I'm sure proud of you, sugar. I knew you had the talent and drive to make it big. Now I tell all my friends I know a famous chef who has been written up in some of those fancy magazines. You must have seen some pretty exciting places. I bet you've seen over half the world by now."

"You know me. My home is where my suit-case is."

"Sugar, that might be fine and dandy for some people, but for myself and most folks round here, being gone from Magnolia Blossom for more than a week is long enough."

"Actually, if everything goes according to plan, I'll be settling down in New York and opening my own restaurant soon."

"Your own place?"

Excited, Rachel leaned forward. "I've got a proposal before some investors. If they agree, I'll be working for myself."

"When will you hear?"

"Hopefully in late July."

Helen glanced toward the kitchen then at Rachel. "How do you think Amy and Shaun will like living in New York?"

Rachel frowned. "Given time, they'll see the advantages of leaving Magnolia Blossom."

"Then you've decided to leave for sure, even if the restaurant deal falls through?" Helen scrubbed a particularly clean spot on the counter.

"I don't know what I'm going to do. That's what's so frustrating. So much depends, of course, on whether I can open my own restaurant. I've dreamed about that for a long time. I'm not usually an indecisive person, but I don't know the first thing about raising children."

"Now, I've never had any children, but from all I've seen I'd say you take it one step at a time."

"I suppose my first step is to call New York and see about the schools available for Shaun and Amy."

Helen cocked her head. "The first step? Don't you think the first step is getting to know them? It's been pretty long since you've spent any real time with them. They have a full life here."

"I know. Everything's a mess." Rachel sighed. "But my life isn't here."

"It was once."

"No, it wasn't, Helen. Magnolia Blossom was only another temporary stopover. Longer than most, but temporary just the same."

"Well, sugar, I'm sure you'll do what's best for everyone concerned." Helen started filling the saltshakers, her glance straying toward the kitchen several times. "You know I saved that magazine with your name in it. Let me see, what did that magazine writer call you?" She snapped her fingers. "The Cajun Queen."

"Sounds like a riverboat, doesn't it?" The second Rachel said riverboat, a vivid memory of Michael's steamboat flashed into her mind and her resolve to forget their confrontation fled. She had instinctively known that if she paused for even a moment she would dwell on him, experiencing again the bittersweet emotions of seeing him. If she stayed in Magnolia Blossom for even a few weeks, she would be inundated with Michael Hunter's presence. Could she risk stirring up old emotions?

"Maybe that's what Michael should call his boat.

'Course, it needs more than a new name. Several coats of paint. A new interior. I think he's considering fixing it up.'' Helen paused. "Hey, sugar, I'm sorry for bringing up Michael. I forgot that y'all were once an item.''

Years of experience had taught Rachel to hide pain and loneliness behind a mantle of deceptive calm, and she utilized that now. "Friends, Helen. That was all.''

"Sugar, I was there when you needed to talk.''

"He's in the past where he belongs. We've both changed, moved on with our lives.''

Helen stared at her for a moment. "Can you honestly say your feelings for him are dead?''

After the scene at the riverboat, Rachel was left with no doubts about Michael's feelings. "Yes.'' She stood, her mantle of calm slipping. "I need to run. Thanks, Helen—for everything,'' she whispered, her voice raw, her throat tight. For years she'd struggled to present a strong, invincible facade to the world, but right now she was having a tough time keeping it in place.

As Rachel hurried from the café, tears crowded her eyes. Again she was accosted by the scorching summer heat, but this time she left her sunglasses on to conceal her glistening eyes. Emotion felt like a coil wrapped about her chest, squeezing the breath from her. She inhaled deep gulps of hot air.

She didn't usually indulge in tears. She hadn't cried when she had been forced to leave friend after friend as her parents had moved from one place to another.

She hadn't cried when her mother had left her and Amy with Aunt Flora. But now she felt her world changing, her life in shambles. She experienced all over again the same hurt she'd felt when her mother deposited her with Aunt Flora. She remembered the confusion of falling in love with Michael while she wanted to pursue her dreams. In the end she had chosen to leave—that was the only thing she knew how to do.

At the only stoplight in town, she sat, indecisive about which way to turn. For one fleeting moment she wished she could turn to Michael as she once had.

Where was Amy? Rachel wondered as she stared at the kitchen clock. It hadn't been that long ago that she had been sixteen, and yet Rachel felt generations apart from her sister. She had been trying to reach her younger sister, to get to know her better, but all she got for her efforts were pouts and Amy's back as she stormed from the room.

Dinner was in the oven, ready for the past half hour. Rachel had been waiting for her sister's return from no telling where. Amy hadn't left a note. That would change the minute she came home, Rachel decided as she checked her Cajun chicken dish.

Rachel thought about eating without Amy, but she really wasn't hungry and didn't look forward to eating yet another meal alone. Earlier Shaun and Garrett had raced into the kitchen, taken one look at the meal she was preparing and fixed peanut butter and jelly sandwiches to eat while playing computer games.

"Isn't a family supposed to sit down to dinner and eat together?" Rachel muttered to herself, not knowing exactly what to do about the situation.

She poured herself a glass of iced tea. The sound of pounding sneakers filled the kitchen as Rachel shut the refrigerator door. Shaun and Garrett came to a screeching halt inches from colliding into her. She eyed the two plates in Shaun's hand, happy this time they had made it to the kitchen.

"We're going out." Shaun started for the door.

"Where?"

Shaun shrugged. "Just out."

"It'll be dark soon. I want you back by then."

"But *all* the kids can stay out later. Garrett doesn't—"

"By dark."

"How 'bout nine-thirty?"

"By dark," she repeated, her voice firm.

Shaun started to argue the point, took one look at her, and instead mumbled something under his breath—which she was glad she didn't hear—and shuffled out of the kitchen with Garrett following.

Rachel watched them leave, her head pounding like their sneakers against the floor. As she massaged her temples, she thought about all the training she'd had to go through to become a chef. She had absolutely no training to become a parent. In only a few short days, the self-confidence she had painstakingly developed had been shaken to its very core.

On the patio, Rachel sank onto the thick red-and-blue cushion on the chaise longue and sipped her tea. Aunt Flora and she used to come out here after dinner and talk. Those had been special times. Her parents had always been too busy to listen. For the two years Rachel had lived with her aunt, she'd glimpsed what it would have been like to have been raised in a normal family, one that didn't pick up and move all the time, one where both parents weren't always working on research that was more important than their children.

The setting sun splashed the darkening sky with vivid colors. Rachel blanked her mind of all thoughts and relished the serenity that settled over the land right before the sun went down. Closing her eyes, she could still see the streaks of mauve, rose and gold weaving in and out of the blue tapestry.

As she let the beauty of the dying day seep into her mind, she relaxed her bone-tired body. Her exhaustion, combined with the humidity, cloaked her like a heavy mantle. A sound penetrated the lassitude that enveloped her. Amy was home. Even as that realization registered, Rachel knew she couldn't face her sister just yet. She needed the restful tranquillity she felt at the moment to give her the strength to remain patient when dealing with Amy later.

The screen door opened then closed. Rachel sensed someone was staring at her and suddenly realized it wasn't Amy or Shaun. Her eyes flew open, and she looked right into Michael's face, devoid of all expression. Tension vibrated in the air between them as he stepped away from the screen door and closer to her.

"Hello, Rachel."

She felt at a disadvantage, lying on the chaise longue, and quickly rose. "Hello, Michael."

As if he needed something to do with his hands, Michael fitted them into the back pockets of his black jeans. Rachel followed his movements, mesmerized by actions that conveyed a smooth athletic prowess. Slowly her gaze trailed upward, lingering momentarily on the bulge of muscles beneath the short sleeves of his black T-shirt. His body was wiry, tough, every lean ounce of him sculpted with a male strength that transmitted leashed energy and supple command. When she finally looked into his dark brown eyes, her pulse sped through her. Memories of their past nibbled at her fragile composure.

"What brings you here?" she asked, thankful that her voice worked, desperate to think of anything but their past.

"I want to discuss Amy with you."

Rachel stiffened and furrowed her brow. "Amy? Is she with you?"

"Yes, I followed her home from Whispering Oaks. She's in her bedroom."

Rachel started for the screen door. "Why was she at your house? Is something wrong?"

"No—yes."

Rachel halted, her hand falling away from the metal handle. She turned, her gaze immediately drawn to his. "What's wrong?"

As Michael moved toward her, Rachel automatically took a step away until she encountered the screen door. She tilted her head in order to look him in the eye, the gesture subtly defiant.

"Amy's concerned about having to leave Magnolia Blossom."

"Why didn't she come to me about her concern?" Rachel asked, and silently wondered, Why did she have to go to you instead?

"I think you know the answer to that."

The rough edge to his voice made her defenses go up. "But I'm her sister."

"Who never came home."

"This isn't my home."

"You're right. I forgot that. You made it perfectly clear that you wanted nothing to do with Magnolia Blossom or…" His jaw clamped shut; his gaze hardened.

"Or what?"

"Me."

Chapter Two

Coldness was embedded in his voice.

He was only inches away, the clean scent of his soap strong and powerful. His nearness made Rachel forget what she was going to retort. Instead, her gaze fastened on the cleft in his chin. She remembered how she loved to caress the dent and run her fingers through his thick brown hair, which held touches of sunlight.

"Why are you here now?" Rachel asked, unnerved by his presence more than she would ever admit.

"Amy overheard your conversation earlier this afternoon with Helen about schools in New York, and she wanted me to convince you not to leave Magnolia Blossom and take her and Shaun away." His laughter was humorless. "Of course, Amy doesn't realize I'm the last person in the world to convince you of that."

"Why does she want to stay here?" Rachel already

had a good idea why her sister and brother wanted to stay in Magnolia Blossom, but she wanted to center the conversation around her siblings and not her feelings for Michael.

"Because this is her home. Because she has only one year left of high school and wants to finish here. Because all her friends are here."

"But New York offers so many opportunities."

"Who are you talking about, yourself or Amy?"

"Both."

"Please, don't kid yourself. Amy isn't interested in New York. When you make your decision, I hope you'll at least consider your sister's needs, too."

"So now you not only know what's best for me but for Amy and, I suppose, for Shaun, too."

"I never tried to tell you what was best for you, but I'll tell you taking those two out of Magnolia Blossom isn't best for them." There was a quiet strength in his voice as he stared at her with a frosty regard. "I care about them."

"And so do I. There are some good schools for Amy in New England or Switzerland where she can make new friends. Those kinds of schools can open so many doors for her. Those places aren't the ends of the earth."

"Now you're talking about Europe! What are you going to do—dump Shaun and Amy in different schools on different continents?"

"If we leave Magnolia Blossom, they'll have a say in what school they'll go to."

"I see. After *consulting* them, you're going to dump them in different schools."

She was reminded of what her parents had done with Amy and her twelve years before, then later Shaun. All her suppressed feelings of abandonment and insecurity surfaced. Her parents hadn't wanted to be burdened with children who got in the way of research. Leaving them with Aunt Flora had been the best thing for them, but the abandonment still hurt, and no amount of logic took the pain away.

"Don't you see, Rachel, both Amy and Shaun need stability right now, not a major upheaval."

"I moved around when I was their age. I survived."

"What's good for you is good for them? Not all people like to pick up and move at a moment's notice. Not all people are as accomplished as you are at leaving friends."

With a flinch she pushed away from the screen door to put some distance between Michael and her. "What I do with them is none of your business."

"Amy has asked me to make it my business. I hope you won't rush a decision because of what happened between us."

"Isn't that presuming a lot?"

A nerve in his jawline twitched as his gaze narrowed on her face. "Then use this time to see things from their viewpoint. You traveled around a lot as a child. They didn't. This is the only real home those two have known. Their friends are important to them, even if they aren't to you.''

His words cut deep. She wanted to deny the feeling; she couldn't. There had been a time in her life when she had wished she had a real home with doting parents and lots of friends—a long time ago. ''I think you should leave now,'' she managed to say in an even voice.

He leaned close. ''I hope you'll really think about what I said tonight.''

She looked him in the eyes and said, ''Contrary to what you believe, I do care what Amy and Shaun are feeling. Their feelings will be considered when I make my decision.''

Amy opened the screen door and stepped onto the patio, turning to Michael. ''Did you talk with her?''

''Yes, he did,'' Rachel answered.

Amy looked at Rachel. ''Well?'' she asked, her pout firmly in place.

''I haven't made any decisions and when I do, you, Shaun and I will sit down and discuss them.''

Amy stared at Rachel for a long moment, her expression hostile, intense. ''Discuss it with us? Don't you mean tell us?''

''I need to head home,'' Michael said.

''No! Please stay for dinner. Rachel has fixed one of her famous dishes. There's plenty for all of us.''

''Sorry. Not tonight.'' Michael started for the screen door.

Rachel hadn't realized she was holding her breath

until he'd declined the offer. Relief trembled through her. He aroused emotions in her that made dealing with everything else more difficult.

"Rachel?" Amy whispered. "Ask him to stay."

Rachel saw none of Amy's earlier hostility in her expression and was tempted to ask Michael to join them for dinner, but the words wouldn't come out. They lumped in her throat, her mouth dry, her palms damp. She couldn't face another moment in his presence, even to please her sister.

While he strode to the front door, Amy spun and glared at Rachel. "I thought he was a friend. Here in Magnolia Blossom we ask friends to dinner. You must do things differently where you come from."

The sound of the front door closing filled the air with renewed tension. "Amy, it's late and—"

"I'm not hungry anymore." Amy flounced into the house, banging the screen door behind her, then the front door as she left.

Rachel started to go after Amy and try to explain. But how can I explain my feelings toward Michael to my sister? I can't even explain them to myself. She sank down on the chaise longue, feeling defeated and alone.

When darkness settled around her, Rachel went inside, deciding to check on Shaun before going into the kitchen to eat an overcooked dinner. She knocked on his bedroom door, but he didn't answer. Opening the door, she glanced about the room to confirm her suspicions. Shaun was still outside.

She looked toward Amy's closed door. It boasted a new sign that read Do Not Enter. Glancing at Shaun's room, she saw total chaos—as though a hurricane had recently swept through. Silence magnified Rachel's feeling of loneliness as she walked into the living room to wait for her family's return.

Rachel sat in the darkened living room waiting for her younger brother. There was no sound of pounding sneakers to alert her to Shaun's presence. This time the sneakers were silent as he came into the house. When he was in the middle of the living room, heading for his bedroom, she switched on the lamp. Shaun froze as if he were playing a game of statue.

Rachel didn't say a word.

Suddenly her eight-year-old brother swung around and launched into his explanation. "We were playing a game of hide-and-seek and no one could find me. I had the best place *ever* to hide. I couldn't come home till the game was over."

For Shaun's sake Rachel was thankful that she'd had an hour to cool off or she would have grounded him for the rest of his life, which she realized was absolutely ridiculous. "Did you win?"

Shaun blinked, nonplussed by the question. Then he flashed Rachel one of the smiles that must have gotten him just about anything from Aunt Flora. "Sure. No one found me. Finally, they all gave up."

"Lucky for you that they gave up so soon." Rachel glanced at her watch. "Let's see. You were an hour late. I figure a fair trade-off is an hour for a week. You're grounded for the next week. I'll let you go to church as well as your baseball games and practices, but that's all. No TV. No phone calls. No friends over.'' Rachel rose and started for the kitchen to clean up her ruined meal, which still smoldered in the oven.

''But Aunt Flora didn't care if I stayed out after dark. This isn't New York. Nuthin's gonna happen to me after dark here.''

Rachel continued walking.

''That's not fair. A week! What am I gonna do in this place for a whole week? I'll die of boredom!''

Rachel pivoted. ''You should have thought about that when you were hiding. You had plenty of time to come up with some ideas.''

''Who are you to tell me what I can and can't do? You aren't my mother.'' Shaun's face reddened with anger.

Patience, she reminded herself. ''I won't argue with you, Shaun. We'll discuss who I am later.''

''But—''

Her younger brother snapped his mouth closed, then stomped off to his bedroom and slammed his door shut. First thing tomorrow morning she would go to the library in Natchez and hope there was a good book on parenting that she could check out.

The ringing of the doorbell a few seconds later made Rachel jump. When she opened the door to find Helen standing on her front porch, she was pleasantly surprised. ''How did you know I was at the end of my rope? Did you hear the doors slamming all the way downtown?''

''No, but Amy paid me a visit as I was closing up tonight.''

''Oh, she did.'' Why does my sister talk with everyone in town except me? ''I can just imagine what she had to say if you decided to come by after a long day at work.''

''I'm concerned, Rachel. I've never seen Amy so unreasonable. The whole time she was in the café she ranted and raved about what she was and wasn't gonna do. The bottom line is she won't leave Magnolia Blossom.'' Helen's smile was sad as she continued. ''That was said as she stormed out of the café without letting me finish a sentence, which is very hard to do.''

''Where did she go?''

''She didn't say.''

Rachel clenched her teeth. ''She thinks she can come and go as she pleases without saying anything to me. I have no idea where she is or what time she'll be home. Surely Aunt Flora didn't let Shaun and Amy do this.''

''No, but then Flora never threatened their security.''

''You think I should give up everything and stay here?'' Wasn't it enough that she had agreed to take care of her brother and sister? Did she have to give up everything?

''It would be easier for Amy and Shaun in the short

run. I can't answer beyond that, nor can I tell you what's best for you, sugar. That's your decision.''

''I feel like I've been cast in the role of an ogre.''

Helen rolled her shoulders. ''I'd better be going or I'll be worthless tomorrow.'' At the front door, she turned and hugged Rachel. ''Sugar, would staying here for a year be too much? You could open a restaurant later. Think about it.''

''Night, Helen.''

As Rachel closed the door, her anger pushed all other feelings to the side. Her life was already turned upside down with the unexpected responsibility of taking care of her sister and brother. First Michael and now Helen wanted her to forget all she'd worked for.

She went into the living room and sat on the couch to wait for Amy's return. They had to talk. But as Rachel waited, her temples throbbed with a headache. She couldn't stay in Magnolia Blossom, not even for Amy.

A persistent ringing gnawed at Rachel's dreamless sleep. All of a sudden her mind cleared, and she bolted up on the couch, snatching up the phone. ''Hello.''

''Rachel, this is Michael.''

Her hand tightened about the receiver as she glanced at the clock on the mantel. Twelve-sixteen. ''What's wrong?'' The pounding of her pulse thundered in her ears as she tried to calm the racing of her heart.

"Shaun's here with Garrett."

"What?" She rubbed her hand down her face to try to clear her groggy mind.

"On my way to bed I passed Garrett's door and heard voices. Shaun was with him."

"I'll be over in a few minutes."

"Rachel, let Shaun stay till morning. Whatever you have to say to him can wait till then. They've both finally gone to sleep."

"I'm coming. He disobeyed me." Without waiting for Michael to say anything else, Rachel slammed down the receiver, berating herself for falling asleep when she should have been alert. Maybe then Shaun wouldn't have sneaked out of the house.

She snatched her purse and started to leave when she remembered Amy. She quickly checked to see if her younger sister was home yet. When she didn't find Amy anywhere in the house, she made a mental note to get Shaun then go looking for her sister.

As Rachel hurried to her car, her thoughts churned with worry. What did Shaun think he was going to accomplish by running to Garrett's? Why couldn't he accept his punishment? Where was Amy at this hour?

When Rachel pulled into the lane that led to Michael's house, she pressed her foot down on the brake. The palms of her hands were sweaty as she stared at the two-story antebellum house ahead. She knew she couldn't barge into Michael's home and start yelling at Shaun, even though that was her first impulse.

Slowly she eased her foot off the brake, and the car crept forward. She couldn't let Shaun think he could do what he pleased. She could remember wishing her mother or father had set limits for her. Instead, they had allowed her to go anywhere she wanted with little supervision. She had often spent hours away from their temporary base, playing in the jungle or on a beach, usually alone. Her parents hadn't cared enough to ask where she'd been when she'd returned to the campsite. Rachel wasn't going to make that mistake with Amy and Shaun. They needed limits.

When she parked the car in front of Michael's house, the door swung open to reveal him standing in the entrance. ''Come in.'' He stepped aside for her to enter.

She started to demand to see Shaun, but the expression on Michael's face stopped her. The air pulsated with his anger as they stared at each other.

''Where's Shaun?'' Rachel finally asked, scanning the foyer, alarmed at how easily he could evoke strong emotions in her.

''Asleep.''

''Then I'll get him.'' She turned toward the staircase, aware that she had no idea where Garrett's bedroom was, but nothing would be accomplished staying and dealing with Michael. She still needed to handle her siblings.

As she placed her foot on the first step, Michael

grabbed her arm and swung her around. "We're going to talk first."

He dragged her toward the den and shoved her into a chair by the fireplace. Rachel couldn't believe his Neanderthal attitude. "I have nothing to say to you."

"Then listen, *really* listen for a change."

She began to rise, but when he put both hands on the arms of her chair and leaned toward her, she sank into the cushion. She felt trapped, surrounded by him. She closed her eyes, wishing she could block his image from her memory; she couldn't. She sensed his gaze drilling into her face and slowly opened her eyes, trying to remain in control.

"The only parent Shaun has really known was Flora. With her death his life has changed drastically. He doesn't understand your coming in and setting down all these rules he's not used to."

"So you think I should let him do anything he wants?" She allowed her rising anger to fight Michael's effect on her.

"No, but move slowly with him. Give him time to adjust to you."

"In the meantime he runs around town wild, going where he wants, coming in when he wants." Rachel shook her head. "A child needs rules to follow."

"Reasonable ones."

"Coming in by dark is reasonable."

"Maybe in New York City, but in Magnolia Blossom that's when all the kids his age play hide-and-seek in the park. Shaun's always been a part of that.

The kids aren't doing anything wrong. They're having fun. It sure beats them sitting around watching TV.''

"When we talked about his curfew, he never said anything about playing hide-and-seek in the park with the other kids. All he said to me was that he was going out.'' Michael's clean male scent accosted her, and she wished he would move away. She didn't want him so close, producing strange sensations inside her.

Stepping back, Michael directed the full censure of his gaze at her. "Sit down with Shaun. Talk to him. Tell him what you expect of him in concise, concrete terms.''

"What in the world do you think I've been trying to do with both Amy and Shaun—tap-dance?'' She stood with both hands planted on her waist, her anger escalating as quickly as the temperature. "It's kind of hard to talk to a person when all you see is his back as he's leaving the room.''

"Talk to or at?''

"Talking is talking!'' Her voice rose several levels. Her head began to throb again. "I ask a question, I expect a straight answer. I say something, I expect to hear something back, not a door slamming.''

"Talking to a person is more than you saying words. It's also listening to him when he's talking and letting him know you've listened, maybe by para-phrasing what he's said.''

"I know how to carry on a conversation.''

"I'm sure you do with an adult, but…''

Rachel hated to admit she had the same doubts, but

she was an intelligent woman who loved her sister and brother. Somehow she would work everything out with them.

"Will you please get Shaun for me?" She met his dark gaze with quiet dignity.

His mouth thinned into a slash. "Rachel, why is it so hard for you to accept help from another person?" He grasped her arms. "Believe it or not, I want this to work with you, Shaun and Amy. I care for those two."

All Rachel could focus on was his closeness. She wouldn't be drawn into his world again!

"Was that help you were offering me? Strange, that's not the way I heard it." Her gaze lowered to his hands still clasping her. "Please let me go."

He released her. His look flattened into a neutral expression as he pivoted and strode toward the stairs without another word.

Rachel held herself taut until Michael disappeared up the stairs. But once he was gone, the trembling started in her hands and spread like a brushfire through her. She hugged her arms to her, rubbing her hands up and down to warm her chilled body.

Rachel had little time to compose herself before Michael appeared with Shaun behind him. Shaun's pout rivaled Amy's as he came to stand in front of Rachel.

"How did you think you'd get away with this?" she asked in a tightly controlled voice.

"What did you expect me to do?" Shaun's belligerent eyes became slits as they locked with Rachel's.

"I expected more of you than this."

"Well, you're not my mother. I'm not doing what you say." He straightened as though ready to fight for what he had declared.

"No, I'm not your mother, but I'm the one taking care of you, and you'll do as I say whether you like it or not. Understand?"

"No, I'll never mind you!"

"I guess you don't think being grounded for a week is long enough."

"I hate you!" Shaun whirled and ran from the room.

Stunned by the violence in Shaun's last look, Rachel was immobile until she heard the front door slam shut. She started toward it.

"I know you're angry at Shaun right now."

She spun as fast as Shaun had seconds before. "Are you going to tell me I shouldn't be?"

"No, everyone has a right to their feelings—"

"Oh, thank you for that." She cut in.

"But I hope you'll think about postponing any further discussion concerning the night's escapade till tomorrow. Give yourself a chance to calm down. As you can see, Shaun needs it, too." One corner of Michael's mouth quirked upward. "Heaven knows, I learned that the hard way. I've said things to Garrett that I've regretted after I had time to think things through."

His half smile affected her senses. For a few seconds she felt as if they had something in common. A strong urge to seek comfort in his arms swamped her. It took all her willpower to stay where she was. She had agreed to be her sister's and brother's guardian and suddenly she realized how ill-equipped she was for that role. Would it be so difficult to ask for help?

"Let me talk to Shaun," Michael said as he walked past her, then stopped.

For an instant Rachel saw regret in his eyes. She blinked, trying to understand the look he was giving her, but as quickly as it appeared it vanished. He continued toward the front door, leaving Rachel alone to gather her composure.

Her life was not in Magnolia Blossom. It was that simple and that complicated. Even if she didn't get the backing for her restaurant, she had every intention of going to New York at the end of the summer. She would give her sister and brother time to adjust to her as their guardian, then close up the house here. She had been crazy to consider staying in this small town where everyone knew everyone.

When she went out, she saw Michael talking to Shaun near her car. Their murmuring voices drifted to her on the jasmine-scented air, but she couldn't make out what they were saying.

As Rachel approached the pair, Shaun looked at her, hostility still apparent in his expression. He mumbled something to Michael, then rounded the front of the car to climb in on the passenger's side.

Rachel faced Michael, uncertain what to say or do. Her inadequacies concerning Shaun filled her with fear. She didn't want to fail with Shaun or Amy. She didn't want them to grow up feeling as she had, unloved, unwanted, frightened to get close to anyone.

"Rachel, just as adults say things they don't mean, so can kids when they are angry or scared. Please give both of you some time to cool off before you decide what you're going to do about tonight. Find out why he stayed out."

"Isn't that obvious? He wanted to defy me."

"I'd rather his reason come from him."

An overwhelming desire to be held by Michael inundated her. If only she could drop her defenses for a while. Because he was standing in front of her waiting for her to say something, she murmured, "I'd better go," but she didn't move toward her car door.

She stared into Michael's face, illuminated by the light from the veranda. Lifting her hand slowly, she touched the cleft in his chin.

Clasping her hand, he stilled the movement.

"It's late. I really should go."

"Uh-huh." He bent his head toward hers.

Chapter Three

The blare of the car horn parted them instantly. Rachel jerked away from Michael. She quickly opened the door, murmuring goodbye, a flush heating her cheeks. Safely in the car with her sanity restored, she was thankful that Shaun had sounded the horn.

On the ride to the house silence dominated the confines of the car. Rachel thought about what Michael had said about waiting to talk to Shaun. Her first impulse was to get it over with and move on, but maybe Michael knew what he was talking about. He *had* been a father for the past seven years.

Rachel entered the house and tossed her purse on the table in the entryway. ''We'll talk about this in the morning after we've both gotten a good night's sleep.'' She slanted a look toward Shaun, who had his arms folded over his chest and a frown on his face.

"Why don't you just get it over with now? You're gonna ground me anyway."

"Frankly, Shaun, I don't know what I'm going to do until I've had time to cool off and listen to your side."

When a puzzled look replaced the anger in Shaun's expression, Rachel knew Michael was right about waiting. For the first time, she felt she had a chance with Shaun.

As Rachel watched her younger brother walk toward his bedroom, she caught sight of Amy's door. She started for her sister's bedroom but stopped when she heard a car pull into the driveway. Rachel stood in the entry hall, trying to remain calm as Amy let herself into the house.

All her good intentions fled when Rachel saw Amy's defiant look. "It's almost two in the morning. Where have you been?"

"Around." Amy began to walk past Rachel.

Rachel grabbed her arm to stop her. "I won't have you going out at night without telling me where you're going."

Amy shook loose. "I'm not Shaun. I'll be seventeen in a few weeks and can do what I want."

"When you're on your own, you can do what you want. Until then you live by my rules."

"And what if I don't?"

"I want the keys to Aunt Flora's car." Rachel held out her hand.

For a tension-fraught moment Amy stared at Rachel before shoving the keys into her hand.

"You'll get these back when you're willing to follow a few simple rules. I want to know where you're going. You'll be in this house by twelve. I'm responsible for you and Shaun now."

"I didn't ask you to be. I can take care of myself." Fury filled Amy's eyes. "Why don't you leave us alone like everyone else has?"

Before Rachel could reply, Amy whirled, ran to her bedroom and shut the door. Rachel stood for a few seconds, shocked by her sister's words, spoken in anger but suffused with pain.

The sound of Amy locking her door propelled Rachel forward. She knocked on her sister's bedroom door. "Amy, we need to talk. Please let me in."

For the longest moment Amy said nothing, then finally she shouted, "I want to be left alone. I don't need you or anyone else."

How many times had she said those very words? Leaning against the wall, Rachel trembled at the intensity of emotions coursing through her. Listening to Amy, Rachel felt as if she had traveled back in time and was reliving the pain of being left in Magnolia Blossom by her parents.

Michael stared at the large white sign that proclaimed June eighth Founders Day in Magnolia Blossom. It had been over a week since he'd talked to Rachel, but in that time he hadn't been able to get her out of his mind. *Lord, why did she have to come back to Magnolia Blossom?* Everything had been all right as long as he thought he'd never see her again. He didn't want her in his life, even temporarily. He didn't need that kind of reminder of what could have been.

Michael searched the field where the townspeople were setting up the tables for the annual picnic and found his son talking with a friend. Garrett looked at him and waved. The heaviness in Michael's chest increased when he remembered the phone call he'd received. His ex-wife had walked out on him and Garrett years before, declaring she wasn't ready to be a mother, that she needed to pull her life together— without them. Now she wanted to share custody of their son after all these years. He felt the edges of his life coming apart.

Heavenly Father, give me the strength to deal with this new problem. I've been there for my son from the beginning. Give me the knowledge to follow Your path in all things.

Garrett raced up to Michael, coming to an abrupt stop inches in front of him. "Dad, have you seen Shaun? We're supposed to practice for the game."

"No. They haven't arrived yet."

"Are ya sure?"

"Yes." Because I've been looking for Rachel ever since I came.

"We're gonna beat the pants off you grown-ups today."

"Wanna make a little bet on that?"

"Yeah. I don't have to do the dishes for a week if y'all lose."

"And when *you* lose, you have to keep your room clean for a week. Nothing shoved under the bed. Deal?"

Grinning, Garrett shook his father's hand. Perplexed, Michael frowned as he watched his son join a group of children and head for the river. He had the feeling Garrett knew something concerning the annual softball game between the kids and the grown-ups, something that swung the odds in the kids' favor.

"I need your help," Helen said, scurrying to Michael. "Max is sick and won't be able to coach our team. Not only is he the best coach we've had but our best player, too."

Michael chuckled. So that was it. Garrett knew about Max because Max's son hung out with Garrett and Shaun. "What do you want me to do?" He had a clean room at stake and had no wish to lose the bet with his son.

"Will you be the coach?"

All except that. "I don't think—"

"C'mon, Michael."

"Why don't you do it?"

"Remember three years ago when I did? Afterward, the town council banned me from ever filling that position again."

"Oh," Michael murmured, recalling the free-for-all during the fourth inning between Helen and one of the base runners who didn't follow the right signal. "If I accept, will I get combat pay?"

"I'll give you one of my pecan pies to take home."

"Two."

"Two it is." Helen lowered her voice and leaned closer. "I do have a few tidbits for you." She began to tell Michael where to put everyone on the team, what the batting order should be and what each player's strengths and weaknesses were.

After ten minutes of listening to Helen, Michael laughed. "Helen, isn't this game for fun?"

"Fun? No way! Not when we're playing the *children*." She stressed the word *children* as if that explained everything.

No wonder she was banned from being the team's coach, Michael thought as Helen marched off to help prepare the food.

"My boy, you're braver than I thought," Robert Davenport said as he approached Michael and clapped him on the back.

"I guess we all have our moments of insanity. This is one of mine," Michael replied while scanning the crowd for Rachel. Speaking of insanity, why couldn't he get Rachel Peters out of his mind? When she'd left Magnolia Blossom ten years before, he had wiped her from his mind out of necessity. Now all of a sudden he couldn't stop thinking about the woman.

"Michael, someone approached me about your riverboat again."

"I want to back off from selling the boat right now.

I've been reminded how important roots are. That riverboat is part of my family heritage.'' Michael plowed his hand through his brown hair, his gaze tracking Rachel as she walked toward the food tables. ''I've been kicking around an idea lately. What if I fixed the boat up for short cruises on the river? It could have a restaurant that served lunch and dinner.''

Robert looked in the direction Michael was staring. ''You'll need someone to help you with the restaurant. Have anyone in mind?''

Michael furrowed his brow. ''Do you?''

''We both know that Rachel would be perfect as a consultant. Of course, I get the feeling she's just biding her time until she leaves for New York.''

The mention of New York produced a stab of pain in Michael's chest, reminding him again of what had happened ten years before. ''It would keep her here for a while. That would help Shaun and Amy adjust to her.''

''You'd have to work closely with her. Could you?''

What would his life have been like if Rachel had stayed in Magnolia Blossom and married him? Lately he'd asked himself that question, but as before he was determined not to pursue the answer. She was out of his system, and he intended to keep it that way.

''I don't know, Robert.'' Michael didn't know if he could work closely with Rachel knowing in the end she would walk away. His frown deepened. Again he tunneled his fingers through his hair in frustration while he glanced toward her. "It was just a thought. I haven't made up my mind yet."

Rachel placed her potato salad on the long table with the other food for the picnic. She hadn't been to this type of affair since she had lived here. When she looked up from inspecting the feast, she caught sight of Shaun racing toward the river. Since the night her younger brother had run away, their relationship had improved. She'd taken Michael's advice and listened to her brother's side. When she'd discovered that some of the older boys had taunted Shaun for having to come in early, she could understand why he had disobeyed her.

She could even understand why he had run away after she'd handed out what he considered an unreasonable punishment. She hadn't retracted the week's grounding, but she hadn't added to it, either. She still had a long way to go with Shaun, but he was more willing to talk to her now.

With thoughts of Michael weaving through her mind, Rachel found herself searching for him in the crowd. When her gaze settled on him, her heart missed a beat. Across the short distance she watched as Michael raked his hand through his hair, then massaged the back of his neck, gestures he used when he was upset. Frowning, he stared at the river for a long moment, then made his way toward the path that ran along the Mississippi.

Something's wrong. Rachel didn't think about the

wisdom of following; she just did. She didn't like to see that vulnerable look in his expression.

As she hurried along the path, she wondered where Michael had disappeared. Rounding a bend in the trail, she collided with him and instantly backed away, her eyes wide with surprise.

"I'm sorry. I didn't see—"

"That's okay. I'm sure this trail is big enough for the both of us. I'll go this way. You go that way." He pointed in the opposite direction.

When he began to move past her, Rachel touched his arm. "Let's walk together."

One eyebrow rose. "Together? Has the heat finally gotten to you?"

Rachel laughed. "No. I came looking for you."

"Why?"

"I think it's time we talk."

"Why?"

"Because of what happened between us ten years ago. Because you know my sister and brother so well. Because I think you need to talk right now." That vulnerability she had glimpsed earlier flashed into his eyes, and she didn't wait for him to say anything. She took his hand and began walking along the path.

At the first lookout point on the path Michael stopped and gently tugged his hand from hers. "Rachel, I think it would be best if we went our separate ways. We hurt each other once, and I personally don't want to go through that again."

"Don't you mean I hurt you?"

He shook his head. "Lately, I've been thinking. I can see now that I demanded a commitment when you weren't ready to give one."

"We wanted two different things in life, Michael. I knew how important Whispering Oaks and Magnolia Blossom were to you, that you wouldn't want to leave them. And I couldn't stay." Rachel clasped his hand, marveling at the strong, warm feel beneath her fingers. "What happened is over, but we shouldn't let it stand between us now."

Again, he removed his hand from hers and strode to the edge of the bluff. "Let bygones be bygones?"

She joined him near the edge. "Exactly. We were best friends once."

"Before we started dating." He glanced at her. A smile touched the corners of his mouth.

She stared at him, memories tumbling through her mind. Vivid pictures of them together pushed all else from her thoughts. The remembered feel of his chiseled cheekbones and roughly hewn features beneath her hands produced tingling sensations in her fingertips as if she were running them over a piece of warm granite. His slow smile touched a part of her that she held in reserve. She was completely lost in the moment, the ten years that stood between them crumbling to dust.

"You want to be friends again?" Michael asked.

That was the only thing possible between them now, Rachel acknowledged to herself, and yet she couldn't quite let go of the intense emotions that had gone beyond friendship. She tried to inject some humor into her voice as she replied. "Well, at least not enemies. Amy and Shaun think the world of you. We should be on speaking terms for the children's sake." Her sentences were rattled off in rapid fire. She felt pulled toward him like the river toward the delta, her actions beyond her control.

"Only for their sake?" His gaze probed hers, stripping away the years of separation.

Disconcerted, Rachel turned away and tugged a leaf off a bush, crushing it in her hand, its fresh scent wafting to her. "No. For mine, too. I've got enough problems facing me here in Magnolia Blossom. I can't handle this tension between us, too. I need a friend." She had never admitted needing a friend to another person. Surprisingly, the admission came as a relief.

Michael placed a hand on her shoulder and kneaded her tensed muscles. "Amy and Shaun can be a handful."

Rachel laughed shakily, wanting desperately to lean back against him, but she'd walked away from having that right years ago. Instead, she stood stiffly in front of him. "That's the understatement of the year. It wasn't that long ago that I was Amy's age, and yet I feel so much older."

"She's extremely precocious and determined to have her way. She reminds me of someone else I knew years ago."

Her eyes closed as his hands continued to massage

the taut muscles of her shoulders and neck. She wanted to give in to the delicious sensations flowing through her but realized she shouldn't, couldn't. Calling on a willpower that had helped her to succeed in a tough profession, she stepped away from Michael's entrancing caresses and turned toward the river as though she had never seen the Mississippi and was enthralled with its discovery.

"And Shaun. He's another story. I haven't been around my younger brother much, and even though we're talking, I don't know if I'm getting through. He's such a—" No words of description materialized as she thought over the past two weeks with Shaun.

"A dynamo."

"Yes! If we could tap into his energy source, we could light half of Mississippi."

Michael's chuckle was low and warm like the night air in the summertime. "Shaun could talk Flora out of anything. In fact, he can talk just about anyone into doing what he wants."

"I can certainly vouch for that. There have been a few occasions I shouldn't have given in to him. He's a future con artist who definitely needs limits set for him."

"Rachel, it'll take time, but you can reach both of them. Your heart's in the right place."

She slanted a look toward him, their gazes embracing. When she saw the tenderness in his dark eyes, her throat contracted. She'd had so little tenderness in her life, a life she had purposefully chosen for herself, she realized. But sometimes it was difficult trying to be so tough and strong.

"Do your parents know what's happened to Flora?"

Rachel went rigid as if she had been hit and was bracing herself for another blow. "I've been trying to get ahold of my parents. Communications between here and the Amazon jungle aren't the best."

"But you haven't heard from them?"

"No. They're probably out stalking some rare tropical plant and haven't returned to their base camp yet." Again Rachel was making excuses for her parents. Part of her was angry that she felt she had to. "They'll get in touch when they can," she added with more conviction than she felt.

Rachel had often wondered why they had bothered to have children in the first place. Neither her father nor her mother had been able to answer her satisfactorily. Eventually her parents would contact her about Amy and Shaun when they got the news about Aunt Flora. But she knew the outcome of that conversation. Even if they wanted to take Amy and Shaun, she knew that wasn't the best solution for her sister and brother. Her parents' living conditions were primitive and temporary. Amy and Shaun needed more stability than that, so the alternative was for her to take care of them. Even Aunt Flora had known that was the best solution. She had left money and provisions in her will for Rachel to take care of her younger brother and sister. Rachel wondered if her parents and aunt had discussed this at one time.

For a few minutes Rachel watched as a barge passed on the river below. She'd seen her mother a few years back when she'd been speaking at a conference in New York, and they had eaten dinner together. In the past four years Rachel had shared three hours of her mother's time. Why was saving mankind more important than her own children? Couldn't someone else do it for a while? Rachel had wanted to ask her mother those questions at dinner that evening. She hadn't. The conversation had been polite and insignificant, ending with a stiff hug reserved more for an acquaintance than a daughter.

"Rachel, are you all right?"

She swung around, pasting a bright, false smile on her face. "Of course, I am. I was just thinking about the softball game this afternoon."

Michael touched her arm, his hand sliding down to grasp hers. "It's okay to admit you aren't all right. You never talked much about your parents. I'm a good listener."

"I'm fine. Really," she quickly said. "Tell you a secret, though." She leaned closer, immediately realizing her mistake when her senses were deluged with his outdoor woodsy scent. She pulled back and whispered loudly, "I forgot how unbearably hot it can get here in the summertime. Since I've been here I've taken more naps in the afternoon than I have in the ten years since I've been gone. Come three o'clock I may just curl up in the bleachers and miss seeing the big event.''

''You aren't playing?''

''Me! I wouldn't fit in. I haven't played in ten years. Surely the coach isn't counting on me.''

''Not anymore.''

Rachel laughed. ''You're the one Helen duped—I mean, talked into being the coach.''

''Afraid so.''

''What persuaded you? I hear it's a thankless job.''

''Someone has to do it.''

''So you did it out of the goodness of your heart?''

''Yep.''

Mischief prompted her to say, ''Liar. She told me she was going to entice the lucky person with one of her pecan pies.''

''Two.''

''Oh, you are a shrewd bargainer. No one else in town would do it for less than four of them.''

''I did it for the team.''

''And not for your sweet tooth?''

''Well, that and to keep the peace.''

Rachel shook her head. ''Remember the time I baked you a three-layer German chocolate cake to get you to take me to New Orleans? You didn't want to go, but after eating the cake, you took me.''

''That's what I wanted you to think so I could get one of your cakes.''

''Oh, Michael Hunter! You may never get another cake from me again.'' Snapping her fingers, Rachel smiled. "Okay, how about that time I wanted to go to that new restaurant in Natchez?"

He grinned.

"The concert in Jackson?"

"That group was one of my favorites."

"I never thought you could be so devious. I can't let you get away with that."

"You can't?" A look of pure playfulness was in his eyes as he began to stalk her. She took one step back then another.

"I should have realized that when I saw one of their albums at your house. A friend's indeed." She chattered, her nerve endings quivering as she tried to push past him.

He blocked her escape, pinning her against the trunk of a live oak, the Spanish moss hanging on its branches concealing them from the world in a green drape. "You enjoyed trying to manipulate me. I just let you think you were and I got to satisfy my sweet tooth, too." His gaze snared hers as he bent closer. "Admit it. It was a game we both enjoyed playing," he murmured, his voice low, smoky.

She nodded once, trapped in a world where only she and Michael existed. She was seventeen again, he nineteen, and they had just discovered they were more than best friends. The kiss that had produced that revelation was still engraved in her thoughts.

Slowly, reverently Michael touched her throat. His eyes locked with hers. "We played a lot of games, you and I. I was always trying to discover what made you tick and never quite succeeding.'' He dropped his hand from her throat, his eyes clouding with bitter-sweet memories.

Rachel watched myriad emotions cross his face as he shoved himself away from the tree trunk, distancing himself physically and emotionally from her. He was different from the young man she'd fallen in love with. She was different, too. She didn't know this man before her. They were strangers with a shared past. It was a mistake to think she could afford to become his friend again. She stepped from underneath the hanging moss. In the end she would leave him behind as she had all the other people before him.

As she stared at Michael's back, she didn't know if she could handle the next several months without some help. Whether she liked it or not, she needed Michael. Having decided she had to take the risk, Rachel approached Michael and laid her hand on his arm.

''I don't want to play games, either. I'd be kidding you and myself if I said I belonged in Magnolia Blossom, Michael. I have a business proposition before a group of investors. If they give me the go-ahead, I'll be opening my own restaurant in New York. I'll be gone by fall, but until then I need someone to talk to about Amy and Shaun. I'm out of my element with them.''

He glanced over his shoulder and smiled, a sadness in his eyes. ''I wondered when you'd quit pretending you might stay in Magnolia Blossom.''

"Over the past two weeks I've been going back and forth on what I would do if my business proposal didn't work out. I've allowed myself to feel guilty about wanting to take my sister and brother and leave. Not anymore. You've made me see that. I have to look at what's best for everyone concerned, not in the short run but the long run. Leaving won't be easy for them, but people move around all the time."

"When are you going to tell them?"

"I want them to get to know me before we discuss leaving town."

"Don't keep this a secret from them. They have a right to know, Rachel, as soon as possible."

"You won't say anything until I tell them?"

"No, but you're wrong to keep it from them."

"Amy had a fit about the call to New York concerning schools. She's still not talking to me. If I say anything now to them about leaving, they'll close their minds completely to me, and I won't have a chance of making us a family."

"Is that what you're trying to do?"

"Yes, of course." Tension began to throb in her temples. Everything about her future, the children's futures, was so up in the air. She couldn't put anything into a neat, little package as was her custom.

"The longer you stay here and not say anything, the more they will think you aren't going to leave. You'll be giving them false hope."

"If they shut me out, I'll never be able to convince

them there are advantages to leaving Magnolia Blossom.''

''What?''

''The world has so much to offer. They can make friends at their new schools. We can travel as a family during the summers and holidays. They'll be able to see so many new things. I'll be able to open up a whole other life for them.''

''When? Running a restaurant will require a lot of your time. Besides, is traveling, seeing the world what's best for them or you?''

''For all of us.'' She fired the words back, the tension in her head intensifying. ''At the moment, Michael, I'm all they have.''

''They're involved in their church, this town. It won't be easy.''

''Since when have I taken the easy route?''

His hard gaze bored into her as though trying to read what was deep in her thoughts. ''I think we'd better head back.''

Rachel needed the conversation to end on a light note. Every time she and Michael had been together since she'd returned they had argued. She attempted a smile she didn't feel and said, ''Maybe if we stay out here long enough, Helen will recruit another coach.''

''And lose my pecan pies! Never!'' He started down the path toward the field. ''You know I probably should have demanded those pies in advance. I may not be in any condition to accept them afterward.

Thank goodness they've outlawed tarring and feathering.''

"It's been ages since I had a piece of Helen's pecan pie. I'm sure you'll want to share it.'' Rachel snapped her fingers. "I've got it. Why don't you bring both pies over after the fireworks later tonight for some coffee and dessert? I'll supply the coffee.'' There was a part of her that was amazed she had asked him to the house, but the other part of her needed his help with her sister and brother.

Michael hesitated.

"I could use your help with Amy,'' Rachel added. She didn't want to spend another evening warring with her sister. Founders Day was a time for family in Magnolia Blossom, and she was determined to observe it with her siblings even if that meant having Michael as a referee.

"Okay, I'll share the pies. After all, you'll be contributing to the adult team.''

"How?'' she asked, relief evident in her voice. Finding reasons to be around Michael wasn't the wisest thing. Surely if she looked hard enough, she could find someone else to help her with her brother and sister. But Michael knew what a family should really be. She'd always prided herself on seeking out the best advice and listening. That was the only reason she'd asked Michael over after the fireworks. Yeah, right, and the moon was made of cheese.

"You're refusing to play.''

"I should be offended.''

"I remember how you used to play."

"Now I *know* I'm offended." She frowned with a gleam in her eyes.

"Sports were never your forte, Rachel. You think a strike is something a union does when it wants more money."

"Well, it is."

Michael shook his head. "You're hopeless. When I tried to educate you, I almost lost my mind. I don't make a mistake more than once."

She heard the warning in his voice but chose to ignore it. She didn't want there to be any tension between them. "Are you going to hold that Atlanta Braves game over my head forever?"

"At least this time you got the name of the team correct."

"I was the chef for a party the owner had for the team. I had to learn real quick."

"Then there's hope for you, after all."

"I know that a player is out if he gets three strikes. I read up on the game when I found out I was going to do that party. I didn't want anyone asking questions I couldn't answer." Rachel was glad that Michael had picked up on her playful tone. "These games used to be fun. Since arriving here this morning, I get the distinct impression I'll be entering a war zone. What happened?"

"Helen took over."

"Oh." Rachel laughed. "I see now. Helen's one of the most competitive people I know."

"You're probably the wisest person in Magnolia Blossom today."

"How come?"

"'Cause you wouldn't allow Helen to rope you into being a part of the team."

A part of the team. Sometimes she had a hard time putting into words why she couldn't put down roots, was afraid to commit herself to anything that seemed permanent. This restaurant proposal was the first thing she had considered that would require her to stay in one place for any length of time. Maybe after ten years—no, twenty-eight years—she was tired of living a nomadic life. But never in her wildest dreams had she considered returning to Magnolia Blossom. The town was too small and too emotionally demanding. She had made her choice years before, and she was determined not to let herself become a part of this town—or a part of Michael's life.

Chapter Four

Rachel spread the blanket on the bluff that over-looked the river. Dusk settled around her as she waited for the fireworks display to begin and for her family to join her. The warm breeze, perfumed with the scent of mowed grass, caressed her face. The sound of the insects vied with the murmurs of people's voices as they prepared for the evening's activity. She closed her eyes and enjoyed the tranquillity.

"You won't believe that neighbor of yours." Helen plopped down on the blanket next to Rachel. "I went by your house to leave you your very own pecan pie and he almost ran me down with that big, gas-guzzling car of his."

"Who?"

"Harold Moon, who else?" Helen drew a quick breath and continued, "And when he almost backed into me, he didn't even bother to say excuse me or anything. He just drove away. Actually, he burned rubber like he was angry that I was in the street in *his* way. I should be the angry one.''

''Maybe he didn't see you.''

Helen gave her an exasperated look. ''Not see me? Who are you kidding? I like my own cooking. You would have to be blind not to see me.'' She scanned the area. ''Where is everyone?''

Glancing over her shoulder, Rachel saw Amy and her boyfriend, Kevin, strolling toward them holding hands. She indicated their approach with a toss of her head. Amy was paying close attention to something Kevin was saying, a look of rapture on her face. She was too young to be serious about a boy. She had too much to see and do before she settled down. Rachel was determined to make Amy see there was more to life than Kevin and Magnolia Blossom.

''Ah, and I see Shaun, Garrett and Michael coming, too,'' Helen announced as Amy and Kevin smoothed their blanket next to Rachel's and sat, Amy smiling at Helen but ignoring Rachel.

Rachel hadn't meant to search the people beginning to populate the bluff, but she did and immediately found Michael among the crowd. Sometimes she wondered if she didn't have a sixth sense when it came to him. There had been a connection from the first time she had seen him on the riverboat. It was powerful, compelling—frightening.

Dark shadows spread along the ground as Michael settled himself next to Rachel, stretched his long legs out in front of him and leaned back on his elbows. "Good evening, ladies. A perfect night for fireworks, don't you think?"

"Sugar, it's a perfect night for much more than fireworks."

"I do believe, Helen, you might be right about that," Michael said, his drawl more pronounced than usual. His glance strayed to Rachel, and he winked.

His impish grin generated a warmth in the pit of Rachel's stomach that expanded outward. She was remembering the night they'd spent on this very bluff— the night he'd told her he wanted to marry her. She'd left Magnolia Blossom one week later when she'd received the offer from the cooking school in Paris.

Rachel was thankful when the fireworks began. A spray of red and green streamed across the heavens like rubies and emeralds scattered across black velvet. Then another spray exploded above them.

The light from the display cast Michael's profile in golden splendor. He turned slightly, and his gaze seized hers for a long moment. The breath in Rachel's lungs caught and held while she was trapped in his look. Gone from his expression was any merriment. In its place was seriousness as though he, too, remembered that night when he'd given her his heart and she'd stomped on it.

She looked away as myriad colors splashed the darkness. Michael rose and walked away. She chanced a look and saw him stop by the line of trees where the cars were parked. He leaned against his truck with his arms and legs crossed while the fireworks continued to light up the night sky. His regard was riveted to her.

She strode toward him. They had to talk about that long-ago evening on the bluff, or it would be there between them anytime they were together. She needed to explain why she'd run away.

She halted in front of Michael. Words dried in her throat as she stared into his eyes. The hard set of his jaw and the tautness of his shoulders attested to his feelings.

"Remember the last time we were here?" he finally asked.

"I don't like to look backward." She knew it wasn't enough. The fireworks continued exploding above her. "My only defense is that I'm not good at relationships, Michael." She didn't explain herself often and had a hard time doing it now, but this was important. If they were going to be friends while she was in Magnolia Blossom she had to make him understand. "I never have been. I gave up after my fifth move as a child. It hurt too much leaving behind people I cared about."

"I'd hoped once that you would trust your feelings concerning us, or trust me at least. I'd hoped you could forget your past. You didn't have to leave me behind."

"Yes, I did. You weren't going to leave Magnolia Blossom for Paris. I had to see if I could do what I had dreamed about for years. You were already doing what you dreamed about. Your roots and soul were planted here in Mississippi."

"I would have waited if you'd asked."

"You didn't mourn me long, Michael. You have Garrett as proof that your life went on. He's nearly eight years old. I can add."

"Ah, so that's what's bothering you."

"No—yes. It didn't take you long to find someone else. Garrett was born a few years after I left." Rachel hadn't meant for the hurt to seep into her voice, but she heard it and knew that Michael did, too. She could remember the pain that pierced her heart when Aunt Flora had broken the news of Michael's marriage. Until that moment, she'd thought about giving everything up and returning to Magnolia Blossom and Michael.

He shrugged. "Think what you like. The bottom line is that it didn't work out between us ten years ago. I don't like to dwell in the past any more than you do. My future is Garrett and, yes, Magnolia Blossom. That hasn't changed. You're right about my roots being sunk deep in the soil of this place."

"Where does that leave us?"

"There is no us. We both agreed on that."

"Michael, if being friends is too difficult for you, then you don't need to feel obligated."

The final burst of fireworks lit the sky with a brilliance that made it appear as if the sun had risen. "I want to help with Amy and Shaun. I care about them. They have been a part of my life for a long time."

She wasn't alone in her battle. "Thank you."

"Don't thank me yet. I'm not worried about Shaun. He'll adjust wherever he is. Amy is a whole different story. I'm not sure she's going to listen to anyone, including me. She's bound and determined to remain here. No telling what she's going to do. She doesn't have wanderlust in her blood like you do, Rachel."

"It's not a disease," she retorted, pulling herself straighter. "Not everyone is like you."

"And not everyone is like you," he countered instantly, pushing himself away from the bumper of the truck and standing a few inches in front of her.

Her heart responded to his nearness by speeding up. She swallowed several times and stepped back to a safe distance, where she didn't feel surrounded by him. "Touché. We agree that we are very different from each other."

"Are we?"

She heard the amusement return to his voice as he moved around her and started toward his son. She whirled and watched him walk to Garrett and tousle his hair, then hug him. The love between father and son was so evident it touched a place in Rachel's heart she didn't think anything could affect. Garrett was lucky to have a parent like Michael.

Pain buried long ago oozed to the surface. Clutching her arms to her stomach, she pressed inward, resolved not to let the tears flow. She didn't cry anymore, had stopped doing that long before she had come to Magnolia Blossom to live with her aunt.

She swallowed the lump in her throat and straightened. She depended on no one, and having to depend on Michael for help was leaving her feeling vulnerable. As soon as she was able to leave Magnolia Blossom and get on with her life, everything would be all right. But first she had to win her sister and brother to her side.

She started for the group and arrived by Helen's side in time to hear Amy mutter, "I'm not going to the house."

"That's too bad, Amy. I was counting on you showing me that new CD you told me about." Michael reached down, scooped up his blanket and began folding it.

"You're coming to the house?"

"Who do you think is supplying the pecan pies? I worked hard for those pies and I don't share them with just anyone."

Amy glanced at Kevin, who nodded. "Well, since Helen made them, I guess I could have one piece."

Helen helped Rachel shake out her blanket, then fold it. "I love hearing people talk about my pies like that."

"Why don't you come over, too?" Rachel asked, realizing that if Helen was there Rachel would never have to be alone with Michael.

"It's been a long day. Winning is exhausting. This is your party. Enjoy. I'm going home to bed and dream of our victory." Grinning as though she had a secret, Helen waved goodbye and strode toward her car.

Rachel fought the urge to run after Helen and beg her to come to the house. Rachel suspected her friend was up to her old matchmaking tricks.

''I want to ride with Garrett. Can I? Can I?'' Shaun asked, hopping from one foot to the other as though he had so much energy he could barely contain it.

''If it's okay with Michael,'' Rachel answered, longingly watching Helen as she drove away.

''Sure. We'll follow you to your house.''

With the plans settled, Rachel headed for her car, aware that Michael and the boys were right behind her. She felt self-conscious as she walked. Even though it was dark, she sensed Michael staring at her. Relieved when she slid into her sedan, she started it and backed out of her parking space.

She had a few minutes to compose herself before she had to entertain Michael. She looked in the rear-view mirror and saw his headlights. Her palms were sweaty, and she rubbed first one then the other on her jeans. She was more nervous tonight than when she'd started dating Michael ten years before.

Once inside her house she quickly took the pies from Michael and prepared the coffee. ''Anyone want vanilla ice cream with their piece?'' she asked. The group sat in the living room, silent, staring at each other.

Shaun and Garrett said yes. Kevin declined, and Amy remained quiet. Deciding her sister's answer was a no, Rachel looked toward Michael. She wished she could accept his help without being in the same room with him.

He smiled, the corners of his eyes crinkling. "Pecan pie was invented specifically for vanilla ice cream. I'll help you."

That was not the kind of assistance she'd wanted. "Fine," she murmured when she couldn't think of a reason to refuse him.

Her hand quivered as she cut the pie. The kitchen was too small for her and Michael, the air charged with a finely honed tension that had nothing to do with Amy. Perspiration beaded on her forehead. She attempted to scoop some ice cream, but ended up bending the spoon, which clanged to the countertop. The sound seemed to echo through the kitchen.

"Here, let me try." Michael took another spoon from the drawer and ran it under hot water, then dipped it into the frozen dessert.

Rachel flushed. She knew better. She was letting him get to her—again. "I wish I had my utensils and equipment here. I didn't think to bring them. This wouldn't have been a problem."

"Do you travel with your own cooking utensils?"

"Yes."

"Then why didn't you bring them?"

"Because—" She hesitated, not wanting to voice her reason.

"Because you didn't think you would be here long?"

"Right. But Shaun and Amy's opinions made me reassess the situation."

Michael didn't say another word. His mouth firmed into a hard slash as he worked to get the ice cream out. After completing the preparations, he handed her two plates to take into the living room while he took the rest.

After the dessert was served to everyone, along with coffee or milk, Rachel sat on the couch next to Michael, the only empty place left in the living room. No one spoke while they ate, and she was glad for the reprieve while she collected herself.

"Now that school is out, Amy, what are your plans for this summer?" Michael asked as he placed his mug on a coaster on the coffee table.

Her sister shot Rachel a withering look. "That all depends on where I'll be. Why plan anything if we aren't gonna be here?"

"You'll be here." Rachel raised her mug to her lips, hoping the action would keep her from having to say anything further.

"Helen wants me to work at Southern Delight again."

"How about the summer arts program in Natchez?" Michael asked as he brought the last of his piece of pie to his mouth.

Amy shrugged. "I don't know if I'm gonna do it."

"What's that?" Rachel asked, again reminded she really didn't know her brother and sister very well.

Michael turned to her. "Amy is a gifted actress.

For the past two summers she has gone through the program to hone her skills. Students from all over Mississippi attend for three weeks in July. Last summer they did *The Diary of Anne Frank* at the end of the session. Amy played the lead role.''

''I didn't realize. You should do it, Amy,'' Rachel said, wanting to encourage her sister.

''Why? What difference does it make?''

''It's an honor to be invited to attend.'' Michael took a sip of his coffee. ''Besides, I look forward to seeing you up on the stage again.''

Amy stared at her hands, which were folded in her lap, and mumbled, ''I'll think about it.''

''The theater is one of the things I love about New York. You can't get any better than Broadway.'' Rachel finished her coffee, satisfied that at least her sister was talking.

Amy's head shot up, and she speared Rachel with a look that was meant to freeze. ''I want to go to Hollywood. That's where *everyone* goes, not New York.''

Rachel realized mentioning New York had been a mistake. Amy seemed to think Rachel had thrown down the gauntlet. Her sister was determined to find fault with the city no matter what.

Amy bolted to her feet. ''Just because I've done some work on the stage doesn't mean I want to leave Magnolia Blossom. Everything I want is here. Come on, Kevin. We're late to meet the rest of the gang.''

''You need to be back by twelve,'' Rachel called

as Amy stalked to the front door with Kevin following her.

Amy jerked open the door while Kevin said, "I'll have her home by then."

After the couple left, quiet reigned for a few minutes in the living room while the two boys finished their pie and Michael drained his coffee. Rachel stood to take the empty plates into the kitchen. Tension knotted her stomach. She didn't think she would ever get used to these skirmishes between her and Amy.

"Can I go outside and play flashlight tag in the park?" Shaun jumped to his feet with a hopeful look on his face.

"Can Shaun spend the night?" Garrett asked, leaping out of his chair with the same hopeful expression.

"That's okay with me if Rachel says it's okay."

"Sure." She drew in a deep breath to calm herself. Every time she was around Amy she was left feeling wrung out. Of course, with Michael sitting only a few feet away from her, the tension was heightened, and she couldn't blame all her exhaustion on the confrontation with her sister.

"I'll pick y'all up at the park in an hour. That should give you enough time to play."

The boys raced for the front door and were gone before Rachel could blink. She sighed and looked at Michael, who still sat on the couch, relaxed as though he had not a care in the world.

"I hope you weren't expecting a miracle with Amy," he said with a lopsided grin.

"No. She stayed longer than I thought she would. Frankly, I wasn't sure she would last two minutes. At least she got the piece of pie eaten." Rachel stacked all the plates and started for the kitchen, needing to stay busy.

Michael followed. She realized she might have to entertain him for another hour until he picked up the boys. The knot in her stomach tightened into a fist, and a band contracted around her chest. In her world she was used to entertaining, but this was different.

"I'll help you clean up."

"Oh, no, that's okay. If you have something else to do before—"

"I don't, Rachel. I helped you make this mess. I'll help you clean it up," he said in that lazy Southern drawl of his.

"Fine. You can dry. The towel is in that drawer."

"It always amazed me that Flora resisted modern technology up to the end. I know that Amy kept trying to get her to buy a dishwasher, but she thought that was a waste of good money, especially since she had Amy and Shaun to do the dishes."

Rachel filled the sink with water and soap. "That was my aunt. Look how long it took her to buy a television. She didn't have one when I lived here. I think the kids went on a hunger strike before she caved in and got one."

Michael laughed. "She loved her radio."

"And her books," Rachel said as she placed the first plate in the drain. "I miss her, whether you believe me or not. I wish I could have made it to her funeral. I wish I could have said my goodbyes." Sadness laced her voice. She knew she was opening herself up in front of Michael and that was dangerous, but she hadn't talked about her aunt with anyone except Robert Davenport. She needed to talk.

"I know."

"Do you? Do you know how much she meant to me?"

Michael put the towel down and turned to her. "I'm sorry I said those things on the riverboat that first day. That was cruel. I know you loved Flora. We all did. She was a remarkable woman."

The tears threatened, but she was determined she wouldn't shed any in front of Michael. "She was like a mother to me." Rachel continued washing the dishes, her blurry gaze fixed on the soapy water. "She certainly was around more than my own mother ever was."

"That's how Shaun and Amy felt about Flora."

"Yeah, I can see why. Shaun has seen his real mother maybe four times since he was a baby and deposited with Aunt Flora. Amy is a little bit luckier, if you want to call it lucky. She was five when she came to live with Aunt Flora. Since that time she's probably seen our mother a dozen times."

"It's never easy for a child to be rejected by his

mother or father. It's hard being shuffled back and forth between two parents, too."

Rachel slid a look toward Michael, noticing his tone of voice had changed. It held a sadness that had nothing to do with Amy and Shaun. Since she and her siblings had never been shuffled between their parents or their parents and Aunt Flora, she knew Michael was referring to something else, something that bothered him deeply. "What's going on?"

Chapter Five

The hardened line of his jaw emphasized the emotions Michael held locked inside. "Mary Lou called a few days ago. Now that she is remarried and lives so close, she wants to share custody of Garrett. She left us. Granted, she has kept in touch with Garrett *lately,* but our lives are just fine without any changes."

"What did you say to her?" Rachel finished washing the last plate and put it in the drain for Michael.

"My first impulse was to slam the phone down. I didn't. We're going to see her this weekend in Jackson."

The steel edge to his voice underscored his displeasure at the prospect of seeing his ex-wife. Rachel knew only a few tidbits about Michael's marriage to Mary Lou. When Amy or Shaun had wanted to talk about him, Rachel had changed the subject. She'd refused to let Aunt Flora mention him after his marriage. Rachel couldn't shake the feeling of betrayal she'd experienced. Even though Mary Lou and Michael's marriage hadn't worked out, he'd married her, loved her and had a son with her. Rachel emptied the water from the sink and kept her face averted, realizing she had no right to feel that way. Michael deserved to be happy, and Rachel had always known being a father and having a family were two important things he'd wanted in life. She couldn't begrudge him following his dream. She knew how important that was.

"How's Garrett feel about it?" Rachel remembered Mary Lou. She had been beautiful in high school and very popular. She'd grown up in Magnolia Blossom but had talked of moving to the big city after she graduated.

"I haven't said anything to him yet." One corner of Michael's mouth lifted. "I'm hoping the problem will go away. I don't trust Mary Lou. When she left us, she made it perfectly clear she didn't want to be a mother. Why is she suddenly wanting to change our arrangement? It's been working well."

"For whom?" Rachel asked, realizing she sounded like she was sticking up for Mary Lou.

Michael scowled at her. "Me! Garrett!" His voice was rough and grim. "Why can't things stay the same?"

Rachel wished she could control her life better, too. "That's not the way life is. You know that." She tilted her head so she could look at Michael. "What happened between you two?"

He slung the towel over his shoulder and began to put the plates in the cabinet. His back was to her, his movements restrained. "It seems Magnolia Blossom wasn't what Mary Lou wanted. I have a habit of picking women who don't like small towns. She wanted more from life than what I or Garrett could offer her. She started drinking. Finally, after she nearly killed herself driving the car, she realized she couldn't stay any longer. She left to pull her life together."

"How does Garrett feel about her living so close?"

"He's excited to see her. That worries me."

Rachel faced Michael. "Are you worried he'll want to be with Mary Lou all the time?"

His smile was rueful "Yeah. Being a parent isn't easy. I have to be tough at times, set down rules."

"Tell me about it. I'm finding that out." She reached out and touched his arm, her fingers closing around it. "You're a great dad. He knows that."

"I don't want to lose him."

"You won't. Garrett knows who has stood by him." Suddenly aware that she was grasping him, she dropped her hand and stepped away.

Michael rubbed the back of his neck and shook his head. "Garrett's my life. I thank the Lord every day for him. I know God will provide me with the right answers when the time comes."

Michael's strong faith had always sustained him. When they had been friends years ago, he'd shown his love of God in many ways. And while in Magnolia Blossom, she'd believed she wasn't alone in the world and that she was one of the Lord's children, too. What had happened to her budding faith? "Are you still involved in your church like you used to be?"

"Yes. Amy and Shaun are, too. I hope you'll come to the service one Sunday. Reverend Williams is still the minister."

"I always enjoyed his sermons."

"Me, too. He has a strong belief in family. When I'm at church, I feel a part of a larger family. It helps to put my life in perspective. The people of this town are good people. My son and I can count on them in times of trouble."

Michael's words made Rachel wish she had that with her own brother and sister. It was her fault there was such a distance between her and her siblings. She had the summer to change that. "Well, right now I could use some pointers on being a parent. I wish parenting came as easily to me as it does to you."

"Came easily? Whatever gave you that idea? It's hard work, but I wouldn't trade my years with Garrett for anything. I want more children. I want to give him brothers and sisters."

Rachel didn't want to consider Michael remarrying and having more children. But she realized that was a purely selfish feeling because Michael was a great father.

He glanced at his watch. "It's getting late. I'd better go and pick up the boys."

"Thanks for your help tonight."

"I don't mind doing a few dishes."

"Not the dishes. With Amy."

"It was no big deal. I didn't need the pies, anyway."

"I hope that isn't because you feel you're overweight? If so, the rest of us are in big trouble. There isn't an ounce of extra weight on you."

He chuckled. "No, I just don't need the sugar."

"But you used to love chocolate and anything else sweet."

"I still do. I just refrain from indulging too much."

Rachel eyed him. "Are you a health-food nut?"

"No, but I have to set a good example for my son. I try not to eat too much junk food."

"Now that's something all cooks love to hear."

He cocked his head, a tiny frown creasing his brow. "It really does fulfill you, doesn't it?"

"I think everyone needs a way to express herself. A creative outlet. Cooking is mine."

"No regrets then?"

"None." She answered too quickly, her throat closing at the intensity in his expression. How could she tell him the hardest thing she'd ever done in her life was walk away from him? But she'd made her decision ten years before and she would stick by it. Her life was her work. "I'll walk you to your truck."

"You don't have to. I know my way."

"That's the least I can do for you since you came tonight to help me with Amy." She began to move toward the front door.

"Tell her, Rachel."

His words halted her, and she turned to face him, the length of the kitchen between them. "You saw what happened when I mentioned New York. We've been through this, Michael. I need more time."

He held up his hand, palm outward. "Okay. I won't mention it again."

She quirked an eyebrow. "Really?"

"Really. You've made your point."

"This doesn't sound like the Michael I used to know. The guy I knew wouldn't have given up trying to convince me his way was the best way."

"Gee, you make me sound like a nag, or worse, a dictator."

"Never. Opinionated, yes. We did have some lively debates."

He crossed the kitchen and strode past her into the living room. "I guess raising a son has mellowed me. Besides, no one stays the same. People change, grow up. We were young back then."

"Yeah, babes in the woods."

Peering over his shoulder, he placed his hand on the front doorknob. "I see your cynicism hasn't changed."

"You forget that at the age of sixteen, when I turned up in Magnolia Blossom, I'd seen more of the world than most people, and the places I'd seen were not your typical tourist spots.''

''Where? You've never talked much about your past.''

''Because it is the past, and that's where it belongs.'' It was one of her cardinal rules. She would not look back. It was a hard rule to follow, though, when a person returned home after being gone for a long time.

Michael stared at her for a moment, then yanked the door open. The air vibrated with his tension. Even ten years ago, he'd wanted to delve into her life as though he had a right to know every minute detail. She sighed and pushed the screen door open.

Out on the front porch, the night air was still hot and humid. It bathed her face in a blast of moist heat that, she kept reminding herself, was one of the reasons she liked living closer to the North Pole than the equator. She watched Michael descend the steps and head for his truck, his movements agile, fluid. She had always loved to watch him. That had not changed, she realized as she followed him to his truck.

With his hand on the door handle, he threw her a glance over his shoulder. ''I'll bring Shaun home tomorrow afternoon.''

''Fine.'' For a reason she couldn't account for, she didn't want him to leave just yet. ''I realize we're two different people, that we've changed in the past ten years.''

He pivoted, crossing his arms over his chest, and regarded her with the intensity she'd come to expect from him. "What you mean is that we don't know each other like we used to, that we're really strangers?"

"Exactly." She looked away, then at him. "But we can make this...friendship work."

"So long as I play by your rules?"

"Michael, you've never played by anyone's rules but your own. I know *that* hasn't changed."

He leaned on his truck. "I think that was a compliment."

She smiled, relishing the light breeze that had kicked up, cooling her flushed cheeks. "Yes. I've always admired your independence, your loyalty and honor."

"My gosh, you make me sound like a Boy Scout."

Rachel laughed. "Not you."

"Now, that didn't sound like a compliment. If I stay too much longer, I probably won't have an ego left. I need to go. The boys are waiting."

"Are you kidding? They haven't thought once about you picking them up."

"True. I'll have to drag them away and listen to them whine all the way to Whispering Oaks."

"The things parents have to put up with. I've come to the quick conclusion everyone who wants to be a parent needs to go to school, then take a long, exhausting exam before they can have children."

He dropped his arms to his side. "Tough, isn't it?"

"Yeah, tough." She hadn't meant there to be a note of vulnerability in her voice, but she heard it and so did Michael.

He took her hand in his and pulled her closer, brushing a strand of hair behind her ear. "I'll help you for as long as you need me to."

Her heart fluttered. "I appreciate it."

His hands tightened about hers. A warmth suffused her. The world spun, and she leaned into him to steady herself.

"Are you okay?" He gripped her by the arms.

"I'm fine. Just not enough sleep. Amy gets in late. Shaun gets up early." She would never tell Michael his nearness still did strange things to her insides.

"I've spent a few sleepless nights worrying about Garrett, and he isn't even a teenager yet." Michael drew her into his embrace. "I'll walk you to the house."

She shook her head against his chest, said, "Really. I'm fine," but she didn't move out of his arms. Instead, she listened to the strong beat of his heart, its tempo increasing. The realization that she was having an effect on him made her bolder and probably, she would decide later, foolish. She wrapped her arms about him and tilted her face to look into his eyes. The illumination from the streetlight cast shadows on his features, but she could read the concern in his expression.

He threaded his fingers through her hair, his gaze

fastened on to hers. "You need to take care of yourself."

"I will," she murmured, licking her dry lips. "Strange bed. Strange house."

"Flora's?"

She nodded.

Silence engulfed them.

Her leaving Magnolia Blossom would always stand in their way. Suddenly, she didn't want that between them, at least not at the moment. She could get very comfortable in his embrace. That knowledge sent a bolt of panic through her, and she pushed away.

An electrified silence crackled between them like heat lightning.

Finally, he opened his truck door and slid inside. Hugging herself, she stood in her aunt's driveway while he backed out and drove toward the park. Coldness embedded itself in the marrow of her bones. She wasn't sure if she could make it to the end of summer living in the same town as Michael. He made her feel things she was determined she would never feel. He made her remember—something she tried very hard not to do.

Rachel rolled over and peered at the clock on her bedside table. Five in the morning. She groaned and snuggled under the covers, hoping to go back to sleep. Fifteen minutes later she gave up and climbed out of bed.

She slipped on a robe and headed for the kitchen

to fix a large pot of coffee. She had a suspicion she would need it. She'd only had a few hours of sleep. Thoughts kept tumbling through her mind, and she couldn't stop herself from thinking—about Magnolia Blossom, Amy and Shaun, but, most of all, about Michael.

She switched on the light in the living room and gasped. Amy sat on the couch in the dark, a surprised expression on her face before her usual sullen countenance fell into place.

"What are you doing up?" Amy asked, bringing her legs to her chest and hugging them.

"I was about to ask you the same thing."

Amy wrapped her arms about her legs. "I like to sit in the dark."

Rachel came farther into the room. "It's soothing, isn't it?"

"Yeah, well, it's time for me to go to bed."

"You've been up all night?"

"Yeah, what of it?" Tension whipped through Amy's words.

Rachel shrugged. "Nothing. Just wondering."

"Well, you can stop wondering if I snuck out of the house. I've been right here for the past few hours."

"I wasn't wondering."

"Why are you up so early?"

"Couldn't sleep. In fact, I was heading into the kitchen to make some coffee. Do you want to join me? We could talk. We haven't—"

Amy jumped to her feet. "I'm tired. I'm going to bed."

She hurried toward her bedroom, leaving Rachel standing in the middle of the living room wondering if she'd even had a conversation with her younger sister. Maybe she had been dreaming, Rachel thought as she padded toward the kitchen and that pot of coffee she so desperately needed.

As the coffee brewed, its wonderful aroma filling the air, Rachel sank onto a chair at the kitchen table and rested her chin in her palm. Her eyelids drooped. The blare of the phone caused her to shoot to her feet, nearly toppling over her chair.

She snatched up the receiver. "Hello, Rachel speaking."

Static greeted her words.

"Hello, is anyone there?"

"Rachel, it's me, your mother. Sorry about this connection. It isn't the best in the world. Is everything all right?"

Through the bad connection Rachel heard the question and closed her eyes. No, my world is changing. "Aunt Flora died a few weeks ago."

"I know. I received your letter and the lawyer's. That's why I'm calling."

"Are you coming back to the States?" When are you and Daddy going to be the parents?

"Not for a while. I don't know when I'll be able to get away, but I'm sure you're taking care of everything. I know I need to sign some papers about guardianship and I will as soon as I can. I'll call you and let you know when I can come.''

Rachel's grip tightened. ''But, Mom—''

More static. ''I don't have long before I have to head back to camp. We're moving it to another location. What are your plans?''

This woman was my role model. No wonder I can't make a commitment or stay in any one place for long. No wonder I'm afraid to be a mother. ''We're staying in Magnolia Blossom until the end of the summer. Do you want me to wake Amy and Shaun so you can speak to them?''

''Can't.'' The static on the phone got worse. ''I'll talk to them another time. We're heading out now. Goodbye, Rachel.''

''Goodbye, Mother,'' Rachel said to a dead line.

Her hands quivered as she replaced the phone on the wall. She was so cold. She hugged her arms to her, feeling the anger building inside her. She had been discarded twelve years ago and rarely thought about since. She felt as though she had lost more than Aunt Flora.

Rachel closed the oven door, set the timer on the stove, then began to stack the dirty dishes by the sink. Cooking was her therapy, she thought as she ran her finger around the inside of the metal mixing bowl and popped it into her mouth to savor the chocolate batter. She had been cooking for a long time and still loved to lick the bowl.

As she placed the dirty bowl into the water, she heard the front door bang open, the pounding of sneakers on the hardwood floor, then the door to a bedroom slam shut. Rachel shook her head. Quiet didn't exist in a household with children, something she would have to get used to.

She picked up a paring knife and was about to wash it when she heard pounding on the front screen door. She raced into the living room and saw a giant. A giant with a look to kill and a baseball bat in his hand.

"Where are those two brats?" Harold Moon's words filled the space between them like thunder filled a stormy sky.

"Who?" she squeaked.

"Your brother and that Hunter kid."

"What's the problem?"

"The problem is those two." His face red, Harold raised the baseball bat as though he was going to smash the screen door.

Show no fear, she chanted silently while she looked to see if either of the boys had at least thought to lock the screen behind them when they had fled into the house. No, there was nothing between her and Harold but a piece of flimsy screen with its latch unhooked.

"If you'll just put that bat down, we can talk about this calmly and rationally," she said, pointing with her knife.

He glared at her, the bat still in his hand. "Only if you get rid of that knife, lady."

"Knife?" Peering at her hand, she saw the parer

and was surprised by the fact she had it in her grasp. They must look a sight, she with her small knife and he with his big baseball bat. Finally, she found some humor in the situation and smiled. She stepped to the table in the entrance hall and placed the parer on it. "Now it's your turn," she said in a soothing voice meant to placate a raging bull.

After tossing the bat into the yard, he turned, a frown etched deeply into his face. "Those two boys hit a ball through my picture window and missed hitting me by mere inches." A vein in his temple throbbed, the red flush in his cheeks deepened, and his already loud voice was getting louder with each word.

"Please come in and let's discuss this calmly." She managed to speak around the dryness in her mouth.

He stormed into the house, his bulk making the entrance hall awfully small. "Where are they?"

Now that she was facing him, she could see no humor in the situation. She didn't know if she could appease this man and she certainly wouldn't be able to stop him from doing anything he chose to. She pasted a calm expression on her face and waved her arm toward the living room. "Let's have a seat in here and talk about this picture window the boys allegedly shattered."

"There is no allegedly about it, lady. I saw them. Plain and simple."

Rachel moved past Harold and sat on the couch, hoping he would do likewise. "Well, then, with that settled we can discuss how to fix it.'' Out of the corner of her eye she saw Shaun and Garrett peeking into the room.

''They should have to pay for it.'' He remained standing with his eyes narrowed to slits.

Thankfully, the man's back was to the boys. There was no telling what Harold would do if he saw Shaun and Garrett. ''I totally agree with you, Mr. Moon. The boys will pay to have the window fixed. Please get it replaced and send me the bill.'' Her neck was sore from looking up at the man. She finally stood when she realized he was not going to sit. ''I'll make sure it doesn't happen again.'' She heard the pounding sneakers making a beeline for Shaun's room as she and Harold approached the entrance hall.

The man started to go after the boys. She placed herself in front of him. Show no fear, she repeated as she felt the anger emanating off him in waves.

''I believe we have concluded our business. I'll be expecting the bill, Mr. Moon. Good day.'' She began inching herself and him toward the front door.

He threw one last glare toward where the boys had been only a moment before, then stalked to the screen door. ''I will. It will cost you a pretty penny.''

''I'm sure it will,'' Rachel muttered as she watched the man storm across the street.

She gripped the screen to steady her trembling body. Shock was definitely setting in as the seconds of silence ticked away. She used the silence to calm her nerves. She glanced at the gaping hole in Harold Moon's picture window.

"I can't believe you stood up to him, Rachel," Shaun said behind her.

Slowly, she turned. Garrett stared at the polished hardwood floor by his feet as if he could see his reflection and was amazed with the discovery. Her brother's eyes were round, a look of awe on his face.

"He was gonna kill us." Garrett's gaze remained fixed on the floor while he scuffed the toe of his tennis shoe into the hardwood.

"Nonsense. I wasn't going to let him." Rachel closed the thick wooden door, locked it, then walked toward the couch before she collapsed.

"Yeah, I know," Shaun said in that awestruck voice.

Garrett finally looked up. "We didn't mean to hit the ball through his picture window."

"Of course not. No one intends to do that. But it did happen, and you two have to pay for it."

"How? My allowance is only five dollars a week. I'd be in debt until I graduate from high school." Shaun plopped down in the chair across from her.

Rachel smiled, relief finally sweeping through her. "Nah. Not that long. I'll talk with Garrett's dad, and we'll work something out."

"When?" Shaun asked, sitting on the edge of the chair.

"I don't know."

"Do it now," Garrett said. "I want to get this over

with. Dad isn't gonna be too happy about this. It's best if he knows right away. Will ya tell him for us?''

Rachel wanted to groan. ''I think you two should be the ones to tell him.''

''We will, but please come with us,'' Shaun said as he jumped to his feet.

''We'll have to wait a few minutes until the cake is finished. I'll be there for moral support only. It's your job to explain what happened.''

Both boys nodded.

As Rachel left the room to see about the German chocolate cake, she felt apprehensive about this meeting with Michael. Her emotions were still raw from the evening before and the phone call from her mother earlier that morning. She needed time between meetings with him in order to recuperate. But she couldn't turn down Shaun's request. The very fact that he'd made it gave her hope that she was making progress with her little brother. Now if only Amy would hit a ball through Harold Moon's picture window and live to tell about it.

Rachel pulled up to Whispering Oaks and parked in the circular drive. When she climbed from her car, she took a moment to look at the place that had once been a familiar favorite haunt of hers. Michael had taken good care of the plantation. The house was freshly painted, and the black fences that kept his horses and cattle in were well tended. The red azalea bushes that ringed his home were beautiful.

She turned slowly as memories inundated her. She could remember watching him ride a stallion in the paddock to the left. She could remember their first kiss on the veranda. From the beginning Michael had been very determined, knowing exactly what he wanted. Rachel looked away, and her gaze fell upon a stone bench in the rose garden to the right of the house. That was where he had told her he loved her. That had been where her panic began to grow. Those words had made her feel tied down to Magnolia Blossom. They had threatened her dream.

Rachel heard the sound of a horse approaching and swung around to see Michael riding toward her. He dismounted. While he strode to her, she shoved the memories to the back of her mind.

"What brings you out here? I thought Garrett was spending the night with Shaun," he said, worry creasing his brow as he glanced at his son to make sure he was all right.

"Harold Moon paid me a visit this afternoon, and he wasn't too happy."

"The man never is." Michael removed his leather work gloves and tapped his leg with them.

"I'll let the boys tell you why."

Garrett stared at his left shoe, which he was digging into the dirt. Shaun looked away as though the horse in the paddock was the most fascinating creature he'd ever seen.

"Okay, what happened?" Michael asked with a sigh.

Shaun looked at Michael. "We were practicing. You should have seen Garrett's hit. The best ever."

"And where did that hit land?" Michael relaxed his stern expression, some of the tension siphoning out of him. "Garrett?"

Garrett quit digging the hole and mumbled, "Through Mr. Moon's picture window." He finally raised his head. "I got under that ball, and you should have seen it sail through the air."

"Yeah, right into someone's living room. Whatever possessed you two to toss a ball near that man's house?"

"You should have seen Rachel. Mr. Moon came over to the house furious. If she hadn't been there, no telling what he would have done to us," Shaun said, awe still in his voice.

Michael's jaw clenched, his regard on Rachel's face. "What happened?"

"Why don't you two go get the computer game you wanted earlier from Garrett's room?"

After the boys raced into the house, Rachel said, "Nothing happened. Mr. Moon was just a little angry that his window was broken. I took care of him."

"Harold Moon is always just a little angry about nothing, so I suspect it was more than a little." Michael shook his head. "They had no business in Harold's yard. They know he doesn't like anyone trespassing on his property."

"They weren't in his yard. They were playing in Aunt Flora's."

"Garrett hit the ball across the street? That's several hundred feet."

"Yeah," Rachel said, remembering she, too, had been impressed when she had pulled out of the driveway and had looked at the distance. The houses in the neighborhood sat on lots of several acres.

Michael whistled. "For him, that is far."

"Well, quit being impressed. We need to come up with a solution to how the boys will pay for the window."

He thought a moment, his head cocked. "I have some chores on the riverboat that need to be done. I was going to hire temporary help, but it might as well be the boys. But Shaun really doesn't have to do anything, since Garrett's the one who hit the ball."

"No, both of them were playing. Shaun pitched the ball to your son, so he's as guilty as Garrett. Besides, it won't hurt either one to do some work this summer."

"Then it's settled. I'll pay for the window, and they can work it off with me. Anything else?" Michael began to put his leather gloves on.

Wishing desperately for the ease they used to have between them, she looked toward the paddock, almost showing as much interest in the horse as Shaun had earlier. "Do you get to ride much?"

"Usually every day."

"I remember that time Ladybug threw me. My bottom was sore for a good week."

He lifted one eyebrow. "Rachel, I'm shocked. I

can't believe you would dwell in the past. I thought it wasn't important to you.''

She speared him with a glance she hoped conveyed her displeasure. ''It's hard not to think about the past when you return home after ten years and every time you turn around you're slapped in the face with it.''

''No one ever stopped you from coming back to Magnolia Blossom. Flora, Amy and Shaun would have loved it.''

But not you? She wanted to ask but kept her mouth shut by clamping down so hard her jaw hurt. ''It would have done no good,'' she finally said.

''Seeing your family or seeing me?''

Chapter Six

"Michael, I thought we agreed not to get into this. Remember, friends?"

"Yeah, you're right. It's been a tough day, and I'm taking it out on you. My apologies."

"What happened?"

In frustration he waved his glove-clad hand. "Mary Lou's making demands. Nothing I can't handle."

First Rachel had reappeared in his life, and now Mary Lou. His orderly routine was completely disrupted. He couldn't keep the anger from churning his stomach. He'd spent years coming to peace with how things had turned out for him and Mary Lou. Rachel had her dreams, but so did he. He had failed in his marriage and in his dream to have a large family. He would not let his son down. He would hold his small family together no matter what. And even though Mary Lou was Garrett's mother, Michael wasn't sure she was good for his son. He could still remember finding her drunk one afternoon while Garrett was crying in his crib. The memory shuddered through him.

Rachel placed her hand on his arm and drew his attention. "Maybe a friendly ear could help."

"I don't know if anyone could help me with this problem." Forgiveness was an intricate part of his faith, but he didn't think he could forgive Mary Lou in this case. That didn't sit well with his conscience.

"Now that sounds like me talking. We can all use a friend."

Remembering all the times he'd been shut out of Rachel's life, Michael clenched his jaw and shook her hand from his arm. He arched a brow. "Even you? I seem to recall you're not big on talking over your problems."

"I'm trying."

Hurt flittered across Rachel's face, but Michael hardened his heart to it. "I'd better get Avenger back to his stall. If he misses his dinner, he's one unhappy horse."

"Speaking of dinner, would you like to come over this evening? I've made a German chocolate cake." The second the invitation was out of her mouth she wanted to take it back.

A look descended on his face that chilled her in the humid, warm air. "No. I really must be going." He spun on his heel, walked to his stallion and vaulted into the saddle. "Send me the bill." He spurred his horse into a canter.

Michael disappeared around the side of the house, and Rachel felt as though he had slammed a door in her face. She wished she'd handled the baseball incident over the phone. She'd wanted to help him, but he had made it clear he didn't want her help. There was a time when he had turned to her. The past few minutes only emphasized how different they'd become.

Rachel stared at the table of food and wondered what army she was going to feed. Shaun and Garrett had begged off the beef Wellington she had prepared and had fixed themselves peanut butter and banana sandwiches. Armed with tall glasses of milk, the two boys had headed outside to eat on the patio since she had decreed no more food in the bedrooms.

After that she'd turned to Amy, hoping her sister would stay home long enough to eat a meal with her. But she should have known better, Rachel thought when she recalled the disdain on Amy's face at the very mention of spending any time with her older sister. So Rachel was stuck eating alone yet again and having mounds of leftovers. Cooking for her family was not doing her ego much good, Rachel decided as she carried a glass of sweetened iced tea to the table.

The sound of the doorbell demanded her attention. When she opened the front door, she was surprised to see Michael standing on the other side of the screen. "What are you doing here?"

"You invited me to dinner."

"And you declined."

"True, but a guy can change his mind."

She'd been crazy to ask him to dinner, and now she didn't know what to say. Her only defense was she'd thought that the two boys would be eating with them. She didn't want to share a cozy dinner for two with Michael, especially after their conversation at his house earlier that day. Forcing a smile, she opened the screen door and allowed him inside.

"When's it ready?"

"I was just sitting down to eat."

He walked into the kitchen and took in the table set for one. "Where is everyone?"

"They took one look at what I prepared and made a mad dash for the peanut butter jar. I guess I'm going to have to start experimenting with peanut butter in my recipes."

"Where are Shaun and Garrett?"

"Out back devouring their sandwiches."

"And Amy?"

"Out with Kevin. Those two are inseparable. I'm worried about what she'll do."

"She fancies herself in love."

"She's not even seventeen."

"Way too young to know what love is."

His sarcasm knifed into her. "I'll share my dinner with you if you can leave the past out. A deal?"

He tilted his head to the side and thought for a moment. "A deal. But you'll have to face the fact that your sister thinks she's in love with Kevin, and she doesn't want to leave Magnolia Blossom to see the world."

Rachel sucked in a deep breath, pressing her lips tightly together. The contrasts and similarities between her and her sister's lives were obvious to both her and Michael.

"We haven't sat down to dinner yet, and I'll have my say, Rachel. You're the one who brought up the subject of Amy."

"So you think she'll do something foolish?"

"That's always a possibility. Just remember when you were her age. You tell me what you think she'll do."

She shook her head. "I'm afraid I can't put myself in Amy's shoes. We're very different people. We want different things out of life."

"Are you so sure about that? Have you discussed this with Amy?"

"Discussed it with Amy? You know I haven't. She won't talk to me about anything."

"If she feels you're backing her into a corner, she'll come out fighting."

Rachel laughed, no humor in the sound. "That's all we do."

"She's trying to preserve the life she wants the best way she knows how."

"Like I did?"

"Yes. You wanted something different from me ten years ago and you went for it. What you have to ask yourself now is do you want the same thing?"

"To be a chef? Yes, of course."

"No. To avoid a commitment to another person."

Her breath caught in her throat, and her heart

missed a beat. Michael had a way of striking below the belt and doubling her over with his words.

His eyes clouded with an expression Rachel couldn't read. "The commitment I'm talking about now is the one you need to make with your brother and sister. I know it's too late for us. We had our time ten years ago. Whatever we develop now wouldn't be the same thing."

No, it wouldn't be. She had been a teenager, a senior in high school. She was a young woman now. Rachel glanced away and gestured toward the food on the table. "If we don't eat soon, it'll get cold. I'll get you a plate."

"Rachel, your life has changed—"

"Don't, Michael. I'm trying."

"Remember the other day when you talked about getting help with parenting? Come to church this Sunday. Talk with Reverend Williams. He has five children and has dealt with many parenting issues. He's always listened to me when I've had a problem."

But she wasn't like Michael. She didn't open up easily to anyone. She'd spent all her life keeping her feelings bottled up. "I'm sure he has, but—"

Michael laid his fingers over her mouth to still her words. "Don't dismiss this. Church is a good place to start bringing your family together."

Rachel blinked, nonplussed by his touch. His gaze drilled into her as though he could convey silently how strongly he felt about his faith. When he dropped his hand, she stepped back. "Shaun said something about it to me. I'd already decided to attend next Sunday.''

Michael smiled. ''I'm glad. You won't regret it.''

His smile, as usual, warmed her and flustered her. She pointed to the chair at the opposite end of the oblong table. ''We'd better eat.''

He sat next to her. That action affected the rest of the meal. Rachel was too near to him for her peace of mind. She had a hard time focusing on what he was saying. She was too busy watching him drink his tea, savor the food she'd lovingly prepared, smile at something she managed to say. By the time dinner was over, her nerves were as taut as a rubber band stretched to its limit. She wondered when she would snap from the strain.

''Let's do the dishes later. The sun's setting, and I know the view from Flora's patio is beautiful.''

Rachel looked at the mess in the small kitchen and remembered the night before. ''I have a better idea. I'll clean up later after you're gone.''

''Sure you don't want my help?''

''Yes.''

''I'd be nuts to pass up a chance not to do the dishes.''

She was the one who was nuts for thinking they could be just friends. It was like jumping into a raging river to save herself from being burned.

Michael refilled the glasses of iced tea and handed Rachel hers. As she walked to the back door that led to the patio, she felt as though she were walking to her doom. The air was warm, laced with the scents of gardenia and honeysuckle, a gentle breeze stirring enough to keep things cool as the sun dipped toward the horizon. Shaun and Garrett, as she knew they would be, were gone to the park to play with the other kids. She and Michael were alone with a riot of colors splashed across the sky, offering a beautiful backdrop to the evening ahead.

Warily, Rachel sat in a chair and took several sips of her tea, relishing the coldness as it slid down her throat. Normally, she enjoyed silence, but right now the quiet eroded what composure she managed to have. "You're going to have Shaun and Garrett work on the riverboat. Have you decided to finally do something about it?"

"Yes." He lifted his tea and sipped. "The boat is a sound one. The repairs it needs are cosmetic. I've decided to renovate it and use it for short trips on the river. There'll be a restaurant on it." He cradled the glass in his large hands and stared into her eyes. "Will you help me design the kitchen while you're here this summer?"

Her hands trembled. She nearly dropped her drink and had to place it on the table. "Why me?" she asked, shocked by the offer.

"Why not? I don't know of anyone more qualified than a chef who is making quite a name for herself. I'll pay you for your services. Strictly business between us."

For a brief moment she was tempted to accept. She couldn't. She would be in constant contact with Michael, and that was a temptation too risky to take.

"Rachel, I know this offer is a surprise. Frankly, it's a surprise to me. But it makes a lot of sense if you think about it. It'll give you something to do while you get to know Amy and Shaun. Don't give me your answer right now. Promise me you'll think it over."

She nodded, still too stunned to do much else. Her mind swirled with the possibilities. The job would help her when she designed her restaurant in New York. Michael wouldn't be able to devote all his time to the kitchen. He was a busy man with a plantation to run and with the rest of the riverboat's renovation to oversee. But nevertheless, she would probably be around him every day.

"When did you decide to renovate the riverboat?"

"I'd been toying with the idea for some time. I need to do something with it. Keep it or sell it. I just couldn't sell it. It was my legacy from my grandfather."

"Just like you can't sell Whispering Oaks?"

"Yes." He finished the rest of his tea in two swallows and put his glass next to hers on the table. "When I ride over the land, I think back to the past and imagine my great-grandfather doing the same thing, or one of my great-uncles working in the field as a young boy. We all had to learn about the plantation by working it right alongside the farm hands."

"A family tradition?"

"Yes. My family has a lot of them. I like the feeling of belonging. I've tried to pass that on to Garrett."

"My immediate family doesn't have any traditions unless you count knowing the best way to pack a suitcase."

With memories of her phone call with her mother, Rachel stared at the sky, the few ribbons of color left merging with the darkness. She was determined not to let her mother destroy the serenity of the moment. Rachel pushed the memories away. She felt insulated from the world as the night edged closer, and for a few minutes she allowed herself to forget her problems and savor the evening's beauty.

"Traditions have to start somewhere, Rachel. You can start some with Amy and Shaun." Michael cut into the silence.

"They'll have their own families soon."

"Shaun still has a few years to go." A chuckle added a richness to his words.

"Hopefully, so does Amy. What kind of person is Kevin?"

"He's a good kid. Plays on the football team. He's part of the same youth group that Amy belongs to at church. He was also on the debate team that won state this year. I think he'll get a scholarship to Ole Miss."

"For football?"

"No, academics. Actually, the way they started dating was he tutored Amy in math last semester."

"Ah, so she's inherited my ability for math," Rachel said with a smile.

The night completely surrounded them now, and the only light to illuminate the patio was what streamed through the living room window. But Rachel didn't have to see Michael's expression to know he was staring at her. She looked toward the dark sky, trying to ignore his intensity. "I didn't realize it was getting so late."

"Yes, and I'd better be going. Are you sure you don't want help with the dishes?" As he rose, Michael picked up the two glasses.

"Yes, you're off the hook. I'm just glad that I had someone to share my dinner with. Eating alone is lonely sometimes."

Rachel followed Michael into the kitchen and stood by the door while he placed the glasses on the counter. He glanced at her and caught her staring at him. Her cheeks flushed and she backed into the dining room as he came toward her.

"The more I think about you designing the kitchen on the riverboat, the more it makes sense. Is there anything else I can say to persuade you to design my restaurant?"

Rachel's steps were halted by the dining room table. "I don't know when my restaurant deal will come through. I might not be able to finish your project."

"If that happens, then you're free to leave. You know me. When I do something, I like the best."

She blushed even more at the compliment. "I'll be gone for sure by the end of summer."

"Then we'll need to get started as soon as possible. Most of the kitchen can be done by then, possibly the whole thing. That's over two months away." He grasped her upper arms and pulled her close.

She breathed in his scent and relished it. She touched her hand to his chest, intending to push him away, and marveled at the steady beat of his heart while hers was pounding. The rhythm of his heartbeat began to increase the longer she stayed in his embrace.

"I can give you a tour of the boat tomorrow morning. How about nine?"

She nodded. She would have agreed to anything as long as he was touching her.

Michael grinned. "Good. You won't regret helping. I'll see you tomorrow at nine."

Rationality slowly returned, and his words sank in. "Nine?" She gripped the back of a dining room chair for support.

"For the tour of the boat."

"Oh, that." Oh, no, she had agreed to help him with his kitchen! One part of her knew that and was elated; the other part was appalled.

"Yes, that," he said and turned to leave.

She indulged herself in what was becoming her favorite pastime, watching him move. She couldn't do it. Look what happened to her willpower just being near the man. She'd agreed to do something she knew was wrong for her. Tomorrow morning she would have to tell him she couldn't design his kitchen.

Michael stood at the railing of his riverboat and watched Rachel pull her car into the parking space next to his. After spending a sleepless night, pacing from one end of his bedroom to the other, he'd finally decided he wasn't totally crazy to have asked her to help him design the kitchen for his restaurant. Only half-nuts, he thought with a derisive laugh. The plain and simple truth, though, was he had never been able to resist Rachel when she had really needed him, and she needed him—even if she was completely unaware of that fact.

Somewhere around three in the morning he'd come to the conclusion that he'd given her the chance because he knew she would have to have something to work on while she was here or she might leave sooner than she had announced. That wouldn't be good for Shaun and Amy. Somewhere around four he had known he had to see if there was anything left between him and Rachel because every time he was near her it felt like there was something between them. But memories of what had happened ten years before wouldn't vanish. How could he trust her not to stomp on his heart again? Somewhere around five he'd decided he could be her friend and keep their relationship strictly professional. And somewhere around six he had declared himself a fool.

They'd had their chance, and for whatever reason, God in His infinite wisdom had decided the two of them wouldn't work. As friends, maybe. As a couple? A bittersweet laugh spilled from his lips.

As she walked toward the riverboat, he watched her long-legged strides. She was beautiful, talented and scared to care about anyone for fear that person would leave her. She liked to do the leaving first. She had spent her life avoiding roots while he had spent his trying to build a stable, grounded life tied to a community, church and family he loved.

If he was going to prove to himself he wasn't a total fool, he had to make this partnership work. Besides, for Amy's and Shaun's sake, he wanted this to work.

Dear Heavenly Father, please guide me and help Rachel to see that making a commitment to her family isn't a bad thing. Commitments are what make life worth living.

Michael focused on her expression and knew she had come to tell him she had changed her mind. He had expected that. He affected her whether she wanted him to or not. That would scare her, threaten all she thought she wanted. Now all he had to do was convince her not to change her mind. She was an excellent choice to design his kitchen.

As Rachel made her way to the riverboat, she set her jaw in determination. She would tell him she couldn't do the job, then leave before he could persuade her otherwise.

She had seen him at the railing on the upper deck, but by the time she arrived at that location, he was gone. She began her search in the main salon. As she passed through the large area, the size of two ballrooms, she saw such possibilities that she almost stopped to appraise it more thoroughly. She had to remind herself she was on a mission. She couldn't think about the beautiful carved moldings, the brass fixtures, the picture windows that afforded a clear view of the river and land beyond.

She headed toward the back of the boat, toward what she knew had once been the kitchen. She came to a stop just inside the doorway. The room was huge, and that would be the only thing she would keep. The rest of it would have to be gutted. There was nothing salvageable, from the antique stoves to the cabinets with missing doors. She visualized the kitchen as it should be. She put a halt to her musings when she pictured herself stirring something on one of the new stoves, everything clean and shiny in the brand-new kitchen.

This was a mistake. She took a step back, intending to call Michael about her change of heart. She should never have come to the riverboat. With another step backward she hit a solid wall of human flesh. Hands gripped her arms to steady her, then turned her.

Her heart plummeted when she saw the endearing grin on Michael's face. She was doomed if she didn't do something fast.

"You're right on time, Rachel. Let me give you a tour. Then we can talk about where you want to start."

"That's not why I'm here." She had to remain strong even though his smile warmed her.

He released his hold on her and started to guide her toward the front of the riverboat.

She halted, forcing him to stop. "I can't do it."

"Are you backing out? Rachel, we have a verbal agreement." He stepped closer.

She tried to move away and found herself trapped between Michael and the doorjamb. "I'm breaking it."

"Why?"

"I don't have the time."

"What are you doing with your time while you're here?"

"Taking care of Amy and Shaun. That can be a full-time job."

"Is it?"

She dropped her gaze and murmured, "Well, no, but only because they have their own lives with not much room for me. I hope to change that."

"Why can't you start on the kitchen design until they want to include you in their lives? I know you, Rachel. You'll go crazy in Flora's house without some kind of direction."

"I'm experimenting with some new dishes."

"Not enough."

"I'm cleaning and boxing up Aunt Flora's things."

"Still not enough."

"Helen wants me to get involved in the church again. I thought—"

He placed his fingers over her mouth to still her words. "I'm all for that, Rachel, but you can do that and still design my kitchen. You've always liked to be kept busy. What better way than doing something you'll enjoy?"

She sighed, knowing when to admit defeat. "Promise me it will be strictly business between us," she said, desperate for him to be the strong one.

"I can promise you nothing will happen that *you* don't want to happen. You are in control." He backed away.

She looked from him to the antiquated kitchen. "Okay. I'll design the kitchen, but as soon as my financing for my own restaurant comes through, I'll quit. You may have to find someone to finish the project."

"You won't back out until then?"

She nodded, feeling as though she had just agreed to her own prison term. "When do you want to start?"

"How about now? Let's take a tour, then we can talk in the main salon."

"I've been on the boat before. We don't have to go on a tour."

"But it's been over ten years, Rachel. I want you to see it, to get a feel for the place before you start your designing. I want to explain some of the plans I have for this old steamboat."

"Okay," she murmured, her interest piqued.

"When the boat's ready, we'll start with lunchtime cruises on the river. The customers will get a chance to eat good food and see some of the beautiful scenery. I plan to stop at a couple of the plantations for tours, too. If that takes off, then I want to do nighttime cruises. Make it romantic, evenings meant for two." He gestured for her to go down the hallway where the staterooms were. "Of course, I always have the option of never leaving the pier, but the engines are in good shape."

Rachel opened one of the doors to a cabin. "What are you going to do with these?"

Michael entered and made a full circle. "Nothing at the moment. Later I could have weekend cruises."

"Then are you going to redo these?" She looked at him and wished she hadn't.

"Yes." He walked toward her.

She had meant to move out into the corridor but felt snared by the intensity in his eyes.

"I want to furnish these rooms with period pieces. Make people feel like they've stepped back in time to the days when steamboats reigned on the river. I have some furniture in storage at Whispering Oaks. The rest I'll acquire. What do you think?" he asked in his Southern drawl that could melt her insides.

Thinking was impossible, she wanted to shout, but her throat was too parched to speak. Time came to a standstill, and all that mattered was Michael. It's happening all over again, she thought with a sense of panic.

The sound of boys laughing forced Michael's attention away. He stepped into the corridor as Garrett and Shaun came to a screeching halt outside the doorway.

"We're ready to work, Dad."

"What do you want us to do?" Shaun asked, looking at Rachel with a perplexed expression.

With a flush staining her cheeks, she brought her hand up to smooth her hair. While Michael gave Garrett and Shaun their instructions, she tried to compose herself enough to make it through the rest of the morning. She and Michael working together was an impossibility that she had to make work, because despite her misgivings, she wanted to design the kitchen.

When the boys raced away, Michael turned to her. "What do you think about all this?"

Rachel took the opportunity to move into the hallway. "I like your plans. You're not biting off too much at once, which is smart. The only thing I want to interject here is if you think I will design a kitchen like the one in this boat's heyday, then you'd better get someone else."

"You mean you don't want to cook on a wood-burning stove?" he asked with a chuckle.

"Afraid not."

"You should use whatever modern conveniences you need. Only the best. I can afford it."

She realized they were talking as if she would be the chef. She needed to make it clear that would never happen. "Do you have any idea who you'll get to be your chef?"

"No, do you have any suggestions?"

"You could advertise in the New Orleans and Jackson papers."

"That's a possibility. Or, Rachel, you could be my chef."

"No," she said instantly. "I have my own plans."

"I know, but I did want you to know you were the first person I thought of for the job."

"Thank you, but the answer is still no," she murmured and strode toward the main salon. She needed to be around other people before she found herself accepting his job offer.

She stopped in the doorway and watched her brother and Garrett removing chairs from the room. They were giggling and talking in lowered voices, and she suspected they were talking about her and Michael. The second the boys saw her they clammed up, but they were having a hard time not grinning.

"How did you two get here?" Rachel asked, hoping to divert their overactive imaginations.

"Our bikes. We ride everywhere." Shaun carried a chair outside.

"Dad, where do you want the lumber?" Garrett picked up the last chair to take to the stern.

"Put it on the lower deck at the back of the boat."

Rachel enjoyed her safety in numbers all of two minutes before the boys disappeared down below and she was left alone with Michael again. She pretended a great interest in the main salon, walking the length of the room, appearing as though she was taking note of the cornices above the windows, the ornamental molding. Her mind, though, wasn't on her surroundings.

She was aware of Michael's every move as he, too, made an inspection of the main salon. She saw him run a hand along the brass fixtures on the counter, then look at her in the large mirror on one wall. He winked.

A dog barked several times, followed by three splashes. Rachel dragged her gaze away from Mi-

chael. "I'd better see what the boys are up to now."
She hurried from the room.

She looked down and found Garrett and Shaun
swimming in the river next to the boat with a big
black dog. Leaning on the wood railing, she heard
Michael behind her and knew she couldn't deal with
him at the moment. She scurried down the stairs to
the bottom deck and bent over the railing, shouting,
"Whose dog is that?"

Shaun treaded water near her. "Don't know. He
just followed us from town."

"Does he have a collar?"

"No. Can I keep him?"

"I don't know, Shaun."

"Please. Aunt Flora didn't like dogs. Only cats."

"I guess you can until we find out who owns him,
then he'll have to go back to his owner."

The whoopee that greeted that announcement could
have been heard clear to downtown Magnolia Blossom.

"I think you've totally won Shaun over, and it
didn't take but a few weeks."

Rachel tensed. "He's the easy one. Of course, he
won't be happy when the owner claims the dog."

"Maybe he was abandoned."

Rachel cocked her head to the side and studied the
black Labrador retriever. "No. He's in great shape.
Someone has been taking care of that dog."

"Then you can get Shaun one of his own."

Rachel faced Michael, who had donned dark sunglasses that kept his eyes hidden. "No. It's too hard to have a dog in New York City."

"Thousands of people do."

"I think a dog, especially a big one, should have a yard to run in, not a small apartment."

"It would be a nice way to allow Shaun to take something from here when he leaves."

The sun beat down on her, and she was forced to shield her eyes from the glare. The hot breeze tangled itself in the strands of her hair, whipping them across her face. "You know I shouldn't be surprised by your advice. That's what's so special about small towns. I would appreciate it *if* I was looking for advice."

Shrugging, Michael grinned. "Sorry. You asked me for my help. Part of that help is advice on what is best, in my opinion, for Amy and Shaun. Darlin', you can't have it both ways. It's all or nothing."

It always had been that way with them. He'd wanted everything from her, and she hadn't been able to give that to him. She dug into her purse in search of her sunglasses. "I'll think about a medium-size dog."

"What happens if no one claims this Lab? What are you going to do then?"

"Give the dog to you as a present?"

"Nope. I've got two already. Don't need another one."

She found her sunglasses and plopped them on her nose. "Then I'll face that problem when the time comes. I have too many problems ahead of that one to get too concerned at the moment."

"Well, then, I'd better warn you that Amy is worse than Shaun when it comes to animals."

"She is?"

"You can always hope the dog is gone before she realizes it's at your house."

Rachel wished she could wipe that grin from his face. He was enjoying her dilemma way too much. "I suppose I could hide him. Since she's rarely home, it might work."

Michael chuckled. "Anything's possible when you want it bad enough."

"Does that sum up your philosophy of life?"

"Sure does."

The dog's barking drew her attention to the end of the pier. "Are the boys through for the day?"

"Yep, until I get things started, then I'll use them more."

"Good. I'll have them follow me home and make posters about the dog. After that, I'll start working on some preliminary plans for the kitchen. I should be able to show you something in a few days."

"I'll be by to pick up Garrett a little later, then."

"Just let him spend the night again."

Michael drew himself up straight, his hands flexing at his side. "Can't do that. I have to take Garrett to Jackson early tomorrow morning."

"To see Mary Lou?"

He nodded, a frown carved deeply into his features.

"You can pick him up early tomorrow morning. I'm usually up by six."

"Okay, if you're sure," Michael murmured, tension threading through his words.

Michael leaned against the railing and watched as Rachel stopped to talk with Garrett and Shaun. His memories of his relationship with Rachel and his failure to keep his marriage together strengthened his desire not to get involved with Rachel again. Even though he'd always wanted a large family, he wouldn't put himself through that kind of pain ever again. He just had to remember that over the next few months.

Chapter Seven

The aroma of coffee brewing greeted Michael when Rachel opened the door to her house. Her hair was wet as if she had just gotten out of the shower. She wore a pair of shorts and a white T-shirt with Born To Cook in big red letters. She looked good to his tired eyes.

She smiled and gestured for him to come inside. "I hope you're hungry. The boys are finishing up their blueberry pancakes."

Michael yawned. He hadn't slept the night before. "All I want is a big cup of coffee. Preferably the whole pot."

"Now, Michael Hunter, I didn't get up thirty minutes early just so you could drink coffee and be on your way. You can have at least one of my pancakes."

"You shouldn't have gone to all that trouble."

"When someone is invited to breakfast, a person has to fix something to serve. Pancakes are easy, and they're something the boys will eat."

"As opposed to beef Wellington?"

"Yes," she said with a laugh. "I'm learning. Last night I fixed a pizza, and they didn't leave one piece." She headed for the kitchen.

As Michael entered the room, Garrett jumped out of his chair, downing the rest of his milk in the same motion. "I'm ready, Dad."

"But I'm not. Sit. Rachel is making me eat breakfast."

"Yeah, did she tell you that it was the most important meal of the day?" Shaun asked while spearing another pancake from the serving platter.

"No, but I did read that somewhere."

"Bet she didn't have to twist your arm much." Garrett grinned, displaying his milk mustache.

"Just about anything Rachel fixed would be tempting." Michael sat in a chair between the boys.

"Just about? What won't you eat?" Rachel handed him a large mug of coffee, then went to the stove to flip the last batch of pancakes.

"Well, let me see. I was never partial to snails. I'm sure you learned to prepare them in Paris."

"Ugh!" Garrett screwed his face into a frown. "Snails? People eat them?"

"I did learn how to prepare escargot, which is really a fancy name for snails. They are very good."

"I think I lost my appetite," Shaun said, scooting

his chair back. "Let's play a video game until your dad gets ready to leave. First one in the living room gets to choose."

"Shaun—" The rest of her sentence would have been spoken to thin air as the boys raced from the room. Rachel shook her head. "Do they even know how to walk? Every time they go someplace it is always a race to see who'll get there first."

"Makes me tired just looking at them." Michael put several pancakes on his plate, plopped a square of butter on top, then lavished maple syrup all over them. He bowed his head and said a silent prayer.

Rachel sat in the chair farthest away from him and sipped her coffee. "Will you be all right today?"

"Yeah," he said with little conviction.

"Remember, Garrett loves you. She can't take that away."

He finished his coffee and went to the counter to pour himself more. "When Mary Lou left us, I prayed she would return. I didn't want Garrett to grow up without a mother like I did. But then Mary Lou didn't—" He swallowed hard, remembering the nights and days being both mother and father to Garrett.

"And now you don't think she has any right to be in Garrett's life?"

"Yeah. She chose to leave and find another life. I know in my heart I need to forgive her, but it isn't easy."

"Forgiveness doesn't always come easily, especially when you've been hurt."

"I'm more concerned about Garrett's feelings than mine. He was the one who was hurt."

"Are you sure that's the case?"

He stabbed her with a narrowed look. "Yes, of course."

"Have you forgiven me for leaving you?"

Silence hung in the air between them, thick, emotion-filled.

"Have you, Michael?" Suddenly she wanted to know more than anything.

"I'm trying, Rachel. That's the best answer I can give you."

She tried not to let his words hurt her, but it was hard. "Perhaps you should talk with Reverend Williams. He may be able to help you."

Michael didn't reply but sat down and took a bite of his pancakes. "This is delicious."

"Thank you. I never tire of hearing people say that about my cooking," she said, sad that he was doing what she did so well—avoiding his feelings.

"Don't tell Helen, but I think these beat hers."

"No way would I say that to her. I value her friendship."

"It's nice to hear you say that."

Rachel stiffened. "What's that supposed to mean?"

"Nothing." He stuck his fork in the last piece of pancake and brought it to his mouth.

"I care about Helen. She's the best friend I ever had."

"I'm sorry, Rachel. I'm tired. I didn't get much sleep last night, and I said something I shouldn't have." Michael rose, taking his plate and mug to the sink. His head was beginning to throb with tension. He turned to leave.

She stood in his way. "Maybe you shouldn't have said it, but it is the way you feel. I may not live here, but that doesn't mean I haven't kept in touch with Helen."

Michael wanted out of there, but short of physically moving Rachel out of his way, he wasn't going anywhere. "A card now and then is not keeping in touch."

Her eyes widened. "I've called her."

"Yeah, on her birthday. That's once a year. And since we're on the subject, you haven't done much better with your own sister and brother."

Rachel sucked in a deep breath. Lines of anger scored her features. She opened her mouth to say something but then clamped it closed.

His head ached, and his pulse hammered against his temples in a maddening beat. "This was not a good idea." He clasped her upper arms and moved her to the side, then he stepped around her and left the kitchen before he made the situation worse.

"Let's go, Garrett," he called, not breaking stride as he headed for the front door.

He strode to his truck and got in, deliberately keeping his gaze averted from the porch. He could feel Rachel watching him. Tapping a fast rhythm against the steering wheel, he waited for his son to climb into the passenger side, then he backed out of the driveway, barely managing not to screech his tires.

His son must have sensed his mood. He remained quiet as they drove out of town. "Are you mad at Rachel?" Garrett finally asked when they were on the highway to Jackson.

"What makes you think that, son?"

"Gee, Dad, maybe the way you left her place."

Michael's grip on the steering wheel tightened. "We had words. Nothing important."

Garrett stared out the side window. "Dad, Mom wants me to come visit more now that she lives so near."

The words tore at Michael's heart. For years Garrett had been the center of his life. Now he had to share his son with Mary Lou. Mary Lou's timing was awful—not that there would ever be a great time to give up custody of his son, but with Rachel back in town his emotions had taken a beating.

"We'll work something out for the summer, son."

For a long moment Garrett was silent then he asked, "Dad, why did Mom leave?"

Michael sucked in a sharp breath. He wasn't sure how to answer. "We got married too young. We weren't ready." The steering wheel, where he gripped it, was wet with his sweat. He couldn't tell his son about Mary Lou's drinking problem.

"Do you think she'll come to one of my baseball games if I ask her?"

"Sure," Michael answered, trying to be positive. He might be angry at Mary Lou for walking out on them, but he never wanted Garrett to feel his mother didn't love him.

"Then I'll ask her today. Maybe I'll be able to hit a home run. Of course, this time it won't go through Mr. Moon's window."

"Please remember that in the future. That's one man I don't want mad at us."

"Why is he so grumpy?"

"I think, son, he wants to be left alone."

"Maybe someone hurt him in the past."

"That's a possibility."

Garrett chewed on his lower lip, thought for a moment, then slanted a look at his father and asked, "Did Mom hurt you?"

"Our marriage didn't work out because we weren't right for each other," he answered, feeling as though he were balanced on a tightrope and any moment a stiff wind would whisk him off.

"Can I play one of my CDs?"

Michael nodded, relieved that his son didn't pursue the topic. He wasn't quite eight and certainly didn't need his illusions tarnished.

Garrett played a CD Michael hadn't heard. After several songs he didn't want to hear it ever again. But for the next half hour he endured the album, draining his mind of all thoughts.

By the time Michael pulled up in front of Mary Lou's two-story house, he was feeling better about the meeting. Maybe everything would work out.

Mary Lou opened the door when Garrett rang the bell. She smiled at her son, then drew him to her and hugged him. Michael hung back and watched the scene between mother and son, trying not to feel as though he was losing his son to Mary Lou. Anger he'd held bottled up escaped, carving a frown into his features.

"Y'all come on in." Mary Lou waved them into her house. "We'll have lunch out on the patio by the pool." She took Garrett's hand to show him the way.

Michael followed. The glass table on the patio was already set for three even though lunch was several hours away. Mary Lou indicated that they have a seat, but Garrett headed for the large kidney-shaped pool.

"You have a slide *and* a diving board. Wow!"

"I should have had you bring your swimming suit today. Next time you should," Mary Lou said.

Michael tensed. His frown strengthened into a scowl.

Mary Lou walked to where Garrett stood. "You know we have some time before lunch. I think I can find a suit that will fit you. Do you want to go swimming?"

"Can I, Dad?"

Michael nodded, not trusting himself to speak. His headache had returned, the pain behind his eyes intensifying.

While Mary Lou took Garrett into the house to change, Michael prowled the patio, too restless to sit. Mary Lou wanted to have a relationship with her son. After nearly six years, she suddenly wanted to share him equally. She hadn't been there when Garrett had gotten the flu last year or when he had gotten into a fight with a boy at school or— Michael shook the angry thoughts from his head. He had to deal with Mary Lou being back in Garrett's life. He had to deal with the anger and mistrust eating at him.

Lord, please give me the strength to deal with Mary Lou. I can't do it without You. I know I should forgive her. But I can't. I can't forget what she did to Garrett. She wasn't there for him when he needed a mother.

When Garrett shot out of the house and raced for the pool, Michael said, "Slow down, son. You know there's no running around pools."

Two feet from the water Garrett came to a halt, then proceeded to walk the remaining distance to the slide. At the top of it, he waved then plunged into the pool.

"You've done a good job with him, Michael."

He stiffened at the sound of Mary Lou's voice. Pivoting toward her, he managed to keep himself from scowling at her. "I had no choice."

"Please have a seat." Mary Lou gestured toward a chair while she sat down. "I thought for this first meeting, Tom shouldn't be here, but later he certainly wants to be involved in Garrett's life."

"Garrett has a father."

"I know that."

"What do you want?" His anger was apparent in his voice.

"Direct as usual. I know you have a right to be angry with me. I walked out on you and Garrett."

"You left without letting me know where you were. For days Garrett cried for you. I thank God every day he doesn't remember that. But I do."

"I was twenty-one and not prepared to be a mother. I couldn't stay any longer."

"And you think I was prepared to be a single father?"

"Michael, you've always been grounded. I knew you would do what needed to be done."

"And that's supposed to make everything okay now?" He looked toward where his son was swimming. His throat constricted with memories of the struggle he had gone through dealing with a two-year-old, trying to be the best father *and* mother his son could have. He'd tried to make his marriage with Mary Lou work even after he'd discovered her drinking problem. He'd made a commitment to her, and their son needed both of them. He knew he could forgive Mary Lou for walking out on him, but he didn't know if he could forgive her for leaving Garrett without a mother. He remembered growing up without his mother and the loneliness he'd felt.

"I'll ask you again. What do you want, Mary Lou?"

"As I told you on the phone, I want partial custody

of Garrett. I'm able to take care of him now. I have a good home and a good husband. I have my life together. I haven't taken a drink in over a year.''

''No.'' Michael shook his head to emphasize his answer. ''You can see him with me present, but that's all.''

''I'll go back to court if I have to.''

The threat hung in the air between them. The pounding of his heartbeat roared in his ears. ''Is that what you want—a fight?''

''Hey, Dad, Mom. Look at this.'' Beaming with a grin, Garrett waved again, then did a flip off the diving board.

''If that's what you want, I can't stop you from going to court,'' Michael said, a tightness in his chest that threatened to seize his next breath.

''I want to spend some time with him. Tom and I want to have him stay with us some weekends.''

''No.'' Michael clipped the word out, then clamped his jaw shut.

Garrett pulled himself out of the pool and came over to the table, water dripping off him. ''Mom, I'm playing baseball next Saturday. Will you come see me?''

Michael clenched the arms of the chair, wanting to snatch the invitation away.

''Of course, I will. Tom and I will be there ready to root for you.''

The smug smile on Mary Lou's face caused Michael to cringe. Short of making a scene, he would have to endure Mary Lou and her new husband's presence at the ball game. First thing Monday morning he would pay Robert Davenport a visit concerning his ex-wife's demands.

"Helen, what a nice surprise." Rachel let her friend into the house. "Do you want some iced tea?"

"Sounds divine, sugar. I'm parched. It's so hot I could fry eggs on the sidewalk outside my café. Of course, I'd probably lose some customers if I did."

"What brings you by?"

"Do I have to have a reason?"

"No, but who's minding the store?"

"Amy is, and she's doing a nice job."

In the kitchen Rachel poured the tea into a glass full of ice, then handed it to Helen. "I'm glad she's working full-time. Keeps her out of trouble."

"If you say so."

"What aren't you telling me?"

"What's she doing with the other forty or so hours a week? When she isn't sleeping or working?"

"Helen, spill it. What's happening?"

"I just hear things from time to time."

"About her and Kevin?"

"They're getting mighty serious." Helen tipped her glass and took several long sips.

"I can't follow her every place she goes."

"No, I reckon you can't. But maybe you should talk with her."

"You know, the problem with that is she won't listen to me."

Helen rubbed the back of her neck. "Yeah, you do have a problem there."

"Maybe I should try to follow her. It would probably be easier."

Helen walked to the kitchen table and looked at the drawings scattered all over it. "Are these for Michael's boat?"

"Yes. I'm almost finished."

"Have you seen him lately?"

"I saw him briefly at church, but we didn't talk." Rachel recalled the way Michael had kept his distance after being the one to encourage her to attend the service. When she'd glanced at him, a look of vulnerability had touched his eyes before a shutter fell in place.

"You know Mary Lou's coming this weekend to see Garrett play baseball."

"No, I didn't," Rachel said, disappointed that she had to hear the news from Helen and not Michael. She knew he didn't owe her any explanations, but the hurt was still there. "I haven't seen Garrett much since he came back. He came over this morning to play with Shaun. But he raced through here with Shaun so fast I'm not even sure what he's wearing. They're out in the backyard right now with the dog they found."

"So you haven't found the owner of the Lab yet?"

"No, I'm beginning to feel the dog will be ours. I had the boys put up posters, but no one has called."

"Well, you know part of the problem is where the boys put up those posters. One is on a telephone pole, but a bush hides it from everyone's view. Another is in my window, but down in the corner behind the newspaper bin."

"Why am I not surprised?" Shaking her head, Rachel took a chair at the table.

"What's going on besides your problems with Amy?"

Rachel ran her hands down her face. "What can I say? Lack of sleep wreaks havoc with one's body. It all boils down to one person. Michael. I shouldn't have come back at all."

"I don't think you had much choice, Rachel."

"And I'm not making the best of this situation. Do I stay away from the man like my common sense keeps telling me? No, instead, I tell him I'll work with him on his riverboat. What's wrong with me?"

"Do you want the truth or do you want me to lie to you?"

"Michael Hunter is just a friend. He isn't even the same person I knew ten years ago, and I'm certainly not, either." With her eyes closed Rachel massaged her temples. Tension clung to every part of her like spiderwebs to a haunted house.

"I think you're falling for him all over again."

Rachel rose, gripping the edge of the table. "I

won't do that to myself. I won't do that to Michael, either. We're just *friends.*"

Helen bent over the table. "Fine. Then what's this problem you're having with sleeping?"

Rachel was so intent on Helen and their conversation that she jumped when she heard the pounding on the front door. "I sure hope it isn't that man again. He doesn't know how to use the doorbell."

"Who?"

"Harold Moon." Rachel started for the door.

"Hold it. Let me answer it. I've been meaning to have a few words with that man since he almost ran me over."

Rachel couldn't have stopped Helen if she had wanted.

Helen planted herself squarely in front of the open door. "Can I help you?"

Harold scowled and held up a poster. "This is my dog."

Helen huffed, shaking her head. "Do you honestly want us to believe you own a dog?"

The scowl lines in his face deepened. "I don't care what you believe. That's my dog, and I have the papers to prove it."

Helen put her hands on her hips, her eyes blazing. "I wouldn't turn any dog over to you without seeing those papers, and then I'm not sure I could do that to a poor defenseless animal."

"Look, lady, this isn't between you and me."

"I'm making it my business."

Rachel decided at that moment she better intervene. "May I help you, Mr. Moon?"

"Yes, get this—lady out of here, then we need to talk about Charlie."

"I'm not going anywhere. I wouldn't leave my friend alone with you if you were—"

Rachel placed her hand on her friend's arm. "Helen, why don't you go out back and get the boys? Please."

Helen stalked toward the backyard, glancing over her shoulder several times. When the door slammed shut, Rachel turned to her neighbor.

"Come in, Mr. Moon."

Harold hesitated before opening the door and coming inside. "All I want is to be left alone, and yet you and those kids keep getting into my business."

Rachel felt sorry for the man. He probably didn't realize how defensive his voice sounded. The touch of vulnerability in his eyes reminded her of Michael's look at church. "Is the dog named Charlie?"

He mumbled yes.

"How come we've never seen you with him?"

"Because there is a leash law in this town and, unlike some people I've seen, I abide by it."

"How long has Charlie been with you?"

"Two years. What does that have to do with anything?"

"I must be certain you're the dog's owner."

"Bring him here. I'll show you."

"That's an excellent idea, Mr. Moon." At the back

door Rachel called to Helen and the boys to bring the dog inside.

The look on Garrett's and Shaun's faces made Rachel hope the dog didn't belong to Harold Moon. She had been afraid of this and wished she hadn't impulsively told Shaun he could keep the animal if they couldn't find the owner.

The two boys trudged inside followed by Helen and the dog. Shaun's head hung down, and his shoulders were slumped. Garrett didn't look much better.

Harold squatted and whistled. "Come here, Charlie."

The Lab's ears perked up, and he loped over to Harold, almost knocking the man back. The dog licked his face, his tail wagging.

Her neighbor glanced up. "Are you satisfied?"

"Yes," Rachel said before Helen could speak.

Tears glistened in Shaun's eyes as he said goodbye to Charlie, then came to stand next to Rachel, his chin touching his chest. She swallowed hard. "Mr. Moon, would it be possible for the boys to come over and see Charlie from time to time?"

Shaun's head snapped up, hopeful eagerness on his face. "We won't be no trouble."

Harold looked from Shaun to Garrett then at Charlie.

"Please. They have come to care about your dog," Rachel added, seeing the struggle in Harold.

"Okay. But not too much." He started for the door,

called to Charlie to follow and was gone before Helen could recover.

The startled expression on her face was still in place as the door shut behind the man. "Did I hear right? He's invited the boys over. Are you out of your mind, Rachel?"

She shot her friend an exasperated look. "No, the man is lonely."

"How can you tell?"

"I can." *Because I've felt the same way,* she silently added, *many times.*

"Rachel, I don't know if we should go. He isn't too friendly." Shaun stared at the front door, his expression almost as shocked as Helen's.

"I grant you the man is not very social. He needs practice."

"Sugar, he needs more than practice. I don't think even Amy Vanderbilt could help him."

"You two will be playing with Charlie out in the backyard. He has said you can come. The decision is yours."

Shaun conferred with Garrett, their whispers animated. "Okay. We'll try it."

When the boys left, Helen felt Rachel's forehead. "I think the heat has finally gotten to you. It's fried your brain."

"You know, Helen, small towns can be a closed society. Has anyone tried to reach that man?"

"Remember? I took him a pecan pie when he first came to town, and he refused it."

"Oh, my gosh, then he's a hopeless case."

"Okay. Maybe he did say something about being diabetic."

"There you have it." Rachel decided it was time to shake up her friend's life. "He's hurting, Helen. I can feel it."

"What are you? Psychic?"

"He's kind to his dog," Rachel explained, as if that said it all.

Helen walked to the front window and looked at Harold's house. "He does have one of the prettiest yards in town."

Rachel smiled as she turned to go into the kitchen. Helen had been alone for too long. And if her friend was busy with her own romance, she would leave Rachel be.

Rachel stared at Michael as he worked on his riverboat. She watched him move some lumber, sweat beading his brow. She felt the energy seep from her and she grasped the railing to steady herself. He picked up a canteen, took a sip, then dumped the rest over his head. Water dripped from his face, catching the fading sunlight and glistening. All she needed to complete the scene was to hear "Ol' Man River."

Michael looked toward her. He grinned and waved. Flushed from the warm greeting he sent her, she clutched her briefcase and strode toward him.

"I have the designs ready," she said in an all-business tone she was sure contrasted with the blush staining her cheeks.

"Oh, great! That was quick. Here, let me take a look." His hand touched hers on the handle of the briefcase.

She released her grip and stepped back, perspiration bathing her face. So much for presenting a business facade, Rachel thought. "If you don't like the design I've come up with, let me know what you don't like about it. I'm sure I can fix it."

He gave her a smile that doubled her heartbeat. "I'm sure you can. I have complete faith in you when it comes to cooking."

"Only cooking?" she asked, hearing the hurt tone in her question. She bit her lower lip, wishing she hadn't said anything.

His look drilled into her. "Let's go into the main salon and have a look. I have a table in there where I can spread everything out."

"How was your trip to Jackson?"

"I'm sure you've heard by now that Mary Lou is coming this Saturday to see Garrett play baseball."

But not from you. She nodded, careful to keep her expression neutral.

The main salon offered a slight reprieve from the afternoon sun. "My, don't you think it's unseasonably warm?"

Michael looked up from examining the designs. "It's the humidity. You'll get used to it."

"Most of the time I feel like a limp noodle."

"Mmm," he said absently, turning his full attention to the papers before him.

Anxiously, Rachel waited, perspiration rolling down her face. She wiped her hand across her brow.

"I like this design, Rachel. The only thing I would change is the area over here." Michael pointed to one wall. "I would move some of the cabinets to here and have the other preparation area along there so the two people don't have to stand so close together." His gaze trapped hers. "In the summer, even with air-conditioning, it can get awfully hot in a kitchen. I think spreading the people out might keep wars from erupting."

"I heartily agree," she said, brushing her hand across her brow again.

He straightened and removed a clean, folded handkerchief from his back pocket. He wiped it across her forehead, down her cheeks and along her neck. "I believe I heard we're having a heat wave."

"Isn't that a song?"

His thumb paused at the base of her throat. "Not any I heard of."

"Ah, yes, you used to be partial to rock and roll."

"Still am. And your favorites are classical and show tunes." He pocketed the handkerchief while the other hand remained on her shoulder, his thumb drawing slow circles where her life force beat beneath it.

"Yes. I see we still don't like the same music."

"But I can think of a few things we still have in common." His gaze linked with hers.

"Like what?" She took an unsteady breath.

"We both like chocolate." His impish grin caused her to think of the past, when he'd made her laugh.

"That doesn't sound like much."

"But it's a start," he replied with a wink.

Rachel laughed, relaxing for the first time since coming to the river landing.

A flash of red, a sound, pulled her attention from Michael. Amy stood in the doorway with a sullen look on her face.

Rachel's tension returned. "Hello, Amy. Did you need me for something?"

"I came to talk to Michael." Her sister peered at Michael as if Rachel weren't there. "Kevin needs a summer job. We were wondering if you needed people to work on the boat." Amy glanced at the door and motioned for Kevin to come inside.

"Good to see you, Kevin," Michael said, shaking the teenager's hand. "I could use some help with painting, sanding, moving heavy stuff."

"That's sounds great, Mr. Hunter. I was supposed to work at the gas station, but Bob's nephew is going to spend the summer with him."

"Well, then, the job is yours. You can start tomorrow morning at seven o'clock."

"I'll be here." Kevin started to leave, but Amy remained.

"Thank you, Michael."

Amy refused to look at Rachel. "Will you be home for dinner?" Rachel asked.

Her sister arched one of her brows. "No, I'm help-ing Helen at the café. I'll be home later."

"When?" Rachel hated dragging information out of Amy bit by slow bit.

"Twelve."

When Amy left, Rachel sagged. "I have to keep repeating Reverend Williams's advice to have pa-tience."

"You talked to him?"

"After church. I looked for you, but you were gone when I came out."

His gaze shifted away, then back. "It was a rough weekend."

"And you didn't feel like talking to a friend?"

"Is that what we are?"

"I hope we are."

Michael dragged his hands through his hair. "If you say so. Frankly, I don't know what I'm feeling anymore. My emotions have taken a beating lately."

She looked him straight in the eye. "Then we have something else in common."

Chapter Eight

"Dad, where's my uniform? You cleaned it, didn't ya?" Garrett yelled from the laundry room.

Michael sauntered into the kitchen, poured himself another cup of coffee and faced his son, who looked as if his whole world was about to fall apart.

"I put it on your bed this morning."

"Oh."

Garrett started to leave when Michael said, "When we talked after our trip to Jackson, everything was fine. Is everything okay now? You seem a little tense."

"Mom's gonna see me play today. I need to look my best. Dad, I need to get dressed or we'll be late. We can't be late!"

Michael drew in a deep, fortifying breath as he watched his son head for his bedroom. Michael took a sip of his coffee, then decided against another cup of caffeine. He was already wired from the six cups he'd had, starting at three o'clock this morning.

He pitched the coffee down the drain and rinsed his cup. Not only were Mary Lou and Tom coming to Magnolia Blossom, but after yesterday with Rachel on the riverboat, he was wound so tightly it wouldn't take much for him to slip over the edge.

The worst part of today would be seeing Rachel in the crowd of people at the ballpark. He ran his hand through his hair repeatedly. Today could be a very long day, he thought as he scooped up his keys.

"Ready, Garrett," he called to the second floor.

His son came bounding down the stairs. "How do I look?"

For the first time Michael could remember, Garrett had combed his hair and scrubbed his face clean without Michael telling him to do so. His uniform shirt was tucked into his pants. His son had never been concerned about his appearance until today.

"Great. Your mom will be impressed."

"She said her husband will be coming, too."

"Nervous?"

"Yeah, kinda."

Michael tousled his son's hair and hugged him to his side. "You don't have to be."

"Dad, you messed up my hair. Now I have to go upstairs and comb it again." He raced up the stairs. "We're gonna be late."

Michael heaved a deep sigh, thinking of the *long* day ahead.

*   *   *

Rachel stared at the massive front door, inhaled a deep breath and marched up the steps to Harold Moon's house. Her hand shook as she reached to ring the bell. The door swung open a minute later, and the man stood in the entrance as though he would fight anyone who dared to cross the threshold. And Shaun was somewhere inside. What had possessed her to ask him to allow her little brother to play with Charlie?

"Shaun said he was coming over here to see Charlie. He has a baseball game."

"He's in the backyard." Harold jerked his thumb in that direction, his usual scowl firmly in place. "Go around by the gate."

She stepped inside the yard and called, "Shaun, time to go."

Her brother glanced up from throwing a Frisbee for Charlie. "Just a sec." He hurried to the back door and knocked.

Her neighbor opened the door a crack. "Yes?"

Rachel's eyes widened at the man's tone of voice. It wasn't soft, but it wasn't gruff, either. And she could swear, even though the door blocked some of his face, that Harold Moon wasn't scowling. Of course, he wasn't smiling, either.

"I hope you can come see me play this afternoon. I'm pitching. We're playing our arch rivals, the Seahawks." Shaun puffed out his chest, proud of the fact that he was the best pitcher on the team.

"Probably not, kid. I have things to do around here." Harold shut the door quietly.

"Why did you ask Mr. Moon to your game?" Rachel asked as they were getting into the car.

"Ah, he's not so bad. You should see him with Charlie. You know, he used to play minor league ball."

"He did?"

"Yep. He even showed me a new pitch."

"He did?"

"Yeah, and he helped Garrett with his swing."

"He did?" Rachel slanted a look at her brother, astonished.

"Boy, is Garrett nervous about today. His mom's coming."

Rachel was very aware that Mary Lou was coming. Rachel had tossed and turned last night with dreams about Mary Lou and Michael. Rachel couldn't have slept more than a few hours, and she was wrung out.

"Is he glad his mother is coming?"

"Heck, yes."

"Most kids would be angry with a mother who hasn't been around much." Rachel thought about her situation and knew she was speaking from experience.

"Garrett isn't like most kids. Besides, Michael explained everything to him a long time ago."

"What did he explain?"

"That his mom needed to find herself. That she had been too young to have a child. That she loved him very much because she left him in Michael's care and knew he would be fine.''

Something in Shaun's voice made her glance at her brother. His brow was wrinkled as though he was thinking. ''What about our mother?''

He looked at her, his eyes clouded. ''Mom loves us. She left us with Aunt Flora. One day she'll come back just like Garrett's mom.''

Rachel's heart swelled; her throat constricted. She wished she felt the way her brother did about their mother and father. Reality would hit one day, and he would learn their parents only cared about their work. Rachel was determined to be there for her little brother when it happened.

She pulled into the parking lot next to the ball field. The second she cut the engine Shaun was out the door and running toward the dugout. She remained in the car, gripping the steering wheel while she composed herself. The mention of their mother had been a mistake. It brought to the foreground feelings she didn't want to deal with today.

When she saw Mary Lou walk past the car, Rachel's grasp on the steering wheel tightened until her knuckles were white. Michael had married Mary Lou eighteen months after Rachel had left for Paris. That had hurt. She had wanted him to pine for her the way she'd pined for him.

You had no right to feel that way, a voice inside her head said.

This had nothing to do with rights and everything

to do with emotions. Rachel realized she had never been totally rational about Michael Hunter, and that had not changed. That was why she had run when he'd declared his love for her. She didn't want to feel intense, all-consuming emotion. Her parents had that, and they excluded everyone else from their lives.

Sliding from the car, Rachel looked toward the stands, which were filling up with parents and friends of the teams. Mary Lou was sitting between a man who must be her husband and Michael. This was going to be a *long* afternoon.

Michael watched Rachel climb from her car and look at him. Their gazes connected.

"Garrett looks good in his uniform."

Mary Lou drew his attention with her statement, and he reluctantly turned his head toward his ex-wife. "He especially wanted to look good for you today," Michael said, hearing the warning in his voice.

"That makes two of us. I think I changed four times before deciding on what to wear."

"Five, dear," Tom interjected with a wry grin.

Mary Lou glanced toward Rachel, who was walking to the stands. "I see I'm not the only one who has returned home."

"Rachel's aunt died a month ago."

"Oh, I'm sorry to hear that. Flora Sanders was always nice to me."

"She was nice to everyone. That was her way."

When Rachel started to mount the bleachers to sit

on the top row, Michael snagged her hand and pulled her toward him. "Sit here." He didn't give her a chance to say no. He tugged her down next to him on the wooden seat. "Rachel Peters, I'd like you to meet Tom Bantam, and of course, you already know Mary Lou."

Rachel smiled and nodded toward both of them, but the look she sent Michael spoke of her displeasure.

"I'm sorry to hear about your aunt." Mary Lou leaned around Michael to talk with Rachel. "What happened?"

"A heart attack. Very quick."

The tight thread in Rachel's voice underscored her leashed anger. Michael realized he shouldn't have asked—okay, forced—her to sit next to him, but he didn't want to spend the whole afternoon listening to Mary Lou.

He bent close to Rachel's ear and whispered, "I need your help. Please."

When the edges of her mouth and the look in her eyes softened he knew she would help. He relaxed his tensed muscles and squeezed her hand, then quickly released his grasp.

"Oh, look, Garrett is first up to bat," Mary Lou exclaimed.

Michael shifted his attention to the field, comforted by the fact that Rachel was sitting on one side of him. Maybe this afternoon wouldn't be too bad, he thought as his son swung and missed the ball.

When his son struck out and tromped off the field, Michael decided he probably should reassess his assumption that everything would be all right. He could taste Garrett's desire for a home run. He had swung at the first three pitches with everything he had. Michael needed to have a word with his son. He started to get up to walk to the dugout when Harold Moon beat him to it. The man pulled Garrett to the side and whispered to him. His son nodded a few times, smiled, then went into the dugout.

Michael frowned. "What's Harold Moon doing with Garrett?"

"Shaun told me he has been giving Garrett a few pointers on swinging the bat."

"He has?" Michael rubbed the back of his neck, shaking his head. "I don't believe it."

"I can't believe he actually showed up. Shaun invited him, but Harold said he had things to do around the house."

"Who's Harold Moon?" Mary Lou asked.

"My neighbor." Rachel didn't look at Michael's ex-wife but kept her gaze trained on the field. Shaun was coming up to bat.

Michael cheered when Shaun got a base run. Rachel's enthusiasm was interesting to observe. When he had played baseball in high school and college, she hadn't cared much for the sport. If she came to the game, she would applaud with everyone else, but that was all. With Shaun she jumped up, clapped and whistled. If Michael didn't know better, he'd have thought she'd changed.

When the Tigers took the field, Rachel straightened, clasping her hands so tightly in her lap that Michael laid his over hers and said, ''Shaun's good. He'll be all right.''

''I know. It's just that the last time the Tigers lost and Shaun was pitching he blamed himself. I couldn't get him to see that no one person was to blame for losing.''

''Shaun has always been more competitive than Garrett.''

''Tell me about it. I actually played one of his video games with him the other night. I have great eye-hand coordination, but there was no way he was going to lose.''

Rachel grew taut as Shaun threw the first series of pitches. She began to breathe easier when the first two batters struck out. She relaxed even more when Helen sat next to her.

''Sorry I'm late. Some customer had a mix-up that I had to see to personally. How's it going?''

''Zero to zero,'' Rachel replied as the third batter hit the ball, and it went sailing out into left field.

When Garrett caught the fly ball, Mary Lou leaped to her feet and yelled, ''That's the way to go. Three up. Three down.''

Helen leaned close. ''So, is this not cozy?''

''Shh.'' Rachel grinned and mouthed the word *behave*.

"Who me? I always do," Helen whispered.

Rachel rolled her eyes and hoped she got through the afternoon unscathed. Between dealing with Michael and Mary Lou and watching Shaun play an important game, she was sure her nerves would be shredded like pieces of confetti by the time the game was over.

By the ninth inning Rachel had bitten two fingernails down to the quick. She glanced at the scoreboard for the hundredth time. The score was still tied, five to five. Nothing magical had changed while she wasn't looking.

"I don't know how much more of this I can take. No wonder I never liked to watch you play, Michael."

He chuckled. "Relax."

Again, he took her hand. She kept telling herself to withdraw it from his, but she couldn't. She enjoyed the contact but wished she didn't.

Garrett was getting ready to bat. Rachel noticed Harold motioning the boy to the fence and saying a few words to him. Garrett grinned and went to the plate. She felt the tension in Michael's grip as his son swung at the first pitch. The sound of the bat hitting the ball reverberated through the park. Rachel stood next to Michael as the ball soared over the playing field. She shouted and clapped when it landed on the other side of the fence.

"A home run! He did it!" Michael wrapped his arms about Rachel and spun her around and around.

When he placed her on the ground, she was dizzy, and that would be her defense if anyone asked why she allowed Michael to kiss her in front of half the town. He pressed her against him and settled his mouth over hers, not in a quick congratulatory kiss but in a long one that curled her toes.

When he pulled back, his gaze captured hers, and for a brief moment everyone else faded from view. They were the only two people in the whole ballpark. His look melted her insides.

"Hey, y'all sit down in front. The game isn't over. Some of us would like to see the rest of the game."

Rachel blushed when she glanced at the people in the stands, every eye on them. She sunk to her seat, wishing she could crawl under the bleachers to hide. Whereas Michael was grinning from ear to ear. The only thing he didn't do was give everyone a high five.

The rest of the inning passed in a blur. The next batter struck out, and the Seahawks came up to bat for the final time—if the Tigers could hold them to no runs. She was aware of everything happening around her, but she felt as though she were in a vacuum, observing the situation from afar.

When the game was over and the Tigers had won, all Rachel wanted to do was get Shaun and head home before someone asked her about the *kiss*. The whole town would have her engaged to Michael before the night was over.

When Mary Lou started talking to him, Rachel saw her chance to escape without having to say anything to Michael. She backed away a few paces, then turned and hurried toward the parking lot. She would wait for Shaun inside the safety of her car.

Turning, Michael started to say something to Rachel, but she was gone. He searched the crowd around the boys but didn't see her. Then he looked toward her car and found her sitting behind the steering wheel with the engine running. He grinned and waved. She glanced away.

Garrett ran up to Michael. "Did you see me?"

"You were awesome, son."

"I was very impressed," Mary Lou said.

Garrett straightened, a big grin on his face. "I've been practicing."

"Tom and I would like to take you out for some ice cream."

"Can we go, Dad?"

"Sure," Michael said, feeling trapped into spending more time with Mary Lou and her husband.

Garrett and Tom walked ahead of Mary Lou and Michael. He was sure she'd maneuvered it that way. He could tell she had something on her mind.

She slowed her step. "I see that Rachel is back in your life. Do you think that's wise?"

"Rachel needed my help with Shaun and Amy."

"I don't want to see Garrett hurt by all this."

"I find your concern just a little late, Mary Lou."

She winced. "Let me say one more thing, then I'll keep quiet on the subject of Rachel. Think long and hard before you fall in love with her again. Has anything really changed with her? Can she stay in Magnolia Blossom? I can't see you any other place but here. Do you want a repeat of ten years ago?''

He ran his hand through his hair and massaged the back of his neck. He was very aware that Rachel wouldn't make a commitment or settle down in Magnolia Blossom. That was why he was protecting his heart against her. The kiss had been a lapse in good judgment. That was all.

Sheltered under the overhang, Rachel stood at the back of the riverboat and watched the rain fall in gray sheets. A thin layer of perspiration blanketed her whole body as she inhaled air laced with the clean, fresh smell of a summer shower.

It had been almost two weeks since the baseball game, and life moved forward, Rachel thought, peering over her shoulder at the beehive of activity in the main salon. The sound of an electric saw and hammering dueled with the sound of the falling rain.

She hadn't seen Michael much since the game and she never saw him alone, which she suspected he arranged purposely. She welcomed the crowd of people who demanded his time. She was able to come to the boat, supervise the renovation of the kitchen, which was progressing nicely, and leave with her emotions intact. It couldn't have worked out better if she had planned it.

''I love to look at the river when it rains, to listen

to it hit the water. Soothing. Calming. Something I need right now.''

At the sound of Michael's voice, Rachel closed her eyes for a few seconds, realizing her reprieve had ended.

He came to the railing and leaned back against it, facing her, one corner of his mouth lifting in a smile. ''I need a break. I've been so involved in these renovations that I feel like I'm meeting myself coming and going.''

''There does seem to be a lot going on around here these days.''

''I wanted the boat ready before the end of summer. I think I'll get my wish, but at what price?''

''Why the push? You've had the boat for years.''

''You know me. When I get something into my head, I don't like to wait.'' He crossed his arms over his chest, his back against a post.

''I feel the same way. That's why I've been on pins and needles waiting to hear from the investors about my restaurant.'' She realized she had brought up the subject of her restaurant as a reminder to him—and herself—that her stay in Magnolia Blossom was temporary.

Michael's expression went neutral, and a subtle tension sharpened the air between them like the atmosphere right before a storm. ''When do you expect to hear?''

''Within the month. A couple of them are out of the country right now.''

"What do you think your chances are?"

"Good."

"Then you'll leave?"

"Yes." Thunder sounded in the distance, and Rachel jumped. The tension between them had honed her nerves to a keen edge.

"Looks like the weather is taking a turn for the worse." Michael faced the same direction as she did, his arm brushing hers.

The casual contact sent a jolt through her as if lightning had struck her body. "How are things going with you and Mary Lou?"

Michael sighed. "We had another big discussion about Garrett. It didn't go well."

For a few seconds his emotions lay exposed. She placed her hand over his on the railing, wanting to comfort and give something to him. He had given her so much.

"Does Garrett know you two are arguing about custody?"

"I haven't told him yet. I didn't want to fight a legal battle over him, but I don't trust Mary Lou." He stared at the rain, the weather a reflection of his mood. He hadn't intended to come out on deck and talk with Rachel, but before he'd realized it, his feet had taken him to her and his mouth had opened and spoken.

"You won't be able to keep this from him for long."

"So I guess we both have secrets we're keeping

from our families,'' he said with a bitter edge to his voice.

''I've decided to tell Amy and Shaun soon, even if I haven't heard from my lawyer about the restaurant proposal.''

''When?''

''After her birthday next week. I don't like keeping secrets. You were right.''

''Which is your way of saying I'd better tell Garrett about what's going on?''

''He doesn't realize what really happened when Mary Lou left, does he? He doesn't know about her drinking problem?''

''He was too young. I could never disillusion him by telling him the truth about his mother. I'm not putting my son in the middle of this.''

''But aren't you doing that with this custody battle? Maybe Mary Lou has changed. Is she drinking anymore?''

''She says no, not for a year.''

''But you don't believe her?''

He stiffened. ''No—yes. I don't know, Rachel. I want to believe her. It would make things so much easier. She sees Garrett on a limited basis with me around.''

''But not alone.''

''No.''

''What are you afraid of? That she will run away with him? Isn't her husband established with a medical practice in Jackson?''

"Mary Lou was always unpredictable."

"Contrary to you?"

Michael pressed his lips together and continued to stare at the gray sheets of rain. The sound on the water usually soothed him, but now he was wound so tightly he was afraid he would snap in two pieces. He let the silence between them lengthen, hoping that Rachel wouldn't pursue the topic of Mary Lou. He was all talked out.

"What are you going to do for Amy's birthday?" he finally asked.

"I'd like to organize a birthday party. What do you think?"

"It's worth a try. I'll even help you. You can have the party on the boat. A lot of the work has been done."

"Thanks. I want it to be a surprise."

"This from the woman who hates surprises?" Michael arched a brow.

"If it wasn't a surprise, I'm afraid she might not agree to me giving her one."

"Aren't things better between you?"

"A little, this past week. She actually had breakfast with me this morning."

"Speaking of breakfast, don't forget the pancake breakfast at the church. Amy is one of the organizers. Great way to be around your sister and help the youth group, too."

"I'll be there," Rachel said, realizing she would also be around Michael.

* * *

"We need more pancakes," Kevin called from the doorway of the church kitchen.

"Where are all these people coming from?" Rachel asked, stirring another batch together.

"They heard you were making the pancakes and they couldn't resist sampling your cooking, sugar." Helen flipped over some pancakes on the griddle.

"I'm not the only one. You're cooking, too."

"But, sugar, they've tasted my pancakes at the café. You're a mystery to them."

"Quit chatting, ladies, and get busy. You have a hungry crowd out there in the parish hall." Michael slid another serving platter toward Helen.

Perspiration beaded Rachel's brow. "And this is for charity?" She felt like a piece of wilted lettuce.

"Yep. The youth group is raising money for their mission trip to Mexico," Michael said, then left the kitchen to give the full platter to a teenaged server.

Amy dashed in and grabbed another pitcher of orange juice. "Two more families just showed up. Kevin is seating them now."

"When you're through pouring the juice, we could use another cook." Rachel slid the mixing bowl to Helen. "We're running low on bacon."

"Be back in a sec."

Rachel stared at her sister as she slipped from the kitchen. "Did you hear that?"

"Yeah, she'll be back in a sec. What's wrong with that?"

"Nothing. It was actually said in a perfectly normal

voice. I may needlepoint those words and frame them.''

''There's only one problem with that. You don't needlepoint.''

''True. But I could take it up.''

Helen nearly choked on her laughter. ''You sit still long enough to do something like that?''

''Do what?'' Michael asked, coming up behind Rachel and snatching a piece of bacon.

She thwacked him playfully across the knuckles with a spatula.

''Ouch!''

''You have to wait like all the other workers until the paying customers have eaten.''

''You wield a mean spatula, Rachel Peters.''

''And you just remember that the next time you try to eat before it's your turn.''

''Oh, look, what's Amy doing?'' Michael pointed toward the door into the parish hall.

Rachel started to turn but stopped and whirled in time to see Michael snitching another piece of bacon. He had it halfway to his mouth when she said, ''I'm ashamed of you, Michael Hunter. You're the youth director. What kind of example are you setting by taking that bacon?'' The corners of her mouth twitched as she tried to suppress her laughter.

Michael hung his head and offered the piece to her. ''It's hard to resist your cooking.'' He slanted a glance at her through lowered eyelashes, a sheepish look on his face. "I'll try to resist, but I can't promise anything."

Rachel rolled her eyes. "I don't want that bacon. You touched it, you have to eat it."

"Oh, really." His expression brightened. He popped the piece into his mouth, an impish grin gracing his face. "It's a sacrifice, but I'll do it."

"Will you two get back to work? We'll never get everyone served—at least not before lunch. And I have a café to run, customers who might want to see me before the end of the day." Helen stood with her hand on her waist, a lethal-looking spatula in her grasp.

Michael saluted. "Yes, ma'am." He grabbed another plate of pancakes and headed for the parish hall, whistling as he went.

That set the tone for the rest of the pancake breakfast. Even Amy relaxed and smiled more than usual. By the time Rachel mixed the last batch of pancakes, exhaustion clung to her, but it was a pleasant feeling. She leaned back against the counter and surveyed the kitchen. The scent of frying bacon and pancakes still laced the air. She felt at home. The sensation took her by surprise.

Kevin entered the kitchen with a tray full of dirty dishes. Amy followed with several empty platters stacked on top of each other. Their laughter filled the room with a warmth that heightened Rachel's sense of belonging.

"Okay, is it our time to eat?" Michael asked, bringing in more plates.

"Yes," Helen announced. "Everyone can grab some food. We'll clean up after we eat."

Several teenagers scrambled to be first in line for the remaining pancakes. Helen patiently doled them out. Kevin and Amy brought up the end of the line, taking their breakfast and following the rest of the youth group into the parish hall.

"There'd better be some left for us adults." Michael held up his plate.

"Don't you mean me?" Helen asked, slipping a stack of pancakes on his plate.

"No, I mean me."

Rachel laughed. "You two are giving me a headache."

When Helen, Michael and Rachel came out of the kitchen to sit with the youth group, Reverend Williams stood up. "This fund-raiser was a rousing success again this year. We owe it all to the hard work of everyone in this room. Having Rachel as one of our cooks was an added treat. I heard members would like to have another pancake breakfast next week. I never knew pancakes could be so delicious. Thank you all for making this a success."

Several teenagers glanced at Rachel. She blushed while applause erupted in the parish hall.

Michael leaned over and whispered, "Looks like you won the reverend's heart as well as the youth group's. Anytime you want to help me with this group, let me know.''

''Sorry, I'll have to pass. The only hearts I need to win over are Shaun's and Amy's.''

''Shaun's you have in the palm of your hand.''

''But not my sister's,'' Rachel whispered. ''Not yet, at least.''

''Amy has volunteered to say the blessing.'' Reverend Williams sat while Amy came to the front of the room.

''Heavenly Father, bless this food we are about to eat and help provide for those who are less fortunate than we are. Guide us in our mission to spread Your word and show us how to reach out to those who need us. Amen.''

Her sister's prayer filled Rachel with a sense of peace. Amy's sincerity and generosity touched Rachel's heart. Even though she and Amy weren't getting along, her sister was a good person whose strong faith would help her adjust to any situation. That realization made Rachel wish her own faith was stronger. Then maybe she would be satisfied with her life. Rachel pushed away that idea. She just needed to get to New York and her dream of having her own restaurant.

Chapter Nine

"Yes, I understand. I'll be there August tenth to sign the papers," Rachel said, jotting a note on the pad next to the phone. "Thank you, Frank. This is wonderful news and sooner than I expected." She hung up, her hand lingering on the receiver.

Wonderful news? Then why wasn't she happier about getting the money for her restaurant? She should be jumping for joy. Instead, she was wondering how she was going to tell everyone the *good* news.

Amy's surprise birthday party was this evening on the riverboat. Rachel couldn't say anything until after that. She had a month before she had to be in New York to sign the papers, then a couple more weeks after that before she had to start the plans for the restaurant. She had some time. She would wait until the moment was right.

"Rachel, I'm leaving for the boat," Shaun called.

Taking her mug of coffee, she walked into the living room. "I'll be down later. Did you get all the invitations delivered?"

"Yeah. She doesn't suspect a thing. She thinks she's coming to the boat to pick up Kevin after work. He told her that his car was having some problems."

She went with her brother onto the porch, taking a deep breath of the fresh air. "It's a good thing she's doing that summer arts workshop in Natchez or I don't know how we could have kept this quiet."

Rachel watched as Shaun rode his bike away from the house. He would be all right about the move, but that still left Amy. Sighing at the task ahead of her, Rachel took a sip of her coffee, then retrieved the mail from the box. As she entered the house, the phone rang. She hurried into the kitchen and snatched up the receiver.

Breathless, she said, "Hello."

"Rachel, it's your mother. I wanted to let you know I'll be coming to the States in a few weeks to testify before a congressional committee on funding for medical research. I thought I would stop in Magnolia Blossom and sign those papers."

Rachel sank onto the chair next to the phone, her hands trembling with anger. Her mother's life went on as if nothing was different, and she supposed, for her mother, it wasn't. She didn't have to worry about her children. That was Rachel's responsibility. It shouldn't be.

"Rachel? Are you there?"

"Yes, Mother."

"I won't be able to stay long because your father and I are at a crucial time in our research. I wanted to take care of the legalities as soon as possible because I have no idea when I'll get back to the States."

Rachel's anger mounted. "How convenient for you that I'm here to take care of your children."

"You know it wouldn't be a good situation to have Amy and Shaun live here in our camp."

"For whom? You and Dad or Amy and Shaun?" Rachel's hand tightened around the receiver until her knuckles turned white.

"For everyone."

"Why did you have children, Mother? You certainly aren't around enough to know what is good for us. First Aunt Flora and now I will take care of *your* responsibilities."

"I thought you were okay about this?"

"How? Did you ever really talk to me about it?"

"I've got to go. The boat's leaving to go back upriver. We'll talk when I get to the States."

Before Rachel could say, "Don't bother," the line went dead.

Tears pooled in Rachel's eyes as she stared at the phone. She didn't understand where the tears were coming from. She had long ago given up crying over a situation that would never change. She and her siblings were a burden. She just hated having it confirmed again. Why was she still trying to have a relationship with her mother when it was obvious that wasn't going to happen?

"Rachel, where are you?" Helen called from the living room.

Rachel rubbed her hand across her wet cheeks, hoping to erase any evidence that she cared what her parents thought or did.

"There you are." Helen stood in the doorway into the kitchen, her eyes narrowing on Rachel. "You've been crying."

"No, I just got something in my eye." Rachel hurriedly stood.

"When you're ready to tell me, I'm all ears. Is it Michael?"

Rachel shook her head.

"Amy?"

Rachel turned and leaned against the counter, her hands grasping its edge. "You aren't going to let this go until I tell you?"

"Confession is good for the soul."

"I'm not ready yet." She had a hard time telling anyone that her parents had rejected her and wanted nothing to do with her, Amy or Shaun.

Helen threw up her hands. "Okay. I'll mind my own business."

"Now, that will be a first."

Helen glanced at all the food ready to go. "I'm sorry I'm late, but I got held up at the café." Helen picked up a box of food. "Here, the least I can do is help you load this into your car. I'm sure there's a lot to do at the boat. We only have a few hours left.''

After Helen helped load the car, she followed Rachel to the pier. Michael came down to the landing and started carrying the boxes of food to the main salon.

''Where's Kevin?'' Rachel asked after everything was on the boat.

''He went to pick up some of the kids,'' Michael said. ''He didn't want a lot of cars near the landing. Do you have everything you need for the party?''

''All except Amy and her friends.''

He stared at her, his gaze intent, probing. ''Something's wrong. What is it?''

Her eyes widened. Michael had always had a sixth sense when it came to her moods. No matter how hard she tried to hide her feelings from him, he could tell. Rachel's teeth dug into her lower lip as she debated how much to tell him. She decided to reveal part of the problem. ''I received a phone call from my mother today.''

''Is she coming for Amy and Shaun?''

Rachel shook her head. ''No, but she's coming to sign the papers Robert told her were necessary for me to be their guardian. She doesn't want them to live with her and Dad. Of course, this shouldn't come as a surprise. Amy would really protest that move, and the conditions my parents live in aren't the best.'' Her chest constricted, and her lungs burned.

Suddenly, she needed some fresh air. She escaped

to the deck and took a deep breath. Michael's hands settled on her shoulders, and he drew her against him. He felt strong, capable—steady. He was a man who would never turn his back on his family. He would do anything for his child.

"Is there something else?" Michael asked, his fingers kneading the tightness in her shoulders.

She flinched and was glad he couldn't see her expression. She wasn't ready to share her good news about the restaurant deal. "Isn't that enough?"

"Are you going to tell Amy and Shaun about the call?"

"No, I don't want them to be hurt."

"Like you?"

"Yes, like me," she murmured, realizing she was finally speaking about her feelings concerning her parents.

Even Aunt Flora hadn't realized the depth of Rachel's despair over her parents' rejection. She'd always tried to put up a brave front when the subject of her parents had come up. She was tired of denying her hurt and anger. Over the past weeks Rachel's idea of family had shifted. It wasn't okay that her parents didn't have time for their children.

"The day my mother brought Amy and me to Aunt Flora's was one of the saddest days of my life. At the time I didn't realize that my aunt would be the best thing for Amy and me. All my life I had been shuffled from one place to the next, never able to make friends because I didn't stay in one place long enough. Then my mother left us with Aunt Flora, expecting us to settle down and be happy and content to make our home with her older sister. It never happened for me. I didn't know how to settle down. I had never learned how to." Tears cascaded down her cheeks.

Not saying a word, Michael continued to massage her tensed shoulders.

She knuckled her tears away, but they still flowed. "As a little girl I used to dream of the Ozzie and Harriet type of family, but I gave that dream up a long time ago. I'm not cut out to be part of a family like that."

He turned her to face him. "Why not?"

"Because I can't make that kind of commitment. You, of all people, should know that."

He took a handkerchief from his back pocket and wiped her tears from her face. "Then what do you plan on doing about Amy and Shaun?"

"What I'm doing now. I'll love them the best way I can and hope it's enough. I'm just not very good at this sort of thing."

"That's how I felt when Mary Lou left me to raise Garrett all by myself."

"Then there's hope. Look at you now. You're a great father. He adores you."

"But it wasn't easy."

"Is that why you're so angry that Mary Lou is back in Garrett's life?"

Surprise flashed in his eyes. "Yes, I think that's part of it. She wasn't around for six years and now she wants to waltz right back in and pick up where she left off without having done any of the hard work it takes to raise a child.''

Rachel cupped his face with one hand and with the other urged him closer to her until their mouths touched. His kiss was a gentle reminder of what kind of person he was. He was a good man who deserved a woman who could love him with no reservations, who could totally commit to him. Times like this she wished she could be that woman.

''You know, we're more alike than you and I ever thought, Rachel. For years after my mother died, I fought my feelings of abandonment. At six she was such an important part of my life that I couldn't understand why God took her away from me. I needed my mother. I was angry at God for a while. Then my father made me realize that my mother would never be gone as long as I could remember her. She was with God, and I would be reunited with her one day.''

Rachel pulled back and stared into Michael's eyes, filled with a sadness she'd glimpsed from time to time. ''But your mother never had a choice. Mine does. She chooses not to be a part of our lives. And you had your father to comfort you.''

''Yes, but when I was six, none of that mattered. My mother was gone. I realize our situations are different, but the emotions are the same.''

''And I made everything worse. I left you not six months after your father passed away. I'm sorry.'' She clenched his shoulders, hoping to convey in her touch how much she wished she hadn't hurt him all those years ago.

He blinked, erasing any evidence of sorrow. "My point in telling you this is that you'll have to deal with your parents' abandonment or it will haunt you and influence everything you do."

"Is that experience talking?"

His nod was curt. "I'm still working on it."

"Because of me and Mary Lou."

"My dream was to put down roots here in Magnolia Blossom and raise a large family—the more children the merrier."

"Whereas I've always run from commitment because of my childhood."

The smile he gave her was mocking. "I guess we've handled our issues of abandonment differently. But, Rachel, praying has helped me through the rough times."

"Our guests are arriving," Helen announced from the doorway into the main salon.

Michael rested his forehead against Rachel's, his hands buried in her hair. "I know you'll do what's right for Amy and Shaun. They're lucky to have you for a sister. We'll talk some more later."

Rachel stepped away from the comfort of Michael's touch. She wished she had his kind of faith. She wished it were as simple as turning to God to erase the feelings churning inside her. Maybe praying could help her, too, Rachel thought, grasping on to a seed of hope and holding tight.

* * *

When Amy walked into the main salon thirty minutes later, Rachel realized all her hard work had been worth it. After her initial shock, Amy had a big grin on her face as her friends swarmed around her congratulating her. Rachel had never seen her sister so happy.

One of the teenagers cranked up the volume on the CD player, and the sounds of pop rock bounced off the walls. Rachel stood back from the group and watched her sister interact with her friends. None of Amy's hostility was evident, and Rachel wished it could be different between her and her sister.

"Do you want to dance?" Michael all but shouted in her ear.

"I never learned to dance."

"There's not much to it. You move to the beat. Anything goes." He tugged on her arms. "Come on. Besides, I bribed them to play a slow dance right about now."

The music changed to a soft melody that Rachel would have called music. Michael pulled her into his arms and began to move to the slow beat. Rachel locked her arms about his neck and allowed the rhythm to flow through her body as she swayed.

"See, this isn't so bad. We can carry on a conversation without shouting." He leaned back slightly to look at her. "I'd have thought you would have learned to dance by now."

"Never had the time."

"What have you been doing with your time besides cooking?"

"Not much else. Sometimes when I'm in a new place, I sightsee, sample the local foods, that sort of thing."

"Have you ever been serious about anyone?"

"No. I'm never in any one place long enough."

"You have been running fast. What's going to happen when life catches up with you?"

Rachel stiffened within the circle of Michael's arms. "It's not going to. I'm very good at evading."

When the music changed to a fast tempo, Rachel slipped from his embrace and made her way to the refreshment table.

Following her, Michael picked up a half sandwich and took a bite. "This is my dinner, I'm afraid."

"You didn't eat before?"

"When? I was too busy getting this place ready. Did you?"

"No, I was too busy getting the food ready."

"Michael, thank you for this party. I was so surprised." Amy gave him a kiss on the cheek.

"Actually, all I did was supply the place. Rachel did all the work. It was her idea."

"Thanks," Amy murmured in a less than enthusiastic voice. "In another year I'll be able to do anything I want. I'll be eighteen and won't have to answer to anyone."

Even though Amy spoke to Michael, Rachel knew the comments were directed at her. She had felt that very same way when she was seventeen. "Well, that may be true, but you still have a year to go."

Amy lifted her chin. "I know some seventeen-year-olds who are on their own."

Rachel regretted being pulled into Amy's argument. She bit the inside of her cheeks to keep from saying anything. Michael gripped her hand and pulled her to his side, his support quietly conveyed.

"And how well are they doing?" Michael asked, squeezing Rachel's hand. "Striking out on your own is a big step."

"They're happy," the teenager declared, louder than necessary. "Kevin's friend Patrick has a job at the supermarket in Natchez. He has an apartment with two other guys. He's doing fine."

"Is that Patrick Johnson?" Michael asked.

Amy nodded.

"When I talked with his dad last week, he was worried about Patrick. He isn't going to finish high school because he has to work two jobs to pay the rent. He's thinking about moving back home."

Amy grabbed Kevin's hand. "Let's dance. This is our song."

Rachel watched the young couple move onto the dance floor. "Thank you, Michael. If I had said anything else, this boat would have been declared a war zone."

"There's trouble brewing."

"I know."

"Why don't you leave her in Magnolia Blossom? She can stay with me."

"No. I won't abandon her. She's had to deal with that one too many times. She'll adjust. Besides, Shaun, Amy and I are all we have. We're family."

Michael twisted to face her. "A month ago I wasn't sure you felt that way."

"I've always felt Amy and Shaun were my family."

"I think you knew it in your head but not your heart. Now, you know it in your heart."

The truth of his words hurt. She had run from the idea of a family most of her life. She couldn't run anymore. "We'd better take up our battle stations before some of these teenagers slip out of here for dark places on this boat."

For the next two hours Rachel stood by the door, feeling like a warden in a prison. She had to turn several couples away from exploring the boat. Another hour, and the party would be winding down, she thought, and began to relax until Helen scurried over to her.

"They're gone!" Helen declared in her melodramatic way.

"Who?"

"Amy and Kevin. They walked onto the deck to get some fresh air, which I've been letting the kids do. I've been keeping an eye on them. Well, I turned to speak with a young man, and that must have been when they slipped away. I can't find them on the deck.''

Rachel tensed. "Do you think they left the boat?"

"No, Shaun and Garrett are playing on the lower deck by the gangplank. No one has gone past them. They're here somewhere.''

"Where's Michael?" Rachel asked, worried that Amy would do something foolish and end up hurt. It wasn't that long ago that she had felt the tender emotions a first love produced. And look at the pain her relationship with Michael had caused both of them.

"He's coming.''

Rachel looked beyond Helen and saw Michael striding toward her. Relief shimmered through her. "You know?''

"Let's check all the cabins first. I have the master key.''

Fifteen minutes later she and Michael had opened and locked every cabin door on the second deck. They climbed to the upper level, Rachel's heart hammering faster each minute. As they walked by the wheelhouse, Rachel heard a noise. She stopped and pointed toward the door, which was slightly ajar.

Michael came up and whispered in her ear, "I'll handle this.''

She shook her head. "She's my sister. I will.''

Taking a deep, fortifying breath, Rachel slid back the wheelhouse door and stepped into the room. Silhouetted against the moonlight streaming through the large windows were Amy and Kevin, standing very close together. They were so intent on each other they didn't hear Rachel come in until she coughed. They jumped apart.

"Excuse me, Amy, but I believe some of your guests are starting to leave. You need to say goodbye to them." Rachel was amazed her voice was level and calm, because inside she quaked.

Amy didn't say a word but stomped past Rachel and Michael, who was still standing outside the wheelhouse. Rachel was glad she couldn't read her sister's expression because she was sure Amy was furious. Rachel could tell by the rigid way her sister held herself as she left.

Michael came up behind Rachel and gripped her shoulders. "This, too, shall pass."

She sighed. "I hope so. Another reason I couldn't leave her here is that I don't want anyone else to have to deal with Amy's volatile emotions."

"That's being a teenager. Up one minute, down the next."

"Amy's issues go deeper than that."

He drew her against him and cradled her in his arms. Their strong feel dimmed her worries for a few seconds. She allowed herself to forget her troubles, to forget that she needed to tell Michael the restaurant deal had gone through. She would soon.

"How could you embarrass me like that?" Amy asked the next morning in the kitchen.

Surprised her sister was up so early, Rachel glanced

up from reading the papers concerning her restaurant proposal, which her lawyer had faxed her. "It's called being a responsible chaperon."

Before Rachel had a chance to turn over the legal papers, Amy plopped down in the chair next to her, her gaze straying to the documents. "What's that?"

Rachel drew in a deep, calming breath. "Details about my restaurant deal in New York."

Amy scowled, her eyes narrowing on the pieces of paper as if she could ignite them with her gaze.

"The investors said yes. They want to meet with me in August. I'll sign the papers then."

"When were you going to tell us?" Amy's voice rose.

"I just found out yesterday myself."

Sleepy-eyed, Shaun shuffled into the kitchen. He halted, took one look at Amy and said, "I think I'll skip breakfast."

"Stay. This concerns you, too." Amy flexed her trembling hands. "When are *you* leaving?"

Rachel inhaled deep breaths that did nothing to calm her speeding heart. "Shaun and I will go to New York on August tenth so I can sign the papers while you're in Mexico on your mission trip. Then we'll return and pack up the house. I want both of you in New York by the start of school."

"I'm not going." Amy's pout descended.

"I can't. Garrett and I have a basketball clinic at school that week."

Both her sister and brother faced Rachel, accusations in their expressions. In that moment Rachel realized she would rather face an angry mob of strangers than her own angry family. "Shaun, don't you want to check out New York before you move there?"

"No." Tears welled into his eyes.

"I know you don't understand now—"

"You got that right," Amy interrupted, rising and putting an arm around her brother as though she would protect him from their older sister. "When were you going to discuss this with us like you promised? Right before you had to leave? The only reason you told us now is because I saw you reading those." She flipped her hand toward the papers in front of Rachel.

"I want us to be a family. We can't be one if we live in different cities." Rachel knew anything she said at the moment wouldn't really be heard by either one.

"Your idea of discussion is quite different from mine. You led Shaun and me to believe we might actually have a say in our own futures."

"I suppose I could go and sign the papers, Shaun, without you. That way you could still go to the basketball clinic."

"How big of you. We're staying come September." Amy shot the words back.

"We're a family. We do this together." After talking to her mother on the phone, she was more determined than ever to keep this family together. She wanted to give her siblings something she'd never had—a real home.

Amy took a step then another until she was only inches from Rachel. ''I will not leave Magnolia Blossom. Ever.'' She brushed past Rachel and hurried out of the room.

The slam of Amy's door reverberated throughout the house like a gong. Rachel winced.

With tears streaming down his cheeks, Shaun yelled, ''I'm not leaving, either.'' He, too, raced from the kitchen and slammed his bedroom door shut.

Rachel started to follow Amy and Shaun, but when she stood in the hallway, staring at the closed doors, she felt the wide rift between her and her siblings. She didn't know if she would ever be able to close it. She had to try. She would give them some time to calm down, then she would talk with each one and try to make them understand.

Rachel sat in the living room in the dark, trying to bring some order to her life. The whole day, her sister and brother had given her the cold shoulder. Neither had left their bedrooms, not even to eat. When she returned to New York, she was sure everything would settle down and her life would be like before—except she would be responsible for Amy and Shaun, and there would be a part of her left in Magnolia Blossom, the part that wished she could make a total commitment to Michael.

She had given Amy and Shaun time to digest her

news. She needed to talk to them and get them to understand. She knocked on Shaun's door, then waited until he said to come in. He was at his computer, playing a game. He didn't look at her as she entered and sat on his bed behind him.

"We should talk about this." Rachel watched him kill a few aliens and wondered where she should begin.

When his man died, he switched the game off. "I don't want to leave Magnolia Blossom. My friends are all here. Garrett is the best friend a guy could have."

"I know. But my work is in New York, not here."

"Amy says you can cook anywhere."

She'd heard those words before—from Michael, years ago. "Yes, but I'll have my own restaurant. That's something I've been planning for ten years. It's one of my dreams. Do you have dreams, Shaun?"

His lower lip stuck out. "Yeah, I want to pitch a no-hitter."

"That dream is important to you. Well, my dream is important to me. You'll be able to make new friends in New York and you can come visit Magnolia Blossom and Garrett. He can come see you and you can show him all the neat things there are to do in New York. He'd probably love to see a Yankees game."

His lower lip quivered; tears pooled in his eyes. "I don't want to leave. I'm scared."

Rachel went to her brother and hugged him. "I

know. Change is scary. But I want us to be a family, to be together, not separated. I love you, Shaun. Please give this a chance.''

He leaned back, swiping the tears from his face. ''I love you, Rachel.''

''I promise you can come visit every summer. I know that Michael or Helen would love to have you.''

He pulled away, straightening his shoulders. ''Do you think I could see the Yankees play? They are one of my favorite teams.''

''Sure, and when the Braves come to town, I have connections. I think I could get you in to meet the team.''

''You can?''

''Yep, anything for my little brother.'' Rachel tousled his hair.

''I don't have to go away to school, do I?''

''Not unless you want to. There are plenty of good schools in New York City.''

Shaun turned to his computer and began to play the game again.

''Don't stay up too late,'' Rachel said as she left Shaun's bedroom.

She halted in front of Amy's door, not really ready for the confrontation. She knocked, her heart beginning to beat faster. Her palms were damp as she lifted her hand to knock again. Nothing. She shouldn't be surprised. Amy was ignoring her, as usual, but they had to talk about this sometime.

Rachel eased the door open. The room was empty,

and the window was wide-open. Panic began to nib-
ble at the edges of her mind. Quickly she made a
search of the house to assure herself that Amy wasn't
around. She wasn't.

Rachel returned to her sister's bedroom and looked
at the mess. Then she walked to the open window and
stuck her head out. The drop to the ground was only
four feet, and the bush under the sill was trampled.
Amy was gone, and Rachel's panic burst forth. She
knew in her heart that her sister had run away.

Chapter Ten

Rachel couldn't keep her hands from shaking as she punched in Michael's number. All she could think about was that her baby sister had run away—possibly with Kevin.

As soon as he picked up, she asked, "Michael, do you know where Amy is?"

"What's wrong?"

"She climbed out of her window tonight and is gone. I have no idea where she is and it's now an hour past her curfew." Rachel glanced at her watch as though that would change the time.

"Did you call Kevin?"

"Yes, he was the first person I called. He's not at home. His mother *thinks* that he's out with Amy." Rachel sat at the kitchen table, her legs too weak to support her.

"It's probably nothing. Amy has lost track of time before."

"You don't understand. My lawyer called yesterday morning. My restaurant deal came through, and Amy knows about it." Even to her own ears she heard the hysterical ring to her words.

"It did? And when were you going to tell me?"

The accusation in his voice cut deep. "I started to tell you last night, then Amy and Kevin were missing and the opportunity passed." Her voice sounded heavy with emotions she wished she could control, but Michael could always expose her feelings faster than anyone else.

"I see."

She heard the distance in his voice as though he were barricading his heart against her. "I'm scared. What if something happens to Amy?"

"I'll be over."

He hung up before Rachel could tell him no. She called him back, but there was no answer. She knew he was ignoring her. After the gentle tone of his voice at the end of the conversation, Rachel wasn't sure she could handle him showing up. Her control was fragile at best.

She placed a call to Helen. "Amy's gone. Do you have any idea where she would be? When she's been at work, have you heard her talking about a place she might go when she's upset?"

"No, sugar. I'll be over to help you look for her. Have you called the police?"

"Yes, but Henry said there wasn't much he could do since she is a runaway. He's doing some checking for me, but I just can't sit here waiting to hear something. I think she's with Kevin."

As she got off the phone with Helen, the doorbell rang. Not wanting to alarm Shaun, she hurried to answer it. He had finally gone to sleep at twelve, and she would prefer he didn't worry along with her.

Michael, with Garrett beside him, stood in the doorway, his appearance disheveled as if he had dropped everything and rushed over. She knew she'd awakened him, and he must have thrown on whatever was near at hand. His shirt didn't match his pants, but to her he looked wonderful. Against her better judgment she was glad he was here. She stepped to the side to allow him and Garrett into the house.

"Thanks for coming. I hate dragging you out at this hour, but—" Rachel swallowed hard. "I'm sure I'm worrying for nothing. She'll probably come strolling in here with some excuse that Kevin's car ran out of gas."

Michael turned to his son and said, "Why don't you go back to sleep in Shaun's room?"

"Is he still up?" Garrett asked Rachel.

"No. He finally went to bed an hour ago."

Garrett shuffled toward Shaun's bedroom. "I won't wake him."

After his son left, Michael combed his fingers through his mussed hair, then rubbed the back of his neck. "I've got a feeling Amy was serious when she told you she didn't want to leave Magnolia Blossom.''

"Then where could she have gone?"

"We'll check some of the teen hangouts."

"We'll have to wait until Helen shows up and can stay here with Shaun and Garrett. Do you want some coffee until then? I know I woke you up."

"Sure." He walked with her to the kitchen. "How did Shaun take the news about the move?"

"Okay. He wasn't happy, but we talked about it."

"You realize when we do find her the situation will still be the same."

"Yes." Rachel poured him some coffee, trying to keep her hand steady as she gave him the cup. "I didn't want to break up the family, but since I've been waiting for her, I've been thinking. I guess I'll have to see if she can stay with someone here in Magnolia Blossom for her last year of high school."

"As I said before, she can always stay with Garrett and me."

"Thanks. I'd hoped that Amy and I would get to know each other all over again, but that doesn't look possible now."

"Rachel, it doesn't have to be like this. The option of you staying is always open."

The doorbell sounded again. Rachel used the excuse of answering it to avoid replying to Michael's statement. She was relieved to see Helen on the porch. Rachel pulled her into the house.

"I'm so glad you're here. Can you stay with Shaun and Garrett while Michael and I go look for Amy?"

"So you called Michael?"

"Yes. I thought she might have gone to see him."

"Sure, Rachel. Haven't you noticed whenever something goes wrong you call Michael? Who did you call first, him or me?"

"Not another word, Helen. I don't need you to play matchmaker now."

"You called Michael. Just as I suspected." Her smile was way too smug as she strode into the kitchen and greeted Michael.

"We're going to try the turnoff on Miller Road. I also thought the park and the bluff nearby. Any other places you can think of, Helen?" Michael asked, downing his coffee in several swallows.

"The dock at the end of the Old Farm Road, your riverboat."

"Helen, if Amy comes home, call me on my cell phone. I don't know when we'll be back." He put his hand on the small of Rachel's back to guide her toward the door.

The dim light of dawn grayed the landscape as Michael pulled his truck up to the bluff that overlooked the Mississippi River. "It doesn't look like anyone is here."

"Let's check around just to make sure. This is the last place. If she's not here, where is she?" Rachel felt weariness in every part of her body. The night had been long and unproductive, and she felt as though she'd lived through a month's worth of nights instead of one.

Michael turned, sliding his arm along the back of the seat. "Rachel, you may have to face the fact that she has left Magnolia Blossom."

"But she wanted to stay. That's what this is all about."

He opened his door. "We'll take a look."

Rachel heard the resignation in his voice and knew he thought searching the bluff was futile. But the alternative was going to Aunt Flora's and admitting defeat. She couldn't do that just yet. Right now she would give anything to find Amy safe and sound.

After making a careful inspection of the area, Rachel met Michael at the truck. The sun peered over the horizon, casting its rosy hues into the blue sky like long fingers reaching for something unattainable. The warm air smelled of grass and pine. Birds sang in the trees along the bluff as though there was nothing wrong in the world.

Rachel couldn't bring herself to open the truck door. "If Amy stays here, I've failed to keep the family together. I didn't realize how much that would bother me until now."

"You have been away for years. Why is it so important to you now?"

She flinched at the question that pierced her armor. "I don't want them to feel they have been totally abandoned by their family. I want them to feel that at least someone cares about them, especially now that Aunt Flora is gone.''

"You're talking about your parents?"

"Yes. It's hard to accept that your mother and father don't want you around. I've been there. I wanted to make it better for Amy and Shaun."

"So you want to be their mother and father."

"I guess something like that."

"But you aren't. Be a sister to Amy, not a mother. Aunt Flora filled that position quite well. And sometimes no matter what we do we can't shield our loved ones from being hurt. Both Amy and Shaun have a strong faith. That will help them through this."

"But I don't? You've always had a way of getting right to the point."

"God is with them. He is with you. Your parents may have abandoned you, but God hasn't. You are never alone."

"I feel that way right now."

"Then maybe you need to turn to the Lord. Let God be there for you."

She wanted to. Something was missing in her life. She realized she needed help. "Let's go back to the house. I want to be there when Shaun wakes up so I can explain what happened."

Rachel remained silent on the ride to Aunt Flora's. She thought over what Michael had said to her. She knew she couldn't be her sister and brother's parent, that she couldn't erase what their mother and father had done to Amy and Shaun. She did feel she could ease the hurt, be there for them. But Amy wanted nothing from her. The gulf between them was as wide as the one between Michael and her. She was good at keeping people at a distance. She had learned from a master, her mother.

Lord, help me to reach Amy. I love her and want us to be a family. I don't know where to begin. Please guide me in what to do.

Shaun and Garrett came onto the porch when the truck pulled up. A troubled expression creased her brother's brow.

"No rest for the weary. I was hoping to shower and change before I had to talk to Shaun about Amy." Rachel climbed from the truck, feeling both physically and mentally exhausted.

"Helen told me Amy didn't come home last night. Where is she?" Shaun chewed on his lower lip, trying desperately not to show how worried he was.

But Rachel saw it in the lines that marked his young face, in the distressed tone of his voice. She placed an arm around his shoulders and guided him into the house. "That's true, Shaun. Amy's left, and we don't know where she is. Do you have any idea where she would have gone?"

He shook his head. "She doesn't tell me much, especially lately."

Rachel listed all the places Michael and she had searched. "Any other hangouts we didn't go to?"

Shaun snapped his fingers. "The church. She has gone there before when she was upset."

"It's worth a look. Rachel, why don't you stay here with Shaun? If she is there, I'll call."

"But I should come with—"

"Rachel, Shaun needs you," Michael said in a low voice. "He's worried about Amy. Your presence will help him. Let me check first."

While Michael headed for the door, Rachel proceeded into the kitchen. "Let's get some breakfast while we wait. Helen, do you want to stay?"

"Yes, sugar. I'll even help cook."

"No, you're a guest. Besides, cooking will take my mind off my troubles. You sit and entertain Shaun and Garrett."

Rachel immersed herself in the food preparation, fixing enough to feed an army. She kept mixing and cooking to take her mind off where Amy could be. What was she doing? Rachel remembered the impulsiveness of youth and the feeling of being invincible. The combination of those two things could get a person into trouble.

You are never alone. Michael's words came to mind. Rachel thought of this summer and how she had become involved in the church and in the town.

Oh, dear God, please let her be all right. I need You.

When the phone rang, Rachel grabbed the receiver so fast she was sure she surprised everyone in the kitchen. "Yes?"

"Rachel, she's here at the church," Michael said.

"I'll be there. Please keep her there." Rachel hung

up before Michael could talk her out of coming. She had to see that her sister was all right with her own two eyes.

At the church she jumped from the car and rushed up the steps to the large double doors. If Amy hadn't wanted to stay, it would have been difficult for Michael to keep her. Rachel prayed he was able to persuade Amy to stick around because Rachel had been going out of her mind with worry about her baby sister.

Michael met her at the doors into the sanctuary. "She's sitting in the back. I'll make sure y'all have some privacy while you work this out."

"Did you talk to her?"

"Yes. She knew I was calling you."

"She did?"

"Actually, it was her idea. I think y'all need to talk."

"I've been trying to."

"She's ready now, Rachel."

The foreboding tone to his words made her apprehension mushroom. "What happened, Michael, to change her mind?"

"Just talk to her." He stepped to the side to let her pass.

When Rachel entered the sanctuary, she wasn't sure what to expect. She halted inside the doorway and searched the back pews for her sister. At first she thought Amy had fled despite what Michael had said. Then Rachel found her sister in the corner, sitting on the floor, looking forlorn. The ache in Rachel's heart expanded, constricting her breathing as she stared at Amy, lost and alone.

Her sister glanced up and saw her. A mutinous expression immediately descended on her face. Amy might be ready finally to talk, but Rachel knew this wouldn't be easy.

She walked over to her sister and sat cross-legged on the floor in front of her. "Are you all right?" She wanted to touch her, pull her into her arms and hug her. Her sister's expression forbade her to do any of those things. The ache in Rachel's chest sharpened.

"No." Tears shone in Amy's eyes, and she immediately blinked them away as though she was determined not to show any emotion to Rachel.

"What happened? Did someone hurt you?" Rachel forced her voice to remain calm while inside she was trembling so badly she had to clasp her hands together in her lap.

Amy laughed, the sound a bit hysterical. "You've hurt me, sister. Everything I care about is here in Magnolia Blossom, and you want me to leave it behind just like that." She snapped her fingers in front of Rachel's face. "I can't. And I don't know how to change that." Amy's voice cracked on the final sentence.

"I realize that Magnolia Blossom is important to you. I was wrong to try and force you to leave. I didn't want to break up the family, and I can't stay."

"Why not?"

Amy's chin tilted at that defiant angle that Rachel had come to expect. The need to be totally honest with Amy—with herself—engulfed Rachel. She scrubbed her hands down her face in weariness, the past twenty-four hours so emotionally draining that she had to labor to put two thoughts together. "I don't know how to explain this to you. It's a long story." *I don't know if I can do this.*

"Maybe you should tell me. Everyone needs some-one." Concern erased Amy's defiant expression.

Rachel stared long and hard at her little sister and realized she needed to start taking emotional risks or there would be nothing left for her. She glanced at the altar and remembered she wasn't alone. Michael was right; God was with her. She could do this. Peace descended.

"Maybe you're right." Rachel sighed. "For six-teen years of my life when I lived with our parents, we moved once or twice a year. We never stayed long in any one place, so it was difficult establishing friendships and making any kind of commitment to anyone because I'm basically a shy person. Moving about was the pattern of life I got used to. With each new place I withdrew further into myself, scared to open up to others, to expose my feelings. Then I came to Magnolia Blossom and actually stayed here for two whole years."

"I wasn't that young that I don't remember some of the moving. I hated it."

"So did I at first, then I slowly learned to accept

it as a way of life for myself. Moving around isn't all bad. I've been doing it for almost my whole life.'' Rachel couldn't even remember how many countries she had visited in the course of her twenty-eight years.

''But coming to Aunt Flora's changed things?''

''For a short time. I began to make friends. I fell in love with Michael. But I got scared of the feelings he created in me. I didn't want to depend on anyone for my emotional well-being. To do that was to give him a great deal of power over me. I couldn't do that a second time in my life.''

''You're referring to our parents?''

A lump lodged in Rachel's throat, and she nodded.

''So you ran.''

''Yes, but I ran toward a dream I'd had for years.'' Rachel moistened her parched lips with the tip of her tongue, then swallowed several times to ease the tightness in her throat. ''I've always wanted to be a chef and to have my own restaurant.''

''You are a famous chef.''

''I'm getting there. This deal in New York for my own restaurant was just another part of my dream coming true.''

''Sometimes dreams we have when we are young aren't right for us when we get older.''

Rachel smiled, feeling every bit of her twenty-eight years. ''When did you get to be so smart?''

''Aunt Flora's influence.''

"Then our parents probably did the right thing leaving us with her."

The tears returned to sparkle in Amy's eyes. "But I'm the reason they left us with Aunt Flora. I'm the reason they abandoned us."

Rachel reached out and touched her sister's arm. Finally, and for the first time since she had come home, she felt there really was hope for her and Amy. "How can you say that?"

"Remember that day I wandered from camp and almost died? It wasn't a week later that our mother brought us to Aunt Flora."

Rachel drew Amy into her arms and stroked her hair, the ache within easing. For all these years her sister had carried that burden inside of her. "It wasn't you that was to blame. It was me."

Amy pulled back, tears streaking down her cheeks. "No, Rachel, you're wrong."

"I was supposed to be watching you. I should have done a better job of it. You could have drowned in the ocean if our father hadn't seen you."

"I sneaked off because I wanted to explore on my own. You aren't to blame."

Rachel brushed Amy's tears away with the pad of her thumb. "Let's make a deal. Let's decide that neither one of us was to blame. It was an accident. Accidents happen."

"Then you don't blame me for what happened?"

"Heavens, no. I never did. I love you. That won't

ever change. We are a family. We'll stick together no matter what.''

Her sister smiled, the moisture in her eyes making them glisten. ''Yeah, we are a family, aren't we?''

''You bet.'' Rachel took her sister's hand. ''Now, can you tell me what happened after you left last night?''

Amy took a long breath. ''Okay. After I left the house, I walked to Kevin's. We came here to be alone and pray. He was the one who talked me out of running away.''

Rachel squeezed her sister's hand. ''I did a lot of thinking last night, and I think you should stay here in Magnolia Blossom. I know now that I can't take you away from your friends the last year you're in high school. You and I are a lot alike, but we are different, too. I couldn't see what I was doing to you because I have no reference to those kind of feelings. I kept telling myself I wanted the family to stick together above anything else, that you and Shaun would adjust because I always had.''

''Who would I stay with?''

''Michael offered, and I'm sure Helen would. Of course, you might have a friend you could stay with.''

Amy grinned. ''You mean it?''

''Yes. I hope, though, you'll come visit Shaun and me in New York during school vacations.''

''I've always wanted to go to a Broadway show.''

''Then that's what we'll do.'' Rachel stood and offered her hand to her sister. ''I'll be busy with the restaurant, but for you I'll make the time." Rachel put her arm around Amy as they headed for the door.

Before leaving, Rachel turned and stared at the altar. Light from the ceiling shone on the cross. Michael's words whispered through her mind. *Let God be there for you.*

Could she open her heart totally and let God inside? She realized that until she did she would have a hard time allowing anyone else in. Tears glistened in her eyes. *Heavenly Father, I have avoided making any kind of commitment. I have run from people all my life. Help me to open myself to Your love. Help me to love.*

"If your dream is to have your own restaurant, Rachel, why don't you open one here or in Natchez? You're willing to settle down in New York, why not Magnolia Blossom?" Amy asked as she pushed the door open.

"In New York I can get lost in a crowd. In Magnolia Blossom everyone knows when I sneeze," Rachel quipped, stating her usual argument against staying.

"Is that the only reason?"

Pausing on the steps, Rachel regarded Amy. She searched the area for Michael, but he was gone, driven away by her. She remembered his wariness about trusting her again. "The bottom line is that I couldn't stay here and be around Michael and not be a part of his life. I don't know if I can be what he wants or give him the family he deserves, but it would kill me to see him with another woman.''

''Why does it have to be another woman?''

She didn't answer her sister's last question, but Rachel couldn't get it out of her mind on the drive to the house. In her profession she had taken one risk after another, but in her personal life she hadn't even taken one chance. Speaking to Amy honestly had been a small first step.

Shaun flew out the screen door and down the stairs when they pulled into the driveway. He threw his arms around Amy's waist. ''You're okay.''

''Of course, shrimp. What did you think?''

''That you ran away. That I'd never see you again.''

''And leave you? No way. My main goal in life is to make yours miserable.''

''Yeah, well, I want that CD you borrowed back.''

Rachel followed the pair into the house, listening to them bicker. This was what family was all about. She didn't realize how much she needed this until she'd almost lost it. Could she take another risk on Michael?

Chapter Eleven

"Okay. Who sprayed me?" Whirling, Amy put her hands on her hips and looked for the culprit.

No one said a word.

With water dripping off her, Amy sighed, swiping her wet hair out of her eyes. "Kevin Robert Sinclair, I can tell it was you."

Kevin lifted his shoulders. "How?"

"You're still holding the hose."

The eight other teenagers laughed.

"She caught you red-handed, Kev," one of the boys said.

Kevin arranged his features into an innocent expression. "I thought you might be getting hot, so I was cooling you off. That's what friends do for each other."

Amy grinned. "Gee, thanks. Let me return the favor."

Rachel stepped over to Michael and whispered, "You better do something fast or they'll never get these cars finished. Six people are waiting. Thank goodness they're patient. Of course, they're parents, so they have to be."

Michael surveyed the cars lined up in the church parking lot. "Who said parents are necessarily patient?"

"Isn't that written down somewhere?"

"In your dreams."

Amy marched over to Kevin and held out her hand for the hose. The boy reluctantly passed it to her, but his hands remained around it. A tug-of-war began, with water spewing everywhere.

"You're her sister. Do something." Michael moved away from the group to keep from getting wet.

Rachel headed for the teens by the black sedan. Over her shoulder she said, "Chicken. I agreed to help because you said this would be a piece of cake."

"You agreed to help because I promised you ice cream afterward."

Michael watched Rachel step into the melee and wrestle the hose from Kevin and Amy. Thoroughly wet, Rachel proceeded to spray both of them.

"I'll control the water from now on, children. Chuck, put that other hose up. If any of you get out of line, you get sprayed. Let's get back to work before these good people make us pay them for the privilege of washing their cars. Remember, this is a fund-raiser for your mission trip. If no cars are washed, no money is made.''

There were a few good-natured grumblings as the teens went back to work.

''I'm impressed, Rachel,'' Michael said with a chuckle. ''You could be a drill sergeant with the best of them.''

''My training is finally coming in handy. You ought to see me manage a kitchen full of temperamental chefs. There were times I wished I had a hose to cool them off.''

''You and Amy certainly seem to be getting along.''

A grin lifted the corners of her mouth. ''Yeah. Since she ran away and we had that talk, things are so much better. Thanks for all your help. I'm not sure we would be where we are without it.''

''Sure you would. Has she decided who she's going to stay with this next year?''

''Not yet. She's having a tough time deciding between you and Helen,'' Rachel said, a wistful tone in her voice. She still wished Amy would come with Shaun and her to New York in the fall, but she wouldn't say anything else to her sister. Amy knew how Rachel felt without her adding pressure.

''But you wish she was moving to New York?''

''You bet. I'll miss her. So will Shaun. I know she's gonna come visit during her school vacations, but it won't be the same.''

''That was a tough decision for you to make.''

"Yes." Rachel moved to the next car and rinsed it off so the teenagers could soap it down. "I'm still hoping I can convince her to come live with Shaun and me after high school. But it will be her decision."

"It wasn't that long ago you felt differently. I'm glad you changed your mind."

Rachel shot him a frown. "People can change, Michael." She sprayed another car, then stepped back to let the youths do their job.

"Maybe."

"You don't think people change?"

"Of course, they can change—if they want to badly enough. But that's the key. Do they really want to? Or are they fooling themselves and others into thinking they do, then revert back to their old ways the first time things get rough?"

"Chuck, will you take over with the hose?" Rachel asked, handing it to the nearest teenager.

"Yes."

When a gleam of mischief entered the tall boy's eyes, Rachel added, "And only spray the cars?"

The gleam vanished. "Yes, ma'am."

After Chuck took the hose and headed toward the next car in line, Rachel faced Michael, her back to the crowd in the parking lot. "Okay. What's going on, Michael? What are you afraid of?"

"What makes you think I'm afraid of anything?"

"Oh, maybe the fact you're not looking at me."

He directed his gaze to her. "I thought at least one

of us should keep an eye on the kids. I can't believe you gave Chuck the hose.''

''And I can't believe you're changing the subject on me. Besides, I'm all wet, so what's the worst he could do to me? Now you, on the other hand—''

''Why do you think I'm watching the young man? I would like to remain dry.''

''Okay. Enough chitchat. What's going on, Michael?''

''Mary Lou has contacted a lawyer concerning custody and visitation rights. She wants equal say in raising Garrett. I don't think I'll be able to avoid a fight.''

''And what do you want?''

He stabbed her with an intense look. ''Frankly, I want Mary Lou out of Garrett's life.''

Shocked, Rachel gasped. ''You usually don't judge people so harshly.''

''I don't trust her. It wasn't that long ago that she was drunk a good part of the day and could care less that Garrett was in the next room crying for her. That's not something I'll forget.''

''Or forgive?''

''Yes.'' Michael clamped his jaws together, flexing his hands then curling them into a tight ball at his side.

''Is she drinking now?''

''No—or so she claims. She belongs to AA. She says all the right things, but I don't trust her.''

Pain and anger laced his words. Rachel's throat constricted. ''You suggested I should turn to the Lord for guidance concerning Amy. Maybe you should turn to the Lord about Mary Lou. If she has truly changed, don't you think she deserves a second chance? Don't you think Garrett deserves a mother? How does Garrett feel about all this?''

''He doesn't know what's happening between Mary Lou and me. I haven't told him. I don't know how.'' Michael raked his hand through his hair, staring over Rachel's shoulder, a scowl knitting his brow.

She could tell he wasn't really looking at anything but was lost in his own thoughts. He was hurting, and she wished she could do something to help him. ''Remember your advice to me? That I should tell Shaun and Amy about my decision as soon as possible? Well, I wouldn't keep this from Garrett for too long. He should hear it from you, not someone else. You know how small towns are. He'll hear it from someone.''

Michael closed his eyes for a few seconds. ''Yes, I know. He's been bugging me about spending the weekend with Mary Lou. They have a boat, and he wants to go skiing.''

''And you don't want him to be alone with Mary Lou?''

''Yeah. I trust people totally until they give me a reason not to, then I find it hard to give my trust again.''

The tightness in her throat expanded. She swallowed several times. They could be speaking about their relationship. Ten years ago he'd felt she had betrayed his love.

A shriek erupted behind Rachel. She jumped and nearly bumped into Michael.

He steadied her, then headed for the youths. "Now you'll see why Chuck was the last person to give the hose to."

There was one car left in the parking lot. The tall boy wet it down, then turned the water on the girl next to him. She took the bucket of soapy water she held and dumped it over Chuck, who proceeded to chase her with the hose. Thankfully, the last car was cleaned before a full water war erupted in the parking lot. Rachel backed away and watched, still troubled by her conversation with Michael.

He came to stand beside her. "I guess this is one way to beat the summer heat."

"Does this happen often?" Rachel asked while Amy produced the hose Chuck had put away earlier.

"Let's just say these guys know how to enjoy themselves."

"How many car washes have you had?"

"Oh, five or six in the past few years."

Suddenly Rachel noticed the quiet. She looked toward the teens, all drenched from head to toe, all staring at her and Michael with silly grins on their faces. She didn't trust her sister's impish expression, nor the fact that Amy whispered something to Kevin who in turn whispered something to the petite young woman next to him. Quickly, whatever Amy had come up with spread to the whole group.

''I think we may be in trouble,'' Rachel murmured, sliding a step closer to Michael.

''I think you're right. Run,'' Michael said the second the teenagers started toward them.

The hoses were turned on Rachel and Michael. They didn't get three feet before they were drenched. Laughter bubbled up inside Rachel while Michael tried to wrestle the hose from the teen nearest him. Finally, he managed to capture it.

''Scatter,'' Amy shouted to the group.

Before Rachel could blink the water from her eyes and flip her wet hair out of her face, the parking lot was deserted. Michael stood ready to do battle with no one to fight. He glanced at Rachel. The gleam dancing in his eyes warned her she was his next target. She backed away, scanning the area for the second hose. It lay five feet away—five *long* feet away.

Rachel dove for the hose and got hit with a spray of water. ''You won't get away with that.'' She grasped the hose and aimed it toward Michael, squeezing the handle on the nozzle. Water dribbled out.

Michael laughed. ''I won't? Looks like I might.'' He blasted her with the full force of the hose.

Rachel peered toward the building and saw Amy push Kevin out of the way then turn the faucet on before hurrying to the one that controlled the flow to Michael's hose. Rachel pressed her handle down and fired water at Michael at the same time Amy managed to shut off his flow, leaving him at Rachel's mercy. She covered him with water from top to bottom. Exasperated because his hose didn't work, he tossed it down and rushed her.

Rachel saw his intent, screamed, threw her hose down and ran for the church. As she wrenched the door open, she heard the giggles of the teens nearby, then the sound of Michael's pursuit. Inside the building she frantically searched for a place to hide.

Before she could move toward the ladies' rest room down the long hallway, Michael captured her. "Now I know where Amy gets her playfulness." He swung her around.

"Uncle. Uncle."

"But I haven't done anything."

"But you're thinking about it. I can tell." Rachel shivered in the coolness of the air-conditioned entrance. "Admit it."

Michael released his hold on her. "The thought did cross my mind—but only briefly."

"Sure. And pigs fly."

"Rachel Peters, are you mocking me?"

"Never." She skirted him, keeping several feet between them. "I need to thank Amy for her help."

"And I thought Amy was a friend."

"She is, but she's my sister," Rachel said over her shoulder as she went outside. Pride swelled her chest at the thought that she and Amy were finally truly sisters.

While she and Michael had been in the building, the teenagers had returned to the parking lot and begun cleaning up their mess. Rachel stopped dead in her tracks, amazed.

"You've done well, Michael. I thought you and I would have to clean this up."

"Well, thank you, ma'am. I'll accept that compliment."

When everything was put away, Amy came to Rachel and Michael. "Are y'all coming with us to get some ice cream?"

"Of course. That's the only reason I agreed to help today." Rachel gestured toward her wet clothes. "But what do we do about these?"

"Nothing. We can get our ice cream and eat outside at the picnic tables," Amy said, walking toward Carol's Sundries, halfway down the block from the church.

Michael and Rachel fell in behind the group of teenagers. Again, she felt that Amy was planning something. Whispers flew among the youths with a few knowing glances thrown toward Michael and her.

"There isn't anything they could do at Carol's Sundries, is there?" Rachel asked when Amy smiled at her.

Michael took a moment to answer. "I don't think so, but your sister is definitely up to something. The last time, I got drenched."

"We'd better be alert, then."

After Rachel and Michael got their ice cream

cones, they left the shop to sit at the picnic tables across the street in the park. There was nowhere to sit except at a lone table under a live oak. The teen-agers lounged all over the benches of the three tables clustered together, leaving no room for Michael and her.

Rachel smiled sweetly at Amy and marched to the lone table. "Now we know what she was planning."

"I think Helen is rubbing off on her," Michael grumbled and sat across from Rachel.

"Do you think? That's all Magnolia Blossom needs is another matchmaker."

Michael's expression went neutral. He concentrated on eating his chocolate ice-cream cone.

"Does that bother you?" Rachel asked, taking a lick of her peppermint ice cream.

He shrugged. "If she wants to waste her time, that's fine by me."

"Yeah, we're just friends."

Rachel slid her gaze away, afraid her feelings were reflected in her eyes. She shouldn't feel hurt, but she did. When had she wanted there to be more than friendship between her and Michael? She was leav-ing, which made it an impossible situation. She had a restaurant deal in New York waiting for her. She had a life outside Magnolia Blossom. She wasn't good at making commitments to others. She had little practice.

But while she ran through all the reasons it would never work between her and Michael, she kept thinking she wished that wasn't so. Would it be so bad if she postponed going to New York for a year to see what developed between them? That way Amy, Shaun and she would be able to stay together. Her restaurant deal could be renegotiated later.

"Yuck! I don't see why I have to go to this dumb play. Boys don't see *Romeo and Juliet*. It's for girls." Garrett squirmed in his seat in the back of the car.

Michael pulled into Rachel's driveway. "The last time I checked, I'm male, and I'm looking forward to the play tonight. Amy is playing the lead, and she's a friend of ours."

"I have one thing to say. Yuck!"

"Well, then please keep your opinions to yourself. I don't want to do anything to ruin Amy's big night." Michael opened the car door. "You stay here. I'll go get Rachel and Shaun."

As he closed the door, he heard his son say, "Yuck! Yuck! Yuck!"

In the past Michael had been relatively assured that Garrett would behave himself at functions like the one they were attending. But lately he wasn't so sure. Garrett was angry a lot of the time. When Mary Lou came back into their lives, Garrett changed. All the more reason to fight her on the custody issue. She wasn't a good influence on Garrett.

Before Michael could ring the bell, the door flew open, and Shaun raced outside.

"He's faster than a speeding bullet," Rachel said

from the entryway. She gathered her purse and stepped onto the porch. "He's been complaining about the play, but the second you pulled up to the house he made a mad dash for the door. Do children ever make any sense?"

Michael looked toward his car, the light from the dome illuminating his child's surly features. "Nope. The day we think we have them figured out is the day they are guaranteed to change again." He opened the door for Rachel, then rounded the front and slid in behind the wheel.

"And if I hear another negative word about this play from either one of you, we'll just come home afterward instead of going out to eat. I'll fix you both one of my specialties." Rachel flashed Michael a grin. "Let's see. If I remember correctly, the boys haven't tried snails. I think it would be a good opportunity to expand their palate. What do you think, Michael?"

"Sounds good to me."

"We don't have any snails," Shaun said from the back seat.

"I could go out in the yard and hunt some down." Michael threw the car into reverse and pulled out of the driveway.

"You wouldn't!" Garrett exclaimed.

"I think I saw something slimy out in our backyard the other day."

"Those were slugs, Dad. Yuck! Yuck!"

"That seems to be his favorite word lately," Michael whispered to Rachel, then said, "this is Amy's night. Be good, boys."

During the short drive to Natchez, Shaun and Garrett were unusually quiet. Rachel felt pinpricks in the back of her head, as though they were staring holes through her. Despite the boys' reluctance concerning the play, she was looking forward to this evening, not because Amy was performing, but because when Michael asked Rachel if she would like to go with him, it felt as if he was asking her out on a date—a crowded date with two young boys as chaperons but a date nonetheless.

At the community theater in Natchez, Michael led them to their seats. While Rachel settled down to watch *Romeo and Juliet,* the two boys wiggled and whispered to each other until she had to intervene and threaten extended grounding. Finally, in the second act, they calmed down, and Shaun fell asleep.

By the time the performance was over, Rachel was in awe of her sister's acting ability. She knew the story, had seen it performed in London by the Royal Shakespearean Company, but watching Amy in the part of Juliet made her realize what talent her sister had. Amy definitely needed to be exposed to Broadway and the theater in New York City.

Everyone crowded around Amy backstage after the play. Rachel's gaze sought Michael's as though it had a will of its own. While the group parted to let Amy see them, Rachel felt trapped by Michael's intense look, a look that told her she was missing out on life, that she was throwing away the best thing she could ever have by leaving Magnolia Blossom.

"What did y'all think?" Amy asked, her eyes alight with happiness.

"You were nothing short of brilliant. Where did you learn to act like that?" Rachel asked, her smile attesting to how proud she was of her sister.

Amy shrugged, suddenly embarrassed. "I just like to pretend."

Kevin came up next to her and took her hand. "Are you ready?"

"Hey, little brother, would you and Garrett like to go get hamburgers with Kevin and me?"

Rachel winced when she heard Amy name a fast food chain. "I was thinking we could celebrate at—"

Amy waved her hand in the air and laughed. "Don't worry, sis. I don't expect you to eat there. Kevin and I made a reservation for you and Michael at one of the plantations in town."

"But—"

"I hear the food is great. Since when would a chef pass up an opportunity to eat good food?"

"This is your evening. We're celebrating your play."

"And I want a hamburger. We're meeting some other kids there."

Michael arched a brow. "And you are voluntarily taking your brother and Garrett?"

Amy grinned. "They'll behave. I can't see them

eating in a fancy restaurant after sitting through the play. I thought I would reward them for coming.''

Rachel narrowed her eyes. ''You're just too good to be true. It's not going to work.''

''Sure it is.'' Amy checked her watch. ''You have fifteen minutes to get there. Come on, Garrett and Shaun. You two better not give me a bit of trouble or y'all will be walking back to Magnolia Blossom.''

''Amy!'' Rachel exclaimed, ready to snatch the two boys back.

Amy glanced over her shoulder and winked. ''Just kidding. Have fun.''

As everyone filed out of the community theater, Michael whispered close to Rachel's ear, ''I think we've been had.''

''I think you're right. We can always go back to Magnolia Blossom. I think Southern Delight is still open.''

''No. Your sister went to a lot of trouble to plan this. I wouldn't want to ruin this evening for her.''

''And she's right. I would like to sample the food at this restaurant.''

''Then we'd better get going.''

Michael touched the small of her back as he guided her to his parked car. The light feel of his fingers sent a tingling sensation up her spine. Now tonight felt like a real date. She knew she would need to say something to Amy tomorrow about trying to match her and Michael, but for the rest of the evening Rachel intended to enjoy herself.

At the plantation house they were shown to a table set for two in a dark, secluded alcove. They each ordered something different so they could sample each other's dishes. When Michael held up his fork, Rachel leaned forward to taste the steak speared on it. The intimate gesture of sharing their meals heightened her awareness of the man sitting next to her. His clean, fresh scent surrounded her and pushed all other delicious aromas away. His deep, masculine voice centered her full attention on him while they discussed the renovations on the riverboat.

"So, do you have a chef for the restaurant?"

"No. I've interviewed several but haven't made up my mind yet. Maybe you could help me decide."

"Possibly," Rachel said, stirring some sugar into her after-dinner coffee.

"I'm leaning toward a young woman who's working in New Orleans right now. I think she's got a lot of possibility. She wants to strike out on her own."

A seed of jealously swamped Rachel, the sudden feeling disconcerting. She busied herself by taking several sips of her coffee while she wrestled with an emotion she had no right to feel. "Has she ever run a kitchen before?"

"No, but I like to give people a chance to grow. And she seems quite loyal. She's been at her present place for four years. She doesn't move around a lot. I like that."

His words held a hidden rebuke, directed at Rachel. He hadn't really forgiven her for what had happened ten years before. Loyalty had always been important to Michael. It went hand in hand with trust.

She took another swallow of her coffee to ease the constriction in her throat. "I'd be glad to help any way I can."

His gaze snared hers. "Then I'll set up a time for you to meet the applicants."

Candlelight danced in his eyes, drawing her in. For a few seconds she fought the desire to tell him she would be his chef. Then she remembered her plans and his earlier comment about trust and loyalty. She realized she loved him, always had, but could she make the kind of commitment he deserved?

"Well, what do you think, Rachel?" Michael sat at a table in the riverboat's newly redecorated dining room.

"I have to agree she has possibilities as a chef," Rachel said, shifting in her chair next to him.

"But?"

"But I'm concerned about her management skills. You'll need someone who can run your kitchen as well as be a good cook."

He tossed the pencil he'd been taking notes with onto the wooden table. "And Paul Fontaine earlier?"

"His experience is with making desserts, not entrées."

Michael rose and began to pace. "There's only one more I'm interested in. Marcus Davenport couldn't come till tomorrow."

"Then I'll be back. What time?"

"One."

"Good. I can oversee the final touches to the kitchen and sit in on your interview with Mr. Davenport."

Michael continued to walk from one end of the dining room to the other. Rachel could understand his uneasiness over hiring a chef, but something else was making Michael as restless as a caged animal.

"Michael, you're exhausting me. Sit. Tell me what else is wrong."

He didn't stop pacing. "I got served with the papers today."

"But you knew Mary Lou was going to go to court."

"Yeah, but I kept hoping she would tire and go away. Leave us alone."

"Have you told Garrett yet?"

He came to a halt a few feet in front of her. "No. I will tonight. If I don't, Mary Lou will."

"You and Garrett have a good relationship. He'll understand. Are you going to tell him about Mary Lou's drinking?"

Michael scowled. "I can't. He's not even eight yet."

"Then what are you going to tell him?"

He ran his hand through his hair repeatedly. "I'll think of something. I don't have any choice. I have to tell him now."

"Remember what you told me about God being

with me. It's the same for you. The Lord is here to guide you, Michael.''

''Right now I feel very alone,'' he murmured, his shoulders sagging as if he had the weight of the world bearing down on him.

Rachel stood and reached out to lay a comforting hand on his arm. Her cell phone rang. She touched Michael, intending to ignore the call. The jingle sounded again in the quiet.

''Please answer it,'' Michael muttered and stepped away from her.

She flipped open her phone. ''Yes?''

''Rachel,'' Amy said in a tense voice. ''You've got to come home now. Mom's here, and she wants us to pack.''

Chapter Twelve

Rachel slammed on the brakes, jumped from the car and raced up the steps of Aunt Flora's house. Her heart hammered against her chest as she thrust open the front door and entered. She came to a halt halfway into the living room. Amy and Shaun sat on the couch, facing their mother, who stood by the fireplace, tall, stiff, frowning.

Shaun leaped to his feet and launched himself at Rachel. "I'm so glad you're home." His arms went around her.

Rachel placed her hand on his back and patted him. "Everything will be okay," she whispered, then looked at her mother. "Hello, Mother. This is a surprise."

"It shouldn't be. I told you I was coming."

Rachel walked with Shaun to the couch and waited until he was seated before facing their mother. "No, the surprise is the part about Amy and Shaun packing their bags.''

Her mother's tanned features were pinched together in a deep frown. ''Weren't you the one who a few weeks ago brought me to task for not doing my duty by my children? I'm here now to take Amy and Shaun back with me.''

Amy shot to her feet, her arms ramrod straight at her side. ''No, I won't go!''

Rachel gave her sister a reassuring smile. ''Amy only has another year of high school left. She shouldn't leave Magnolia Blossom right now.''

Her mother quirked a brow. ''And you're staying here?''

Amy pushed past Rachel. ''This is my home. You can't make me go with you.'' She left.

Shaun rose, tears brimming in his eyes. ''Me, neither!'' He ran from the room.

Her mother sighed. ''I thought this would make everything better.''

''How?''

''Weren't you the one who said I should take responsibility for my children? That's what I'm doing. Your father and I talked it over. They can come live with us.''

''How generous of you.''

''I don't need your sarcasm.''

''Why did you have children?'' Rachel desperately wanted an answer to the question that had been eating at her for years.

"Your father wanted a son to carry on his name. At least that's why we had you and Amy. Believe it or not, Shaun was an accident. By that time we'd realized raising children and doing our research didn't mix well. It wasn't safe for children in our camp. Our lifestyle didn't go well with parenthood."

"So you discarded us."

"I gave you the best home I could. My sister always wanted children and couldn't have any."

"And now suddenly the camp is safe for children?"

Her mother looked away, shifting her weight from one foot to the other. "It's better than before. I should be able to keep Shaun and Amy safe."

"That's not good enough. We're a family now."

"What do you mean a family? They've always been your sister and brother."

Rachel advanced toward her mother, locking gazes with her. "Until recently I didn't realize what the word *family* really meant. Now I know. For family you make sacrifices if you must. For family you stick together through the good and bad times." She drew in a deep, cleansing breath and added, "Yes, Mother, I am staying in Magnolia Blossom at least until Amy graduates from high school. Go back to the Amazon with a clear conscience. I want to take care of Amy and Shaun because we are family."

Her mother blinked, backing up several steps. "You want to stay in this town?"

Rachel lifted her chin and met her mother's direct look with one of her own. "Yes."

"But what about your plans for your own restaurant?"

"They can wait. Amy and Shaun come first." Not until this moment had Rachel realized she'd committed fully to her siblings, and it felt as right as did her decision to stay.

Her mother squared her shoulders, snatched her purse and headed for the front door. "Then I'll sign the guardianship papers Robert has." She paused at the door and faced Rachel, a strained expression carving tired lines about her eyes and mouth. "If you're sure?"

"Yes, very."

She turned to leave.

And be ye kind one to another, tenderhearted, forgiving one another, even as God for Christ's sake hath forgiven you. The Bible verse popped into Rachel's thoughts, showing her what she must do to be at peace with herself. How could she expect Michael to forgive her if she couldn't forgive her parents? "Mother, why don't you stay for dinner?"

Tossing a glance over her shoulder, her mother hesitated. "Are you sure?"

"Yes, very. We don't get to see you nearly enough."

Her mother peered at her watch. "It'll have to be an early dinner. I have to make a late flight from

New Orleans for the congressional meeting in Washington.''

"Dad, Mom wants to take me deep-sea fishing this weekend. Can I go?''

Michael turned from staring out the window into the darkness. His son's eager expression faded to a frown as Michael wrestled with what to say.

"We get to spend the night on the boat. She even said I could invite Shaun to go with me.''

"Not this weekend,'' Michael finally answered, bracing himself for the ensuing battle.

"Why not?'' Standing in the middle of the den, his son stiffened.

"We need to talk, Garrett. Have a seat.'' Michael gestured toward the couch.

His son remained where he was, his frown deepening.

Michael heaved a sigh and moved away from the window. "Your mother and I—'' He searched for the right words and decided there was no easy way to tell his son the truth. "We don't see eye to eye on some things. We're going back to see the judge to help us make some decisions.''

"What kind of decisions?''

"When your mother can see you and how often.''

"Why can't I see her whenever I want? Whenever she wants? She's my *mother*.''

Tension bore deep into Michael's neck and shoulders. "It's complicated. I'm not sure it's best that you stay with your mother a lot."

"Why not?"

Because she might start drinking again. Because she left you and me years ago. Michael couldn't say what he wanted, and no substitute words came to mind. "It just isn't."

"That's not fair! You have to let her see me. She won't love me if she doesn't," Garrett shouted, then he spun on his heel and ran from the room.

Michael placed his hand over his chest to ease the tightness constricting it. Each breath he drew hurt his lungs, and his heart pounded a mad beat. He was losing his son and he didn't have any idea how to stop it from happening.

He started to follow Garrett but decided against it. Instead, he stood in the middle of the den. Mary Lou kept trying to see Garrett, knowing how Michael felt about it. At least he could be thankful she hadn't told Garrett about the custody hearing. Michael plunged his hand into his hair. But then maybe it would have been better if she had. He'd certainly made a mess of it.

The sound of the doorbell rang through the house. He wished he could ignore it. He had no desire to see anyone tonight, but it chimed again. Determined to send the person away as quickly as possible, he headed for the front door and wrenched it open.

The light from his veranda illuminated Rachel in a

soft glow. She smiled, the gesture reaching deep into her eyes to enhance her natural beauty.

"I hope I haven't come at a bad time. I couldn't wait until tomorrow to talk to you."

Michael stepped to the side to allow her into the house. "What couldn't wait?"

She pivoted toward him. "I decided to stay in Magnolia Blossom this year while Amy's finishing high school."

"And then what?" He quietly shut the door, resisting the urge to slam it.

He walked toward the living room, needing its formality to remind him not to get too comfortable around Rachel. She moved to the sofa and sat. He remained by the brocade wing chair, his hands gripping the back.

"That will depend. I haven't made any plans beyond that. I only made the decision to stay this evening."

"Why?"

"Why am I staying?"

He nodded, his fingers digging into the brocade.

"Mother came today to see us. She was going to take Amy and Shaun back with her to the Amazon."

"That would be an answer to all your problems."

She flinched at the sarcastic bite to his words. "But it wouldn't be what's best for Amy and Shaun. Magnolia Blossom is their home. We're a family. I convinced Mother that I wanted to be their guardian and live here."

"And you really do?"

"What's wrong? I thought you would be happy about my decision. This is what you've wanted all along."

"Is that why you're staying, because I wanted it?" His anger infused his voice.

"No. I want it. But I would be lying if I denied you weren't part of this decision."

"How nice. And when you begin to feel trapped, you can blame me right before you leave again."

The color drained from her face. She rose, clasping her hands in front of her. "Is that what you're worried about? That I'll blame you if something goes wrong? Or is it something else that's bothering you?"

"Oh, don't get me wrong. I'm ecstatic for Amy and Shaun. But what about your restaurant? What are you going to do this next year?"

She took a deep breath. "I'm putting my plans for a restaurant on hold." She paused and drew in another fortifying breath. "I was hoping you would offer me the chef position on your riverboat."

"What happens when you leave in ten months?"

She glanced away, then brought her gaze to his face. Her eyes shone. "I wanted us to start over. See if we could be more than friends."

"Again the question, what happens when you leave in ten months? Am I supposed to pick up the pieces of my life like I did ten years ago? Forget about you? Forget about any feelings I might have for you?"

She trembled. Hugging her arms to her chest, she

said, "I know I haven't been very good at making a commitment, but I'm learning. I care about you, Michael. Very much. You're important to me, and I want to see if we have a future together."

He ached to hold her, to wipe away the haunted look in her eyes, but he couldn't. He remembered the anguish, the loss, he'd experienced when she'd left him. He knew his limits, and he'd reached them. He couldn't deal with losing Rachel on top of everything else happening in his life. "But I don't, Rachel."

Pain flickered in her eyes before she veiled them. When she looked at him, her expression was neutral. She'd always been good at hiding her emotions behind a mask. She hadn't really changed.

"If this wasn't so tragic, I'd laugh. You've always been willing to take emotional risks, whereas I never have. And here it is, our roles are reversed."

"I'm tired of exposing myself to those emotional risks you say I take." He pushed himself away from the wing chair. "I don't trust your sudden change of heart."

"That's what it boils down to. You don't trust me. You can't believe that I might have really changed. People do. And people deserve second chances, but of course, you have to forgive a person to give her a second chance."

With her shoulders back, she walked past him into the foyer. He wanted to stop her, to tell her—what? At the moment he felt as though his life were falling down around him. Each brick resounded with a warning to protect himself from further pain.

''You don't need to say anything else to me, Michael. Without trust and forgiveness we have nothing. Goodbye.''

The sound of the front door closing echoed through the house, announcing to the world that he was letting go of the best thing that had ever happened to him. He shuddered, cold to the marrow of his bones. Kicking Rachel out of his life would only cause him to suffer more. But then denying Garrett his mother was causing his son to suffer. When Mary Lou had left them, the one thing he'd vowed he wouldn't do to his son was cause him undue pain.

He peered at the door, then up the stairs where Garrett had disappeared. Michael had to start putting his life back together. He suddenly remembered the nursery rhyme about Humpty-Dumpty and wondered if he could piece himself back together. The task seemed overwhelming. He trudged up the stairs, viewing his son's closed door and remembering the sound of Rachel walking out of his life. The coldness burrowed deeper into him.

Almighty God, ruler of all things in heaven and earth, hear my prayer for guidance. Strengthen my faith and help me to forgive those who have wronged me and to right the wrongs I have committed. Open my heart to Your love and mercy. Grant me the ability to love and show mercy, through Jesus Christ our Lord. Amen.

With each word he whispered, he drew nearer to Garrett's bedroom. As he knocked on his son's door, a calmness washed over him. God was with him. God would show him the way. Michael would be all right.

"Go away! I don't want to talk," Garrett shouted.

"I'm not leaving until we talk, son."

Seconds stretched into a full minute. When the door swung open, Garrett hid behind it. Michael stepped into his son's bedroom and pivoted toward him. Garrett shoved the door closed, the sound reminding Michael of Rachel's departure and the hurt stamped on her expression.

Where to begin? A momentary surge of panic flashed through Michael. The Lord was beside him every step of the way. He closed his eyes for a few seconds, visualizing peace and forgiveness.

"Being with your mother is important to you?"

Tears welled in Garrett's eyes. "Yes. I missed her while she was gone."

"You never said."

"Because you never liked to talk about her. I didn't want to hurt you."

Michael's heart expanded with all the love he had for his son. He could learn a lesson about forgiveness from Garrett. He never held a grudge for long.

His son plopped down on the nearest twin bed, his shoulders slumped, his hands clasped between his legs. "She needs me."

Surprised at Garrett's words, Michael blinked. "Why do you say that?"

"She wants to make up for leaving me. That's important to her."

"Did she tell you that?"

"Not in so many words, but I can tell. She did tell me that she did some bad things and that she had to ask God for forgiveness. If God can forgive her, why can't you?"

Michael sucked in a deep breath as though he had been punched in the stomach. "I—" He clamped his lips together and tried to think of the best way to reply to his son. "I don't know. I'm trying."

Garrett lifted his head, tears running down his cheeks. "I want to get to know her. Please let me."

For a long moment Michael stared at Garrett, frozen, unable to move or say a thing. Tears continued to fall from his son's eyes, unchecked, as they stared at each other.

Michael was across the room in two strides. He scooped his son into his arms and held him tight, tears misting his eyes. "I love you, son."

"I know that. I love you, Dad, but I love Mom, too."

"I can't promise I'll change overnight, but I'll call your mom and talk to her about you going deep-sea fishing this weekend with them. Okay?"

Garrett pulled back, wiping at his tears. "You mean it?"

Michael nodded, a lump the size of the Gulf in his throat.

"Do you think Shaun can go, too?"

"You'll have to ask him."

"I'll go call him right now." Garrett hurried toward the hall, stopped halfway to the door and said, "No, wait. You'd better call Mom first, then I'll talk to Shaun."

Michael smiled. "I'm going to. Don't worry. I won't change my mind."

Garrett blushed. "I know you won't. I just want to make sure everything is still on for the weekend before I invite Shaun."

"Do you want to talk to her after I do?" Michael tousled his son's hair as he passed him.

"Sure. Just let me know when you're finished."

Michael arched a brow. "You aren't going to listen?"

"No. I know you have things to talk over that are private. I'll wait here."

Michael paused in the doorway. "When did you get to be such a smart kid?"

With a huge grin on his face, Garrett shrugged.

"Well, that's done." Rachel replaced the receiver in its cradle and twisted to look at Amy. "And you know what? It felt good to tell my lawyer to hold off on the restaurant deal."

Amy downed the last of her soda. "Then you really don't mind staying in Magnolia Blossom this year?"

"No." Rachel fingered the newspaper at her elbow. "But I'll need to see about getting a job. I'll have to travel to Natchez or Jackson, possibly even New Orleans.''

"What about Michael's restaurant on the riverboat?''

"He's interviewing someone else today.''

After the evening before, working with him wasn't a possibility, Rachel thought with a touch of sadness. She couldn't be around him all the time in a work situation, or a situation of any other kind. The idea that he couldn't totally trust her hurt her deeply. Granted, she had given him reasons to feel that way, but she had changed. She had learned to make a commitment.

"Maybe it won't work out.''

"Amy Peters, no more matchmaking. One Helen in Magnolia Blossom is enough. Besides, Michael isn't interested.''

"Does that mean you are?''

Rachel held up her hand, palm outward. "Stop. Don't go there. Whatever we had once is over. Period. No more.''

"Thou doth protest too much.'' Amy rose and put her glass in the kitchen sink. "Are you through with the renovations on the riverboat?''

"I'm going over later this afternoon to meet with the carpenter about a few last-minute details, then I'm basically finished.'' Thankfully, Rachel thought, trying to ignore the pain threatening to overwhelm her.

Amy leaned against the counter. "You know we didn't get to talk last night after Mother left. You ran out of here so fast you made my head spin. Are you sure about what happened?"

Rachel's smile came from the depths of her heart. "Yes. We're a family. It took me some time to really realize what that meant, but I must say, you, Shaun and Michael have helped me with that."

"Were you as surprised as I was about Mother's offer?"

Rachel laughed. "Shocked."

"Do you think she was serious?"

"Yeah, or believe me, she wouldn't have made the offer to take you two with her."

"Why did she do it?"

Rachel looked away from her sister for a few seconds. "I believe because I said something to her that last time she called about being your guardian."

Amy's eyebrows shot up. "But I thought you and Aunt Flora had talked about it several years ago."

"Yes, but I got angry at Mother for not doing what I thought she should as the parent."

"Oh." Amy hung her head, staring at the floor.

Rachel stood and went to her sister. "This summer I've done a lot of thinking. Getting involved in the church again has helped me to sort out my feelings concerning our parents. I've always felt abandoned by them, and in a way we were. But you know, Amy, I feel they did the right thing by leaving us with Aunt Flora. Their medical research helps thousands of people. I'm not excusing how they handle everything, but I understand. I can forgive them. I can move on."

The words, said out loud, felt so right. Rachel pulled her sister into her embrace and hugged her.

"I love you, big sis."

"I'm glad, because you're stuck with me. I'm not going anywhere."

Rachel stood on the landing, peering at Michael's riverboat. A man was positioned over the back of it, painting the name. So far there was a big black *C*.

She saw Michael's truck parked nearby and hoped she could meet Brandon, the carpenter, and leave without running into Michael. Her heart ached too much to see him right now. Maybe later, with time, she could feel as though she weren't coming apart if she met him on the streets of Magnolia Blossom. Somehow she had to pull herself together enough to live in the same small town for at least the next ten months. For Amy and Shaun, she would do it. She was through running away from her emotions and denying they existed.

With a heavy sigh she walked toward the gangplank. She would use the back way to the kitchen. In and out. Thirty minutes tops. Then her professional connection with Michael would be cut.

But never her emotional one, she thought as she climbed to the second deck. When she stepped into the kitchen, she was surprised to find it deserted. A feeling of coming home inundated her as she ran her hand along the gleaming stainless steel. She visualized herself standing in front of the stove, stirring one of her cream sauces, the scents and smells of a kitchen enveloping her. Onions sautéing. Bread baking. Coffee brewing.

She gripped the counter and leaned into it. She quivered with the vision she knew was just out of her reach. If only she had learned how to make a commitment earlier—ten years ago.

"Rachel."

With her back to the door, she slid her eyes closed, her breath bottled in her lungs. *Please not now, Lord. I can't handle seeing Michael.*

"I was afraid you weren't going to meet Brandon."

She spun. "I always finish a job, Michael. I have changed, but not totally."

Michael moved into the kitchen, his face no longer in the shadows.

Rachel sucked in a deep breath at the haggard lines around his mouth and eyes. She wanted to smooth them away, ease what torment had put them there. She remained where she was, aware that a large wall stood between them, originally erected by her, reinforced by him.

"I told Brandon you would meet with him another day."

"Why?"

"Because we need to talk."

"I thought you had said all you wanted to last night."

"A guy can change his mind."

Hope vied with her natural wariness. Her hands on

the counter tightened. "Yes, just as a gal can. What do you want to talk about?"

"Us." He took a step closer.

"There is no us. Haven't you said that enough these past few months? I've finally gotten it, Michael."

He tunneled his fingers through his hair. "I was wrong last night about a lot of things."

Her heart began to pound.

"I want you to be the chef on the riverboat."

"No."

"Why not? I thought that's what you wanted. Have you changed your mind about staying in Magnolia Blossom?"

"No."

He shook his head. "Then I don't understand."

"Ten years ago I ran because I couldn't give you what you wanted, and yet I knew I could never watch you fall in love with another woman, marry and have a family. I'm staying in Magnolia Blossom, but I won't work for you. I made a promise to Amy and Shaun, but I know my limitations."

The frown that furrowed his brow vanished. "You won't work for me because you have feelings for me?"

"I love you. I now realize that hasn't changed in ten years."

"Good." The tension in his body melted. He moved one step closer.

"Good?"

"I love you."

"But last night—"

He placed his fingers over her mouth. "When you came back to Magnolia Blossom, I fell in love with you all over again. With you as you are today, not ten years ago. What I feel for you now far outshines those feelings."

The pounding of her heart thundered in her ears. Her throat contracted, making it difficult to draw air into her lungs.

"I've been up all night, trying to work through my problems. I did some soul-searching with God's help and realized a few things about myself." He rubbed his fingers across her lips.

The sensations created from his touch made the world fade. Her every sense became centered on the man standing in front of her.

"I do trust you. I have from the beginning. You were the one I turned to when things were heating up with Mary Lou. The past few months I have opened my heart to you, and that's not something I've done in years. You know me better than anyone. That doesn't happen without trust, Rachel. I was just being too stubborn to realize that."

Tears flooded her eyes and spilled down her cheeks. Michael wiped them away, but more fell.

"You aren't supposed to cry."

"Tears of joy. I didn't think I would ever hear you say you trusted me. Does that mean you have forgiven me for leaving you ten years ago?"

"For a time I'd forgotten the power of forgiveness. You taught me how freeing it is to forgive another." He cupped her face, leaning closer. "Yes, I have forgiven you. Will you forgive me for being so pigheaded?"

"Mmm. I don't know."

He brushed his lips across hers. "Is there anything I can do to change your mind?"

"Perhaps."

He wound his arms about her and brought her against him. His mouth settled over hers. His kiss rocked her to the depths of her being.

When he pulled back, his eyes gleamed with happiness. "Well?"

"Not a bad start."

"Then I guess I'll have to spend the next thirty or forty years trying to convince you."

"Oh, it probably won't take *that* long." She laughed and tightened her embrace, drawing him close to her.

"Will you marry me?" He kissed her lightly on both sides of the mouth.

"I thought you'd never ask."

"Is that a yes?"

"Yes. Yes. Yes."

"Will you be my chef on the *Cajun Queen*?"

"The *Cajun Queen*?"

"I decided to name the riverboat after you." He grinned and snuggled closer, nibbling on her ear. "I want the very best, and you, my love, are that."

"How can I turn down a proposition like that?"

"You can't, since I'm giving you the *Cajun Queen* as a wedding present."

Rachel gasped. "Giving me the boat?"

"Do you honestly think I'll have the time to run the restaurant with my plantation and other business ventures?"

"But, Michael, it's been in your family for several generations."

"And you'll be family, so it will stay in it. It'll be something you can pass on to our children."

She knew how much family and traditions meant to him, and the gesture took her breath away. "I don't know what to say."

"How about yes? I started this riverboat project to give you a reason to stay in Magnolia Blossom. At the beginning I told myself it was for Amy and Shaun's sake. Now I know better. It was for me."

She leaned her head on his chest and listened to his strong heartbeat. "The only thing I can say is yes."

Epilogue

❦

Two years later

Rachel searched the restaurant full of diners for Helen and Harold. She saw them in front of the picture window and strode to their table, so glad her best friend had given Harold a chance. He'd turned out to be such a dear man and perfect for Helen.

"I hope the dinner was to your satisfaction."

"Are you kidding?" Helen placed her hand over Harold's. "It was a delicious prime rib."

"Only the best for your first anniversary."

Helen smiled. "What are you going to do about your second one coming up in three weeks?"

Rachel laid her hand over her rounded stomach. "Hopefully, be in the hospital delivering this sucker."

"Are you sure you trust me in your kitchen while you're on maternity leave?"

"Well, it was you or Michael. And he told me in no uncertain terms he would be too busy taking care of me and the baby."

Helen squeezed her husband's hand. "Aren't men grand?"

"Harold, you better watch out. She wants something," Rachel said with a laugh.

"I've learned how to handle this woman." He winked at Helen.

"I think that's my cue to leave you two lovebirds alone."

Rachel headed toward the kitchen, stopping at tables on the way to say a few words to the customers. When she reached one couple, she smiled and said, "I'm glad you and Tom could come this evening, Mary Lou."

The woman returned her smile. "I thought it would be a perfect way to top off a great week, since we had to bring Garrett and Shaun back."

"I haven't seen them yet. Did they have fun at Disney World?"

Mary Lou's eyes sparkled. "I didn't realize how much energy they had. We were up at dawn and went all day—not *one* break. I believe I wore out a pair of tennis shoes."

Rachel laughed. "I know what you mean. Enjoy the rest of your evening."

Rachel paused at the entrance to the kitchen to scan

her restaurant. Pride straightened her shoulders as she noted every table was full. People came from all over to sample her food. She and the *Cajun Queen* had been written up in the New Orleans and Jackson newspapers. But all this wouldn't mean much without Michael and his love.

As she entered her domain, she was captured from behind and pulled against a hard body. She snuggled against the man holding her, his familiar, comforting scent wafting to her.

Michael buried his face in her hair. "Mmm. You smell like garlic and onions."

"I'm not sure that's a compliment."

"To a chef, I'm sure it is." He turned her around, his arms still loosely about her.

"You know I'm busy."

He looked over her shoulder at the workers in the kitchen and drew her to the side so a waiter could get through the door. "I won't keep you. I just wanted to check and make sure you were all right before heading home."

She cupped his face. She loved how he fussed over her even to the point that the riverboat had remained at the pier for the past two weeks and would until after the baby was born. "I realize you've been gone all day to Vicksburg, but honey, I have your pager number as well as your cell phone number. Believe me, if I go into labor, you'll be the first person I notify, even before the doctor."

"Do you think that's wise?"

"In this case, yes. You'd think this was your first child, not mine."

Michael placed his hand on her stomach, stroking it. He felt a kick and smiled. "He wants out of there."

"His mother wants him out of there, too. I think I've put on thirty pounds."

His gaze linked with hers. "You're the most beautiful woman in the world."

Tears thickened her throat. "You're going to make me cry, and I still have work to do."

"Then I'll leave. I'll be back to pick you up." He slid his hands into her hair and brought her mouth to his.

His kiss, full of all the emotions he felt, shook her to her very soul. Right in front of all the kitchen staff, she returned his kiss, her arms winding about her husband's neck.

When they parted, the staff clapped. Rachel blushed while Michael gave her another quick kiss, then left. Content and happy, she walked to the sink to wash her hands before cooking. She had everything she could ever want.

* * * * *

Dear Reader,

This was my fourth book for the Love Inspired line. I had so much fun writing it because it brought back memories of my childhood in Mississippi.

In this story I wanted to explore a woman's fear of opening herself up to love. Once Rachel allowed the Lord into her life, it wasn't long before she was able to see that she could love her siblings and a man. Love can be scary. We open ourselves up and sometimes we do end up getting hurt. But love is what makes life rich and wonderful—from the love of God to the love of a partner to share your life with.

I hope you enjoy Rachel's journey toward finding her soul mate. Michael is a hardworking man who has a strong faith and believes in family. Rachel learns some valuable lessons from him, but he in turn learns how to forgive, which is such an important part of our faith.

I would love to hear from you! If you want to be added to my mailing list, please write to me at Margaret Daley, P.O. Box 2074, Tulsa, OK 74101.

May God be with you,

Margaret Daley